All I Need Is You

Boulder Beaumonts Book 3

Nika Rhone

Book Cover Design by 100 Covers

Published by Park Nine Publishing

"Be who you are and say what you feel, because those who mind don't matter and those who matter don't mind."

Dr. Seuss

Chapter 1

IT WAS OFFICIAL. HER brother was one of *them* now.

After all this time, she should have been used to the bitter pinch of betrayal. But now, watching Rafe spin his new wife around the dance floor with that ridiculous gooey-eyed expression on his face, there was a sense of finality to it there hadn't been before.

Not that she'd really expected any other outcome once he put that diamond on Lillian Beaumont's finger all those months ago. But until they'd said their vows, there had always been the slightest sliver of hope to hold on to. Hope that *something* might happen to derail the wedding. Like cold feet. A return to common sense.

A plague of locust.

But the event had gone off without the smallest hiccup to ruin—or save—the day. So here they were, celebrating the new Mr. and Mrs. Raphael Delgado like it was the most wonderful thing in the world her big brother had tied himself to *that woman.*

And through them, the Delgados to the Beaumonts.

Forever.

"Bella, why aren't you dancing?" Dropping into the chair next to her sister at the otherwise empty dais table, Brianna fanned herself with an abandoned napkin. "The band is incredible!"

"Of course it is. Money can buy the best of everything, and the Beaumonts would *never* accept anything less than the very best." Like the delicious wine she polished off in a large swallow from her glass.

Smooth. Mellow. *Rich*.

A bottle probably cost more than she took home in a week working at the family restaurant. And it was being poured for guests as if it were water.

"Oh my god, will you please stop grinding on that?" Bria groaned. "So they have money. So what? We were wrong about Lillian. She wasn't some rich snob looking to have her fun with Rafe and leave him with a broken heart when she got bored and moved on. She loves him like crazy."

It took everything she had not to flinch at those words. They were too close to ones she'd heard before. Words that had been a lie.

"I just worry he's making a mistake, and now it's too late."

"Rafe's a big boy, *hermanita*. He knows what he's doing, and what he wants. He certainly doesn't need us sticking our noses into his love life. In fact, he expressly forbade it. Remember?"

This time, she did flinch. Not at the reminder of how very furious Rafe had been with her, Bria, and their brother Cris after discovering their part in sabotaging his and Lillian's budding relationship. But at the stab to the heart of him choosing *that woman* over his own family. It was enough to make a girl want to cry.

Or get drunk.

She reached for the untouched glass of wine at the place setting beside her and took a large sip. Taking someone else's drink was probably some major etiquette *faux pas* or something, but she honestly didn't care. "Have I done or said anything to cause trouble today? All week?"

Because god forbid the wedding festivities be limited to a single day. Or even two.

Oh, no.

It had been an entire week filled with spa days and shopping trips and a joint bachelor/bachelorette wine-and-cheese party at one of the local vineyards that, even she had to grudgingly admit, had been pretty fun.

Or it would have been, if she hadn't been surrounded by Beaumonts.

"It's not what you say with your mouth. It's what you say with this." Bria drew a circle in front of Bella's face.

"I can only smile so much before my face cracks. What more do you want me to do?"

Bria sighed.

"You can let go of whatever grudge it is you're still holding on to." She gestured toward the dance floor. "Look at him, Bell. He's happy."

He *was* happy. And that seemed the cruelest cut of all.

Because when the three Beaumont brothers had taken their own shot at breaking up the happy couple, it had been because they thought Rafe wasn't good enough for their precious little sister. And in thinking Rafe wasn't good enough, by extension it meant the Delgados weren't, either.

And that was an insult she just couldn't forget.

Even if it seemed everyone else had.

"Don't worry, I'll continue to be on my best behavior the rest of the night. I won't embarrass the family." She pasted a toothy smile on her face to prove it. When her sister gave her a doubtful look, she went for her weak spot. "Won't Alejandro be looking for you?"

A gooey expression that rivaled Rafe's came over Bria at the mention of her boyfriend. "No, he knows I was coming to drag you out onto the dancefloor."

Which was sister-code for 'he knows I want him to dance with you when you get there so you don't feel left out because you didn't bring a date.'

Yeah, no.

"Actually, I'm kind of danced out right now. I think I'll just sit and finish my wine first, and then I'll be out."

Bria's burgundy-tinted lips pressed into a pretty pout. "Promise?"

The "mmhmm" was half-lost in the depths of her glass as she took another long sip. It wasn't really a lie if she didn't say the word, right?

"Well, okay. But make sure you're out there soon."

She watched her sister disappear back into the sea of people laughing and dancing and having a wonderful time in their expensive gowns and designer suits and glittering jewelry. All right, that was only some of them. There were plenty of regular, non-glittering people out there, too. Relatives from their side of the family, and Rafe's friends.

Which kind of said it all about the great divide no one but her seemed to see.

Her gaze zeroed in again on her brother, who was currently slow dancing with his wife—the word still left a nasty aftertaste—despite the fact the band was playing a fast-tempo song.

A shaft of melancholy despair speared through her chest.

She was glad Rafe was happy. She was. Truly.

She just wished it had been with someone else. Someone she could be sure wasn't going to one day rip his life apart by deciding things 'weren't working out.' That he wasn't 'enough' for her. That he wasn't a 'good fit' in her world.

The world where money was everything, and people were judged by how much they had.

And everything they didn't.

The wine didn't taste as good going down this time. It didn't mix well with the bitterness of old resentments. Not that it stopped her from finishing it off.

Some things were better faced through the gentle fuzz of alcohol.

Like hearing the music come to an end for the announcement of "All right, it's time for the bouquet toss. Let's have all the single ladies out on the dancefloor!"

Nope. That was a hard pass.

Chasing the last drops from her glass, she slipped the beaded strap of her tiny purse over her shoulder and made a not-so-graceful escape to the restroom. The floor-length, blush silk bridesmaid dress might be the most gorgeous thing she'd ever worn, but it was still a pain in the butt to walk fast in.

Or maybe it was the combination of heels and alcohol giving her trouble.

Either way, she made it to her destination without face-planting. After she was done, she lingered in the cozy anteroom with its subtle floral potpourri and damask chairs and fainting couches. Not that she was hiding or anything. She was simply taking a break from all of the people and noise and smiling till her cheeks ached.

Okay, she might be hiding.

But in her defense, she deserved the respite. It had been one of the longest days of her life, and she'd been on her best behavior for every second of it. Even when she'd been forced onto the floor with her wedding party partner for the dreaded first dance. Three minutes in Peter Beaumont's arms had left her feeling strangely off-balance and prickly.

Stranger still was the sensation of loss after he'd let her go.

She hadn't liked either feeling one little bit.

Sitting beside him at the dais table after that had been a torture of discomfort. Made worse every time he'd tried to engage her in conversation during the meal.

Not because he was boring. A lot of his comments had been witty and even interesting. And if he'd been anyone else, she would have totally enjoyed his company.

But he was *that woman's* brother. Her twin brother, no less.

Somehow, that made it worse, even though they couldn't have been more polar opposites. Lillian was petite, with an oversized personality which made her seem so much larger. Peter, for all his broad shoulders and impressive height, could almost fade into the background with his calm, easy-going disposition. She'd seen it happen more than once over the past few days.

Not that she didn't think he had it in him to be forceful when he wanted to be. He was a Boulder police officer, after all, just like Rafe. There had to be something more to him than dimples and boyish charm.

Not that she cared about either of those things. He was still the enemy.

Okay, maybe not the enemy, exactly. But still one of *them*.

A faint cheer came through the restroom door. A signal the bouquet had been caught by some poor woman who'd now be subjected to the indignity of having a strange man—or worse, a relative—stick his hand under her dress to slide a garter onto her leg while everyone watched and cat-called and laughed.

She shook her head as she got to her feet. Why did anyone still think that was fun?

Her steps faltered outside the restroom as she heard the announcement calling the bride and groom to the dance floor. Did she really want to watch her brother getting all sexy and cute with Lillian as he removed the garter from her leg before throwing it to the bachelor horde?

The answer didn't even require a moment's thought.

Her feet took a sharp right turn toward the staircase. Clutching the long skirt in one hand to keep from tripping, she made her careful way up to the hotel's main street level. Which was unsurprisingly crowded.

The majority of the downtown Boulder hotel might have been taken over by the wedding—the downstairs ballroom for the reception, and most of the pricey rooms for the guests, including the entire wedding party. But the lobby-level restaurant and bar were both still open to the public.

Perfect.

Her original intent, decided when she'd started perspiring halfway up the staircase, had been to step outside to the patio for some fresh air. Instead, she headed for the door into the bar in the street-facing corner of the lobby.

One drink. Maybe two, depending on how much cash she'd tucked into the purse with her ID, lipstick, and room key. That should be more than enough time for the whole bouquet/garter circus to finish playing out before she went back downstairs.

If nothing else, it would be good to have a few minutes of peace and solitude where she didn't have to smile and play nice for anyone.

"Well, *hello* beautiful."

Barely suppressing a sigh, she stopped and looked at the guy who'd popped up like a prairie dog from his seat to step into her path between the bar's dozen or so tables. Tall, auburn-haired, sort of good looking, maybe about ten years older than her in his early thirties. The slacks and button-down gray shirt rolled up to the elbows said after-hours businessman rather than tourist. Just the kind of guy she'd normally let chat her up in a bar on a Saturday night.

Tonight, she just didn't have the bandwidth for it.

Offering him a neutral smile, she murmured "Thank you," and moved to step past him. Which would have worked if the second guy hadn't stood up next to him to block the way.

"Hey, hey, hey, where you going so fast, sweetness?" A little taller than his friend, dark hair styled with probably as much product used to tame her own into its elaborate up-do, he reeked of some musky cologne that made her nose twitch.

A tingle of unease chased up her spine.

This one wasn't like the first. In fact, he was the kind of guy she actively avoided on the nights she and her friends went bar-hopping.

The dangerous kind.

Adrenaline did wonders to clear the wine-buzz from her head as she assessed the situation. She could try to get them to move, or she could retreat. Although judging by the predatory gleam in the dark-haired guy's eyes, he'd take either as a challenge.

Damn it.

She would've been better off hiding in the restroom.

There was nothing she could do now except try and make herself a less appealing solo target. She summoned up her best imitation of confidence. "Excuse me, please. I'm meeting someone at the bar."

"Well, that's their loss, isn't it, since you met us first." The words might have sounded playful, but the tone didn't match the intent in his expression. He'd cornered his prey, and he wasn't letting her go easily.

"I'm meeting *my boyfriend.*"

If she'd hoped that would make a difference, she was doomed to disappointment.

And not a little concern. There was something ugly in the one guy's gaze, and not just because he was currently ogling her breasts like they were treats on display in a candy shop's front window.

"Don't worry, sweet thing. When we're done rocking your world, you'll forget all about your boyfriend." He licked his lips.

Eww.

Revulsion rippled through her.

She'd been right. This one was dangerous.

Time for Plan B. Retreat.

Not that he looked inclined to let her leave any easier than he'd allowed her to pass.

One hand flexed at her side. She'd hate to get blood on her gorgeous gown, but if he laid a finger on her, she was more than willing to shove her palm into his nose the way Rafe had taught her.

Before she could decide whether to risk turning her back on them or not, a deep voice said "Excuse me" in a way that had the two jerks making a hole between them. Probably before they even realized what they were doing, if their expressions of surprised chagrin were anything to go by.

Her plan to latch onto whoever was leaving and follow them out dissolved into disbelief as her unintentional savior's face came into view.

Peter freaking Beaumont.

All six-foot-four of him.

Who, rather than walking on by, stopped beside her as if it had been his destination all along.

What the hell?

The red-haired guy looked a little slack-jawed as he stared up at the tuxedo-clad mountain before him. But the other one was too busy ogling her chest again to care.

"Do you mind, buddy? We were talking to the lady."

And just when she thought the universe couldn't get any weirder, Peter spoke again in that same 'don't fuck with me' voice that sent a shiver down her spine.

"As a matter of fact, I do mind. Because the lady's with me."

***

"Our dearest Lillian makes an absolutely *exquisite* bride."

Despite his melancholy mood, Peter Beaumont grinned at the effervescent man who'd joined him leaning against the wall in the hotel's massive ballroom. With his dark eyes, Mediterranean coloring, and larger-than-life personality, Des made it impossible not to respond in kind to his bubbly nature.

"Due in large part to the dress you designed to keep my pipsqueak of a sister from looking like a satin-smothered cupcake." Lil was more than a foot shorter than him at five-twoish. Even with her usual four-inch heels—which he was pretty sure she'd already kicked off somewhere when the dancing started—she was still a pixie-sized squirt.

A *married* pixie-sized squirt.

His head still couldn't wrap itself around that.

Hand to his chest, Des acted as though Peter had thrust a dagger into his heart.

"As if I would dress anyone in anything less than complete perfection. A DF Original will never be anything other than sublime." He banked down his hallmark theatrics to add, "And I would design nothing but the absolute best for my darling kitten and her entourage on her most special day."

"Well, you certainly succeeded there." Even a fashion clueless guy like him could see that. His brothers might live in designer suits, but his closet was more Under Armour than Armani. The only reason he even owned the tux he wore was because of all the charity events his mother insisted he attend on the family's behalf.

Over-blown animation flowed back into Des's expression as he preened at the compliment. "I did, didn't I? Not that it was easy, what with all of the baby bumps to work around."

His lungs locked up on a wheeze. "The what?"

Des had the nerve to chuckle. "Oh, your face right now! Where is that photographer when you need him? No, dear boy, our lovely bride isn't *enceinte*. I was referring to the two married ladies in the wedding party. Having to take both Amelia's reducing after-baby body and Thea's increasing baby bump into account, creating a flattering design for all four ladies and doing last-minute alterations to make the fit perfect was quite the challenge. But, as always, one I rose to with stellar aplomb, if I do say so myself."

Oh, thank god.

He'd barely come to terms with his sister getting married. He definitely wasn't ready to think of her as pregnant. She was his little sister, for fuck's sake.

Okay, technically, she'd been born ten minutes before him.

But he'd always watched over her as if she were the baby of the family. A protective urge borne not just from her petite stature and sometimes capricious nature, or even being the only girl, but from her status as his twin.

They'd always had a special bond between them. Neither had inherited the Beaumont business-sense that made their father and brothers so successful. Both had chosen paths different from what their parents might have imagined for them, Lillian into art and himself into law enforcement. And they shared an undeniable and abiding love of sweets.

They could fight like cats and dogs and enjoyed the hell out of teasing each other whenever possible. But at the end of the day, they'd always had each other's backs. Been there for one another.

And now she was gone.

Dramatic much, Beaumont?

Yeah, okay. That was overstating things a little. But from the second he'd seen Lil walking down the aisle toward Rafe with a look of pure adoration on her face, a look mirrored on Rafe's for her, it had finally registered she wasn't his anymore.

Oh, she'd always be his sister, sure. But that "us" feeling, the special twin-bond they had, would now take a backseat to the new bond she was creating with her husband.

The man she was currently in the arms of, twirling around the dance floor with a radiant expression. Like they were the only two people on the planet. He'd never seen his sister this happy before.

He rubbed at his chest. There was that tiny pinch again.

The one he'd been ignoring all night.

Des laid a hand on his arm, startling him out of his moment of ridiculous introspection. He started to make a joke about being caught navel-gazing like his brother Theo often did, but the knowing look in the other man's eyes stilled the glib words on his tongue. He didn't know how, but Des always seemed to see straight to the heart of a person.

He gave a helpless shrug. "She's my sister."

"I know. It's hardest to let go of the ones we love most. But she's in the best of hands." With an understanding squeeze to Peter's arm, he smiled and walked away.

He was absolutely right about that. Rafe Delgado was a great guy. The best. He loved Lil. Cherished her. Hell, he practically worshipped at her dainty little feet. Not to mention as a fellow Boulder police officer, he was more than qualified to keep her safe, even from herself.

Peter couldn't think of a better man for his sister.

None of that seemed to matter to his heart, though. Which was still feeling that uncomfortable pinching sensation as he watched them move across the dance floor.

It wasn't jealousy. No, he was happy for Lil. This was more like feeling...abandoned.

Which was absolutely ridiculous.

But still absolutely true.

Not only was Lil now married, but both his brothers were engaged to the women who'd won their slightly cynical hearts as well. Hell, even Des and Michael had recently tied the knot in a surprisingly understated—for Des—New Year's Eve ceremony.

Which all left Peter odd man out.

Again.

Disgusted with his whiney inner-toddler, he snatched a glass from a passing waiter's tray. After only a sip, though, he put it down on a nearby table and headed toward one of the bar stations. This much self-pity called for something a lot stronger than champagne, or even the excellent vintage of wine he'd left untouched when he'd abandoned his seat at the dais table after the meal was over.

Seeing his mother in his path, he changed directions and headed for the stairs instead. One benefit of the landmark downtown hotel hosting the reception was the bar on the lobby level. And while the drinks there might not be free, at least he'd be able to drown his ridiculous case of the sads far from the prying eyes of his family.

Especially his mother.

Des wasn't the only one with uncomfortable levels of perception.

Lucking into a seat at the L-shaped mahogany bar, he ordered a beer and a shot of Jameson, which he downed the instant it appeared. As the whiskey burn slid through his body, he took his first almost-easy breath of the day.

He loved his family. He did. They could just be a lot to take *en masse* for extended periods of time. Especially with his mother hyper-focused on making sure her only daughter's wedding went off without a hitch.

Throw in the Delgado siblings—one in particular—and it was a wonder he hadn't started drinking the hard stuff hours ago.

Tipping back his beer, he drained half before coming up for air. That particular mess was one of his own making. Well, his and his brothers'. Although Rafe's brother and sisters weren't without blame, either.

For reasons of their own, each set of siblings had conspired separately to break them up early in their relationship. A fact none of them was proud of, and had spent quite a bit of time trying to make up to Rafe and Lillian. Fences had been mended, forgiveness dispensed, and everyone had moved on.

Mostly, anyway.

But today, the six sibs had been in continual forced proximity as members of the wedding party. They'd had to smile and pose endlessly together for the photographer, travel in the limos together, sit together, eat together, dance together. All while Lil subtly reminded them in a dozen different ways how close they'd come to keeping this day from ever happening.

It had been like dripping lemon juice on a not-quite-healed paper cut. Uncomfortable, drawn out, and impossible to ignore. Just as Lillian had wanted.

His twin was nothing if not an expert at exacting her revenge, even if it took two long years to deliver.

He lifted his bottle in salute to his sister's diabolic little mind and drained it. Whatever retribution Lillian felt appropriate, he'd take without complaint as being well deserved. He really had been an ass back then. He was just glad his relationship with her, not to mention his friendship with Rafe, had survived his assholery.

Downtown Boulder on a Saturday night in June meant high tourist traffic. Good for the city and the bar, but it made getting the bartender's attention for a second round an exercise in patience. While he waited, he let his gaze drift over everyone packed into the small space, picking through the droning buzz of conversation around him. People watching and situation assessment was an occupational hazard he couldn't seem to shut down, even off-duty.

Which was a good thing, as it meant he caught the aggressive body language of two men halfway from the bar to the door.

They were both standing with their backs to him as they talked to someone he couldn't see in the aisle between the crowded tables. Someone they were keeping from passing, if the way they stood shoulder to shoulder was any indicator.

Radar on red alert, he tensed as the two idiots postured even more. That kind of body language meant there was probably a woman on the other side of that wall of swagger.

Shit.

Alcohol and attitude didn't mix well.

Add in testosterone and you got a potential powder keg.

He might not be on duty, but it didn't mean he could ignore the situation. Chances were, whatever was going on would resolve itself and blow over in a minute. But if it went in the other direction, he'd have to step in and deescalate things before they got ugly.

Please blow over.

The last thing he needed was to explain to his mother how he'd gotten involved in a bar brawl in the middle of his sister's wedding reception.

He got to his feet just in case, eyes locked on the men, trying to get a better read of what was going on. Then one of them shifted enough for him to catch a glimpse of the woman they were blockading.

He groaned.

Fucking wonderful.

Isabella Delgado.

Rafe's baby sister. His prickly wedding party partner. And the one person he least wanted to spend any more time with than he already had.

Even so, it was no longer a matter of wait and see. She wasn't a stranger, she was family. Sort of. Which meant he needed to intervene.

Now.

People moved out of his way like water around a large, tuxedo-clad boulder as he forged through the crowd near the bar. Using that same energy, he came up behind the men, who were busy bragging about how they could rock Isabella's world and make her forget all about her boyfriend, and uttered a firm "Excuse me."

As he'd hoped, the deep-voiced words, spoken with an air of authority, had both men shifting aside for him to pass out of reflex. Stepping between them, he stopped beside a scowling Isabella and turned back to face the two men who, thankfully, didn't appear to be nearly as drunk as he'd feared.

Or as smart as he'd hoped.

"Do you mind, buddy?" the dark-haired one on the right said. "We were talking to the lady." He might have said 'lady,' but the way he leered at her when he did made it clear his thoughts were a lot less polite.

Something inside him spiked hot and hard.

"As a matter of fact, I do mind, because the *lady* is with me."

Chapter 2

NOT THE WORDS HE'D planned to say.

He'd *planned* to use a calm tone and neutral body language to avoid creating a defensive response. To open a dialog in as non-threatening a way as possible. To listen without seeming judgmental or confrontational. All the things he'd learned at the academy and done a hundred times since to deescalate a tense situation.

Not come off sounding like his oldest brother Richard when he was at his autocratic best in the boardroom, ready to rip someone a new asshole.

Well, shit.

Not surprisingly, the guy bristled in true pissing-contest fashion. But his ginger-haired friend—clearly the brighter of the two—took the time to assess Peter and the potential threat he represented.

Unlike his brothers, who were sleek-muscled and sport-toned, he spent a good portion of his free time in the gym. And it showed. He wasn't muscle-bound like some lifters he knew, but the size of his chest, shoulders, and biceps did make it necessary to have his uniforms custom-tailored in order to fit right. Not even the tux could disguise the fact he could bench-press either one of these idiots without a problem.

Ginger Man seemed to reach the same conclusion. He jabbed his friend with his elbow and jerked his head toward the table they must have been sitting at when they spotted Isabella.

Dark Hair, aka Dead Man Walking, flicked another glance at her like she was the last pork chop on a buffet he was being forced to leave behind before muttering, "Whatever." With a final dirty look for Peter, he and his buddy melted out of the way.

Concealing his relief at the best-case outcome, he looked at Isabella. If he was expecting to see gratitude, though, he'd have a long wait. Tossing her head even though her long, brown curls were currently secured in some kind of fancy pinned-up hairdo, she set her lips in an annoyed line.

"I didn't need your help." When he cocked his head and waited, she let out a beleaguered huff. "Fine. Thank you." The words were right, but the expression and tone made it clear they were grudging at best.

Ungrateful brat.

"Let's go." He touched a hand to her shoulder to start her in the right direction.

So of course, the obstinate woman had to dig in her heels and ask, "Go where?"

He leaned closer, as if whispering sweet nothings in her ear, when in reality he was trying to hide the fact he was clenching his teeth hard enough to snap a pool cue in half.

"For starters, away from the two idiots who are still watching you like a tasty treat they want to unwrap and share. We're supposed to be together, remember?" When she still hesitated, he added, "Unless you *want* them to 'rock your world'?"

She stiffened her spine so fast her head almost cracked into his jaw. "Fine. Where to?"

"Right side of the bar."

Rather than walk at his side, the annoying woman stepped away from his touch and strode ahead, leaving Peter to follow with a swallowed growl of annoyance. At her. At himself. At the two idiots still staring at her ass.

At Des, for designing a dress which somehow managed to be both demurely modest and decadently sexy. The scooped back was strung side-to-side with loose beaded strands that swayed in time with every step she took, revealing tantalizing hints of skin between them with every movement.

Skin he couldn't avoid touching when they'd danced, no matter how hard he'd tried.

Skin which even now drew his eye in teasing glimpses despite him knowing it was totally, completely, one hundred percent forbidden territory.

Fucking hell.

There was more than one reason it had been a long, uncomfortable day. Nothing like a little inappropriate lust to put your conscience on edge. An irony not lost on him, considering his knee-jerk response when he'd first found out Rafe had slept with Lillian was a right hook to his friend's jaw.

It seemed the universe was giving his sister some extra icing on her revenge cake.

Someone else had taken his seat, probably five seconds after his ass had left it. But in a stroke of good timing, his first of the day, a group of three women vacated their stools almost right in front of where he was standing. He got a proprietary hand on two of them before anyone else could.

Before sitting, he watched the women leave to make sure they didn't get harassed on the way out. Thankfully, they made it past the two idiots' table without incident. Either they'd learned some manners, or they weren't interested in prey that outnumbered them.

Having seen their type before, he was leaning toward the latter.

Civic duty discharged, he dropped onto a stool and motioned to the bartender for another round before realizing Isabella was still standing. He gestured to the seat beside him. "I'm assuming you came looking for a drink. So, sit and have one."

"With you?"

The disbelief in her words helped quell any lingering tingle of attraction, and reminded him they didn't like each other very much.

"Why not?" It was such a loaded question the air practically crackled with the possible comebacks she could spear him with.

To his surprise—and maybe a little disappointment—she slipped onto the stool without taking her shot. At least if they were sniping at each other, he wouldn't be thinking about her skin. Or any other parts of her body. Her sweet, curvy, cinnamon-scented body.

Jesus, what was wrong with him?

Delivering Peter's drinks, the bartender gave Isabella a smile. One a little too friendly to be professional, in his opinion.

"What can I get you?"

She gestured to the bottle of locally brewed Fat Tire beer. "I'll have one of those, and a shot of Mad Dog, please."

"Sure. I just need some ID."

She pulled her license from the miniscule purse slung over her shoulder and showed it without complaint. After tilting it to the light in a gesture Peter was well familiar with, the bartender handed it back and stepped away to get the drinks.

She caught him staring at her and bristled. "What?"

"I'm surprised he asked for it is all, looking the way you do."

A tiny sneer curled her lip. "Like I'm someone rich?"

God, did she ever give it a rest?

"No. Like you're older than you are. With all that makeup and the hair and dress, you don't look twenty-three." Something he'd do well to remember. Sexy skin or not, she was still Rafe's *baby* sister.

Although the five years between them weren't really all that—

He gave himself a mental bitch-slap.

Rafe's. Baby. Sister.

The bartender returned with her drinks. He looked like he wanted to linger, but lucky for his future tip—not to mention his face—he had to move off to fill another drink order. Peter studied the bright red shot, trying to puzzle out its contents.

"Okay, I give up. What's in it?"

"Vodka, raspberry syrup, and a few drops of hot sauce." She downed the shot with a flick of her wrist and let out an 'ah' of appreciation before sliding him a sly look over the empty glass. "Want to try one?"

An involuntary shudder rumbled through him.

His body had about zero tolerance for anything spicy. Something she knew perfectly well, since she'd been there the day his brothers had egged him into trying the new habanero sauce at her family's Cuban-American restaurant. They'd almost had to break out the fire extinguisher to keep him from bursting into flames.

"Pass." He tossed back the whiskey, careful not to let a hiss out through his teeth as the burn slid down his throat to detonate in a tiny nuclear explosion in his belly. He let it simmer for a minute before dousing the heat with his beer.

"So, why didn't you bring him?"

She gave a confused look. "Who?"

"Your boyfriend." Reason number five hundred twenty-seven to keep his thoughts about her on the straight and narrow. "The one you told your admirers about?"

"Oh, that. We broke up a few months ago. I only said it to get them to back off. Not that it worked," she muttered into her beer. "What about you? No pretty socialites available to hang off your arm this weekend?"

There it was again. That sneering tone he'd grown to loathe. The one that always seeped into her voice whenever any mention of money came up.

Funny thing was, she was usually the one doing the mentioning.

Annoyed, he let his sarcasm flag fly high. "No, Paris Hilton was out of the country, and the Kardashians were all busy washing each other's hair."

She snorted into her beer before cocking her head ever-so slightly. "Do you really know…"

"Jesus." He rolled his eyes, a bad habit he'd picked up long ago from his sister. "No."

"Oh. Too bad."

It was. Not that he was interested in any of those plastic people or anyone like them. He'd never admit it to Isabella, but he had a similar aversion to hers for the majority of those inhabiting the moneyed upper-circles of society.

His family might fit in with them when they wanted to, but he never felt he did. Not comfortably, anyway. And with every year that passed, the more out of step with that world he seemed to become.

So no, he didn't want a Kardashianesque woman. But it would have been nice to be with *someone* tonight. Anyone. Truth was, he hadn't had a girlfriend in a while, but he hadn't really felt the lack until now, watching his sister and brothers with their soulmates, looking all cozy and complete.

Ignoring the now-familiar pinch in his chest, he decided it was time to change the subject.

"So, what dragged you away from the festivities, anyway? My mom didn't get the band to start playing Eighties music, did she?"

Isabella let out a surprised laugh. "I have a hard time picturing your mother dancing to Michael Jackson and Cyndi Lauper."

"Oh, if only it were that tame. You haven't been truly scarred until you've walked in on your parents dirty dancing to Marvin Gaye's "Sexual Healing" in the living room."

"Oh my god!" Her hands rose to cover another laugh, this one a little more horrified than the last.

"Right?" Her reaction gave him a sense of vindication. She got it, while his own sister never really had. She'd thought it was 'adorable' their parents would be that affectionate after so many years of marriage. "I was probably about seventeen, and I *still* can't listen to the song without cringing a little."

And why had he told her that?

The first rule he'd learned from having big brothers: never give anyone something they can use against you to make your life miserable. And here he was, offering up a juicy personal tidbit not only about himself, but about his parents, to a woman who didn't particularly like any of them.

Beaumont, you are a freaking dumbass.

Before he could decide if there was any hope of mitigating his lapse in judgement, Isabella blurted out, "I walked in on my parents having sex last year."

He just stared. "Holy. Shit."

She nodded, blinking rapidly as though trying to scrub away the memory of the sight with her eyelids. "I mean, I didn't *see* anything, thank god, but I *knew*..." She shuddered. "And the worst part is, I can never un-know it. Ever. You know?"

"I do." He could totally commiserate with her about that. There were just some things which stayed with you for life.

"The one good thing is they have no idea it happened. Which is the only reason I can still live in the same house with them and not die of mortification every day." The look of horror that suddenly came over her face told him she'd realized the same thing he had a moment ago about sharing potentially damaging information with the enemy.

And there it was. His 'get out of stupid' card.

"Don't worry, I'll never breathe a word about it, as long as you don't, either."

She seemed to grasp his meaning right away. "Deal."

They tapped bottles to seal their pledge of mutually assured destruction and drank until they were empty. He gestured to the bartender for another round.

"So, what *did* make you leave the reception?"

"Honestly? I'm avoiding the whole bouquet and garter thing. And my sister," she added after a slight pause. "I love her to death, but if she makes her boyfriend dance with me one more time…" A tiny growl escaped her throat that he found oddly adorable.

"My future sisters-in-law, too. They might think they're being nice by asking me to dance, but really, they're just making it worse."

"Yes! I mean, if we really wanted to dance, we would."

"Exactly." And he had. He'd asked his mother. And his sister. And his aunt. And…

Okay, maybe he hadn't danced all that much. But the point was, he would have if he'd wanted to.

"This is weird."

He cocked his head. "What?"

"Us, agreeing with each other."

It was.

Part of the reason he'd abandoned his seat at the dais table to hold up a wall instead might have been to deter Amber and Rachel from asking him to dance—he refused to use the word hide.

But he'd also been stuck sitting there alone next to Isabella, trying to make awkward conversation. Which, at the time, had seemed a fate worse than having sandpaper rubbed over his balls.

Now, though, he felt an odd sense of kinship displacing the vague annoyance which usually came from being in her presence for more than thirty seconds.

"Yeah. It is weird. But…it's not so bad, either."

At least he thought so. Since she remained silent as their drinks were delivered, he wasn't so sure she shared the sentiment.

Then she surprised him.

And herself, too, judging by the look on her face as she said, "No, I guess not."

Would wonders never cease?

Their shots were downed with an unspoken toast to their newfound camaraderie. Or, if not that, then at least a temporary ceasefire. Either would make the next morning's family brunch with the newlyweds a lot less tense than the rehearsal dinner had been. The last thing he wanted was Lillian upset before she went off on her honeymoon.

"Do you have indigestion or something? You keep rubbing here. All day, actually."

His mouth went dry as Isabella pressed her fingers right between her breasts to demonstrate, forcing the silky fabric taut enough to show the sweet globes in loving detail. "Was I?" He cleared the blockage from his throat, wishing he could vanquish the vision of those breasts as easily. "No. I was just thinking…" Yeah, no. Telling her the truth was a bad idea, ceasefire or not. "…that you look amazing in that dress."

Her mouth dropped open. "What?"

Yeah, what?

"I mean, not that you don't always look nice, because, you know, you do. But that this dress makes you look, um, extra nice." Extra nice? Talk about lame. "Really pretty, I mean." Still not right. "Sexy." Okay, that might have been a little too on-the-nose. "Sorry! That was totally out of line, so…yeah, I'm going to just stop talking now."

He shoved his beer between his lips to make sure he did.

What the actual fuck?

Why would he say something like that? To *her*, of all people?

Even if it was true.

A groan made it as far as his mouth before it was washed back down with a heavy swallow of beer. So much for their tentative truce. If anything, she was going to give him more grief than ever now.

Only this time, he'd deserve it.

"You think I'm sexy?"

The soft question made his head snap toward her in surprise. She didn't look pissed like he expected. She looked...fascinated. Pleased, even.

Warning bells began to clang, but he still nodded. "Oh, yeah."

"Really?"

If it had been one of those socialites she'd teased him about asking that, he'd say it was a coy play for more compliments. But there was something on Isabella's face, something vulnerable and real, that said she honestly didn't believe in her own level of hotness.

Did the woman not own a mirror?

Leaning in so he could lower his voice, he caught her gaze and held it. "Sexy enough to have me thinking inappropriate things about you. All. Damn. Day."

He probably deserved to be beaten senseless for admitting that to her, but it seemed his common-sense filter had shorted out somewhere between the second and third shots. And he couldn't find it in himself to care. Especially not when her eyes darkened and the pulse in her neck began to jackhammer in speed.

Pink tongue flicking out to moisten her lips, she let her gaze drop to his chest before coming back to meet his. "And I've been thinking you fill that tux out really, really well."

Whoa.

Talk about a bombshell.

Never in a million years would he have guessed at any point during the day Isabella Delgado had been eyeing him with any thought other than how difficult it would be to shove him into Boulder Creek while the wedding photographer wasn't looking.

A slow smile tugged at his lips. "Yeah?"

Her head gave a lazy nod as her eyes took another trip, this time a little further down than his chest. "Oh yeah."

Son of a bitch.

Had she just...

No. There was no way she'd just checked out his crotch. That would be...

Dangerously intriguing.

His body certainly seemed to think so. Blood rushed under his skin, setting nerve ending ablaze and tightening areas his tux wasn't cut to disguise. Those warning bells started banging louder, although he could barely hear them over the rush of his own heartbeat throbbing in his ears.

But he heeded them anyway.

Hell, one of them had to. And judging by the way Isabella's breath was coming in soft little pants as she moistened her lips again, it wasn't going to be her.

Wrapping iron restraints around his rampaging libido, he pulled himself back from the edge before he gave in to the fierce impulse to lean just a little closer and see if those lips tasted spicy or sweet. But it was damned hard.

"We should probably get back to the reception." God, was that his voice? It sounded like he'd been gargling pinecones.

Her chest rose and fell in a long, slow breath, doing absolutely nothing for his resolve. "We probably should."

Neither of them moved.

"Someone's probably noticed we're gone by now."

Her head gave a tiny fraction of a nod. "Probably."

God, her mouth was right there.

Right.

Fucking.

There.

With a strength of will he didn't know he possessed, he pulled his gaze from her slumberous brown eyes and rolled his shoulders, trying to snap the tension banding his body into a quivering tuning fork. The bartender came at his gesture, and he charged the tab and a generous tip to his room before forcing himself to his feet.

They blew by the idiots' table, out the door, across the lobby. Not talking. Not touching. Not even looking at each other. It was as if they both needed to focus every ounce of concentration on putting one foot in front of the other. On doing what they ought to do, rather than what he damn well knew they were both thinking about doing.

They were within steps of the sweeping staircase leading down to the ballroom when Isabella stopped as though she'd walked into a wall.

"I don't want to go back to the reception."

Foreboding, and maybe a little anticipation, prickled over his skin. Going down those stairs was the right thing to do. The smart thing. But he wasn't feeling especially smart at that moment. More like hungry. Predatory. Greedy.

Lonely.

"What do you want to do, then?"

She stared up at him for one heartbeat. Two. Three.

"You."

The blunt declaration hit him like a stun gun, scrambling his brain. Dissolving the tight leash he'd held on himself. Blowing all his good intentions to dust.

He grabbed her hand, squeezing it with gentle care so as to not crush her fingers.

"Are you sure?"

In response, she smiled and turned toward the elevators, tugging him into motion behind her as though he were a pull-toy on a string. Not that he put up any resistance. His head was still playing catch-up with this sudden turn of events.

Did he really want to do this? *Could* he do this?

The answer to both was *fuck yeah*.

There had been an empty, aching spot in his chest all day watching the rest of his family. Feeling left out. Alone. A part, yet apart. And it might not fix things, not in the long run, but a few hours of incendiary sex would definitely make them a little more bearable. For tonight, at least.

As they stepped out of the elevator on the third floor he paused, looking down the hall in each direction. His room was one way, hers the other.

Isabella shook her head at the unspoken question.

"Bria's spending the night with her boyfriend, but technically for my parents' sake we're sharing a room. So, her stuff's there and she has a key. She could come in at any time."

His room it was.

Begrudging every second it took for them to walk to the end of the hallway, he yanked his keycard from the tux's inner pocket and opened the door. But all of those seconds had given him unwanted time to start second-guessing and what-iffing himself about what they were about to do.

About what he *hoped* they would do.

A whisper of hot cinnamon floated up to tease him as Isabella brushed by to go inside, making his mouth water. God, how he wanted to take a bite out of her. But he held himself in control one more time as he stood in the open doorway.

"Last chance to change your mind." His fingers tightened on the cool door handle as he rasped out the warning. "You've been drinking. We both have. If you're not a hundred percent sure you want this, if you're having any doubts and want to turn around and leave, I won't stop you. And I won't hold it against you."

He'd be in fucking hell, but he'd respect whatever choice she made.

The ambient light from the street coming through the open curtains wasn't enough to clearly show her face where she stood in the center of the room, bathed in shadows. But it was more than enough to see her dress as it slid down her body to pool in a shimmering pile around her feet.

His breath left his body on a groan. Of their own volition, his fingers released the door. It thudded shut with the finality of a judge's gavel. Judgement made. Case closed. No more appeals. This was what they both wanted.

And god help him, it was what they were both going to get.

Chapter 3

I'm such an idiot.

Hurrying down the silent hallway to her room in her wrinkled dress, shoes in hand, the refrain pounded through Bella's head in time with her frantic footsteps. With every door she passed, she kept expecting one to pop open despite the ungodly hour of four-something a.m., catching her in her jog of shame.

Dear god, what had she been thinking?

The easy answer would be, she hadn't been. That she'd been too muddled by the alcohol she'd imbibed, too swept away by the heady burn of lust that had consumed her, to be in full control of herself or her decisions.

But it wouldn't have been the truth.

No, she'd known what she was doing every step of the way. From the moment she'd gotten into that elevator with him to the moment the door to his room had slammed shut, she'd been completely and entirely in control.

And that was why she was an idiot.

"Why him?" she whispered to herself as she fished the keycard from her ridiculous little purse. "*Madre de Dios*, of all people, why him?"

Easing the door open, she held her breath and closed it as quietly as she could behind her. The gauntlet of her relatives' rooms wasn't the only obstacle to keeping her evening's activities a secret.

On tip-toe, she eased into the dark room. A whoosh of relief expelled from her lungs when she saw it was empty.

A relief which was short-lived when she realized Bria would be making the same pre-dawn trek back to their room at any time now. Her sister might be twenty-five and in love, but she was still sneaking around like a teenager. Bella had urged her more than once to just tell their parents she was a grown-ass woman and would sleep with her boyfriend whenever and wherever she wanted to.

Feeling like a hypocrite since she wouldn't be admitting her own sleeping arrangements to anyone, and *definitely* not her parents, she stripped off the dress and carefully hung it in the closet. There was a pang of remorse for its wrinkled state, but that's what a night on a hotel room floor would do.

She went to the bathroom to wash her face, staring into the mirror as she blinked in the sudden light.

And that's what a night of wild sex on a hotel room bed would do.

Her long hair hung haphazardly down her back, the dozens of pins which had anchored it scattered somewhere in the dark when Peter had tugged them out, whispering he liked it better down. Any makeup left around her eyes was smudged, and her lips had a bee-stung fullness.

But it was the overall sense of sexual satisfaction lighting those eyes and tilting those lips that made her look like someone she'd never seen before.

Or at least, not for a long, long time.

After scrubbing her face clean and combing some of the tangles from her hair, she was about to go get into her pajamas and crawl into bed when she caught a whiff of herself. Oh dear lord, she smelled like sex. A shiver rippled through her as the musky scent brought on a visceral memory of tangled limbs and deep, dark hunger being satisfied over and over.

And over.

The shiver turned to a tingly ache. *Stamina* should be the man's middle name.

Or maybe *insatiable.*

Much as she longed for sleep, she couldn't risk Bria's nosy nose picking up on that huge clue and outing her secret. She turned on the shower, grabbed the bottle of fancy body wash the hotel provided, and lathered up.

Which might have been a mistake.

That tingly ache only worsened as she ran her hands over her body. Nerve endings which had quieted fired to life again as the glide of her fingers echoed the sensual touch of Peter's inquisitive investigation.

Their first time had been hot and heavy, but the second...

She let out a soft moan as her fingers grazed the tip of her breast. The second time had gone on forever. A gluttony of touch and taste and slow, intimate discovery.

Exploring. Experimenting. Titillating.

Bringing up her other hand, she cupped her breasts and squeezed, letting out a gasp as her body responded with a rush of heat that shot straight to her core. He'd worshipped at these breasts. With his hands. His mouth. His praise. She'd never thought of them as anything special, but he'd given her a whole new perspective on them. On her entire body.

On herself.

No man had ever treated her with such focused reverence during sex before. It had always been a mutually enjoyable activity—admittedly sometimes less mutual than others. But it had never been more than two bodies coming together in order to feel good.

She'd never felt special. Never done half the things she'd done. And she'd certainly never been worn out to the point of falling asleep.

Which was why she'd never before known the pleasure of being awakened by the sensual warmth of a man's mouth on her.

Right.

There.

She moaned as her fingers found the spot, tender but still humming with the aftermath of more orgasms than she could count.

Okay, five. It had been five glorious, star-spangled explosions that left her wondering why she'd ever thought one-and-done was all there was.

Man, what she'd been missing!

Not like she hadn't given as good as she got. Oh, no. She wasn't that selfish. She'd done some tasting and exploring and titillating of her own. Her knowledge wasn't exactly kama sutra-worthy, but instinct and a healthy imagination had done the job, if the moans and groans and whimpers she'd gotten from him were anything to judge by.

She'd liked the whimpers the best.

Having such a large, powerful man reduced to mewling putty in her hands was headier than the expensive wine served with dinner. Seeing his arms straining as he fisted the sheets while she licked and teased. His broad, muscular chest heaving for breath as she brought him right to the edge, but no further.

And the part of him she'd held between her lips. Oh, sweet mother of god, that had been *glorious*. Long. Thick. Hard. She bit her lip to hold in a moan. It hadn't just been the size of him, though. It was the fact he knew what to do with it.

Very, very well.

Her body tightened as the memory aided her fingers in pushing her over the finish line. But the orgasm was only a weak echo of the others. Because her body had already reached its limits, of course. It had nothing to do with the fact it had been her hands doing it and not his.

Which it could have been, if she hadn't left him sleeping in his bed and snuck out of the room like a thief in the night.

Which made her not just an idiot, but a coward, too.

This time, she did groan.

"Stupid, stupid, stupid." She turned off the water and grabbed an oversized towel, rubbing her body dry in brisk, jerky movements. "What kind of woman walks away from a man like him after a night like that without even leaving a note?"

The desperate kind, it seemed.

Because it wasn't until she'd woken up sometime after their third round and spent who knew how long looking at the man lying next to her, boyish face lax in sleep and a goofy little smile on his lips, she'd remembered. Who he was. Who she was.

Who *they* were.

And she'd panicked.

Because she knew, absolutely knew, if he'd opened those long-lashed brown eyes right at that moment and given her that smile, the one laced with wicked, naughty thoughts, she would have happily gone right back into his arms and stayed there for as long as he wanted. And that couldn't happen again. None of it could.

Ever.

She pressed her fingers to her sternum as a pang of something burned from within.

"Just indigestion," she muttered, wrapping the towel around herself. She wouldn't let it be anything else.

Wrung out in more ways than one, she turned off the light and went back out into the room, more than ready to crawl into bed. Instead, she nearly jumped out of her skin at the sight of her sister lounging across one of the beds.

"God, Bria! You scared me!" Heart hammering, she let out a nervous laugh.

Already dressed in her pajamas, bridesmaid dress nowhere in sight, Bria gave the kind of smile that reminded her of the old tabby they used to have. Pepper loved to play with his food, too.

"Soooo, what have *you* been up to?"

"Up to? Nothing." Was her voice a little too high?

"Really? Then where'd you disappear to?"

"Disappear?" She gave her best 'I don't know what you're talking about' look.

"Last night? From our brother's wedding reception? You were supposed to come dance with me?" she prompted when Bella just kept staring at her.

"Oh, that." Damn, she'd forgotten. "I was, um, a little warm from all the dancing I'd already done, and I went to get some fresh air and cool off. Then after that I was going to go back, but I was, you know, feeling pretty tired—"

"From all the dancing."

Bella gave her a narrow look, recognizing the taunt beneath the helpful tone. Lying to your siblings was so much harder because they knew you so well.

Great, so now she was an idiot, a coward, *and* a liar.

"Right, from all the dancing, and, you know, the whole day. Having to be nice and smile and everything. So, um, I decided to call it an early night before I did or said something to make anyone mad."

Bria made a humming noise that could have been anything from agreement to channeling Pepper preparing for the kill. "Then how come your bed hasn't been slept in?"

Her gaze snapped to the still-pristine mauve duvet molded over the queen bed that mirrored the one her sister had draped herself over. "I...made it already when I got up."

"Before you took your shower."

"Yes."

"At five o'clock in the morning."

"Yes."

"In a hotel with maid service. That we're checking out of today."

She struggled not to squirm as the list of increasing unlikelihoods grew, but there was no backing down now. "Yes."

"How industrious. And look, you even put the complimentary chocolate back on the pillow when you were done."

Her eyes widened as she spotted the distinctive gold-foil wrapper nestled on the center of the pillow.

Damn it.

"Um…"

Her sister's expression said 'gotcha' even though all she said aloud was, "Huh." If she were Pepper, she'd be flicking her tail in triumph. Being Bria, she conveyed her smugness after climbing beneath the covers of her bed by ripping open the chocolate from her own pillow and savoring every delicious bite.

Brat.

She wanted to be annoyed, but how could she when she would've done the same thing if their roles were reversed? Or worse.

Dropping the towel, she dragged on panties and her pajamas, turned off the lights, and crawled into her bed with a weary sigh of relief.

"Hey Bella?"

"Yeah?"

"I thought you were getting up for the day."

She gritted her teeth. She loved her sister, she really did. But this was why they no longer shared a room at home. "Hey Bria?"

"Yeah?"

"Shut up."

Snickers filled the darkness. She ignored them, along with the nagging sensation the comfortable bed was too big. Or maybe it was just a little too cold and empty. The whys of either she refused to examine too closely, since she'd decided she was just going to pretend the entire thing with *him* had never happened.

Somehow, she managed to doze off.

It wasn't a good sleep, but at least she wasn't a walking zombie when she dragged herself down to brunch a few hours later with Bria and Alejandro, who had come to collect them at their room like a good, lovesick puppy.

And if she kept glancing down the hall while they stood waiting for the elevator, it was out of an abundance of caution, not regret. No, the last thing she needed was Peter Beaumont sneaking up on her unawares. Especially with her sister there. Not when she didn't know what he might say when he saw her again.

Or what she would say to him.

What *could* she say? Good morning, thanks for some of the best sex of my life I have to pretend didn't happen, do you think they'll have frittatas on the menu?

All she knew was nothing, absolutely *nothing* could be said in front of Bria. She was already suspicious. One whiff of weirdness between Bella and Peter and she'd draw all the wrong—or rather, right—conclusions.

She breathed a huge sigh of relief when the elevator doors closed behind them. Only to have her nerves go back on red-alert as they walked into the private dining room filled with both extended families and she realized this was so much worse than just her sister. Potential disaster lay literally everywhere.

She stopped so suddenly Bria walked right into her.

"Bella, what the hell?" Untangling herself, Bria gave her a grumpy scowl before smiling up at Alejandro, who put a protective arm around her shoulders and tugged her close.

"Sorry," Bella muttered. "I forgot..." Her mind went blank as she caught sight of Peter seated at a table against the wall. With him were several tall, good-looking men Lillian had introduced as their Beaumont cousins from Louisiana, but all she saw was him.

"Forgot what? How to walk?"

"What? Oh, no, I, um, I forget."

"You forget what you forgot?"

With more effort than it should have required, she dragged her attention back to her sister. "What are you talking about?"

Bria made a tiny sound of annoyance. "*Dios*, I need caffeine." Alejandro obliged by leading her to a nearby table. Bella trailed along behind until she noticed they weren't joining anyone else, but had taken an empty table for four.

Nope. Too early to be playing third wheel.

Looking around, she spotted her parents nearby. "I'm going to sit with *Mami*." At least then she wouldn't have to pretend not to notice anyone playing footsie under the table.

The secret she'd shared with Peter the night before about walking in on her parents doing more than footsie popped into her head like an uninvited guest. She groaned and changed directions. No way could she sit with them with that memory fresh in her mind.

Looking around, she saw her brother Cris, but he was sitting with the eldest two Beaumont sons and their fiancées, smiling and looking like he was enjoying their company as much as the food he was shoveling into his mouth.

Traitor.

She spied her cousins, but it looked like they were getting ready to leave. Another table with her aunts and uncles didn't have an empty seat. Hoping not to look as desperate as she was starting to feel, she kept moving. Other than sitting alone, being a third wheel was beginning to look like her best option.

"Come sit with us, kitten."

She smiled as she answered the summons of the elegant hand gesturing in her direction from a nearby table. Aside from having made the incredible bridesmaid dress she'd worn, Desmond "call me Des, darling!" Finkle was a devout regular at her family's restaurant and one of the most interesting people she knew. He was brash, and funny, and moved in so many directions at once he was sometimes dizzying to be around.

He was also one of Lillian Beaumont's closest friends, but she didn't hold it against him. Couldn't, really. He was just too nice a person not to like.

"Thanks." With a silent sigh of relief, she sank into a chair at the four-top table and smiled at Des and his husband, Michael. "I didn't think it would be so crowded this morning."

Des, bless him, ignored the fact she'd passed up quite a few empty seats before reaching them. "Good food and good company are always a big draw."

"I guess so." She picked up the menu and saw he was right about the food. There were offerings representing both sides of the now joined families, from Cuban to Cajun to New York kosher deli, mixed in with the more traditional brunch fare. Her mouth watered. She'd always wanted to try a beignet.

A waiter appeared, pad at the ready.

"Have a mimosa," Des suggested, waving his half-empty glass. "They're quite divine."

"I wish, but I have to be at the restaurant in a few hours." She ordered regular orange juice instead, along with coffee, then ignored her inner craving and went with the Belgian waffle and huevos rancheros.

Her principles were worth more than a plate of sugary fried dough.

A deep laugh from across the room tingled along her skin and buzzed in her belly, reminding her she'd already sold those out for a different sort of indulgence last night. The sweaty, masculine, bliss-inducing kind.

"Bella?"

Her attention snapped back to Michael, who was looking at her with a slightly concerned pinch to his expression. "I'm sorry, what?"

"I asked if everything was okay. You sort of zoned out for a second."

Had she? "Oh, sorry. I was just...thinking about things that are bad for you."

But still felt oh so good.

Down girl.

Des raised his glass to his lips, dark eyes sparkling with speculation. "Those can be the best kinds of things, kitten. Don't knock them till you've tried them."

She had.

That was the problem.

Another of those baritone laughs rang out to the accompaniment of several others. Without her permission, her gaze pinged across the room to the source. Head thrown back in laughter, Peter looked less like the dark, sensual lover of the night before, and more like the frat boy he'd most likely once been. No doubt leaving a trail of battered hearts in his wake thanks to that laugh and those looks and all that money.

And suddenly, it was a lot easier not to like him again.

As she turned her attention to the steaming cup of salvation the waiter delivered, she caught Des giving her another of those speculative looks. "What?"

"Well, since you asked...if I might make an observation?"

"Des..." Michael gave him a look, which Des waved away with a flap of his hand.

"I can't help it."

She looked between them in confusion. "Help what?"

"Meddling. Well, I *can't*," he said in response to Michael's beleaguered groan. "It's part of my DNA or something."

"As a doctor, I can say with one hundred percent certainty that's not how it works."

"Well, it should. Anyway, as I was saying, kitten, it seems to me there might be a little bit of...*tension* happening between you and a certain Beaumont offspring you've been in close proximity with of late."

Her heart did a quick trip up her throat. How could he know?

"No, there isn't." She gave a nervous laugh. "Why would you say that? Me and Peter? That's ridiculous."

"Well, *I* was referring to the cold shoulder the two of you gave each other for the better part of the wedding festivities." He leaned forward, elbow on the table and chin on his hand as he pinned her with a speculative look. "But I think I'd much rather discuss whatever it is *you* thought I meant."

Damn.

"No, um, that's what I meant, too. What else would I mean?" She gave another laugh, but this one sounded even more manic than the last.

"What else indeed." His dark eyes bored into her like he was mentally peeling a grape. One that happened to be her brain. "Of course, it's true one kind of tension often does beget another, if you know what I mean."

"Not a clue." It was tough, but she held his gaze without flinching.

Much.

"Hmm." Looking unconvinced, he sat back. "Still, you might want to do something about this"—he stroked a finger over his own neck while staring at hers—"before you go to work."

She slapped a hand to her neck, feeling the tender prickle of what she could only pray was beard burn and not a hickey. "Hives."

A smile twitched on his lips. "Of course."

Thank god the waiter showed up with their food.

She dug into her eggs almost before the plate hit the table. Her stomach might be cramped by nerves, but that didn't stifle her appetite. Plus, keeping her mouth full seemed the safest way not to say anything else stupid or incriminating.

They all ate in blissful silence for a few minutes. The food was good, but nothing like what her mother could make. Lucia Delgado's brilliance in the kitchen was the cornerstone upon which the family business had been built. Along with her husband's skill and bull-headed determination, together they'd made Bayamo one of the most popular dining destinations in Boulder.

And soon, she was going to help make it even more of a success.

The giddy thought made the months of crunching numbers and gathering data worth it. The only thing she had to do now was actually sit her parents down and present her idea to them. And since the wedding and all its related distractions were now over, it was finally time.

Her time.

With a happy hum, she scraped up the last of the syrup and popped the final bite of waffle in her mouth, wishing there was more. She should be full, but for some reason she was absolutely starving this morning.

Okay, she knew why. She was just ignoring it.

Like the mind-reader he was, Des nudged a plate with several delicious-looking treats in her direction. "Go on. Have one."

"Oh, thanks, but I couldn't."

"Of course, you could." *Nudge.* "You know you want to."

She really did. Which was why she shouldn't. She was not a slave to her impulses.

But darn it, they looked *really* good.

"Maybe just one." After an agony of indecision, she moved her choice to her plate. "Thank you." Trying not to seem too eager, she forked up a bite of the rolled cannoli-filled French toast and nearly died on the spot. "Oh. My. God!"

Des didn't even try not to look smug. "What did I tell you? Sometimes the things you don't think you should want can turn out to be the best decision you ever made."

For a second, she had the strangest feeling he wasn't talking about the food. But then he turned to cajole his husband into sharing half of his hubcap-sized cinnamon bun, and she shook the odd sensation off and went back to enjoying her creamy-sweet treat. Because yeah, it was probably the best decision she'd made all morning.

All week, maybe.

Unlike, say, her *worst* decision, who once again drew her attention despite her best efforts to ignore him. But as he and his cousins all left their table, it was as though she couldn't *not* watch that mass of masculinity as it made its way through the dining room toward the exit.

Okay, she couldn't not watch *one* mass of masculinity in particular. His cousins might all be big and good looking, but he was still the one who stood out in the crowd, and not just because of his muscles.

She tensed as they drew near. If he turned his head just a little, he'd be looking right at her. What if he caught her staring like some lovesick fool? Not that she was one. But what if he thought she was?

She should look away. Ignore him.

But she just couldn't do it. It felt too much like admitting she had something to hide. Or regret. Which she didn't. At all. She'd had some satisfying sex, and that was it. There was nothing more to read into it than that. And if he did, well, it was his problem, and she was more than happy to set him straight.

Firm in how she'd handle things, she waited as Peter neared their table.

And walked out of the dining room without a single glance in her direction.

Outwardly, she refused to show any reaction whatsoever. But inside, she deflated like a bad souffle. All that worry for nothing. The man never even noticed her.

Not like she cared. At all. In fact, she was glad. It made everything so much easier. To go on as though last night had never happened.

Yes. She was damn glad.

And look at that. She was still a liar.

Chapter 4

This was a really bad idea.

Peter adjusted his numb ass in the driver's seat of his Tahoe and told himself for the hundredth time to forget it and go home. To do this at another time, another place. But like the other ninety-nine times, he ignored that wise bit of advice and stayed put.

If he'd just been able to talk to Isabella that morning, it wouldn't have come to this.

He'd had a simple plan. Grab a table in the dining room where he could watch the door. Catch her attention when she showed up. Have her join him so they could talk like two rational adults about what had happened.

Except then his cousins had descended on him, tossing that option right into the dumpster.

Worse, they were all intelligent, and uncomfortably observant. Freakishly so. Even though he was skilled at discreet surveillance, they'd still noticed him noticing Isabella the second she'd entered the dining room. And being the tenacious bastards they were, it had been damn hard throwing them off the scent.

Especially when he'd already agreed to spend the day tour-guiding them around Boulder before they headed back home to Louisiana tomorrow morning. Thankfully, they'd been distracted enough by their sightseeing stint that the question of his interest in Isabella had been forgotten.

By them, anyway.

For him, it was a living, breathing problem which had led him to staking out the employee parking lot of Bayamo at almost midnight in search of answers.

To questions like why had she slipped out of his bed and left without a word? Why hadn't she even glanced his way once during brunch? Why—and this was the biggie—couldn't he seem to stop thinking about her?

All. Freaking. Day.

Yes, the sex had been hot. *So* damn hot. He'd been totally blown away by what a little firecracker Isabella had turned out to be in the sack. But he'd had hot sex before and never felt this lingering fascination that wouldn't go away. This sense of unfinished business.

It was driving him mental.

So here he sat, skulking in the shadows like a perp casing the place, waiting to get some answers, tie up loose ends, and move the fuck on.

Because whatever had happened between them, it couldn't happen again. Ever. Hell, it shouldn't have happened in the first place. Because the one thing his lust-driven brain had managed to make him forget last night was the most important: Isabella was his friend's baby sister.

He'd crossed a line. One he couldn't uncross, no matter how hard he wished he could. But he could make damn sure it was a one-time transgression.

The rear door of the restaurant opened.

Finally.

Most of the staff had trickled out over the past half hour, including both Isabella's brother and sister. Only two cars were left in the lot. One was Isabella's blue Kia hatchback, the other a brown Chevy two-door that must have belonged to the guy who was standing next to her as she locked the door behind them.

A little too closely.

They exchanged a few words, probably goodnights, before each heading to their cars. Peter rested his finger on the ignition button. But rather than get into his car and leave, the guy stood next to it and waited until Isabella had closed her door, started the engine, and backed out of her spot.

Fuck.

While he approved of the guy's protective measure—which only slightly lessened his annoyance at Cris for letting his little sister stay to close up while he went home—it totally screwed up his plan to pull into the lot and talk to her before she left.

"Why should the day end any fucking different than it began," he muttered, pulling away from the curb across the street.

Since he knew where she lived, he hung back as they cruised out of downtown and headed north into the tree-lined neighborhoods of the suburbs. It would be a real cherry on his day if she got spooked seeing his headlights follow her all the way home and called the cops on his ass.

As if he didn't have enough to live down at work already.

Parking at the curb in front of her parents' two-story Craftsman, he saw the moment she recognized his SUV. She stopped at the foot of the porch steps she'd been about to climb and crossed her arms, scowling as he made his way up the walkway toward her.

"What are you doing here?" Despite her obvious annoyance, she kept her voice low, likely in deference to the neighbors and the extremely late hour.

"I thought we should talk."

"No, I mean, what are you doing *here*? What would my parents think if they saw you?"

"Your parents are in Denver with some of your relatives until tomorrow. They were talking about it at the reception," he added at her look of surprise.

"Well, my sister—"

"Is probably taking advantage of them being away to stay with her boyfriend tonight."

"Did you hear that at the reception, too?"

Ah, there was that sarcasm he was coming to know so well.

He gave a small grin, knowing it would annoy her. "No. I saw her reapplying her lipstick and spritzing some perfume on in her car before she left the parking lot. Not something you do if you're just coming home to go to bed."

She looked disgruntled at his observation, but didn't refute its accuracy.

"So...can we go inside, or should we have this discussion out here?"

"Fine, I guess you can come in. For a minute."

Wow, so gracious.

He swallowed the comment back as he followed her to the door. No need to give her an excuse to change her mind about letting him come in. But as he crossed the threshold, he couldn't hold back the question that had been nagging at him.

"Does your brother always leave you to close the restaurant alone?"

"I wasn't alone. Fernando stayed with me." She turned from the alarm pad, surprise widening her eyes. "Wait, were you spying on me?"

"I wasn't *spying*. I was waiting for you to finish work so we could talk. About last night."

Her surprise turned to guarded wariness.

"What's there to talk about? We had sex. What do you want, a performance critique? Okay, you get an eight out of ten. Happy?"

Only eight?

He ignored the bleat of his affronted ego. "Ecstatic. No, smartass. I wanted to make sure..." He cleared his throat. "That you were okay. About what happened. That you weren't...having any regrets."

Which had been his first panicked thought when he'd woken to find her gone. She'd seemed sober enough to make an informed decision when she went into his room with him last night. But he'd been drinking, too. Had his own judgement been impaired enough he'd been mistaken?

The possibility had dogged him all damn day, wearing at his conscience like a river of regret until he'd found himself sitting in the dark outside the restaurant rather than in his bed getting some much-needed sleep.

"Nope," she chirped. "Not a one. Are we done?" She gave the door a hopeful look. Like she was imagining him on the other side of it.

You're not getting off that easy, sweetheart.

"Not until you tell me why you snuck off the way you did."

"I didn't sneak. You were asleep. And I had to get back to my room before Bria did."

That made sense. Had, in fact, been one possibility he'd tried to soothe his guilt-scoured conscience with. And yet...

"Fair enough. But why not wake me up and tell me that?"

"Because you...looked tired." Her lips pressed together, like she was trying hard not to let them curve into a smile. Maybe at the memory of how he'd gotten that way?

He felt no such reluctance, giving free rein to a wolfish grin that had her blinking. "I was *exhausted*." He drew the word out, imbuing it with all kinds of dark, sensual undertones.

Isabella swallowed. "See?" It came out on a squeak.

The proof he could affect her like that was a balm to his still sulking ego. But it did nothing for his growing annoyance.

"That doesn't mean I wouldn't have wanted to know you were leaving. Not to mention, you shouldn't have been walking through the hotel in the middle of the night by yourself. Do you realize how dangerous that was?"

"My room was right at the other end of the hall! It took me like thirty seconds to get there. And besides, everyone on our floor was a member of one of our families. I was perfectly safe."

The logical part of him agreed her points were sound. But the part of him that had seen bad things happen to people in a lot less than thirty seconds, the part that had seen bad things happen to his own *sister*, was harder to talk down.

He did, however, know when to pick his battles. And this wasn't the hill he wanted to die on. Not tonight, anyway. They still had a few other things to clear up first.

But they'd definitely be circling back to her lack of safety consciousness at a later date.

"So, you didn't sn—um, leave because you were having morning-after regrets about what you did?" He needed to be sure.

"What *I* did?" She crossed her arms and tilted her head up at him, eyes flashing. "Don't you mean what *we* did? There were two of us in that bed, you know. Maybe you're the one having regrets."

Something about the way she pushed made him want to push back.

He took a step closer. "Oh, I have regrets, sweetheart. Lots of them. I regret you sneaking away meant I couldn't slide right inside you again this morning the way I wanted to the second I woke up. And I regret not being able to kiss those breasts and taste every inch of your luscious body one more time."

Her lips parted at his deliberately graphic words.

He was way out of line. He knew it.

But he couldn't seem to stop himself.

Dropping his voice lower, he took another step, invading her personal space, yet giving her plenty of room to slide away if she wanted to. "And I really regret not getting to hear those panting little moans you make, and the way you say my name right before you come. Just one. More. Time."

A little like she was panting right now.

"You...you do?" She sounded confused, and more than a little turned on.

Good, because so was he.

"Oh, yeah." His gaze zeroed in on her mouth. "Fuck yeah." He started to lean in. One little taste to remember her by wouldn't hurt. Right?

"Then why wouldn't you even look at me this morning?" she blurted out.

That stopped him cold. "What?"

She muttered something under her breath and ducked around him while he stood there like a dumb ox. "Nothing. Forget it."

"Forget it?" He swung around and stalked after her. "Like hell. What do you mean, I wouldn't look at you? When? We both agreed I was asleep when you left."

She stopped at the bottom of the stairs to the second floor, gripping the curved bannister as though physically restraining herself from running up them. After a few seconds of what looked like painful internal debate, she groaned and sank onto the steps.

"I shouldn't have said anything. It's stupid."

"It's not stupid if it's bothering you, which it obviously is." Reining in both his arousal and his frustration, he sat next to her. "Tell me." He made it more of a request than a demand.

Which seemed to work, since she actually answered.

"In the dining room at brunch. When you were leaving. You passed almost right by my table, and I thought maybe you'd at least say hello or something, but..." She shrugged. "You just ignored me and walked by like you weren't even aware I was alive." She tucked her feet up on the step below her and hugged her knees. "Like I said, stupid."

For the second time in as many minutes, he felt like he'd been smacked in the head with a big stick. Ignored her? Wasn't aware she was alive? Was she *kidding*? If anything, he'd been hyperaware of her every second they'd both been in the same room, and trying like hell not to let it show.

Clearly, he'd done too good a job of it.

"No, it's not stupid," he said, shifting a little so he could look at her as he spoke, even though she wouldn't do the same. "But not very accurate, either. I knew you were there from the second you came in with your sister and her boyfriend. And I was very definitely aware of you when I walked past on my way out."

"Bull."

"Truth."

"Then why didn't you even look at me?"

"Are you forgetting who you were sitting with? Do you really think Des wouldn't notice us doing the whole eye-contact thing? Or that he wouldn't have had something to say to you about it afterward?" The man was almost as big a meddler as his mother.

That brought her head around as alarm flared in her eyes. "God, you're right."

"I usually am."

"I wouldn't go that far."

They shared a rare smile as some of the tension between them eased.

"Plus, I was with my cousins, who are the nosiest bunch of bast—uh, well, they're nosy as hell, and I didn't want them asking any questions, either. Especially not before I had a chance to talk to you and make sure everything was okay between us."

He paused. "*Is* it? About this, anyway," he added with another grin, this one at his own expense. "You're totally free to keep not liking me in every other way. I just want to be sure we're good about last night."

A tiny snort accompanied a softening of those expressive brown eyes that had spent so much time glaring at him the past few days. "I guess maybe you're not *all* that bad."

"Wow, careful, that much praise might kill me."

She snorted again and bumped his shoulder with hers. "Take what you can get. And yes, we're good about last night."

"Good." He bumped her back. "And for the record, I guess you're not so bad, either."

"Gee, thanks."

Somehow, their shoulders stayed touching. He probably should have moved away. But it was a companionable kind of contact, so he told himself it was okay to stay where he was. They'd just reached some sort of weird détente, and he was going to enjoy it while it lasted.

And if he also enjoyed the warmth of her body seeping into his, and the subtle aroma of the cooking spices she'd been around all evening which clung to her hair and skin, well, that was just a bonus.

"You know it can't happen again, right?" He hated it, but it needed to be said.

"I know."

"It shouldn't have even happened at all." For so many reasons. None of which he could quite think of at the moment. But he knew they were there.

"I know."

Was it his imagination, or did she sound a little wistful?

"But I don't regret that it did." Holy shit, had he really just said that? Out loud?

He must have, because he could feel Isabella's body tense against his.

Shit.

Well, there went détente.

"Neither do I."

At the soft words, his head swiveled toward her so fast his neck gave an audible crack. She was already looking at him. Their gazes met, held, and something that definitely wasn't détente crackled to life between them.

It was sharp, and hot, and achingly familiar.

Before he could remind himself again why he shouldn't, he pressed his mouth to hers in a hungry kiss, half hoping she'd either push him away or, better yet, hit him. Instead, she groaned and threw her arms around his neck, pulling him even deeper into the abyss. Logic vanished. Reason retreated. Lust ruled. Nothing else mattered.

It was last night all over again. Except she had too many clothes on.

They both did.

Pressing her back against the stairs, he dragged the hem of the white button-down blouse from her black trousers with one hand and snaked it underneath to the bare skin of her stomach. Sliding along that stretch of warm satin, he felt her breathing hitch against his mouth, becoming a groan of approval as his questing hand found the soft mound of her breast.

This is crazy, this is crazy, this is crazy...

That small voice of warning might have had a chance if her fingers hadn't closed over the erection straining under his jeans and squeezed.

With a growl that would have done his dog Roscoe proud, he attacked the buttons on her blouse, peeling the two halves aside and staring down at the treasure he'd revealed. Last night, those glorious breasts had been wearing a delicate scrap of blush-colored silk and lace. Yet somehow, tonight's plain white cotton was just as sexy.

He palmed the firm mounds with both hands, enjoying the purr she made as she squirmed under his touch. God, she was responsive. Even with only that little bit of contact her nipples were hard and threatening to press right through the sturdy fabric, seeking more.

Well, he was happy to oblige.

Right before he slid a hand around to her back to do just that, though, he saw the clip nestled at the base of Isabella's sweet cleavage. He grinned. Front clasp bra.

Best invention *ever*.

It took a hot second to free her breasts from their confinement, and even less time to close his lips over one of those delectable hard tips. Surprise, or the hot suction of his mouth—maybe both—made her back arch up from the steps on a moaning gasp.

Music to his ears.

He played there a few minutes before giving equal attention to her other breast. By the time he dragged his tongue up the column of her neck to her mouth, she was quivering like a racehorse at the blocks waiting for the starting bell to sound.

Her hands found their way under his shirt as he lingered over the kiss, scoring his back as she tried to pull him into closer contact with her lower body. He obliged, shifting onto his knees to press his jean-clad erection into the welcoming juncture of her thighs.

The groan that vibrated into his mouth from hers almost did him in.

He moved against her, hips slowly working as though there weren't several layers of clothing between them. As if he were buried deep inside her heat. Taking. Giving. Repeat.

The memory of how tight she'd been around him last night, how wet and wild, was almost enough to put him right over the edge.

Fuck it. He didn't care if he came in his pants like a horny teenager. If this was as close to Isabella as he was going to get, then he'd take it. He was so…damn…close…

She wrenched her mouth from his. "Wait."

Everything in him froze at that one small word. Everything except the pain in his balls at being denied the release that had been no more than four strokes away. Maybe only three. That continued, like a vise tightening crank by crank around his sac.

But still he pulled back, breathing hard as he perched on all fours over her on the stairs, blood pounding in his veins as he stared into her dark eyes. Waiting, just as she'd asked.

"Condoms are upstairs."

It took several long seconds for the husky words to register. When they did, the pounding of his blood turned into a roar, obliterating all thought. He was entirely on primitive auto-mode as he prowled behind her up the steps. Down the hall. Into the room.

Her room.

Her bed.

His inner primitive howled. But he stood stock-still, still doing what she'd asked. Still waiting. For some sign, some command which would release him from this punishing level of self-restraint and allow him to finish what he'd started.

What they'd started.

Stopping beside the bed, she stripped away her blouse and bra as she turned to face him, sending both to the floor like a dropped flag at a racetrack.

As signs went, it was pretty damn indisputable.

With an almost violent yank, he tore his shirt off over his head. By the time he'd kicked his sneakers away and jerked off his jeans and underwear, he was hanging on by a thread. One that snapped the second her panties hit the carpet, leaving her gloriously bare.

All for him.

His first impulse was to toss her onto the bed and pick up right where they'd left off on the stairs. Instead, he dropped to his knees in front of her, where he pressed a worshipful kiss to the sweet swell of her belly. God, he loved her curves.

Another kiss. And another. His mouth trailed down over her navel, where he dipped his tongue inside to make her squirm. To her hip and the filigreed heart tattooed there in delicate strokes of black and blue ink. Along the crease of her thigh and right to the sweet little jewel that made her mewl like a newborn kitten when his mouth found it.

She must have been as primed as he was, going off like a Roman candle before he'd spent more than a minute pleasuring her. He made sure to wring every last whimper from her before sitting back on his ankles. The satisfied smile curving her lips as she looked down at him said clearer than words she'd enjoyed herself.

Or maybe she just liked him on his knees.

The thought of worshiping at sexy Isabella's feet for eternity cranked his engine more than he would have thought. But if he didn't get her on that bed and get into her in the next thirty seconds, he was going to lose his ever-fucking-loving mind.

As he rose to his feet, she seemed to read his thoughts, backing toward the bed with a come-and-get-it look.

He didn't need to be told twice.

In three strides he was up against her, tumbling them both to the soft mattress. There was no more time for preliminaries, though. Pausing only long enough for her to dig out a condom from her nightstand drawer, it was game on.

It was almost a shock he didn't let go on the very first pump. But it seemed his dick had gotten its second wind, and was planning to make the most of the unexpected opportunity to revisit this particular slice of heaven.

By the time the warning tingle began at the base of his spine, they were both sweaty and straining. The muscles in his arms were tight as boulders as he held himself over her, hips rocking harder and faster as he raced for the finish line.

When the orgasm hit, it was like reaching the heights of that heaven.

Followed by a quick descent into hell.

Because in the quiet aftermath as they lay panting, boneless limbs entwined, the overload of testosterone flushed from his system and thought once more reared its annoying head. And with thought came unwanted clarity.

That this wasn't supposed to have happened again.

That instead of fixing things, he'd only made them worse.

That he was a rotten fucking friend.

Because even knowing it was wrong, knowing he should be putting on his clothes, should be getting as far away from Rafe's sister as he possibly could, he also knew he wouldn't be doing any of that anytime soon.

Not without having her at least one more time.

And even then, it wasn't going to be nearly enough.

Chapter 5

Getting her family together in one place for one purpose was a lot like herding cats. Only without the built-in cuteness to keep you from wanting to kill them.

First, she had to drag her brother and mother out of the restaurant's kitchen, where they were locked in deep discussion over some new dish they were thinking of adding to the menu. Then it was getting her dad away from his receipts and ledgers.

Bria was the only one who showed up in the office without coercion. Bella's initial swell of gratitude dimmed, however, when she realized her sister was more interested in texting with her boyfriend than in paying attention to what she had to say.

Not the auspicious start she'd hoped for.

Undeterred, she squared her shoulders and focused on projecting confidence and professionalism. She'd worked long and hard to get to this point, and she had every intention of dazzling them all with her proposal. It was finally time to make her own mark on the family business.

Nervous excitement raised goosebumps on her arms.

Showtime.

"Thank you for coming so I could talk to you all together like this. I know you all have things you'd rather be doing—"

Cris shifted his body as though to stand. "Actually—"

"—but all I need is twenty minutes of your time, so I appreciate your attention to what I have to say." She may have kept smiling, but she put every ounce of steel she had into the glare she focused on her brother. With an exaggerated sigh, he slumped back in his seat.

First point to the cat herder.

"What is it, *mija*?" her mother asked. "You have our full attention."

"Thank you." Although she would have appreciated it more if her mother hadn't looked at her watch, as though marking the time. She took in a deep breath and slowly let it out.

You can do this.

"So, as you know, the restaurant has been doing really well. And with our expansion into catering small off-premise events the past few years, we've been able to extend our reach even further to people who might not have otherwise known about Bayamo, or had heard of us but not been motivated enough to come give our food a try."

"Yes, Cristiano and Brianna have made that venture quite the success." Lucia Delgado beamed at her two middle children.

And me, she wanted to whine. *I've been right there helping, too.*

Tossing her inner toddler a cookie, she pushed the well-worn slight aside and forged on. "Which is why I believe the time is right for us to continue building on that success and expand the business even further, into another new market."

This time it was her father who shifted as though preparing to get up.

"Isabella, we've already discussed the idea of opening a second location, and the costs involved were—"

"Not feasible, I know. But that was for another brick-and-mortar site. What I'm proposing is much less cost-prohibitive, with the added benefit of reaching an as-yet untapped market for us." She took a bracing breath.

This is it.

"I think we should open a food truck."

Crickets.

If in the future she was asked to pick a word to describe the overall reaction to that one simple sentence, she'd have to go with horrified. To be honest, she'd expected a fair amount of negativity to the idea. Definitely a lot of pushback, especially from her parents. Maybe even some scoffing and ridicule.

She hadn't expected to render them all speechless.

Not a good sign. Especially since she was pretty sure it wasn't because they all saw her idea as so brilliant and innovative, they couldn't believe they hadn't thought of it already themselves. That would be waaay too much to ask for. Kind of like getting equal credit for the time and effort she put into the catering.

No, this was an are-you-out-of-your-mind, why-are-you-wasting-our-time kind of silence. Which meant she had about five seconds to get in front of the avalanche of criticism and disapproval about to break loose and rain down over her, smothering her idea before it even had a chance.

Ignoring the prickle of sweat building under her arms, she grabbed the stack of spiral-bound presentation packets and started doling them out around the table like a Vegas dealer, talking fast.

"The food truck industry isn't stale sandwiches and bad coffee anymore. Far from it. In fact, it's a highly lucrative, highly competitive business that offers customers a wide range of high-quality food, everything from standard staples to gourmet specialty fare. It also happens to be the fastest growing segment in the overall food industry, increasing at almost sixteen percent a year for the past five years. And those start-up costs you were worried about? They'd be less than a quarter of what opening another brick-and-mortar location would be."

She paused to catch her breath and read the room. As she'd hoped, hard numbers had snagged her business-minded father's attention. He wasn't hooked, not by a long shot. But at least he wasn't walking away.

Not yet.

Cris looked like he was about to say something. She launched into the next part of her pitch, cutting him off.

"Boulder is a prime location for a food truck to thrive. Besides the tons of tourist foot traffic downtown, especially on the Mall, there's also the local breweries to consider. A lot of them are partnering with food trucks that complement their brand to set up shop near their tasting rooms. And it's not only the tourists who are potential customers. All of those college kids? And the workers in the business district? They need to eat. And they want something quick, reasonably priced, and most importantly, *good*. We can give them that."

Bria frowned. "There's, like, a sea of food trucks down in Flatiron Park every weekday already doing just that."

"But none serving *our* food. People get tired of the same choices all the time."

"Which means they'd get tired of us, too. It's a static market."

Bella smiled. "But that's the beauty of having a mobile restaurant. You can cycle in and out of locations whenever you want. In fact, it's something I would recommend we do. Often."

"Right," Cris scoffed. "Because making it harder for your customers to find you makes great business sense."

Her smile got a little more strained, but she hung on to it.

"It does, actually, from a marketing standpoint. It can help create buzz. Once a truck has established a following, people will track it from one location to another. All we have to do is post where we're going to be on any given day on our social media and website, and they'll show up. Heck, they'll be *waiting* for us. The more we interact with customers, the more word spreads, and the more people want to check us out." She flipped her hands out in a *ta-da* motion. "Buzz."

"*Our* social media," Bria repeated. "Meaning you'd want to piggyback off of the restaurant's name and reputation."

"You make it sound like they're not two parts of the same whole. The food truck would be an offshoot of the restaurant, the same way the catering is."

"Not the same," Cris snapped. "People know what to expect from our name. The food we use for catering is exactly the same as what we serve here in the restaurant. There's no cutting corners. No sacrificing quality. No chance of diluting our brand, or worse, damaging it."

Wow. She'd expected to be defending her position to her parents, not get tag-teamed by her brother and sister.

The pain of that cut a lot sharper than she'd have thought.

"There wouldn't be any corner cutting or loss of quality. If you look at page fifteen of the business plan I gave you, you'll see the proposed menu items which, with only a few minor modifications—"

"So, not the same."

"—would make ideal options for minimal preparation and packaging. Plus, there's been a clear shift in consumer preference toward unique and adventurous food concepts. With the way you like to experiment with new dishes, I'm sure you could come up with a few signature items specifically targeted to the mobile dining crowd that would stand head-and-shoulders above the competition."

She'd hoped playing to his vanity would help win him over. Only it backfired.

"Right, because that's exactly why I went to culinary school and spent all these years learning my craft to become a chef. To create roach coach cuisine." He made a sound of deep disgust. "I don't think so."

"I told you," she said through clenched teeth, "they're not 'roach coaches' anymore. Some food trucks bring in over four hundred k in sales a year. Not to mention more than a few have been successful enough their owners have gone on to open their own restaurants."

"Which we already have, so it's a moot point." Cris pushed the packet away as though that was the end of the discussion.

At least their mother did her the courtesy of actually looking at the list of menu items she'd agonized over putting together. Even so, she didn't look any more swayed than her son. "I don't know, sweetheart..."

Bella's stomach dipped. Her brother might be a chef, but her mom was the indisputable ruler of Bayamo's kitchen. If she shot the idea down, that was it. Without food, there was no food truck. End of story.

End of dream.

Panic sent her stomach into another rollercoaster loop-de-loop, making her wish she'd skipped that third cup of coffee. She threw a desperate look at Bria, hoping for a little sisterly backup. But her gaze was firmly fixed on her lap, where she was no doubt busy texting with Alejandro. Again.

Thanks, sis.

Daunting as it seemed, that left her father as her only potential source of support. She looked across the table at him. As she talked, he'd been flipping through the bound packet, stopping here and there to give a page a cursory read before moving on. And all the while, his expression never shifted from the brows-down serious look she'd always secretly thought of as his business face.

It had never seemed intimidating until it was focused on her.

"Dad? Thoughts?"

Blunt forefinger tapping on the packet, he mulled his words over for a long moment. "This is a very professional, well thought out business plan."

A spark of excitement lit in her chest.

"Thank you. I've been working on it for months."

And thank you, CCD, for your entrepreneurship program.

"It shows." *Tap. Tap. Tap.* "I just wish you would have brought the idea to me first before you put all that time and energy into it."

Her excitement flickered like a flame sputtering in a strong breeze.

"I wanted to be sure you had all the information you'd need to make an informed decision." Not the stubborn gut-reaction one she could see in his eyes.

Damn it.

"There's a lot more detailed information in here I didn't talk about yet. About the potential financial benefits to our existing business by increasing our visibility to an entirely new demographic segment. And then there's things like merchandising, and—"

"Jesus!" Cris shoved his chair back with a screech. "I've heard enough of this crap."

"Cristiano." Her mother clucked her tongue. But the admonishment was clearly for the language, not the angry words.

"It's not crap!"

"Isabella..."

"I'm sorry, *Mami*, but it's not. This is a good, solid business idea. Is it a little outside our usual scope? Yes. But so was catering when we first started doing it, and look how well that's gone. If we're going to grow the business, we have to be willing to think beyond the box."

She thought, just for a second, her words might have made a difference.

Then the phone on her father's desk rang. As if it was some kind of signal, everyone scattered. Her father went to answer the phone. Cris and Bria both left the room without a backward glance.

Only her mother bothered to pause long enough to pat her arm with a sympathetic smile. "You did a very good job, *mija*."

And then she was gone, too.

Stunned, Bella looked around the vacated table and the four bound packets left behind, two of them never even opened.

That was it? All that work? All those months of research and planning? And *this* was what it got her? Some angry words and a quick group brush-off?

The third cup of coffee started to percolate in her belly again, leaving a sour taste in her mouth. Vaguely aware of her father's voice rumbling in the background as he spoke to someone, she grabbed her purse and left the office. Her only thought was to get as far away from the restaurant—and her family—as she could before the numbness wore off.

And the real pain began.

"Isabella, wait."

She turned at her father's brusque call, the tiny spark still inside her reviving. "Yes, *Papi*?"

"You need to come in tonight and work the late shift in the dining room. Marisol just called out sick." Without waiting for a response, he disappeared back into the office, shutting the door behind him.

As if some spectral breeze from the finality of that action had blown it out, the spark inside her sputtered one last time and died.

Right along with her dreams.

⚬

"He didn't!"

Sitting on the floor of her best friend's apartment, back propped against the couch, Bella nodded and dug her chopsticks into the container of spicy Pad Kee Mao she'd stopped for on the way over. "Of course he did. He had a hole in the schedule that needed to be filled, so he expected me to fill it. What else is new?"

Beside her, Kinzley Takei shook her head as she chewed her food, poking her own chopsticks in the air until she could speak. "But this is different! After he just shot down your entire proposal without so much as an 'I'll give it some thought,' he asks you—no, he *tells* you—to come in on your day off and work closing? Unbelievable!"

No. Sadly, it was totally believable.

The restaurant had a problem, and her father had dealt with it the same way he always did. Need an extra waitress? Call in Bella. Short-handed in the kitchen? Have Bella sub. Last-minute catering job? Bella to the rescue. She was their utility player extraordinaire. Their go-to girl when things went sideways.

But go-to just wasn't good enough for her.

Not anymore.

No, she wanted her own niche in the family business. A real one. One that gave her a place and a purpose. That said she was just as important as Cristiano and Brianna. Not that her parents meant to play favorites. But Cris was obviously his mother's son, with all her love of and instincts for creating great food. And Brianna had the managerial skills of their father, who would no doubt one day leave the business in her capable hands to run.

All of which left Bella...exactly nowhere. And nothing.

No parent's footsteps to follow in. No predestined role to assume.

No way to prove, to herself as much as to her family, she was an integral piece of the Bayamo machine, and not just a useful spare part.

Not unless she made one.

That was the realization which had started it all. Sitting in this very spot, eating Thai take-away from their favorite food truck, both of them bitching about the limitations and frustrations of working for their respective family businesses. About wanting something more, but not knowing what. And then *bam!*

An idea had been born.

"You're not going to do it, are you?" Kinzley dropped her head back and gave a dramatic sigh, the ends of her blue-tinged black hair brushing the cushions. "Of course you are. You always do what they ask you to."

Bella gave her friend a dirty side-eye. "Like you're the queen of saying no when your parents tell you they need you at the store last minute. Two words: opening day."

"Hey, don't judge. At least you still got to go to the game. *And* I gave you my ticket to bring someone. I, on the other hand, spent the day wiping fingerprints off of display cases and selling stupid souvenirs to tourists instead of munching hotdogs and drinking beer and watching our team kick some Diamondback butt."

There was that. And as a bonus, she'd gotten to spend a great day with her brother. Rafe had been the only person both a Rockies fan and available last minute on a weekday, thanks to his weird police schedule. It had been a long time since they'd done something fun together, just the two of them.

Like, since before he'd gotten engaged to *that woman* long.

The thought of Lillian brought with it thoughts of Lillian's brother. Of how good he'd looked laying sprawled naked across her bed. Of how even better he'd felt sprawled naked across *her*. And under her. And—

Damn.

She'd managed to go the whole day so far without thinking about Peter. Which was way better than yesterday, when she'd had near constant daydreamy flashbacks about the hours they'd spent driving each other crazy in bed. Or the day before that, when the flashbacks had been both visceral as well as mental.

Nothing like having an unplanned party in your panties at the breakfast table in front of your parents and your much-too-observant sister.

Awk-ward.

Resetting her 'no naughty thoughts in this many hours' counter back to zero, she refocused on the issue at hand. Then had to bite her lip and shove away the memory of big, strong hands doing all sorts of deliciously devilish things to her quivering body.

Focus!

"Yes, I'm going in tonight, and not just because it wouldn't be right to leave everyone shorthanded when I don't have any particular plans, anyway." If you didn't count lying in bed, reliving her most recent fall from her high horse in vivid detail. "If I want my family to take me and my idea seriously, I can't act like a pouty brat because I didn't get what I wanted on the first try."

Kinzley's noodles slipped from her chopsticks back into the container. "What? Does that mean you're not giving up?"

"That's exactly what it means." It had been a few hours before she'd gotten past her initial reaction of hurt and frustration. But by the time the second round of tears had tapered off, leaving her feeling drained and empty, a different emotion had crept in and taken hold.

Determination.

"I put way too much effort into this business plan to let it be shot down after barely two minutes of consideration. And not just because it's my idea. I really think the restaurant will benefit from diversifying into a new market. *This* new market."

"Well, for what it's worth, I think you're right. I think it's a killer idea. This"—she hefted her container of Pad Thai—"is great eats, but a truck with food by Bayamo?" She made exaggerated yummy sounds.

Bella started to laugh, then pressed her lips together in thought. "Hmm. Food by Bayamo. That's not bad."

"Not bad for what?"

"A name for the food truck." She tapped the chopsticks on the edge of the container. "Food by Bayamo. Bayamo Food. Bayamo Bistro."

"Bayamo Bites."

The tapping stopped. "Oh, I like that one. Although…"

"Yeah, I just heard it, too. Maybe Bites by Bayamo?"

Bella waffled her head side-to-side. "Yeah. Maybe."

"Or how about Bits of Bayamo? Bayamo's Bits?"

"The best thing you'll ever put in your mouth."

They looked at each other before both dissolving into a fit of giggles. More name ideas flew as they dug into their food, each one getting sillier and more outrageous until there was more laughing than eating going on.

Wiping tears of laughter from her cheeks, Bella leaned into her friend and gave her a tight side-hug. "God, that felt good. Thank you. I really needed something to laugh about."

Kinzley returned the hug with a fierce one of her own. "Laugh. Cry. Bitch. Whatever you need, I got your back, girlfriend."

"Back atcha."

After cleaning up the remains of their meal, they squeezed out onto the apartment's minuscule balcony. The only view was of the CVS across the street, but the fresh air was a welcome antidote to the post-carb lethargy threatening to take hold.

"I could get used to this," Bella sighed, sinking into one of the plastic chairs.

"I'm so glad to hear you say that." There was a mischievous lilt to Kinzley's tone, matched by the quirked half-grin on her lips when Bella turned to look at her. "Since I may have heard from a certain unnamed source, *cough*Wilson*cough*, there may be an apartment opening up in the building as soon as next month. And that the application of a certain set of sisters, who shall also remain nameless, *cough*youandBria*cough*, is top of the waiting list."

If there had been room, she would have fallen out of her chair.

"Are you kidding?"

"Nope."

"And you're only mentioning this *now*?"

"Well, I wasn't sure I should mention it at all, since it's not a hundred percent done deal yet. But I figured after the day you had, you could use some good news, even if it's only a maybe."

"And because you can't keep a secret."

"And because I can't keep a secret."

They both laughed, because it was the truth. In fact, despite what she'd said, she was impressed her friend had been able to hold on to the news this long. And wow, what news! She and Bria had put in their application for an apartment in Kinzley's complex months ago, after they'd finally convinced their parents nothing horrible would happen to them if they moved out of the family home and got a place of their own.

Overprotective didn't begin to describe their father when it came to his two little girls.

Not that they were so little anymore. Or that they needed their parents' permission to move out. But it had seemed best for everyone to ease themselves from the family nest in as low-drama a manner as possible. And that meant agreeing to a few conditions. One of which was having Rafe vet whatever building they planned to move into.

It should have been easy.

Instead, he'd found something wrong with every one of the apartments they'd considered. No locks on the lobby doors. Inadequate lighting in the parking lot. Too close to the college. Too seedy. Too nice—whatever *that* meant.

Every place they'd found, he'd found a reason to nix it.

All but Kinzley's building. Which would have been ideal except for the fact there'd been no two-bedrooms available, and they had to go on a waiting list with no idea of when one might open up. It could be a few months. It could be a year.

And Bella couldn't help but wonder if that was part of the reason Rafe found it so acceptable.

It wasn't as though he was *trying* to be a jerk. She knew her big brother's heart was in the right place. Most of the time. Unfortunately, his need to protect his family was a deep-seated one, and it sometimes made him act like a bit of an ass.

Not without reason. The vicious robbery that had left their father pistol-whipped and bloody had made an indelible mark on a teenaged Rafe. So much so that he'd pursued a career in law enforcement rather than joining the family business as was expected of him.

It had left its mark on the rest of the family as well. But in Bella's opinion, there was a fine line between being careful and being caged. And it had definitely been the latter feeling she was trying to escape when she made the single most stupid mistake of her life.

Four years later, and she still wanted to go back and smack some sense into her naïve eighteen-year-old self. God, she'd been stupid. Too trusting. Too blind.

Too in love.

Time hadn't healed her heart so much as allowed enough scar tissue to build up so that it didn't hurt anymore. Now it was more of a numb ache that pulsed whenever she needed the reminder to not make the same mistakes as before. Being stupidly blind could only be forgiven once. Anything more than that made her an idiot.

A vivid image of Peter Beaumont's naked body as it drove against hers nearly sent her falling out of her chair for the second time. Sex. That was only sex. And sex didn't count.

He didn't count.

It wasn't like there was any danger of her developing feelings for him other than simple, raw lust. He was the very embodiment of her Big Mistake. Rich. Handsome. Well-connected.

Did she mention rich?

No, she'd never risk her heart on someone like him again. Burned once, only a fool would put her hand back into the same fire a second time and expect a different result. And she might be many things, but she would never be a fool again.

Chapter 6

"WELL, IF IT ISN'T Mr. Society Page!"

Fuck my life.

With patience unfortunately borne from years of practice, Peter ignored the taunting words and continued to unbutton his uniform shirt as if he didn't have a care in the world. Which hadn't been true even before his worst nightmare—aka Detective Charlie Lister—showed up in the precinct locker room.

What had happened over the weekend with Isabella was a problem. A huge one. One he had yet to find a solution to. At least one that didn't include locking both of them in his bedroom and making love to her until neither of them could walk straight.

But he'd learned a long time ago how to put his personal crap in a box while he was on the job. Being distracted while on patrol was the surest way to a three-quarters disability retirement. Or, worse, a full-honors funeral.

Too bad for him Lister was part of his work crap. And there wasn't a box anywhere near big enough to stick that much bullshit into. God knew he'd tried. But no matter how hard he ignored the bastard, the guy just wouldn't stop riding his ass.

Like now.

"Saw your picture in the paper this weekend. Must've been nice, rubbing elbows with all of the city's most rich and famous." Lister pushed off the doorjamb he'd propped his shoulder on and sauntered further into the locker room. "Oh wait. Your family *is* one of the city's most rich and famous. Isn't that right, *Beaumont*." He pushed on his name, as though some of the other guys stripping off their uniforms after shift change might need a reminder.

Peter popped his locker open and shrugged out of his shirt, jaw aching from how tightly he had it clenched. He hated when Lister tried to use his family to beat his 'Beaumont is a spoiled rich boy, not one of us regular guys' drum with. But he hadn't said anything yet that wasn't one hundred percent true, so he held his temper and his tongue. Sometimes, when he didn't get the reaction he wanted, the guy got bored and went away.

"Where can I get me one of those swanky tuxes you were wearing? Did you have it made special, or is that just part of your required millionaire's-club wardrobe?"

It didn't look like today would be one of those lucky days.

Again, he didn't respond. But then, Lister didn't need him to. He was on a roll, *and* he had an audience.

"I bet it was custom. Golden Boy here looked too damned pretty for anything off the rack. Am I right, boys?"

That fucking nickname again.

A couple of guys made varying sounds of amusement. Not agreeing with Lister, exactly. More like enjoying the trash-talk show they were getting, something all of them did with each other pretty much every day. But it was all the encouragement he needed to keep going.

"I mean, why wouldn't you have a custom tux when all your uniforms get tailored special for you?" He snorted and looked to the others. "Talk about a prima donna."

Peter didn't respond. Didn't bother to defend himself.

Sam did it for him.

"Yeah, well, you'd have to get your shit tailored, too, Blister, if you had guns like Beaumont does." He made a point of looking at

Lister's arms, which were no match for the impressive biceps Peter sported even without flexing.

There was another round of snickers and grunts of amusement, this time at Lister's expense. Rather than take it with good grace as Peter had, his face darkened, eyes narrowing in anger.

"Yeah, well, you'd better watch it, Beaumont. Steroids will shrink your nuts to raisins if you're not careful."

Slamming his locker shut, Peter spun and glared at him. "And you'd better fucking watch your mouth about that kind of shit."

A normal person would have shrunk under the ferocity of Peter's fury. Lister just gave one of his smarmy smirks and held up his hands in the surrender position. "Hey, take it easy there, big guy. No need to go all Hulk on us."

"Fuck you, Lister. Making accusations like that is some serious shit." Especially since using steroids could get him fired. Not that he had, or ever would. But even a whisper of the illegal performance enhancer could permanently taint his reputation within the department and destroy any chance for advancement.

"Geez, relax. I wasn't accusing you of anything. It was a joke. Lighten the fuck up." He once again looked to his audience for support, this time with a chuckle and a 'can you believe this guy?' roll of his eyes.

And damned if a few of them didn't grin and shake their heads in agreement.

Fuck this.

Grabbing his gym bag, he somehow ignored the triumphant gleam in Lister's eyes and called goodbye to a few of the guys before exiting the locker room. No doubt there'd be a few more comments about him flung around after he left. There was nothing he could do about it, so he tried not to care.

But he did. He couldn't help it.

There had been a lot of prejudgment from his fellow officers when he first got on the job seven years ago. That he was just some spoiled rich kid looking for the power trip that came with the badge and gun. That he would use his family's connections and influence to get plum assignments or promotions.

That he was a joke.

He'd worked his ass off to prove every one of those preconceptions wrong. And not just wrong, but *dead* wrong. It had taken time, but for the most part he'd stopped being Peter Beaumont, youngest son of a financial investment dynasty to his co-workers, and simply became Officer Beaumont, damn good cop and the guy you'd want with you in a tight spot.

Lister was one of the outliers. Which wouldn't have mattered so much if he hadn't made it his mission to make Peter's life miserable at every opportunity. The only thing that made it bearable was Lister getting promoted to detective two years ago. At least now they only rubbed up against each other during shifts change.

And some days even that was almost too much to deal with.

Kind of like today.

As he walked through the precinct parking lot, he heard someone coming up fast behind him. A few seconds later, Sam Garcia caught up. Despite being a good half foot shorter than his own six-four, Sam still conveyed an image of solid 'don't fuck with this' which served him well on the streets.

"Thanks for the clapback in there." Even if it had made things worse. It was still nice to know his friend had his back.

"Forget it. He's an ass."

"Yeah, he is. But I still shouldn't have let him get under my skin like that. I know better. But he crossed the line with that steroid shit. I couldn't stop myself."

"And that's why he's a blister. He just keeps on rubbing you raw about something until you finally pop." His right hand opened wide to illustrate the explosion.

Peter laughed, and some of the tension in his shoulders loosened. "You do realize you called him Blister to his face, right?"

"Did I? Oops." He didn't sound worried about it.

But he should be. If anyone understood how long and far that asshole could carry a grudge, it was him.

"Hey, a couple of us are heading to the Downer tonight for a few. Wanna join?" Sam waggled his eyebrows. "It's Ladies Night."

It was tempting. A few hours at the local dive bar playing pool and talking up some hot chicks over cheap beer might be exactly what he needed to put this Isabella thing into perspective. Or at least get it out of his head for a little while.

Get *her* out of his head.

"Yeah, sure. Sounds good."

"Great. See ya later, Guns o' Steel." He play-punched Peter in the arm, then shook his hand as though it hurt.

"Asshole." But he was grinning as he said it.

After tossing his bag into the backseat of his Tahoe, he slipped on his sunglasses and drove the short distance from the precinct to his apartment. When he moved into the complex two years ago, he'd chosen it for its combination of awesome amenities, pet-friendly status, and proximity to both a dog park and a veterinary clinic.

The quick work commute had been a happy bonus.

Riding the elevator from the underground parking garage to the fourth floor, he checked his watch. Still plenty of time to give Roscoe a good, long walk before he was due to meet his friend John at the gym. He unlocked his apartment door and braced for impact.

Seventy pounds of fur and muscle smothered him with love and sloppy kisses as he struggled to get the door shut behind him. "Okay, okay, I missed you, too, ya big dope." He laughed, turning his head to avoid getting tongued. "Geez, enough already. Roscoe, down. *Sit.*"

With a whine, Roscoe's butt hit the hardwood, the thickly muscled boxer/Lab mix's body quivering, tail slashing like a windshield wiper on extra-high speed. Adoring brown eyes stared up at him in anticipation of the next command in their daily welcome home ritual.

"Leash."

With a chuffing sound, the dog spun and galloped through the apartment to the spare bedroom-slash-home office-slash-dog stuff catch-all. Peter ducked into his bedroom and secured his weapon in the gun safe there. When he got back to the living room situated between the two bedrooms, Roscoe was waiting, blue nylon leash clenched proudly in his mouth.

"Good boy. Hold." While Roscoe stayed stock-still under the command, he ran a hand down the dog's back in an affectionate rub before clipping on the harness he'd grabbed from the back of his door. "Give." The leash was released before he even finished the word. He attached it with a chuckle. "A little eager, are we?"

That was his fault. With everything going on with Lillian's wedding the previous week, he'd had almost zero free time to spend with the pooch. And while Roscoe adored Gina, the neighbor who sometimes took him for walks with her Yorkie, Bubbles—who Roscoe adored even more—it just wasn't the same as the energy-burning exercise Peter gave him.

And Roscoe had a *lot* of energy to burn.

Despite that, he was a perfect gentleman in the elevator, even when the Edler twins climbed him like a furry version of the Flatirons that loomed in the southwest horizon. It wasn't until they got to the street corner and Peter tried to turn them right instead of crossing over that he got stubborn. And when seventy pounds of muscle didn't want to move, nothing much short of a forklift was going to budge him.

"Roscoe, no, we're going this way. Come on." The firm tug he gave the leash didn't so much as dent the dog's focus on the opposite side of the street. Which was the route they took when they went to the dog park a few blocks away. A visit he'd planned to skip today since they'd gone for the past two days in a row.

Because while Lister might wave the Beaumont name like a red flag, he was right about one thing. His family did hold billionaire status, and all that went with it. Good *and* bad. And while he didn't live that lifestyle, pretty much avoided it entirely aside from participating in his mother's numerous charity events, there was no avoiding his name.

A name which made him—and every member of his family—a big, fat, juicy kidnap/blackmail/random psycho target.

That meant a life of being more safety-conscious than most people. Even other cops. Varying his routine was one of the fundamental lessons drilled into him by the head of the family's security team when he was a teenager.

But judging by the way Roscoe was locked and loaded toward the crosswalk, it was a rule he was going to be breaking today. That long walk through the neighborhood he'd planned wasn't happening.

Not unless he picked Roscoe up and carried him the whole way.

"Okay, you win, buddy. Dog park it is."

It wasn't a good precedent to set with how intelligent and strong-willed Roscoe was. But, as he watched him race around the enclosed grassy area with a few of the other large dogs he was familiar with, giving in had been the right call.

Or maybe that was his guilt talking.

Roscoe had been an apartment dog since the day he'd brought him home from the shelter as a big-ass puppy. He had plenty of room, and got multiple daily walks, even in the dead of Colorado winter. But sometimes Peter found himself wishing he had the space of a house and yard like his brother Theo did for his two dogs.

Not that he'd want a huge place like the mini-mansion Theo and Rachel called home. Smaller would suit him better. Something cozier. Homier. Maybe a two-story Craftsman with a sweet porch and stacked stone columns out front, and the scent of home-cooked meals stuffing the inside like a comfy blanket made of warmth and love.

And damned if he hadn't just described the house where Isabella lived.

Forty-five minutes later, after depositing a well-run Roscoe back in the apartment with a bowl of fresh water and a chewy bone, Peter was hitting the first of the machines at his gym with an extra sense of ferocity. Sneakers pounding on the treadmill, music blasting in his earbuds, he was determined not to think about Rafe's sister and focus on his workout.

But the thing about trying *not* to think about something was, it usually guaranteed you *did*. So, the more he told himself to forget—the feel of Isabella's mouth opening beneath his, the salty tang of her skin on his tongue, the urgent little sounds she made when she was about to come—the deeper he got sucked into reliving each and every memory in full sensory detail.

He notched up the speed and incline, feeling the immediate extra burn in his quads and calves. He might not be able to outrun his brain, but he could definitely give it something else to think about. And pain trumped pleasure in the synapses department every time.

About halfway through his run, John stepped onto the neighboring treadmill. Peter gave a quick nod to acknowledge him. His friend returned it along with a questioning look, probably because he was already dripping sweat like a leaky dam, but he slipped on his earbuds and started his own workout without comment.

Needing a longer than normal cool-down period at the end of his vicious run meant they both got off their machines at almost the same time. After sucking down half his water bottle, he gave another nod to his friend. "Hey. You're late."

"Yeah, we had a call right before shift change."

As a Boulder firefighter, John's schedule was even crazier than Peter's, so he could sympathize. There was nothing worse than getting to the end of a long shift only to end up on a last-minute call that kept you there even longer.

"Catch any work?"

"Nah, just an electrical short. But it could've turned into something if the old lady hadn't ignored her husband and called nine-one-one when she did. He swore she was imagining things when she said she smelled something burning, right up until we found the melted power strip under the bed."

"Fuuck."

"Yeah." John's teeth gleamed against his sweat-dampened dark skin as he grinned. "She was giving him a real earful about it when we left. Gonna suck to be him for a while."

Peter chuckled as they moved to the weights and started loading up barbells with the appropriate plates for the next round in their leg-and-abs rotation. "No doubt. But he's damn lucky she called."

An involuntary shudder went through his body. It hadn't been all that long ago his sister had been trapped inside a burning building, along with Rafe and his brother Cris. Thinking about how close they'd all come to burning to death still gave him nightmares.

And still left a bad taste in his mouth over how he'd blamed Rafe for the whole thing.

Unfair, yes. Not to mention untrue. But he'd needed someone to redirect his sense of helpless terror onto, and Rafe had been the most convenient target. Their friendship had cracked a little under the strain, but luckily not broken.

Rafe's brother and sisters had been harder to win back over, but time and the fact they'd all be seeing each other over the holiday dinner table from now on had helped. Isabella had been the last true holdout in that six-way grudge. Although he'd have to say they'd definitely made some deep strides in working past it this weekend.

Deep, deep strides.

Aaand he was right back to thinking about sex with her again. *Damn it.*

"You okay?"

He glanced up from tightening the collar on the end of the bar. "Sure. Why?"

"You just looked a little…weird. Well, weirder than usual," John added, laughing at the middle finger Peter flicked up in reply.

"Just the usual shit." Positioning himself under the standing bar, he settled it across the back of his shoulders and straightened, lifting it free of the rack. After three controlled steps backward, he sank down into a deep squat, keeping his core tight and chest braced, before driving back up through his heels to the start position.

The burn hit in all the right places as he continued through his reps. By the time he replaced the bar in the rack, his quads and glutes were close to weeping with relief.

Mopping up sweat with his towel, he watched John complete his last set of weighted straight-leg sit-ups, where he held a barbell over his head as he came up and went back down again. It was damned impressive. Peter might lift heavier and have the biceps to show for it, but John's abs were ripped to the point of eight-pack territory.

"You're a fucking beast, Easton!"

John grinned at the catcall from someone over on the leg machines, breathing hard as he ran a towel over his sweating face and neck. "Damn, that felt good."

"Now I know you're crazy." Hands dried, Peter went to work removing the plates from his barbell and settling them back in their spots on the weight rack.

"Pot, kettle, dude." Getting up from the mat, he started the same process of removing and re-homing plates. "So, wedding shit, work shit, or family shit?"

They'd been working out together since they played football in high school, so having a conversation in fits and starts between sets was old habit for them. "When is it ever just one?"

"Ah, let me guess. You caught flak from Detective Dick over the spread the Post did on your sister's wedding."

"Good guess. Maybe you should have been a cop."

"No thanks. I'd rather run toward burning buildings than assholes with guns." They swapped spots, John putting his preferred weight on the barbell while Peter grabbed a dumbbell and got on the mat to start a set of Russian twists.

"Hardly ever happens."

They worked their sets, then both collapsed onto a bench and chugged water to recover.

"It'll happen even less once you make detective," John said, picking up the thread of the conversation again. "And I *know* that'll make your mother happy. You're what, up against only two people for the promotion?"

A familiar sense of conflicting emotions threatened to swamp his endorphin high.

"Yeah."

John twisted to look at him.

"What?"

"I dunno. You're usually a lot more enthusiastic when the subject comes up."

"Yeah, well, I guess I've been having...I don't know, maybe some second thoughts lately."

The look John gave said he'd lost his mind.

"About taking the promotion? Now who's crazy? You worked your ass off for over a *year* studying for the test. The entire week before the list got posted you nearly puked from the tension, it meant that much to you. And when the finish line's finally in sight, *now* you're thinking maybe it's not for you? What the fuck, dude?"

Damn, it did sound crazy when he said it like that.

But it didn't change his problem, which could be summed up in one word.

"Lister."

John stared at him a long second, then cursed as he made the connection. "If you take the promotion, you'll be working with Detective Dick again."

"Got it in one. And if the universe decides it *really* wants to screw with me, he could even end up as my training partner." A fate assured to be almost worse than death.

No, he took it back.

Death would definitely be better.

"Look, I get the guy is a major asshole to the tenth power. But are you really willing to let him scare you off from a job you want as bad as you want this one?"

"I didn't think so. But I kind of let myself forget just how bad it could get with him." Occasional locker- and break-room ambushes were usually the worst he'd had to deal with since Lister moved to the detective squad.

But before that, the daily interactions had been pure misery.

"Today was a slap-in-the-face reminder nothing's changed. He still gets his kicks riding my ass over shit I can't change. And I still can't seem to keep him from getting under my skin when he does it. And if I make detective, I'll be back to dealing with his crap every damn day."

He paused. "And it won't only be proximity that'll make it worse, either. I'll be the new guy on the squad."

The horror of understanding lit his friend's eyes. "Shit."

"Yeah." Lister would no doubt make the rookie-hazing crap he'd gone through after the academy seem like a pajama party.

"So…does this mean you've been giving the other thing another think?"

"Not really. Maybe." He sighed. "I don't know."

"Wow, good non-answer. See, you'd fit right in with the Feebs." He ducked as Peter flung a soggy hand towel half-heartedly in his direction.

"Let's just say it's an option I'm keeping in my back pocket for now." But while the idea of joining the FBI gave him the same inner buzz the thought of making detective did, he couldn't find much enthusiasm for the kind of transient lifestyle it would require. Unlike his brother Theo, who'd tramped practically all over the world in his quest for high-adrenaline thrills, Peter had barely ever left his home state of Colorado.

And he was totally okay with that.

Then, of course, there was his cousin Remi. Aka FBI Special Agent Remi Beaumont. The last thing he needed was a whole new set of whispers about nepotism and favor-calling clouding yet another career path. The ones he already dealt with were bad enough.

Breather over, they got back to the second half of their workout. He welcomed the distraction. By the time they finished up, his body was pleasantly wrung out, endorphins running high, the issue of what to do about Lister and his potential promotion tucked neatly back into its work box to worry over another time.

After showering and getting dressed, Peter zipped up his ripe workout clothes in his gym bag and slung it over his shoulder. "Some of the guys are heading to the Downer tonight. Wanna come?"

"Sure. How about dinner first? I could chew the leg off a fucking chair."

Since his own stomach was grinding on his backbone, he was in full agreement. "How about Jax?" The fish and oyster place was right down the street from the bar.

"Or we could go to Bayamo." John's words held the hopefulness of a kid asking for a favorite treat. When Peter groaned, he added in a wheedling tone, "Come on. You know we always get something special when we eat there. Mrs. Delgado loves feeding you."

"She loves feeding everyone." But it was true. Dishes of the most amazing food he hadn't ordered always showed up at his table. And so did Mrs. Delgado.

That was the problem.

He really liked the woman, and her food. He just wasn't sure how he'd feel coming face-to-face with her after sleeping with her daughter.

Scratch that. He knew.

It was going to be damned uncomfortable.

"We can walk to the bar from Jax."

"And Bayamo is only like two more blocks away." John paused in zipping his gym bag shut. "Unless something happened at the wedding you didn't tell me about, and you're looking to avoid one or all of the Delgado clan." He made it into a question.

Damn it.

The guy really should have been a cop.

"Fine, we'll eat at Bayamo." He'd just have to suck it up and deal.

He'd gotten through worse. And it would be good practice for when he had to face Rafe after he got back from his honeymoon. If the guy ever found out all the wicked things Peter had done to his little sister, his head would explode.

Right after he ripped Peter's spine out and beat him to death with it.

As he climbed into his Tahoe and followed John out of the parking lot, he thanked god for the one thing he had going in his favor. It was Wednesday. Isabella's day off. At least he didn't have to worry about running into her tonight.

Because he might be able to fake his way through dealing with the rest of her family, but he was nowhere near ready to handle seeing her again.

Chapter 7

THE SAME TANTALIZING AROMAS that had filled Isabella's house the last time he was there welcomed Peter as he pushed through the restaurant's dark wood door. Memories of that night of wild, sweaty sex weren't exactly what he wanted uppermost in his mind when he stepped up to the hostess stand to greet her sister.

"Bria, hi."

"Peter! *¿Qué bola?*"

"Good, thanks." From the natural smile on her face as she leaned in to kiss his cheek, he was pretty sure Bella hadn't spilled the beans about their extracurricular activities.

Thank god.

The night was already looking up.

She smiled at John. "It's nice to see you again. Welcome back to Bayamo."

"Thanks. You, too."

"So, we don't have a reservation, but I was hoping since it was a weeknight we might still be able to get a table?"

"Don't be silly. There's always a table for you. You're family."

He tried not to wince. What he and Isabella had been doing made the label more than a little distasteful. But maybe it was just the reminder he needed. If it felt wrong, that meant it *was* wrong.

Right?

Bria led them to the curved booth in the back of the dining room nearest the kitchen, the one always held in reserve for friends and family. She left them with menus and the promise their waitress would be right with them. Peter flipped his menu open, then realized John hadn't done the same.

He snapped his fingers in front of his friend's face.

"Hey. Eyes off her ass, bro."

It took a long second, but he complied. "Mmm, mmm, mmm. She's one fine looking woman."

"She's got a boyfriend. And a brother with a gun." Something he would do well to remember himself.

"Okay, okay." With one last quick glance at Bria's retreating form, he settled his concentration on the menu.

Annoyed, both at John for ogling his sort-of sister-in-law, and at himself for being a big freaking hypocrite, he looked over the food choices and prayed for the waitress to get there. Soon. He needed a fucking beer.

"Peter?"

Every nerve ending in his body reacted to the soft utterance of his name. He looked up, already knowing who he'd see standing beside their table.

Because of fucking course she'd be here.

He unpeeled his tongue from the roof of his mouth. "Isabella. Uh, hi."

At least she looked as thrown off-balance as he felt. But she recovered faster, pulling out the pad from the pocket of her black slacks. "Can I get you something to drink?"

Oh wait. It got even better. She was going to be their waitress.

Fuck you, universe.

"Um, yeah, I'll have a beer. Whatever IPA's on tap tonight." He willed her to look up from writing the order he knew damn well she didn't need to record to remember.

"I'll have the same."

Isabella nodded and scribbled some more.

Look at me again, damn it.

"I'll be right back with those." With a vague smile and zero eye-contact, she turned and hurried away.

John watched her go, though lucky for him not with the same avarice as he'd watched Bria. More like confusion. "So, that was awkward."

You have no idea.

"I guess you two didn't manage to smooth out your shit with each other, even with the wedding."

"No, we did. Kinda." They'd just created new shit to deal with in its place.

"Sure didn't seem that way to me."

Ignoring the too-curious look his friend was leveling him with, Peter went back to his menu, though he wasn't seeing a single word on it. All he could picture was the instant his gaze had met Isabella's.

For that split-second, everything else had dropped away. All he'd seen was her, and the spark of surprised joy in her eyes. Then it was like a light being flipped off, and whatever she'd been feeling had first dimmed, then hidden altogether by her refusal to look up from that damn order pad.

Infuriating woman.

Not that he had any idea how to interpret any of it. And he hated not knowing what she was thinking.

Had she simply been as surprised to see him as he'd been to see her, or had it been something else? They'd left things unspoken when he'd finally crawled out of her bed in the wee hours three nights ago. A lot of things. Had that left the impression there might be more sweaty, naked nights ahead for them? Did she want there to be?

Did he?

Before he walked through the restaurant door, he'd have said a firm, fat 'no.'

But now...

"Here you go." Isabella placed their beers on the table, then whipped out her order pad again. Before she could start rattling off the day's specials, he jumped in.

"Isabella, I don't know if you've ever met my friend John?" He knew she had. He just wanted her to look up from that damned pad.

Which she knew, if the glare she shot him before smiling at John was anything to go by. "Yes, I have. It's nice to see you again."

"You, too." His wide smile caused hers to grow as well.

Which in turn caused a nugget of something unpleasant to flare up in Peter's gut. "You know what?" He closed his menu. "Why don't you bring us whatever you'd recommend from the kitchen tonight. I'm sure you know what I like." The smile he gave her bordered on wicked, and held a hint of challenge as her gaze snapped to his.

Finally.

"Yeah, sure, why not." John closed his menu and handed it back to her. But he looked like he regretted it the moment she left their table.

"Don't worry, she won't poison you." Him, he wasn't as sure about.

Because that glimpse he'd finally gotten from her had held a wealth of information, and even more questions. She'd been annoyed, probably at his inappropriate smile and double entendre. Or maybe just at him in general.

But there had also been something else. Something...sad. Or a little hurt. He couldn't be sure.

Or maybe it was none of those things.

For someone trained to read people's tics and tells to help figure out what they were thinking, he seemed to be running into a rock wall when it came to the one person he most wanted to understand.

When the food arrived, it was a little of everything he would have ordered for himself. In fact, it was everything he *had* ordered for himself in the past. All of his favorites.

Coincidence? Or something more?

"Oh, man, I'm in heaven!" Not waiting, John started helping himself from the over-loaded platters. He piled several of the *costillitas* on his plate, the sweet and tangy glaze glistening on the fall-off-the-bone baby back ribs.

Peter's mouth watered in anticipation.

"This all looks great, Isabella. Thanks."

"Of course." She laid one final dish on the table in front of him. A black ceramic salsa bowl filled with a familiar-looking reddish sauce.

A tentative whiff and the slight tearing of his eyes confirmed what he'd already suspected. Habanero. The same concoction that had stripped a layer from his mouth, esophagus, and entire digestive tract when his brothers had egged him into trying the 'mildly spicy' dipping sauce once before.

He barely refrained from breaking out in a sympathetic sweat.

When he looked at Isabella, this time it was her smile that held the hint of a challenge to it. "Enjoy your meal." She gave the food a meaningful glance before walking away with a bounce in her step.

He eyed the various platters with a newfound sense of trepidation. She wouldn't have put any of the sauce in the food. Would she? Probably not. Not when he was sharing family-style with John.

But that smile had made damn sure he'd be wondering about it with every single bite. It was the perfect payback. One worthy of his sister Lillian, and that was saying a lot.

He had to admire that kind of deviousness, even if it was at his own expense.

As predicted, Mrs. Delgado made a table visit to ensure everything was satisfactory with the meal. He had a mouthful of smoky, juicy pork when she arrived, but John picked up the slack and went into rhapsodies over every dish in loving detail.

"And I can't get enough of these little fried cheese balls with the ham inside." He matched words to action by popping another in his mouth and groaning his pleasure. "So good!"

"Ah, *bueno*! I'm happy to see you enjoying my *croquetas*. But make sure you both leave room for dessert. We have *Brazo de Gitano* tonight." She added a wink for Peter, as if knowing the rolled sponge cake with cream and guava filling was his favorite.

Clearly, he'd been eating at Bayamo a lot more than he'd realized.

By the time they finished the last crumb of the dessert sampler platters Mrs. D had insisted on bringing, both of them were ready to be rolled out the front door. Peter's fingers tapped an impatient tattoo on the table, waiting for Isabella to show up with the check.

Other than a few drive-by how-is-everythings and clearing the plates as they emptied them, she'd been making herself scarce all evening. Not that she could have hung around and chatted. She was working. But even so, he still felt a little...neglected, somehow.

Wow, needy much, asshole?

A sharp prick of disappointment stabbed him when one of the other waitresses appeared to drop the slim black folder on the table with a smile. Counting out bills from his wallet to cover his half, he mulled over the possibilities. Isabella could just be on her regularly scheduled break. She could have gone home early.

Or she really could have been upset with him.

Damn it! He shouldn't have teased her. Should have found a way to talk to her, privately. To ask her...what? He wasn't sure, but it felt like he'd handled things wrong. Even if he didn't know what those things even were.

After he said goodnight to Bria at the hostess stand, John made a point of doing the same, giving her another of his trademark 'great sex found here' smiles. The kind Peter knew he'd be putting to good use down at the bar in a little while. Seeing his friend use it on Bria pissed him the fuck off.

"Tone that shit down, Romeo," he snapped after the door swung shut behind them. "Rafe's sister, remember?"

"I remember. Do you?"

"What's that supposed to mean?" They crossed at the corner, heading east along Pearl Street.

"It means you've been acting weird all night, especially when Isabella was around."

His skin prickled at the mention of her name.

"She wasn't around all that much."

And didn't he just sound like a sulky brat.

"You think I didn't see the way you were watching her while she waited on the other tables? It was kinda creepy, dude. In fact, if I didn't know better, I'd think..."

Peter kept walking

"Holy shit. Did you sleep with her?"

Damn it. The guy really missed his calling as a cop.

"Say it a little louder, the people on the other side of the street didn't hear you."

"Son of a..." He pulled Peter to a halt, jamming up the flow of foot traffic as people behind them had to check up and go around. "Tell me you didn't."

When he remained silent, John groaned, grabbing his head like it hurt. "You did, didn't you? You slept with your friend's—no, worse, you slept with your *brother-in-law's* sister. What were you thinking?!"

"I wasn't, okay. It was..." He blew out a breath and moved them both off to the side out of the way, lowering his voice. "It was at the reception. We were both drinking...we weren't drunk," he emphasized when John's mouth opened. "Buzzed, yeah, but totally compos mentis. We were both feeling a little alone and sad,

I guess, and we got to talking, and then one thing led to another and…"

"Jesus. And I didn't think you two even liked each other."

"Neither did I. But like I said, we talked, and it was…nice. *She* was nice." Once you got past all the prickly thorns she was always jabbing him with.

"Okay. Okay." John's brain seemed to be stuck in a buffer situation as he processed everything, staring at the ground next to his feet. "Okay," he said one last time, looking up. "It happened. It was a consensual, and more importantly sober, decision by you both. And she's over legal age…" He raised a brow.

"She's twenty-three." It annoyed him his friend would even question it.

"Okay. Good. So, all-in-all, it's a no-harm, no-foul situation. A mutual one-time lapse in judgement. I mean, it's not like it's going to happen again, right?"

He started walking rather than answer. John cursed and caught up.

"Seriously, dude?"

"I didn't mean for that to happen either, okay? I went to see her Sunday night to make sure she was okay. That she wasn't upset about anything that happened."

"And?"

"Use your imagination. No. On second thought, don't." The last thing he wanted was his friend having any thoughts involving Isabella and sex.

"So, you went there to talk to her and, what? Decided to double-down on your big-ass mistake?"

"I just told you, I didn't mean for it to happen. Neither of us did. There was just this fucking chemistry. I couldn't keep my hands off her." And neither could she. Which made him feel only marginally better.

"Man, you are so screwed."

"You think I don't know that?" He was pretty sure he was going to hell.

"What're you gonna do about it?"

"Fuck if I know."

"Yeah, well, I do. You're going to hang out with your friends, shoot some pool, find some hot chick to take home, and screw her brains out until you've scrubbed Isabella right out of your memory banks. Just forget it ever happened. Got it?"

"Yeah. Good plan."

It was a shit plan. But it was the best he had at the moment, so it was how they were going to roll.

And for the most part, it worked. They hung with friends at the Downer. He took Sam for twenty bucks at the pool table. Lost it back to John on darts. Flirted with a few of the regulars who staked out the place in hopes of a hot hook-up with a cop. Badge bunnies weren't really his thing, but desperate times and all that.

Hailey—or was it Harley?—was the one who ended up plastered against his side at the bar as he watched John and Sam school some summer-term college kids on playing Cricket at the dartboard. She was pretty, with a great rack and a waist he could probably wrap both hands around. And she'd made it more than clear she wasn't only ready and willing to go home with him whenever he wanted.

She expected it.

Maybe it was the cloying sweetness of her breath from whatever pink frou-frou drink she'd been sucking down all night that put him off. Or maybe it was the mercilessly styled blonde hair. Or her blue eyes. Or the way her bony hips made him want to buy her a freaking cheeseburger.

Or maybe it was time to admit she was just the wrong woman.

Because when it came time to close out his tab and take her home to seal the deal, he just couldn't do it. The mere thought of getting naked with her made his dick roll over and play dead. And if that wasn't a sure sign of the apocalypse, he didn't know what was.

Harley—Hailey?—wasn't exactly a good sport about the change of plans.

Paying her outstanding bar tab helped, but she made sure he knew how she felt about him wasting her time. Right before she slid down the bar and up against one of the cops who'd shown up after second shift had ended at eleven.

As he watched her drape herself all over the guy the way she had just been on him, all he felt was relief. Which could only mean one thing.

John was right. He was *so* screwed.

———◆◇◆———

SHE REALLY WAS A coward.

It was an uncomfortable truth to discover about yourself. But facts were facts, no matter how much you might hate them. And the fact was, she, Isabella Maria Delgado, was a one hundred percent, grade-A wuss.

What other explanation was there for the way she'd practically begged Katie to bring the check to Peter's table for her? Not that she had to beg very hard. Actually, she hadn't even finished asking before Katie had given a great big 'yes!' and grabbed the folio from her hands.

Yeah, that hadn't been annoying at all.

Rolling over in bed, she punched the pillow into a more comfortable shape. No, what had been annoying was the weird little flutter she'd felt in her belly every time she'd gone near his table. The first time she could pass off as surprise. The last person in the world she expected to see sitting at the family booth tonight was Peter freaking Beaumont.

But all the other times? Those she didn't have a good explanation for.

Even when she hadn't been serving or clearing for him and his friend, working the rest of her section and ignoring them as hard as she could, she'd still felt as though there were fingers whispering over her skin. Phantom touches at her neck. Her back. Her legs.

No man's mere presence had ever affected her that way before. She'd been so distracted she got two different drink orders wrong, and that *never* happened.

It had to be the sex. Knowing what his hands felt like on her body. His lips. His—

With a groan, she flopped onto her back and tossed the covers aside, suddenly overheated. This. This was the problem. After three days, she shouldn't still be feeling so...so...hot and bothered by the mere memory of him.

If he were anyone else, she'd probably just call him up and ask if he wanted to get together for an encore performance. But he wasn't anyone else. He was Peter freaking Beaumont. Hunky cop. Insatiable sex god.

And the guy who'd most likely whipped out his unlimited AmEx Black card when the check showed up with as much thought as she'd show using her coffeeshop rewards card.

Bad enough she had to serve him. That was her job, and she wasn't ashamed of it. But taking his money—and his tip—would have been just one rung too far up the humiliation ladder to bear.

It had been a timely reminder of the things she kept letting herself forget every time they got naked and crazy together. He was a Beaumont. One of *them*.

Rich. Entitled. Dangerous.

For some reason, the familiar mantra didn't pack the same punch it had just a week ago.

From her nightstand, her phone chirped to announce a new text.

"Really, Kinz?" Because her friend was the only person on the planet who would be texting her past midnight. Most likely to find out if her parents had mentioned anything tonight about her lead-balloon food truck idea.

Spoiler alert: they hadn't.

Not that she'd expected some miraculous one-eighty come-to-Jesus from them. But some acknowledgement she'd come in on her day off after they'd shot her down so hard this morning would have been nice.

Rolling over with a sigh, she grabbed the phone off its charger. Then did a double-take at the text on the screen. And who it was from.

Would you have lunch with me tomorrow? Please?

Peter freaking Beaumont wanted to have lunch? With *her*? Seriously?

One of those stupid flutters went through her belly, making her press her fingers against it to make it stop. No. She wasn't going to feel all squishy about this. This wasn't squish-worthy. At all. It was...weird. And random. And a spectacularly bad idea to even be considering.

Was she considering it?

She stared at the screen, dozens of conflicting thoughts and emotions swirling through her mind like an out-of-control teacup ride. Why was he asking? Why now? Did lunch mean lunch, or was it code for a booty call?

She should tell him no. Hell no. In fact, she should just tell him to go to hell, period.

That was what she should do.

But she didn't.

Without examining her reasons too closely, she typed back a one-word response and hit send.

Ok.

There. Done. No taking it back. She was having lunch with Peter freaking Beaumont, of her own free will. The world truly must be coming to an end.

And not even that could stop the belly-flutter the thought of seeing him again caused.

She covered her eyes with her arm and let out a soft moan.

"I am in so much trouble."

Chapter 8

As Bella pulled into the parking lot alongside the Rayback Collective, she asked herself what the heck she was doing. Going to lunch with Peter Beaumont had to be the stupidest thing she'd done since...well, since she'd had sex with Peter Beaumont.

Except worse. Because this time she didn't have the excuse of rampant, raging lust to bail her out. This had been a clear-headed decision she could only blame on herself.

At least he'd let her pick where and when. Which would hopefully go a long way toward tilting the playing field in her favor for whatever game he had in mind.

Getting out of her car, she allowed herself a tiny grin at his expense. If nothing else, watching Mr. Billionaire Black Card navigate a sea of food trucks for lunch would make for an entertaining afternoon.

And serve as a reminder why he wasn't someone for her.

A few parking spots away, Peter emerged from his big SUV. As he approached with that solid, no-swagger stride of his, her grin dried up, along with her entire mouth. *Dios mio*, why did he have to be so damn good looking?

She slipped her sunglasses back on to try and dull the effect. Nope, no help there.

Needing to distract herself, she said, "I hope you didn't have any trouble finding the place."

"Are you kidding? I come here all the time. It's great!"

"Really?" Like she was buying that.

"Yeah. They've got food, drinks, music, *and* corn hole. What's not to like? And bonus, the outdoor areas are pet-friendly." He actually looked eager. "Ready?"

"You bet." She hung back to let him take the lead. But rather than look lost the way she expected, he walked them past the "Cheers & Chills" sign and into the enclosed yard area like he actually did know the place.

Huh.

Okay, maybe he had been here once or twice for drinks. But as they came into the 'backyard' behind the converted plumbing supply building, she mentally rubbed her hands together. This would be the payoff.

"Hope you're hungry."

"Starving." He turned and looked around.

She could barely contain a smile. He was so going to bitch about the food choices. Wait for it...

"Yes! I was hoping they'd be here today."

"Who?" She looked at the other people sitting at the picnic tables enjoying their meals, but Peter ignored them and headed for the food trucks set up to serve lunch. She hurried to keep up.

"Rollin' Bones. Do you like barbeque?"

"Um, yeah, I guess."

"You'll *love* this, I promise." He hesitated, visibly reining in his enthusiasm. "Unless you'd prefer Greek?" He nodded at the other truck.

"Um, no, barbeque is fine." What was happening?

"Great!" Rocking back on his heels like an excited teenager, he got onto the short line for the food truck styled with weathered wooden planks and a curved canvas roof to resemble an old-fashioned covered wagon. More specifically, a chuck wagon. She'd noticed it around town for that very reason, admiring the kitschy, brand-appropriate look.

From the delicious aromas drifting from the huge smoker on the back of the truck, the food promised to be as good as the marketing.

Standing next to Peter as he started rattling off the favorites he hoped were on the day's menu, she was doubly glad she was wearing her sunglasses. Otherwise, it would have been super-obvious she was staring at him like he was speaking in tongues. Who was this person, and what had he done with her pretentious rich guy?

After dithering over the choices on the whiteboard beside the order window, he went with the pulled pork BBQ sandwich and tangy coleslaw as a side. Bowing to his enthusiastic endorsement, she got the same, minus the pickles.

"My treat," Peter said as he took out his wallet.

She bristled. "I can pay for my own food."

"I know you can. But I asked you to lunch, remember?" Before she could snap back about it not being a date, he added, "How about if you get the drinks? Fair?"

Well, that took the wind out of the sails of her 'you can stuff your money' fury.

"Yeah, okay."

Choosing a picnic table away from the other customers, he sat and looked at the spread of food in front of him like it was pirate booty. "I know it's rude, but I can't promise to wait until you get back before I start eating."

"As long as you don't eat mine, we're good." Heat bloomed in her cheeks—and other places—as his lazy gaze slid up her body to meet hers. "My *food*," she emphasized, although for him or herself, she wasn't sure.

"No promises." The wink he gave said he knew exactly what she'd been thinking.

Her cheeks warmed even further.

"What do you want? To drink," she added quickly. Who said she couldn't learn?

Luckily, the line inside the building was short, so she was back with his soda and her lavender iced tea before he'd eaten more than a few bites of his sandwich. Dropping onto the bench opposite him, she didn't waste any time grabbing her own foil-wrapped bundle and taking a bite.

The heavenly flavors of the lightly toasted brioche bun and smoky, tangy, tender pork exploded on her tongue, making it impossible not to let out a moan of appreciation. "Oh my god, this is so good!"

"Told ya."

Okay, he got to be smug, just this once, because he had. And he was right.

They ate in companionable silence for a few minutes. She couldn't help looking at him as they did, trying to puzzle him out. Who was Peter Beaumont? Every time she thought she'd put him in the proper slot, he popped back out again and surprised her by being something entirely different from her expectations.

It was kind of annoying.

But also a little intriguing.

"You keep staring. Do I have barbeque sauce on my face or something?"

Evidently the sunglasses weren't doing their job as well as she'd thought.

"No. Sorry. I was just, I don't know, trying to figure you out, I guess."

"Not that hard. I'm pretty much a 'what you see is what you get' kind of guy."

She snorted. "Not hardly."

But maybe...maybe he was. The more time she spent with him, the more it seemed to be true. And yet, she just couldn't reconcile that with the harsh lesson she'd learned from Nathan and his father. That people with the money made the rules, and the rest of the people, the insignificant ones like her, either fell in line, or got run over.

She still wore the skid marks on her heart that proved it.

"Go ahead. Ask me anything."

It was too tempting an opportunity to pass up. She wiped her messy fingers on a napkin as she thought. "Okay. Let's start with how the heck you know so much about food trucks."

"Are you kidding? They're some of the best eats in town. No offense to your place, of course," he added with a sheepish grin. "But when you're on the go and looking for something quick, like when I'm on a meal break at work, they're great. You know, you can even track some of them on an app if you want."

She couldn't help it. She laughed.

"No, really." He started to reach for his phone, but she waved him off.

"No. I mean, I know. It's just...this is going to sound weird, but I was just having a conversation about exactly that with my family yesterday." For all the good it did. "I was trying to explain to them how popular food trucks were, and how people even followed them on social media."

"Oh yeah. I have my favorites set to give me a notification alert when they're going to be in my neighborhood. Although I have been known to drive halfway across town for a Better Off Fed grilled cheese when the mood strikes."

"The Mediterranean," she groaned, practically salivating.

"Yeah. You too?"

"God, yes." They grinned at each other like a couple of idiots before she looked down at her food, breaking the moment and the weird little connection they had going. "Maybe I should have had you there to give a testimonial as part of my presentation."

"Presentation? So, not just a conversation."

Crap.

She could have blown him off. It was family business, not his. But for some strange reason, she found herself wanting to tell him about it.

"It was actually more of a business proposal. I had the idea of possibly branching the restaurant out into the food truck business." She waited for him to smirk, or make some flip comment like her brother had.

"I think it's a great idea."

She blinked, certain she'd heard wrong. "You do? You don't think it would tarnish the restaurant's reputation or dilute the brand?"

"Are you kidding? With the kind of food your mom and brother cook? No way it wouldn't be a raging success. Plus, you'd be serving an entirely new group of people who prefer takeout to restaurants. I don't know anything about the business, but I'd think that would be good for the bottom line."

"Right? Exactly what I told them."

He gave her a shrewd look. "I'll take a wild guess and say they didn't agree?"

"No." She stabbed her plastic spork into the coleslaw and shoveled it into her mouth. Groaned at the gloriously crisp tang. And shook her head, picking up the thread of the conversation. "They barely even listened to what I had to say before they shot it down. I put months into working up an in-depth business plan, and then..." She snapped her fingers.

"*Nobody* thought it was a good idea? I mean, I can see your folks maybe being resistant to changing things up. I know my brothers have had that problem with our dad a few times. But what about your brother and sister? They'd know what the trends are, what's up and coming."

"You'd think. But Cris couldn't get his great big chef's ego out of the way to see the true potential in what I was saying. And Bria..."

She snorted. "She couldn't put her phone down long enough to even pay attention." And that still hurt.

"So, make her."

"Make her what?"

"Pay attention. Look, like I said, I don't know the restaurant business, but I do know something about siblings who act like because you're the youngest, your voice counts the least. If you can make one of them an ally, you've already doubled your odds of success. And once you've got one ally, the others tend to fall like dominos. Strength in numbers and all that."

"Why does it sound like you're speaking from experience?"

A far-too-adorable smile made his dimples pop out. "Family vacation, third grade. Everyone wanted to go camping in Yellowstone Park, but I had my heart set on going to a dude ranch and riding horses with real cowboys. First, I got Lil to back me. Then we both worked on our brothers, who were older than us and a lot harder to convince."

"But you did."

"Eventually. It was probably all the whining." They shared a chuckle. "And together, the four of us convinced our parents. It wasn't easy, but like I said, strength in numbers. And persistence. That's key. If you want it, you have to be willing to fight for it."

His words resonated inside her like a gong. She *was* willing to fight. She just hadn't had time yet to formulate a plan of how to go about doing it.

But this...this was good.

She and Bria had already joined forces once about breaking free of the nest and getting their own apartment. This could be just like that. Unfortunately, that had been something which benefited Bria personally. She'd been on board from the start.

The food truck would be a more uphill battle.

Way uphill.

She shouldn't care, but she had to ask.

"So, was it worth it? Going to all that effort to change everyone's minds about the dude ranch?"

His soft brown eyes crinkled at the edges as he laughed. "I got a stomach bug the first day there and never even got to sit on a horse. I was stuck inside the whole time. But everyone else said they had the best vacation ever. So yeah, it was worth it if only because I got them to listen to me."

One of those squishy feelings invaded her belly at the thought of Peter as a sick little kid, face pressed against the window watching the rest of his family having fun on *his* dream vacation while he was stuck inside puking. It made her want to give him a hug.

Which was *so* not how she'd expected this afternoon to go.

Needing to change the topic, which had strayed way too far down the personal path, she picked up what was left of her sandwich. "So, next question. You mentioned you liked they were pet-friendly here. Does that mean you have a dog?"

There was a momentary beat as he gave her a look that said she'd been less than smooth with her abrupt swerve into a new lane of conversation. Then he sucked the remaining sauce from his fingers. "Yeah, Roscoe. Seventy pounds of pure, undiluted love. Unfortunately, a lot of that love is for food, which is why I don't bring him here too often."

She tamped down the flames that licked between her thighs as his fingers slid between his lips. "Too much temptation?" She could sympathize right about now.

"He won't snatch food, which is good, but he has perfected the art of the beg. One look from those big, soulful eyes, and he's got people eating out of his hand. Well, metaphorically. Literally, it's the other way around. One look and he's got them doing what they know they shouldn't."

Kind of like his owner.

Because she knew she shouldn't be here with him like this. Shouldn't be enjoying his company. Shouldn't be comfortable with him, or sympathetic, and definitely not squishy. Yet, here she was, feeling all of those things, and more. So much more.

Today was supposed to have been her proof he was totally wrong for her. A typical rich jerk. Instead, she was the one being proven wrong, over and over again. Because Peter Beaumont was turning out to be nothing like who she thought he was.

And everything she'd thought she might want him to be.

A total anti-Nathan.

"What about you? Any pets?"

Glad to be jarred from those oh-so dangerous inner musings, she shook her head. "Not for a long time. We had a dog and a cat when I was little, but my parents always worried about fur hitching a ride to the restaurant on their clothes. So, after they were gone, we never got another."

"Oh. I guess that makes sense, but it still kind of stinks."

"Yeah, it does. I miss having a furry friend around."

But maybe she'd be able to get one when she and Bria got their apartment. She made a mental note to check with Kinzley to see if the building allowed pets. And to talk to Bria about the news about their impending freedom, which she hadn't had a chance to share with her yet. They'd barely spoken two words to each other the night before at work, and Bria had already been gone from the house when she got up that morning.

A flashbulb went off in her head.

Maybe that was her in. Get Bria excited about them finally getting to move out on their own, then use the same 'we're in this together' angle to make her actually listen to what her business plan was all about.

As the two youngest, and the only girls, they'd always had to work the hardest for every scrap of independence they got. Usually by working together. Thick as thieves, her mother used to say. Maybe she just needed to remind her sister of that.

"Then, would you be at all interested in extending our lunch to include a walk in the park with Roscoe?"

The suggestion, spoken in such a hopeful tone, tempted her more than it should have. A little distance to try and make sense of all the unexpected feelings and discoveries that had cropped up since getting out of her car would be a much smarter choice.

"Sure, I'd like that."

Clearly, smart was not part of her vocabulary today.

"Yeah? Great!" They gathered up their trash and dumped it on their way back to the parking lot. "My place isn't far from here, if you want to follow me there. And I'll text you the address, in case you catch a light."

He wasn't kidding when he said he lived close. Less than five minutes later, another of her assumptions bit the dust as she followed his SUV down into the garage under a large apartment complex to the east of downtown. She'd expected them to head south, where the luxury condos with their million dollar views were.

As they rode the elevator up, Peter gave her what she could only describe as an uneasy look. "So, remember how I said Roscoe's seventy pounds of love? Well, he's also all muscle, which can seem a little off-putting at first, until you get used to him. But he's really just a big, harmless goofball."

"Oh, so he's kind of like you?" She softened the tease with a grin.

"Ha, ha." But he returned the grin, dimples peeping out.

Squish.

Damn it.

As they walked down the hallway, Peter digging his key out of his pocket, she was hit with an overwhelming sense of déjà vu to that night in the hotel. Following him to his room...and everything after.

She plucked at the neckline of her blouse to dispel the hot flash that swept through her body at the memory.

Thankfully, he was too busy talking to notice.

"Just hang off to the side for a second until I get him corralled and calmed down, okay? He has great manners when we're outside somewhere, but he doesn't have much experience with new people coming into the apartment, so I'm not sure if his excitement at seeing you will short-circuit his training or not." He sounded like an anxious parent.

"Okay." She stayed in the hall as he walked through the door to the accompaniment of some whines and scratching noises and a weird thumping sound she couldn't quite figure out. Peter laughed and talked to the dog for a few seconds until the sounds quieted.

"Okay, you can come in now."

Stepping into the open doorway, she looked past Peter who was down on one knee to the furry bundle of energy he had by the collar. Even sitting he was huge, his brown and black fur a beautiful brindled jumble of genetics. She knew the second he sensed her. His body froze, head swiveling from Peter to lock eyes on her with laser focus.

If Peter hadn't assured her the dog was friendly, she'd probably be peeing her pants right about now.

"Hey, Roscoe." She kept her voice soft and cheery.

It must have worked, because his entire body began to quiver, his tail ratcheting back and forth in a frantic wag, striking the wall on every counter-stroke. Well, that explained the thumping noise.

Encouraged, she approached and held her hand out for him to sniff.

"Company manners, buddy." Peter's voice was soft but firm.

Roscoe whined, stretching his body toward her hand as far as he could without lifting his haunches from the floor. He wuffled against her fingers before giving them a wet, sloppy lick.

"Sorry about that." His voice held a hint of laughter. "He's a little on the drooly side when he gets excited."

"I guess I'll take it as the seal of approval." She surreptitiously wiped her hand on her shorts. "Is it okay to pet him?"

"I don't think he's going to let you by unless you do."

She wasn't sure if he was joking or not. But judging by Roscoe's size and muscular build, he would be a very effective road block if he wanted to be. With a slow hand, she reached out and ran her fingers over his large head, the short fur surprisingly soft. She scratched behind one floppy ear, earning her a groan of approval.

"You can keep petting him while I go get his l-e-a-s-h, or come in and look around if you want." He said it over his shoulder as he walked further into the apartment like it didn't matter, but there was that slightly anxious tone to his voice again.

Did he *not* want her to see where he lived?

Not about to pass up what might be a once-in-a-lifetime opportunity, she followed him in past the kitchen on the right, taking everything in as she went. The curved quartz peninsula with its two barstools looked like it got a lot more use than the table off to the left, which hosted a few pieces of mail, an unopened case of protein shakes, and a half-finished jigsaw puzzle. Which, on closer inspection, had no picture on it, but was all blank, white pieces.

Talk about being a glutton for punishment.

The living room held only a few pieces of furniture, but they were all large and comfortable looking, especially the deep blue couch with the recliners on both ends. A big-screen TV hung on the opposite wall, along with several items of sports memorabilia.

Signed, of course.

Straight ahead, sliding glass doors led to a balcony which was definitely bigger than the one Kinzley's apartment had. She stuck her hands in her back pockets and looked up at the coffered ten-foot ceiling. Everything here was bigger, with lots more light and way better finishes. But it wasn't huge, or flashy. It was...nice. Very bachelor-masculine.

Coming out of what she guessed was the bedroom, Peter asked, "What's wrong?"

"Nothing. I really like your place."

"But?"

Hating she was so transparent, she shrugged. "I guess I was just expecting it to be flashier. A big penthouse with a view or something."

"That would be Richard's place. Which is great and all, but not my style. Although you *can* sort of see a tiny slice of the Flatirons from the balcony, if you stand in the corner and lean out as far as you can. But I wouldn't recommend it."

"Duly noted."

Damn.

One more illusion shattered. Was there anything she'd thought about this man that was even close to being right?

"So, before he notices what's behind my back, would you rather go to the d-o-g p-a-r-k and watch him run around, or drive to the people p-a-r-k and walk around the lake with him?" He sighed as Roscoe tensed. "Crap."

"What?"

"I slipped and said the magic W word." He brought his hand out from behind his back and started buckling the nylon harness around Roscoe's quivering body.

"Do you really need to spell in front of him? I mean, is he really that smart?"

"You'd be surprised."

She looked down at the man hugging his not-purebred dog in his not-penthouse apartment, getting ready to go toss a ball at the dog park and, if the little plastic tube on the leash was what she thought it was, prepared to pick up his own dog's poop if need be. Just like a regular, not-billionaire guy.

"Yeah. That seems to be happening a lot lately."

Chapter 9

"So, this is nice and close to your place. I'm surprised it's not more crowded, though." Bella leaned back against the fence encircling the part of the dog park dedicated to the big dogs. And she did mean big. One pooch currently playing some doggy version of catch-me-if-you-can with Roscoe looked like it might weigh more than she did.

"That's the beauty of having a rotating shift and days off during the week. I wouldn't even try to bring him here on the weekend. Too many dogs, too many chances for a problem to happen. Especially since that's when most of the dog dorks are out."

She snorted out a laugh. "Dog dorks?"

"The ones who haven't figured out how to socialize and play well with others yet. They can be super annoying to the other dogs, and that can lead to some bad interactions. So, we stick with off-hours here and hit the dog-friendly people parks the rest of the time. Roscoe!"

He gave three sharp whistles, which snagged the dog's attention away from a friendly sniff of a Golden Retriever's butt which looked like it might have started to get a little *too* friendly. Roscoe waited, tongue lolling, and when no other command came his way, he forgot about the retriever and went back to playing with the monster dog again.

"What *is* that beast?"

"Irish Wolfhound. But don't let his size scare you. Mac's a pussycat."

"I'll take your word for it."

Pussycat her ass. More like a saber-tooth tiger.

"There's, um, something else I hope you take my word for. It's kind of why I asked you to go to lunch today in the first place, actually. No, not kind of. It *is* why I asked. I wanted to tell you that I didn't mean to make you uncomfortable by coming to the restaurant last night."

"Why would it make me uncomfortable?" She'd totally been uncomfortable. "You come in all the time."

"Yeah, but...not since we..." He blew out a breath. "Not after everything that happened between us this weekend. Especially what happened Sunday night, which we haven't had a chance to talk about yet."

"Why would we need to talk about it?"

"Because...because it's us. And...it's weird, right? At least a little bit?"

"Yeah, a little bit." A whole lotta bit.

He looked relieved she thought so, too.

"So, I wasn't sure if me showing up might have felt awkward for you. Because I know it did for me."

"It did?" Strangely, that made her feel better.

He nodded. "And that was the last thing I wanted to happen."

"So, why did you, then? Come to the restaurant, I mean."

"John wanted to eat there, and I figured it would be okay because it was your day off. Or, at least, I thought it was."

He knew what her days off were? How? She certainly didn't know when his were.

"It is, but I had to cover for a waitress who called out sick."

He quirked another of those adorable half-grins, one dimple popping. "Timing, huh?"

Timing. Fate. Bad luck.

Okay, maybe not that last one, despite how she might have felt last night. If he hadn't come in, and she hadn't been there, and they hadn't made each other uncomfortable, he wouldn't have texted her to have lunch today.

And if they hadn't had lunch, she might never have known about his love of barbeque. Or seen his nice-but-normal apartment. Or met his big goof of a dog.

She suddenly had a burning desire to find out what else she didn't know about him.

"Speaking of lunch, is this like a continuation, where I can still ask any questions I want?"

"Ask away."

"Why did you become a cop?"

"Wow, right to the big stuff, huh?" The laugh he gave as he ran a hand along the back of his neck sounded a little nervous. "It wasn't any one reason, really. I guess part of it is that when I was a kid, I was my sister's self-appointed guardian. I don't remember ever making the conscious decision, you know? It's just the way it was. I was bigger, so I needed to protect her, even if I got a bloody lip or two in the process."

She could think of a few times Rafe or Cris had come home looking scuffed up and bloody after some boy had given either her or Bria a hard time. Especially after they'd hit puberty and started to develop. "Yeah, I can see you playing knight in shining armor."

A faint stain of pink colored his cheeks before he looked away. God, could he get any more adorable?

"I don't know about that, but I did my best. And not just me. My brothers did the same. But since we were in the same grade, I was the one who was around the most. She was my responsibility."

"No, she wasn't. You were a kid, too."

"Yeah, you ask your brothers about that sometime. Anyway, it was more than that. I liked watching out for her. It felt good. Important."

"Knight in shining armor," she sing-songed, making him roll his eyes.

"Maybe it had something to do with her being my twin. I can't really explain it, but...it's different from just being brother and sister. There's this extra closeness. Not like identical twins have, but I guess more from doing everything together when we were little, since Richard and Theo were older. It's part of why it was so hard to..." He shook his head and sighed.

"What?"

"Never mind."

"No, what?"

"It's stupid, but that's kind of why I was feeling so conflicted about her getting married."

She immediately bristled.

"Because my brother's not good enough for her?"

"What? No! I never thought that. That was my brothers, and it was a knee-jerk reaction and an opinion they've long since revised. They have no problem with Rafe marrying Lil, and neither do I, so put your thorns away. I meant I felt like I was losing the special bond the two of us had always had."

Thorns?

"You did think it, though. That they shouldn't be together."

"To be fair, that was because I was pissed she nearly got killed on his watch. Which was also a knee-jerk reaction since revised. It wasn't his fault, and he knows I know it. It's forgiven and forgotten, as far as we're both concerned."

She'd heard that before. But now, together with his admission he'd been his sister's self-appointed protector for most of their lives, she could understand why he might have overreacted and blamed Rafe the way he did. It didn't make it right, but it seemed a little more excusable. And Rafe did seem to have gotten over it.

Maybe it was time she did, too.

"I maybe kinda felt like I was losing my brother a little, too." It was a reluctant admission, but the truth.

"Because he was marrying a Beaumont."

She could try to deny the subtle jab, but why bother?

"I guess maybe marrying her wasn't the worst thing he could have done," she grumbled. "I mean, you're not so bad. Maybe she isn't, either."

He let out a bark of laughter. "Wow, talk about damning with faint praise."

"I can always take it back."

"No, please don't. And for the record, you're not so bad yourself."

Roscoe came galloping up and nosed the collapsible bowl by Peter's feet, which he filled from his water bottle. After slurping up half, the dog gave them a happy grin and raced back out to play some more.

"Sorry, I can call him back if you want to go," Peter offered.

"Are you kidding? You haven't finished your answer yet."

"I thought you might have forgotten about that." He only sounded half joking.

"Not a chance. So, you got the protective gene because of your sister. Was that what led you to a life of fighting crime rather than sitting in a cushy corner office like your brothers? And that wasn't a dig," she added quickly. "It's a legitimate question."

Although a few days ago, it would have totally been a dig.

"Actually, no. I knew pretty early on I had zero interest in what they do. Richard and Theo? They love the investment business. Working with numbers is in their blood. Me and Lil? Not so much. I did try, though, because it meant a lot to my dad. But that summer I spent interning at the firm during high school only proved I wasn't cut out for following in my family's footsteps. Which kind of sucked, because I didn't have any idea what else I was supposed to do instead."

That would suck. She couldn't imagine being so directionless.

Unlike him, she'd always known she'd become a part of the family business one day. Never questioned it. Never even considered what she might have done if not filling the preordained role expected of her, the same as Bria and Cris.

Except...she didn't have a preordained role, did she? She was just another cog in the machine. A spare cog at that. Wasn't that the whole problem? And if she didn't have a particular role to play in the restaurant, her own personal niche, then what exactly was she doing with her life?

And wow, who'd have thought she might actually sympathize with Peter freaking Beaumont?

"So, um, how did you figure it out? What you wanted to do?"

"Well, lucky for me, we had a crazy-good career counselor in school. And he sat me down and asked me two things: what did I really like to do, and what was I really good at. Turned out, they were basically the same thing. I liked solving puzzles. Any kind of puzzle. Board games, books, movies...I almost always figured out the whodunnit before the end. And if I didn't, I had to go back and figure out what I'd missed. I was sort of relentless."

"Bet you kicked butt at Clue."

He waggled his eyebrows like a cartoon villain. "In the bedroom with the big pipe, Miss Scarlet."

Darn her fluttery girl parts. He shouldn't be able to get them all revved up with just a suggestive look and some cheesy innuendo.

But maybe it was more than that. Maybe it was that she'd stopped filtering him through her "rich asshole" lens and was seeing the true, unedited man for the first time.

There was definitely a lot there that was flutter-worthy.

"So, um, how did you make the leap from reading about fictional murders to wanting to solve real ones?"

"The career counselor gave me a whole list of jobs which involved problem and puzzle solving. Most of them happened to be in the criminal justice field. For a while, I thought maybe I'd like to join the FBI and be a part of their profiler program, but as much as I enjoy solving mysteries, I like living here more. So, joining the Boulder PD with the goal of becoming a detective looked like a way to have the best of both worlds."

"But, it's not that simple, is it? I mean, don't you have to get appointed or something?"

"Yes and no. There are requirements to be eligible. Then there's a written test and an interview. They take all that, add in your seniority and a few other things, give you a score, and make a list. And then you wait. And wait, and wait," he added with a wry tone.

He might play it off as no big deal, but it was clear to her it was.

"For how long?"

"Until someone transfers, retires, or gets promoted, and a spot opens up. Which hopefully happens before the list expires and you have to start the process all over again. Most people go through it a few times before they finally get promoted."

"That sounds really frustrating."

"Oh, it can be. But it'll be worth it once I get that gold shield." He checked his watch and called for Roscoe.

"You sound pretty confident that's going to happen."

"I'm one of three people tied for the top spot on the current list. So yeah, I'm feeling pretty good about my chances, even though it's only the first time I'm up for it. Barring any bizarre, unforeseen setbacks like Santos deciding to pull back his retirement papers and *not* take his wife on the cross-country RV trip like he promised, of course. Then again, she'd probably kill him if he did that, so I guess there'd still be an opening in the squad either way." He gave a cheeky grin.

She narrowed her eyes. "Yeah, well, she'd be within her rights if she did. There's nothing worse than a liar, especially if it's at someone else's expense."

"That's why I don't lie. It'll always come back and bite you in the ass."

"I would never lie to you, Bella. I don't care what my family thinks. I love you more than anything, and I want to be with you forever. There's nothing that'll ever change my mind, I promise."

Her fingers pressed hard against where the blue and black heart was inked near her left hip as the phantom words whispered through her memory. Nathan had been a world-class liar. Not just to her, but to himself. He hadn't stood up to his family for two whole seconds, much less forever.

When it came down to an ultimatum between money or her, he'd chosen the one he'd truly loved the most.

But as she watched Peter pour some more water into the bowl for a panting Roscoe, the familiar tug of attraction and a less familiar tug of something else overshadowed those old echoes of pain and resentment.

Peter wasn't Nathan. Wasn't even close to anything like him. So maybe it was time she stopped trying to manufacture similarities where there were none, and put that ghost to rest where it belonged.

The thought was as liberating as it was terrifying.

As he straightened from snapping the leash onto the dog's harness, she took a breath and spoke before she could think herself out of it.

"Okay, so, one last question. Do you want to go back to your place and get naked?"

PETER FROZE IN THE act of wrapping the leash around his hand.

Had she really just said that?

"Are..." He cleared his throat as his voice cracked. "Are you serious?" Because, holy fuck. That didn't just come out of left field. It came from a whole other freaking ballpark.

On Mars.

The eyes that met his were filled with desire and something a little wild he couldn't quite identify. "Don't you want to?"

Of course he wanted to. He always wanted to with her. Even when he knew he shouldn't. That was the problem.

One of them, anyway.

The answer should be no. Hell no, in fact. That wasn't why he'd asked her to go to lunch. Wasn't why he'd given in to the impulse to extend the day and invited her to come with him to the dog park.

Although if he had to assign an actual reason to it, he didn't think he could come up with one that made any sense. All he knew was he hadn't wanted their time together to end. He still didn't. He just wasn't sure sex was the right way to go.

But fuuuuck, was it tempting.

To buy himself some time, he held out his hand to her. Relief flashed through her eyes, followed by what looked like a bloom of shy happiness as she put her hand into his. But he must have been mistaken, because there had never been anything *shy* about Isabella. Bold, forthright, stubborn, intriguing...but never shy.

Fingers linked, they took the leisurely walk back to his place in silence. His mind raced the entire way, feeling like a hamster spinning on its little metal wheel. Lots of motion and energy, but getting nowhere fast.

By the time they hit the lobby, only one thought had risen clear of the rest. Bad idea or not, he was going to sleep with her again. The attraction between them was just too strong to ignore.

Isabella seemed to feel the same way. The door had barely locked behind them when she launched herself, her mouth devouring his as her hands slid up his chest, over his shoulders, to the back of his head as she pulled him even closer.

Dropping the leash, he wrapped his arms around her, pulling her body flush to his, his erection pressing into her softness and eliciting a moan he felt roll through his skin and into his bones.

That was all the encouragement he needed.

Urging her legs up around his waist, he carried her to the bedroom without once breaking the kiss. The feel of her against him was so perfect, so right, all his other reservations slid away into silence.

After standing her on her feet beside the bed, they watched each other as clothes were stripped off, piece by piece, until they were both naked. The late afternoon light shining through the window highlighted the exquisite peaks and curves and every other delicious inch of her body.

He savored the view, which had been mostly hidden from him the last two times. Lamplight and moonlight just didn't do her the same justice as sunlight did.

She seemed as fascinated by her perusal of his body, her gaze caressing him from neck to toes before she leaned forward to run her fingertips through the light covering of hair on his chest. A shiver ran through him as the touch slid lower, over his abs, circling his navel, and then it was Houston, we have liftoff as she curled her hand around his throbbing penis and gave it a firm, gentle squeeze.

That was the end of any restraint he'd hoped to hang onto. Which, judging by the smile curving those delectable, devious lips as he tumbled them both to the bed, had been her intent. Oh well, they'd go slow the next time around.

Which came as they lay in bed after catching their breath from their first bout of fast and furious. And it wasn't just slow. He made sure it was torturously glacial, taking his time to tease every single inch of her, even the spots not normally associated with being erogenous.

Who knew toes could make a woman squirm like that?

The sex was just as unhurried and deliberate as the foreplay, a careful orchestration of glide and pull that stoked a fire inside him like he'd never felt before. It was like the difference between an erupting volcano and the steady flow of molten lava down its sloping side. Both were hot. Both dangerous. But the lava flow took its time, filled every space it touched, coating it, until no spot was left unaffected and unchanged.

By the time he pulled the sheet over their sweat-coated bodies to rest, that was exactly how he was feeling. Changed. Whatever this was between them, it transcended just good sex. He wasn't going to call it love, because shit, it had been less than a week since they'd stopped not liking each other. Mostly, anyway.

But damned if he didn't feel like there was something more going on here.

"You know I'm going to get even for that," she murmured against his shoulder, eyes at half-mast and a sated smile on her kiss-swollen lips.

"What, you didn't like?"

"Oh, I liked. If I liked any more, you'd be getting noise complaints from your neighbors." She pressed a kiss to his damp skin as he chuckled. "Still getting even, though. When I can move again."

Just the thought of Isabella doing anything to his body was enough to make his wrung-out bits give a little tingle of anticipation. Unfortunately, that was about all they could do. He was well and truly wiped.

Even his eyes felt exhausted, drifting shut despite his best efforts, not wanting to waste a minute of this time with her. He pulled her closer, inhaling her unique, spicy scent with a sigh.

"Looking forward to it."

Chapter 10

WHEN HE OPENED HIS eyes again, the angle of the sunlight filtering through the curtains had barely changed. A quick check with the clock on his nightstand said he'd only been out about forty-five minutes. His typical power-nap when he needed a quick recharge.

But waking up next to Isabella?

Anything *but* typical.

He couldn't remember the last time aside from Isabella—twice now—he'd actually fallen asleep with a woman after sex. Lounged, maybe. Usually in hopes there'd be a round two. But actual hard sleep? That had always felt a little too...intimate.

And right now, with the woman curled against his side, her long, soft hair scattered across his pillows and wrapped around his arm like a silken rope, it also felt a little too right.

Which should have been the moment panic set in. Should have sent him fleeing from the bed. The room. Hell, from the apartment.

Except, of course, it was his apartment.

And he wasn't feeling the need to go anywhere. It was a little unnerving, but all he wanted to do was stay right where he was, with Isabella in his arms, for as long as he possibly could.

It was a rare opportunity to observe her when she wasn't being her usual intense self. Normally in the past, she'd always seemed completely focused on something, even if it was just ignoring him and his brothers.

But seeing her face like this, soft and relaxed, the fine lines of tension that usually bracketed her mouth erased by sleep, she looked so much happier. Younger.

His conscience tweaked him on that, but he pushed it aside. She was twenty-three, not a kid. And for damn certain she knew her own mind. That self-assuredness was one of the things he admired most about her.

Even when it had made her a painful thorn in his ass.

With a soft exhale of breath, her eyes fluttered open. A look of confusion filled the velvety-brown depths for a second before recognition took over and a shy smile curved her lips. "Hi."

"Morning, sunshine." He'd meant it as a joke about falling asleep, but she nearly drove her elbow through his ribs jerking upright with a gasp.

"What? No! It can't be morning."

"Ow." He rubbed his abused side. "Relax, it's not. It's barely six." Her eyes flared with panic, so he added, "P.M."

"Oh, thank god." She slumped back against the pillow, then rallied herself and swatted his arm. Hard. "That wasn't funny."

"I'm getting that. Sorry." So much for no tension lines. "So, I guess that means staying the night isn't an option?" He felt just as surprised by that as she looked. First falling asleep with her, then having her spend the night? What other unwritten rules was he planning to break today?

You mean besides sleeping with your friend's sister?

Fucking conscience.

It was probably the first time, ever, he'd seen Isabella at a loss for words. And if it hadn't had to do with him and his stupid ask, he might have found it entertaining. Instead, watching her flounder for a response made his ego, which had never felt fragile before, start to deflate like a three-day-old birthday balloon.

"No," she said finally. "Not while I'm living under my parents' roof. Which may seem old-fashioned to you, but I have to respect their rules." She finished on an unmistakably defensive note.

"Put your hackles down. I get it. I had to follow some rules when I was still living at home, too. That's why I got my own place not long after college."

And because he knew he'd never be taken seriously by anyone in the department if "home" was a gated estate where the pool house was bigger than the homes some of his fellow officers lived in.

Her chin tilted slightly. "I'm getting my own place soon, too."

Now that piqued his interest, since it opened up all kinds of possibilities for the future. But before he could ask for any details, a loud growl emanated from her stomach. He chuckled as she slapped a hand over it, her eyes widening in embarrassment.

"I think that means I need to feed you." He hesitated. "If you can stay for dinner?"

She hesitated, too.

Realizing his mistake in saying *need* to instead of *want* to, he did a quick backtrack.

"You don't have to stay, but I'd really like it if you did." He knew he'd read her right when that small smile once again peeked out and she nodded.

"Yeah, okay. I'd like that, too."

"Great. I can order in pizza. Or gyros. Or we could go out for something."

"Or we could just cook something." She looked so hopeful when she said it, he hated to burst her bubble.

"I'm not sure there's anything but a bunch of odds and ends that need throwing out in the fridge, since I never made it to the grocery store this afternoon as planned." He gave her a meaningful look to remind her of why that was.

A hint of color hit her cheeks. "Um, well, why don't we check anyway. I'm pretty good at cooking up just about anything into a halfway decent meal."

"I wouldn't count on it with what I have, but you're welcome to try."

"That almost sounded like a challenge."

It hadn't been. But the fire that flashed in her eyes lit an answering heat inside of him. A reminder of the sparks they'd always struck off each other. Only now he was starting to wonder if some of that friction hadn't been sexual right from the start, and both of them had been too stubborn to notice.

He grinned. "My kitchen is all yours. Do your best. Or worst."

The small taunt caused the heat in her gaze to flare and a confident smile to curve her oh-so delectable lips.

"Watch me." As though energized by the thought of proving him wrong, she bounced out of bed and started pulling on the clothes left strewn around on the floor in their frantic haste to get naked.

Disappointed as the glorious view of her body disappeared, he rolled upright and dragged on a pair of workout shorts and a t-shirt. If he was going to be watching her work, he had a feeling he'd need something a little roomier than his jeans to do it in comfort.

He followed her out of the bedroom, pausing where Roscoe dozed in front of the balcony door to remove his harness and give him a quick scratch. Roscoe thumped his tail, but otherwise seemed content to bask in his shrinking patch of sunlight.

For now, anyway. Once the first scent of food hit the air, that would change in a hurry.

In the kitchen, he found Isabella standing in front of the open fridge, staring inside with a puckered press of lips and a furrow in her brow. He slid onto one of the barstools and rested his arms on the counter, trying not to smirk too much.

"I did mention it was slim pickings."

"Are you kidding? There's plenty in here to work with." Suiting action to words, she started pulling things out onto the counter.

Eggs. Milk. Butter. A plastic bowl of leftover mashed potatoes. Some sadly wilted spinach which never made it into one of his power shakes. The nub ends of a few about-to-turn-moldy-but-not-quite-there-yet cheeses. A cardboard doggie-box from the Roadhouse with the Godzilla Double Bacon Burger he hadn't been able to eat the other night. Probably because it had been his third.

His sister's jokes about his eyes always being bigger than his stomach were sadly true. When he liked something, he tended to overindulge.

It seemed the same held true when he liked some*one*, too.

Because he should be sated to the point of exhaustion right now. But watching Isabella rifle through his cupboards, pulling out spices and whatever else she thought she could use, was the ultimate turn-on.

The only thing that kept him from dragging her right back to the bedroom was knowing both of them needed to refuel first, or nothing much of anything was going to happen when they got there.

Then he'd drag her back to bed, and they could work all those calories off together.

Evidently, 'watch me' hadn't been a literal invitation to observe. With the firm hand of a seasoned taskmaster, she put him to work dragging out the various pans and utensils she asked for. Then he somehow found himself at the cutting board chopping the sad-looking spinach. Then chopping it again when his first attempt failed to pass inspection.

Being bossed around in his own kitchen should have annoyed him. Instead, he followed her lead, knowing this was her dance and only she knew the steps to it. He still had his doubts anything edible would come from the hodgepodge of things she'd scrounged together, but he was willing to let her take her best shot.

Saying *I told you so* would be much sweeter that way.

Only she was the one who ended up saying it after he practically inhaled the loaded mashed potato cakes and muffin frittatas she dished up. Not with words. But her expression as he scraped the plate to get the last of the cheesy, bacon-y goodness said it loud and clear.

And he was a big enough man to admit when he was wrong.

Especially if it would get him a second helping.

"I don't know how you did it, but damn, this is good." He watched with gleeful anticipation as two more frittatas went onto his plate, along with another potato cake. "Thanks."

Her expression held more than a hint of satisfaction, not to mention pride. "So, I guess that's challenge met."

"Met, exceeded, and annihilated. This"—he pointed to his food—"is incredible. You definitely inherited your family's talent for food." He shoved a forkful of fluffy frittata in his mouth, savoring the way the bacon and onion she'd repurposed from his leftover burger jazzed up the egg, cheese, and spinach into something spectacular.

For some reason, what he'd meant as the highest of compliments had her looking a little sad rather than pleased. "Nah, I just learned a lot from watching my mom and Cris. It's pure imitation, not skill."

Now, that just pissed him off.

"That's bull, and you know it. I didn't see you calling and asking anyone how to turn the crap from my fridge into this." He jabbed his fork into a hunk of frittata and held it up. "This is good because *you* had the skill to make it good." He snatched the food off his fork with a decisive snap of his teeth.

Isabella looked a little stunned by his declaration. And pleased, if the hint of color climbing her neck meant anything. "Thank you."

"I mean it. You should be in the kitchen at Bayamo with your mother and brother, not waiting tables."

Wrong thing to say.

"They don't need me in the kitchen," she said hotly, stabbing at her food. "They don't need—" Stiffening, she shoved some potatoes into her mouth, stopping the flow of words.

But he could fill them in on his own. "You think they don't need *you*." When she refused to look at him, he knew he'd guessed right.

Well, shit.

"Hey, you know that's not true."

"Forget I said anything, okay? It's just me being stupid."

"No, it's you being honest. And I appreciate you'd trust me enough to say something like that to me."

"It wasn't on purpose," she muttered.

That stung a little, but he still had to grin at her truculent expression. She looked like a sulky sex kitten. With wild bed head.

"Even so, I'm glad you did. It's obviously been bothering you, and not just today." A lightbulb went off. "Your food truck idea. That's where it came from."

She squirmed in her seat. "Like I said, me being stupid."

"And like I said, no, you're not. I think it makes even more sense now."

"It does?" She looked surprised. And a little suspicious.

"Sure. And your family will, too, when you tell them *why* it's so important to you—"

"No."

"But if they understood how you feel—"

"*No.* Just...drop it, okay?"

"But—"

"Drop. It." If the tone she used wasn't enough of a warning, the jut of her jaw and fire spitting from her eyes as she glared at him were like red flags waving frantically in his face to try and steer him away from the cliff he was about to drive himself over.

Having seen a similar look a time or two on his sister, he was smart enough to know when to back away, hands in the air, and live to fight another day.

"Okay, sorry. It's dropped."

It took a few tense seconds before she seemed to believe him. The rigid line of her back eased a bit, and she nodded. "Good."

They continued to eat, but some of the joy was gone from the meal, the silence no longer as comfortable. He wracked his brain for something to talk about that wouldn't put her back on the defensive. Which pretty much left out family, work, and food.

He considered asking about the tattoo on her hip. But since she'd distracted him from it during his earlier exploration of her body—again—it probably fell into some other red zone he didn't want to enter right now.

Before he could figure out another topic, she spoke softly, still staring at her plate.

"Do you really think—"

The knock on his door stopped her words like they'd been flash-frozen.

Fucking hell.

He ignored it, willing her to finish what she'd been about to say. The knock came again. Desperate, he tried to prompt her. "Do I think…"

"You should get that."

Damn it.

With a disgruntled growl, he slid off his stool and stalked to the door, frustrated enough to yank it open without checking the peephole the way he normally would.

And paid the price.

"Mom." He stared at her like she was a bomb left on his doorstep. Judging by the sound of a fork clattering against a plate behind him, it was a fitting analogy, since her arrival meant two parts of his life he'd prefer to keep separate—at least for now—were about to collide with one hell of a bang.

Somewhere, his conscience was howling with laughter.

An amused smile lit his mother's face. "Don't sound so thrilled to see me." She leaned in to kiss his cheek, then bent down to pet Roscoe, who'd all but galloped to the door and stood at his side vibrating with barely contained excitement.

Unfortunately, that allowed her to look past him into the apartment. "Oh, I didn't know you had...company." There was almost a visible question mark after the word. And no wonder. It was no secret the youngest Beaumont and Delgado children weren't exactly besties.

Except...that had changed over the last few days, hadn't it? They were...

Well, he wasn't really sure what they were at the moment. But it was certainly more than they'd been before.

His mother, being who she was, brushed right past him as he stood trying to formulate a reply and walked to Isabella. Who'd gotten to her feet and looked, to him at least, like she'd been about to make a run for it.

Good luck with that.

His mother was a force of nature no one could outrun.

"Isabella, how nice to see you!"

"Mrs. Beaumont, hi." She accepted the light embrace and cheek-kiss with wide eyes for him over his mother's shoulder. He could only offer a helpless shrug in return. Fuck if he knew what they should do.

"I've told you, dear, call me Patricia. What a lovely surprise, seeing you here. Having dinner. Just the two of you." Her smile widened, making her eyes crinkle at the edges. "I guess that means you're finally getting along."

"Yes," he said at the same time Isabella said "No."

When his mother looked between them in confusion, Isabella let out a nervous laugh. "I mean, this isn't what it looks like. I mean, it is. It's dinner, of course. What else could it be? But it's, um, it's not a *dinner* dinner. It was a bet. I lost a bet. With your son. And I had to cook him dinner to pay up. So, here I am. Cooking. You know, dinner."

"I see." But his mother's wrinkled brow and confused tone said she didn't.

And neither did he.

Not a *dinner* dinner? What did that even mean? Obviously, they hadn't had time to consider what they might say to anyone in the family about their newfound whatever this was between them. And it would be beyond uncomfortable for his mother to find out this way, with both of them fresh from his bed. But to make it sound like nothing more than some kind of impersonal business transaction?

He didn't like it. Not one bit. It grated on his nerves, in fact.

But he couldn't contradict her without making her into a liar. So, he'd back her play. For now. At least until he got rid of his mother and could ask what the hell was going on.

"Right." He looked at Isabella. "The bet."

His mother did another back-and-forth look. "And what bet was that?"

Panic flared in Isabella's eyes. "Um..."

"The one she lost." He mentally rolled his eyes at his own reply. So weak. "Mom, what brings you here, anyway?"

For a long second, it didn't appear like she'd let herself be so easily diverted. Then she seemed to shrug her curiosity off and smiled at him. "Well, that would be you, actually."

His 'oh shit' radar went off with a *ping*. "Me?" That couldn't be good.

"Yes, dear, you. I was just at the foundation meeting finalizing the details about the picnic, and—"

He tipped his head back with a heartfelt groan. "And I forgot. Shi—oot."

Her smile grew. "I told you that you didn't have to be there."

"But I wanted to be." And it had totally slipped his mind. *That* was what Isabella did to him.

"I know. Which is why I stopped by to go over what we discussed."

The fundraising picnic the Everbrite Foundation had organized was something he'd been personally invested in from its inception a little over a year ago. But as much as he hated missing out on one of the last strategy meetings before the upcoming mid-July event, the only discussion he was interested in having right now was with Isabella.

"Thanks, Mom. But do you think we could talk about this tomorrow sometime? Maybe over lunch?"

Understanding bloomed in his mother's eyes.

"Oh, of course! I didn't mean to interrupt. I'll just—"

"You're not," Isabella blurted. "Interrupting, I mean. Anything. At all. In fact, I'm the one who should be going." She gave a patently false smile and grabbed her purse from the table where he'd put it after finding it abandoned on the floor from their rush to get in and get naked.

Now it was like she couldn't wait to get out.

"But your dinner," his mother began.

"We were done. Bet all paid off. So, time to go." She stopped babbling long enough to take a breath. "It was nice to see you, Mrs. Beaumont. Peter..." She faltered as she finally looked at him, her voice going a bit unsteady. "I hope you enjoyed the food."

"I enjoyed *everything*." Okay, yeah, maybe it was shitty of him to say it with such obvious innuendo. But, damn it, he hated the way she was bailing on him like this instead of letting his mother leave so they could talk.

Then again, he had a feeling that was exactly *why* she was bailing.

She gave a nervous laugh, her grip on the purse strap whitening her knuckles. "Okay, well, um, bye."

And she was gone.

He didn't realize he was staring at the closed door until his mother put a hand on his arm, jerking him back from fantasies of ripping it open and going after her. "Sorry, Mom, did you say something?"

"No, I'm sorry. I shouldn't have dropped by without calling first."

"No, it's fine." It so wasn't fine. But what else could he say? "So, what was it you wanted to talk to me about?"

She studied him, lips pursed.

"You know, I think I'll tell you when I take you up on lunch tomorrow instead. In fact, why don't we make it brunch? I don't get to spend nearly as much time with you as I'd like. I think you have something else you'd rather be doing right now."

He did, but she couldn't know that.

"I don't know what you're talking about."

She smiled. "Why, cleaning up your kitchen, of course. What else could I possibly mean?" With a pat on his cheek, she turned for the door. "Better hurry, though, dear. You know how it is with dirty dishes. If you let them sit for too long, things have time to get hard and stuck on, and it's much more difficult to clean them up." With one last smile and—was that a *wink*?—she left, leaving him staring at another closed door.

Dishes his ass.

He'd never been good at keeping things from his mother. It was why she'd always come to him first when trying to find out what mischief he and his brothers had been up to. He never even had to say a word. She just always *knew*.

Much as he'd like to obsess about what, exactly, she thought she knew about him and Isabella, she was right. He did need to clean some things up, and fast.

He called her cell and got dumped to voicemail.

Damn.

"I guess you're already in the car, so please call me as soon as you get home."

Waiting for her to call back, he wrapped up the two remaining muffin frittatas for the morning, and started stacking the dishwasher with the dishes and pans they'd used. Roscoe got the remains of the burger patties crumbled in with his food, which he ate with rapturous tail wags to show his appreciation.

After waiting some more, he called again. And once more went right to voicemail.

Son of a...

He typed out a quick text.

Please call me. We need to talk.

Nothing.

A little niggle of concern chewed on the corner of his brain there might be a more unpleasant reason she wasn't replying. That she *couldn't* reply. He'd like to blame it on paranoia being an occupational hazard. But he'd played this worst-case what-if game with himself long before he'd worn a badge. Usually when it came to his often spontaneous, sometimes reckless, sister.

He didn't like the feeling any better now when it was Isabella causing it.

Call me or I'm coming over and knocking on your front door to make sure you're okay.

Finally, the little bouncing dots that meant she was typing appeared on the screen. The rock in his gut fell away, only to be replaced by the burn of annoyance. So, she'd been ignoring him on purpose.

The dots paused, then bounced, then paused, then bounced again.

What was she writing, a novel?

I'm fine.

He stared at the two words. That was it? After all that dot bouncing? She must have erased whatever else she'd written and replaced it with that pithy little reply.

"Oh, I don't think so, sweetheart."

Call me or I'm coming over.

His phone rang a few seconds later.

"Don't you dare threaten me." Even through the phone, the snarl in her voice was loud and clear.

"I didn't—" Shit. He had. Pinching the bridge of his nose, he sighed. "I'm sorry. I just...this is something we should talk about in person and not by text, don't you think?"

"What's there to talk about?"

"Don't." The edge of the phone cut into his palm, forcing him to relax his grip. "Don't try and pretend something important didn't happen today."

"Oh, you mean like having your mother show up?"

He winced at the shrill rise of her voice.

"I'm sorry about that, but it's not like I knew she was coming." He paused. "Why tell her it was a bet?"

"It was the only thing I could come up with that made sense."

"Why did we need to come up with anything in the first place?"

"So, what? We just tell your mom we were having an afternoon of scorching hot sex and got hungry?"

Even though technically that was exactly what had happened, he hated hearing it put that way. Reduced to simple biological impulses and nothing more. "We could have just been having dinner. People do that, you know. Even without the sex."

"Well, we don't."

"We could."

"We could what?"

"Try going out to dinner. Together. Without the sex part to confuse everything."

The silence was beyond deafening.

"Isabella, could you please come back over, so we can talk about this face to face?" Her thoughts and feelings were always so clearly on display. He felt at a distinct disadvantage not being able to see them. Especially for this conversation.

The silence continued for another long, unnerving moment.

"No," she said finally. "I just got home. If I leave again, my mother's definitely going to ask questions I don't want to answer."

Much as he hated to admit it, she had a point.

"Okay, how about tomorrow, then? Before you have to go to work." He cursed. "I already agreed to have brunch with my mom. What about tomorrow night, then, after you get off work?" It would be late, and he'd have to get up early for work the next morning, but for something this important, he could suck down a few extra energy drinks to get by.

"You know, why don't we give it a few days. Give things time to settle and then see what we want to do."

"Saturday, then," he countered, his mother's dirty dish analogy dancing through his brain. "That's your early shift day, right? Meet me after you get off, and we'll have a late dinner somewhere. Or drinks. Coffee. Whatever you want."

Just please say yes.

"I guess that would be okay." She didn't sound so sure, but he'd take what he could get and run with it like the high school varsity tight end he once was.

"Great! I'll touch base with you Saturday, then."

He tried to feel optimistic when he hung up, but his mother's words kept playing in a loop inside his head. Forty-eight hours. That was a long time to let this particular dish stay dirty. He could only hope it wouldn't be long enough for Isabella to harden her resolve into something too stubborn for even him to soften.

Chapter 11

Morning brought with it one of those rare rainy days, the sun hidden behind a thick layer of swollen, soggy gray.

It matched her mood completely.

Throwing the covers off with a sigh, Bella forced herself upright despite the deep desire to burrow back under them and hold the pillow over her head instead. Not that she needed more sleep. Despite the certainty she'd be up all night staring at the ceiling, she'd actually gone out quick and slept hard. Probably thanks to all that good fresh air she'd gotten yesterday.

Riiight. That was why.

She covered her face with a groan. Okay, it was probably all the good hard sex she'd gotten yesterday. But she was trying not to think about that. Or, more to the point, about the man she'd had it with. Because whenever she thought about him, it felt like something was short-circuiting inside of her brain.

She'd spent so long not liking Peter Beaumont. Now all these new feelings, this revised version of him that was so different from who she'd thought he was, were all making her head spin like a pinwheel in a tornado. And if that hadn't all been confusing enough, in walked his mother to make it all even more crazy.

Or maybe more real. Because the second Mrs. Beaumont had come through that door, the happy little bubble that had formed around the day popped with the force of a nuclear explosion and the real world came rushing back in.

And she'd run.

Not her proudest moment. But to be fair, she'd been acting on pure survival instinct. The last time a rich family had caught wind of her relationship with their son, everything had gone right to hell. Logic said the Beaumonts wouldn't react like that. Their precious little princess had already married a Delgado, after all, and the world hadn't ended.

And yet.

Logic wasn't in control during that moment of adrenaline-fueled fight-or-flight. It still wasn't, not entirely. And every time she remembered the shrewd, all-knowing gaze from eyes the same silky chocolate brown as her son's, she shuddered to think how the conversation with Patricia—nope, still didn't feel right—with Mrs. Beaumont would have gone if she'd stayed.

Not well, if she had to guess.

And she had zero idea of how she was going to explain any of that to Peter without sounding either shallow, paranoid, or insulting. Or all three. She would have liked a little more time to try and figure it out, but all things considered, two days was probably the best she could have hoped for.

He might be the quiet Beaumont, but he was just as tenacious as the rest of them.

After zoning out in the shower long enough to have her sister banging on the bathroom door to tell her breakfast was already on the table, she sat in the kitchen and did her best to carry on a normal conversation with her parents. Thank god Bria was in an unusually chatty mood and carried most of the load.

As she ate, she couldn't help but compare the sweet, delicious sour cream pancakes to her improv frittatas. Peter was delusional if he thought she could come close to her mother's brilliance in the kitchen. But he'd seemed like he believed it, believed in *her*, so...maybe she wasn't such a hack, after all.

Breakfast dishes washed and put away, she trailed her sister upstairs. Buoyed by the memory of Peter's encouragement, the time felt right to put step one of her plan into action.

"Bri, you have a minute? I've got something I want to tell you."

Her sister nodded, an odd gleam in her eyes. "Me, too."

Bella followed her into her bedroom. Her nose twitched from the strong fragrance of carnations that filled the space. It was sweet Alejandro gave her sister a small bouquet of them every week, but she wished he'd pick something a little less cloying.

After closing the door, Bria took a deep breath and let it out in a shaky rush of words. "Alejandro is going to propose."

"*What?*" Okay, probably not the reaction she'd been hoping for, but geez, talk about out of left field! "I mean, that's fantastic." She hugged her sister, mind whirling. "Wow. But...isn't it just a little quick? You've only been dating for less than a year."

"Maybe a little. But when you know he's the right one, you know, so why bother wasting time?"

This, from the woman who made lists for her lists?

"Okay. Well, if you're sure, then, that's great."

"Of course, I'm sure." Bria crossed her arms and huffed. "Why aren't you happier for me?"

Oh, crap.

"I am. I really am. I just want to be sure *you're* sure. It's such a big step. And with Rafe getting married, I can't help but worry—just a tiny bit—that maybe what you're feeling is some kind of...leftover wedding vibes or something. Like, you got caught up in all the love and happy ever after stuff, and maybe started thinking what it would be like to have that for yourself?"

Wait. That wasn't what was happening with her and Peter...was it?

Bria scoffed, flinging a hand in the air. "Don't be ridiculous. That has nothing to do with anything. Alejandro and I have been together long enough to know what we're feeling. It's not some kind of wedding hangover."

Bella really hoped that was true.

She enveloped her sister in another hug. "Then I'm really, really happy for you." Or, at least, she would be. Once she wrapped her head around it a little more. First Rafe, now Bria. Everyone was moving on with their lives. It was stupid, but she kind of felt like she was being left out of some special club because she didn't know the secret handshake.

"Thank you," Bria whispered into her ear before stepping back. "So, what did you want to tell me?"

A renewed hum of excitement lit in her belly.

"Remember the list we've been on for an apartment in Kinzley's building? Well, she found out there's one opening up soon, and it's all ours. We could be moved in by the end of the summer! Can you believe it?"

She couldn't stop smiling at the thought. Freedom from constant parental scrutiny. It was a ridiculously small goal, but now that it was within reach, she could hardly wait.

The fact it would make it easier to spend time with Peter with no one knowing had nothing to do with it. Not at all.

A frown tugged at Bria's mouth.

"Bella, I just told you. I'm getting engaged."

"So?"

"So, I'll be moving in with him."

"Yeah, when you get married. Which won't be for what? Like, a year, maybe more?" A lot more, if their father had anything to say about it. Javier Delgado was the quintessential over-protective patriarch when it came to his daughters.

The problem was, every annoying, frustrating thing he did, he did out of love. Which made it almost impossible to defy his old-fashioned, sexist rules and ideas without flinging that love right back in his face and breaking his heart.

Total Catch-22.

"Well...actually, we've talked about me moving in with him sooner than that."

The first tendrils of unease started to slither around her excited buzz, dampening it.

"How much sooner?" She knew she wouldn't like the answer the second she saw her sister's guilty expression.

"Like, right after the engagement's official."

"*What*?" Okay, this time she wasn't apologizing for her outburst. "No. We had a plan. You and me. We worked on getting *Papí* to be okay with us moving out for over a *year*." A heck of a lot longer than Alejandro had been in the picture, that was for sure.

"I know that was the plan. But things change."

"Things change? That's all you can say about ripping the rug out from under me like this? *Things change?*"

Bria crossed her arms, a mulish expression filling her face.

"I knew you'd be this way."

"What way? Surprised? Upset? Betrayed?"

"Oh, god, stop with the drama already. This is *exactly* why I didn't mention anything to you about it before now. I knew you'd get all bitchy and self-righteous, and make it all about you."

"All about..." Heart thrumming with building fury, she sucked in a careful breath to hold back the scathing words that wanted to come out.

"It is about me, Brianna," she said through clenched teeth. "Because your decision affects my plans, my life, too. So, it's not all about *you*, either."

If she'd hoped throwing her sister's words back at her would help, she was sadly mistaken. If anything, the mulish expression dug in deeper, unwilling to give an inch.

Then an important fact occurred.

"Do you honestly think *Mami* and *Papi* are going to be okay with you moving in with Alejandro before you're married, engaged or not?"

Uncertainty colored Bria's expression for the first time

"Not at first. But I know we can get them to change their minds."

"We?" Why didn't she think Bria was talking about her and her soon-to-be fiancé?

"Like you said, we talked them around once already about us moving out. It shouldn't be too hard to do it again about this."

Flames flickered at the edges of her vision in time with her pounding heartbeat as her temper soared.

"I can't believe you're actually using *that* as a reason I should help you screw me over!" Was her sister stupid as well as selfish?

Bria let out a frustrated sound and stomped her foot.

"Don't be a brat. I need you to be on my side and back me up on this."

"Oh? You mean like the way you were on *my* side and backed *me* up when I was pitching my food truck idea?"

"What? That's not even close to the same thing. This is important!"

Wow.

She couldn't even form words as she absorbed that blow, staring at her sister in disbelief. This was important. *This.* Not her ideas for the restaurant. Not their plans to move out together. Only this. Only her.

Brianna, you selfish bitch.

Bria drew back, outrage darkening her expression. "I am not!"

Oops. She must have said that out loud.

Sorry, not sorry.

"Did it ever even enter your mind how moving in with Alejandro would screw up me being able to move out of the house? Or do you just not care?"

"Nothing's stopping you from still moving out."

"Well, there's not having someone to move in *with*, for starters."

"You can find someone."

Bella flung her arms out. "Who? Kinzley already shares a place with her sister"—she put emphasis on the word—"and I don't have any other close friends who aren't already in their own places." She and Bria had been the last in their social group to still be stuck in the nest.

And now it was going to just be her.

Something a little like panic fluttered in her chest.

"You could get your own apartment, then."

Like it was that easy.

"Right. Even if I could find a one-bedroom that was miraculously available in a Rafe-approved building"—which was highly unlikely—"*and* if I could afford the rent all on my own"—a very huge if—"have you forgotten the whole reason we were moving in together in the first place? Because I haven't. And if you think *Papi* will suddenly be okay with one of his *ángel dulce* 'living all on her own in this dangerous world', you're lying to both of us."

"Well, I don't know what to tell you, Bell. You'll need to figure it out for yourself, because I'm moving in with Alejandro." Her face and tone said her mind was made up.

Well, so was Bella's.

"And you'll need to figure out how to convince *Papi* to let you do that for *your*self, because I'm not helping." Ignoring her sister's sputtered words of disbelief, she left the room, careful to close the door quietly behind her.

Slamming it would have been much more satisfying. But it also would have brought their mother upstairs, and she didn't have it in her at the moment to not lose what was left of her shit if she asked what was going on.

Ducking into her room only long enough to grab her purse and keys, she got in her car and started driving with no real destination in mind. All she knew was she needed to be away. To think. To lick her wounds. To come to terms with the massive betrayal she hadn't seen coming.

Although in hindsight, maybe she should have at least had a clue.

Brianna had been so wrapped up in Alejandro the past few months, either being with him or texting him practically every minute of the day. And she'd risked being caught staying overnight with him not once, but twice in the last week. She should have realized things were reaching critical mass between them.

But she still never in a million years would have guessed Bria would jump from the sneaking around stage to moving in together before marriage. Yes, Rafe had lived with Lillian, even before they were engaged. But he was a man. And as much as she hated it, in the Delgado house that meant he and Cris both got a different set of rules from the ones she and Bria were expected to follow.

So unfair.

And yet, that very unfairness might end up working in her favor for a change.

Because as the bubbling pot of emotions inside her cooled to a simmer, the more clarity came to her thoughts. And she realized the very simple fact she'd been overlooking all along.

No matter how hard Bria tried, their father would never be okay with this.

To his old-fashioned way of thinking, good little Catholic girls, especially *his* little girls—even if they were both grown-ass women—went to church every Sunday, honored their parents, and, the big one, didn't live in sin. Period, full-stop, do not collect two-hundred dollars, go directly to the confessional.

And no matter how much she might want to, Bria wouldn't openly defy their father's wishes. She had too much respect for him, first off. And if that wasn't a big enough reason, there was also the restaurant to consider. Any discord at home would translate directly to work, and Bria was too invested in her position in Bayamo's hierarchy to mess that up.

Even for Alejandro.

The tight knot of muscles in her neck started to unravel and relax. Right now, it didn't matter that by telling her sister she wouldn't back her play she'd basically destroyed any chance she had of Bria coming on board with her food truck idea. That was a worry for another day.

Today, all she cared about was her sister's crazy idea wouldn't send her whole world into upheaval the way she'd first thought. She wouldn't be left odd woman out.

Again.

Bria would ask, their father would put his foot down and forbid it, and everything would go back to the way it was supposed to be.

All she had to do was wait.

***

PATRICIA BEAUMONT WAS A lot of things. Smart. Resourceful. Caring. A staunch friend and devoted wife. The best, most loving mother any kid could ever hope for.

She was also a master manipulator who excelled at getting what she wanted. And she was driving Peter crazy.

Not because of anything she was saying.

Oh, no.

It was what she *wasn't* saying that had his nerves all twitchy and on edge. Not once since they'd been seated for brunch at her favorite restaurant had she mentioned the one thing he'd been absolutely certain would be the first topic on today's agenda.

Isabella.

But here they were, halfway through their meal, and she hadn't brought up what she'd walked in on last night even once. It was as if she didn't care at all that she'd found the two of them sharing a cozy dinner together. Like she'd accepted Isabella's excuse at face value despite it being thin enough to read a book through.

Which was what he'd wanted, of course. Just not what he'd expected.

Not from the woman who'd always been able to know, at a single glance, when he or his brothers had been up to something they shouldn't have.

It was unnerving as hell.

"You still haven't told me if you have a preference which booth you're manning at the picnic." His mother paused in cutting through a thick slice of French toast to look across the table at him, a mild hint of concern in her eyes. "You did put in for the day off, didn't you?"

Right. The picnic.

"Put in and approved." Not that it had been easy. Summer weekends were always a bitch to get off since there were so few vacation spots available and so many people wanting them. His seniority wasn't all that high yet, so he usually never bothered trying.

But this year, the Everbrite Foundation, the charity arm of his family's financial investment company, was hosting the first ever Paws for Vets Picnic. Raising money for the training of service dogs for local veterans and first responders had been his idea.

And while his mother and the foundation had done all the heavy lifting to create an event to make it happen, he still felt a special connection to the project. He really wanted to be there and have a hands-on part in seeing it come to fruition.

So, he'd put in a request for the day off, even though it had already been full. Thankfully, it had somehow been approved. Which Lister would no doubt find a reason to comment on, bitching about special treatment for the "Golden Boy."

Asshole.

Even so, the cause was well worth the aggravation.

His mother's face relaxed into lines of relief. "Oh, good. So, preferences?"

He shrugged. "Put me anywhere you need me, I guess." His fork paused halfway to his mouth. "Except maybe not with the cotton candy." He'd manned that station once before at another event, and spent two whole days blowing spun sugar out of his nose.

It had totally ruined cotton candy for him.

Lips twitching, his mother scrolled down the checklist of meeting notes she'd been going through on her phone. While she did that, he devoured the rest of his Philly cheesesteak omelet. It was delicious, but it just couldn't compete with the leftover egg frittatas he'd warmed up earlier that morning.

Of course, he might have been the tiniest bit biased because of the cook.

"Well, I think that's everything." With a pleased hum, she picked up her coffee, cradling the cup in her elegant hands. "We'll have one more planning meeting a few days out from the event to handle any last-minute crises that come up, because they always do. But otherwise, I do believe we're ready."

Knowing his mother, he didn't doubt it for a second.

"Thanks, Mom. It really means a lot to me, you taking on something else to champion when you've already got so many things on your plate. And I know Vic appreciates it, too."

She waved the gratitude away. "Oh, please. I'll always have room on my plate for a worthy cause. I'm just glad you brought this one to our attention." She hesitated. "How is your friend doing? Is he still planning to attend?"

"Vic's good." A fellow officer, he'd come back from his third National Guard deployment overseas with not only physical wounds courtesy of an enemy IED, but a severe case of PTSD. So severe, he'd ended up having to take early retirement from the force.

It was at his retirement party Peter had first heard him talking about his disappointment in how long he had to wait for a service dog trained to help him with his condition. There were lots of organizations around the country who provided them. But it seemed there were always more people in need than dogs to match them with, thanks to the steep cost involved in raising and training them.

By the next day, an idea had been born.

"As for him coming...he says yes, but it'll probably be early, and only for a little while. Even with Molly, he's still not very comfortable around crowds yet." The yellow Lab was Victor's new best friend, and the greatest thing that could have happened to him. Even after only a few months together, he could see the difference she'd made in Vic's quality of life.

"Well, good. I hope he does. I'd love to see him again. He was a lovely man."

He stifled a snort. Only his mother would think that. Vic had barely spoken two words when Peter had brought him to meet her during the early planning stages for the fundraiser. Of course, that had been B.M.

Before Molly.

He really hoped Vic would feel up to coming. It would be a wonderful example of the true impact service dogs could have if his mother could see him now compared to then.

Their dishes were cleared, but before he could request the check, his mother asked for a refill on her coffee. Stifling a sigh, he took one as well. It seemed they weren't finished talking just yet, after all.

After the waiter withdrew, his mother stirred in a dollop of cream and tapped her spoon gently on the edge of the cup. "Now, about the foundation's next event."

Damn.

He should have seen this coming.

"I know it's still quite a few months away, but it's never too early to start lining up this year's bachelor auction participants." She looked at him with an expectant expression he knew all too well.

"Um...no."

As in *hell* no.

"Peter..."

"Mom..." As amusing as it was to tease her by parroting her tone, this was a serious negotiation. One he couldn't afford to lose. "I told you last year I didn't want to do it anymore."

It had been fun at first. Strutting on stage, having women bid stupid amounts of money to spend a day with him. But after a couple of years, the shine had come off that apple, even if it was for charity.

"Besides, for that kind of cash, those women want a night out with a doctor or a CEO, not some street cop."

"Oh, please. There are plenty of women with hot cop fantasies."

He choked on his coffee. "Mom!" Did she seriously just say that?

"What?" She sniffed. "I read. I'm mature, not dead, you know."

He did know. And he had the Marvin Gaye dirty dancing images burned into his brain to prove it.

"Not helping your case, Mom. You know, you should probably be trying to get someone like Jesse or Nolan to take part." Two of his brother Theo's friends who happened to be a doctor and a lawyer, respectively. "They'd bring in big bucks."

By the speculative glint in her eyes, he'd piqued her interest.

"Hmm, yes. Fresh faces. And maybe your friend John," she mused, tapping a finger against her cup. "Do you think he'd be interested?"

Not wanting to get into a discussion about hot fireman fantasies—god help him—he offered his friend up without a qualm. "I'm sure he'd love it."

"Excellent." Over the rim of her cup, she gave him a smile. "Which means you have no excuse not to take part, too."

Did he mention she was a master manipulator?

"Of course, if you were, say, in any kind of relationship with someone, I wouldn't even be asking..."

And there it was. Finally.

"You know I'm not seeing anyone right now."

One brown brow raised. "Really? No one?"

It was impossible to keep images of Isabella from popping into his head. As soon as he banished one, another took its place. Isabella at the dog park. Isabella cooking in his kitchen. Isabella naked in his bed. Under him. Over him. Beside him.

"Nope." He wasn't really lying, since he had no idea what the hell it was they were doing. But it sure tasted like a lie, anyway. He took a sip of scalding coffee to rinse the sourness away.

"So, last night's dinner was just...dinner?"

"Yup. Just dinner." Now, that one *was* a lie. It had been so much more.

For him, anyway.

She didn't ask any more probing questions as she finished her coffee. But the gleam in her eyes as she looked at him over the rim of her fine china cup said he hadn't been as convincing as he'd hoped.

Damn her mother superpowers.

Dabbing her lips with a napkin as he signed for the meal, she said, "Oh, I almost forgot. Did Richard call you yet?"

"No. What about?" If it was to warn him about their mom's bachelor auction ambush, he was a little late.

"I'm not sure, honestly. He just mentioned something on his way out of the office yesterday that he'd gotten a call from someone at the hotel, and your name had come up."

He shrugged as he pulled his mother's chair out for her.

"Maybe I left something in my room when I checked out." But why would they have contacted Richard? "I'll give him a call later and see what it was about."

The lousy weather washed out his plans to take Roscoe to Pagosa Park. Instead, they had to make do with a few quick walks around the block in between downpours. It was a poor substitute and left both of them in grumpy moods.

So, he wasn't in the best frame of mind when he remembered his mother's mention of Richard and picked up his phone to call him.

"Mom said you wanted to talk to me?"

There was a brief silence before his older brother spoke.

"Is there anything you want to tell me about what happened with you and a certain young lady on Saturday night?"

His lungs seized at his brother's words, like all the air pressure had suddenly been sucked from the room. He knew. Somehow, Richard knew.

Oh. Fuck.

Chapter 12

"I...WHAT?" PETER FORCED OUT a laugh that sounded phony even to him. "What are you talking about?"

There was another silence. He recognized the tactic, because it was one he used himself when talking to suspects. People were uncomfortable with silence as a rule. More so when feeling guilty, and usually they tried to fill it even when they shouldn't.

The question was, what exactly did Richard suspect him of, and how much proof did he have? He didn't regret bringing Isabella back to his hotel room that night. But his brothers were likely to take a much dimmer view of him debauching their newly minted sister-in-law while the wedding festivities were still going on a few floors below.

"Are you going to tell me you weren't in the hotel bar with this young lady Saturday night?"

Shit.

"Yeah, we were there for a little while." No sense in lying about it.

"And did you get into an altercation with one of the other patrons there?"

It took a second before he remembered the dark-haired dick he'd had to liberate Isabella from when she'd first walked in. "I wouldn't call it an altercation, no."

"Then what would you call it?"

'Popping a zit on the ass of humanity' came to mind. But something in Richard's tone said levity wouldn't be appreciated right now.

"He was giving her a hard come-on, not taking no for an answer or letting her get by him, so I intervened."

"How?"

A shiver of unease at the sharp question rode up his spine.

"I pretended to be her boyfriend and got him to back off. Why? What's going on?" Because something clearly was, and he was starting to think it wasn't at all what he'd believed it to be.

"Did you ever touch him?"

"Touch him?" What the hell? "The bar was crowded. I guess I might have brushed shoulders with him when I walked by."

He didn't think he had. But he'd been so focused on getting to Isabella's side, he hadn't been paying all that much attention to what would have been a normal occurrence when walking through a crowd.

"That's it?"

"Yeah. I told them Isabella was with me, he and his buddy went back to their table, and that was it."

"Wait. *Isabella*? As in, *our* Bella?"

His first instinctive reaction was *my Isabella, not yours*.

His second was to curse to himself when he realized Richard hadn't known she was the "young lady" in question. And he'd just handed the information to him on a golden platter. He might as well have put a noose around his own neck.

"Yes, that Isabella."

Richard gave a grunt which could have meant anything from confusion to satisfaction Peter had taken care of someone now considered part of the family.

"What about after you left the bar?"

The noose tightened.

"What about it?"

"Where did you go? Because I know it wasn't the reception."

Which meant his absence had been noticed, even though no one had commented on it the next morning. His stomach sank. Had Isabella's been noted as well?

"I called it a night and went back to my room."

"Alone?"

Fuck.

"What the hell kind of question is that?"

"The kind where I'm hoping you have someone you met in that bar who can give you an alibi about how and where you spent the rest of your night after you left public view."

"Alibi? What the hell do I need..." Pieces started to fall into place. Very bad pieces. "Richard, tell me what the fuck is going on. Now."

This time, the silence was different. More like surprise at Peter's barked order than a power-play tactic.

Richard's sigh was clear through the phone. "The manager of the hotel contacted me right before I left work yesterday. He said someone had called looking for contact info for a 'very big brown-haired man in a tuxedo from a wedding party' who'd been in the bar this past weekend."

"That could describe half our cousins." But he knew it didn't.

A certainty confirmed when Richard said, "Only the three of us were wearing boutonnieres, which he also mentioned. And neither Theo or I went into the bar."

Shit.

"When the manager told him he couldn't give out guest information, the guy said it had to do with an assault that had occurred on the hotel property, and if they didn't want a lawsuit, he'd give him the information."

One word stood out from the entire explanation.

"Assault?" It came out as a snarl. "What the fuck is that supposed to mean?" But put together with Richard's earlier questioning, he had a sick feeling he knew.

"You're the one with the criminal justice degree. You tell me."

"It means the son of a bitch is lying."

"Does it?"

The question hurt, even though he understood why he had to ask it.

"Yeah, it does. What exactly did he say happened?"

"I don't know yet. I turned the matter over to our lawyers. Just like any other time a spurious claim is made against someone in the family, looking for a quick payout. But I wanted to talk to you so you'd know to expect a call from them about it."

"And to find out if it might be true."

"That, too." The admission was grudging, but honest.

"Jesus." He sank onto the couch, scrubbing a hand through his hair as he absorbed the implications. "I swear to God, I never touched the guy." No matter how much he'd wanted to.

"And Bella can corroborate that?"

"Our interaction in the bar, yeah. Along with dozens of other people who were there. Like I said, it was packed. If I'd punched him, don't you think someone would have noticed?"

"If he's saying it happened in the bar. I don't know the whole story yet. Which is why I'll ask again, do you have someone who can be an alibi for after you left?"

Damn it to hell.

"No." Not one he could use, anyway. If she didn't even want his mother to know they were having dinner together, then she sure as hell wouldn't want everyone knowing they'd spent the night in his hotel room.

"Shit. Just this once, little brother, I wish you'd relaxed that Boy Scout mentality of yours and had yourself a quickie bar hookup. It would make squashing this claim a hell of a lot tidier."

It would.

And he had.

But he wouldn't throw Isabella under the bus like that. Especially when he knew he hadn't done anything wrong. It might make the lawyers' jobs a little tougher in the long run, but that was what they made the big bucks for.

They talked for a few more minutes, during which he decline an invitation to dinner at Richard and Amber's place. He wasn't exactly in the best frame of mind to be good company for anyone.

Not to mention the fact his brother would no doubt take the opportunity to grill him in more detail about Saturday night. And while he might not be as good as their mother at digging out the truth, Peter wasn't willing to risk making a slip.

At the end of the call, Richard hesitated. "Pete? As much as I hate this is happening, and as big a pain in the ass as it'll probably be before it's done, I'm still glad you were there to watch out for Bella. She's part of the family now. Even though I'm sure she'd hate to hear me say that," he added with a rueful chuckle.

Peter wasn't so sure about that anymore. But he knew *he* didn't like hearing it.

The last way he wanted to think of Isabella was as family.

But the reminder that was how his brothers felt reinforced his decision to keep her name out of things as much as possible. At least until he could talk to her. If this thing between them was just sex, then it needed to end. That much was clear.

But if it was more...

Then he was willing to wait as long as it took for her to decide if they were worth the risk.

THIS WAS A HUGE mistake.

She knew it, but that didn't stop her fingers from tingling as she pulled into the small parking lot behind the burger place she'd picked for her meal with Peter.

Meal, not date.

She refused to call it that, even to herself. It was just dinner. In public. For no other reason than to spend time with the guy who'd been occupying way too much of her daytime—and definitely nighttime—thoughts.

A nervous ripple went through her belly.

Because she shouldn't be doing this. Not because she was excited about seeing him again. Which she totally wasn't. Because that would just be asking for trouble.

Okay, even she knew when she was protesting too much.

Taking a fortifying breath, she left the safety of her car. She'd seen his truck in the lot, so she wasn't surprised he was waiting inside the restaurant's door. What did surprise her was the way her body felt drawn toward his as soon as she saw him, like he was a magnet and she was a helpless hunk of metal caught in his pull.

Not a good start.

"Hi." The smile on his face as he greeted her only made the tug even harder to resist.

But she did.

"Hi." There was an uncomfortable second where she thought he was going to hug her. When he didn't, she couldn't decide if she was relieved or disappointed.

Relieved. Definitely relieved.

Mostly, anyway.

"I hope you didn't have any trouble finding the place. I know it's sort of out of the way, but they make really great burgers." Which they did. But it was the 'out of the way' part that had been more of a deciding factor in her choice.

The university campus was practically across the street, making it a popular spot for the students and faculty. Hopefully making it *not* the kind of place anyone in his family might patronize.

One surprise drop-in by a Beaumont was already one too many.

"It was pretty easy, actually. I used to eat here all the time when I was at CU. Although it had a different name then, so I didn't realize it was the same place."

"Oh." *He* went to the University of Colorado?

They studied the big board with the dozens of uniquely and sometimes hilariously named burger platters available, then stepped up to the counter to order and pay. They chose a spot toward the back of the dining area, away from the few occupied tables. The laminated cards with their order numbers went on the tall metal stand at the center of the table so the server knew where to deliver their food when it was ready.

"It's a good thing the university is in summer session, or we'd probably be waiting half an hour for a table." Peter stripped the paper from his straw and stuck it into his drink. "I guess since you know the place you went to CU, too?"

"No, CCD." She stabbed her straw into the plastic lid, emotions flaring as they always did whenever she thought of that time in Denver during her first semester. Which she tried hard not to do.

"There's nothing wrong with community college."

He said it like he thought she was being defensive about the difference in their academics. Which, for once, hadn't even entered her mind.

"I know. CCD was a great school. That's not why...there's just some other stuff that happened around then I don't like to think about, is all." She knew she'd made a tactical error when his eyes narrowed the way Rafe's did when he went into cop mode.

Crap.

She scrambled to shift the conversation off herself before he could start digging. "So, you went to CU. I'm surprised. Didn't your brothers both go to Ivy League schools?" As soon as she said it, she wondered if she'd poked a sore point. Just because he had the money to get in didn't mean he had the grades to qualify.

Although, there were probably ways around that.

Money could buy just about anything.

He gave an offhanded shrug. "I was accepted to a bunch of schools, but I chose CU. It has a great criminal justice program." He hesitated. "And honestly, having a Harvard degree would have just given people one more reason to think of me as the entitled rich kid playing at being a cop."

She blinked. "Do they really think that?"

"Some do. A lot less now than when I first joined the force, but there's still a few who enjoy giving me a hard time too much to ever admit they were wrong." He said it like it wasn't a big deal, but she could tell it bothered him.

"Well, they *are* wrong. Rafe says you're a great cop. And he should know, since he's one, too."

Peter grinned. "Which? A cop, or great?"

"Both, of course." She returned the grin, trying her best to ignore the twin dimples on his face. Dang, he was adorable when he smiled. "And I'm not just saying that because he's my brother."

"You're right. He is a great cop. And I'm not just saying that because he's my friend. Or that as Sergeant Delgado he now outranks me. He's got something special, this bone-deep desire to help people. To keep them safe. It's like he was born for the job."

She nodded. Rafe had been set on the path to protect the weak from the day their father was rushed to the hospital, bloody and beaten, but it was more than that. "When he told our parents he wanted to become a police officer rather than work at the restaurant, he said he felt it in here." She pressed a hand to her chest. "That it was what he needed to do. His calling."

"It shows. Which is why I've always tried to use him as a role model for what kind of cop I want to be."

Their food arrived, giving her time to absorb that shocking admission. Peter Beaumont considered Rafael Delgado a role model? In what universe did the son of a billionaire admire the son of a Cuban émigré restauranteur?

Thankfully oblivious to the mental spin he'd just put her into, Peter tore a huge bite from his Have A Cow triple cheeseburger and let out an appreciative rumble. "Mmm, that's as good as I remember."

Bella bit into her Burgatory burger, the topping of jalapeño and habanero peppers biting back with a spicy snap. "Oh, yeah. That's perfect."

He dipped a fry in ketchup before pointing it at her. "You know, one of these days you're going to burn all of the taste buds out of your mouth."

She laughed.

"Not likely. My mother says I liked to gnaw on raw peppers when I was teething as a baby."

"You are so not normal." The teasing was accompanied by a mournful shake of his head and a glint in his eyes that made her smile and take another big bite to tease him back.

And wonder when it had become a goal for her to make this man smile.

After swallowing another bite from his ridiculously large burger, he asked, "So, what was your major?"

"Business." She made a face to show what she thought of that. "But I also got certificates in Dining Services, Bartending, and Entrepreneurship. Those were a lot more interesting." Not to mention more useful, since it looked like she might be working the dining room and catering jobs for the foreseeable future. As in, the rest of her life.

He let out a low whistle. "Wow, overachieve much?"

"Pfft. Right." But a rush of warmth filled her at the compliment.

"At the risk of spoiling what's been a great night so far, I have to say that with all that academic muscle backing you up, I'm even more surprised about your parents not giving your idea the consideration it deserves."

She stiffened. Lucky for them both, she had a mouthful of food that took a few long moments to chew and swallow before she could say anything. By the time she did, her initial knee-jerk anger had subsided enough for her to consider his words.

And realize he was right.

Her parents had been the ones to steer her toward a degree in business management. Why bother if they wouldn't give any true weight to her input about the restaurant?

"You're right. They should have." She was pretty sure she'd surprised him by agreeing. "And I'll be pointing that out the next time I sit them down to talk about it."

"Good. Remind them you're not just a pretty face, but a pretty damn smart woman."

The pleasure of the second compliment in as many minutes was tempered by the anxious itch of waiting for him to bring up the *other* thing she'd said about her business plan. The unfortunate slip in admitting it came about because she felt unneeded in the grand scheme of things. The spare tire for a well-oiled machine.

But seconds ticked by, and he didn't say anything. Relief trickled through her.

For a minute, anyway.

There was still another uncomfortable subject yet to be brought up, and it looked like she was the one who was going to have to do it.

"So, um, did you and your mom talk about whatever it was she stopped by for the other night?" Okay, it was a wimpy lead-in. But she needed to work up to what she was really dying to ask.

"Yeah. She just wanted to bring me up to speed on the foundation's latest fundraiser. Not that I'm really all that involved in the planning process. But I guess I'm kind of an honorary team member since it was my suggestion that got the ball rolling."

"Right, your friend who needed the service dog."

"You know about that?" He looked as surprised as he sounded.

"Your mom was talking about it the night of the rehearsal dinner." She might have resented the Beaumonts for their wealth, but she couldn't deny Patricia—still nope—Peter's mother did a lot of good for the entire Boulder community through the Everbrite Foundation. And she hadn't been able to say no when the topic of volunteers had come up.

"She was supposed to let me know when the sign-ups start for assignments."

This time, he looked both surprised and pleased.

"I think the emails are going out Monday. Did you have a preference about where you want to work? I kind of have an in with the person in charge."

A week ago, the sly wink over getting preferential treatment would have felt like cayenne pepper in her underwear. Now, she could take it as the joke it was meant as, even if it was true. Because really, didn't everyone use their connections to get a little something extra once in a while?

Her mother used her long-standing friendship with Mr. Isakson at the farmer's market to guarantee she got first pick on the fresh produce that came in. In return, he always got a table, even if the restaurant was fully booked. And Kinzley used her sister's boyfriend to get them into the places his band played without having to pay the cover.

So, maybe it was time she stopped being a hypocrite, whining about how only the rich and entitled played the system to their benefit. One hand washing the other happened on all levels, big and small.

"I don't know what assignments there are to pick from. It's probably a lot to ask if it could be something *not* to do with food, since it's a picnic, but if that's possible it would be great."

"I'll see what I can do."

"Thanks." She dipped a fry into the little cup of ketchup and dug deep for a nonchalant tone. "So, did your mom have anything else to say?"

"You mean, about you being at my apartment?"

So much for nonchalant. "Yeah."

"Not directly."

Which meant yes.

Her stomach cramped, and she dropped the soggy fry to the plate. "Do you think she suspects anything was going on between us?"

There was a slight pause. "Would it be so bad if she did?"

"Of course it would!" Then the quiet way he'd asked made her backtrack. "Don't you think so?"

"Not really."

"So, you're okay with your mom knowing we were having wild afternoon delight sex right before she showed up at your door?"

He winced. "Not when you put it like that."

"How else would you put it?"

"That we were spending time together. Because we like each other's company." His hand moved to cover hers on the table. "Kind of like we are right now." His thumb swept over the sensitive skin on the back of her hand. "Aren't we?"

The sensation of his calloused thumb moving in a slow, steady rhythm made nerve endings tingle and her pulse kick up a notch. "Yeah, I guess." She tore her gaze from their hands and met his intense regard, which only made her pulse race even faster. "Yeah, we are. I am," she amended.

A smile eased the solemn lines of his face. "So am I."

"But your mother—"

"Has nothing to do with anything. This is me and you, and nobody else." His hand closed tighter around hers. "Don't you want to see where this could go?"

Damn it, she did. But she was also a realist.

And maybe still a bit of a coward.

"You know it wouldn't work. We're too..." *Different.* But that felt too much like a lie, now that she'd gotten to know him a little better. "...connected. Our families, I mean."

"Lil and Rafe being married doesn't make us off-limits." He sounded adamant about that.

"No, but it does make things trickier."

He frowned. "Why should it?"

Was he really that dense?

"What if we get involved, and things don't work out?

"But what if they do?"

"But what if they don't? Think about the uncomfortable family get-togethers."

"More uncomfortable than when we didn't like each other in the first place?"

He had a point. Although she hadn't known what he looked like naked then. That would definitely add a few new degrees of awkward to things.

She tried a different tack.

"What about everyone else, though? Say we do go out, and things end badly between us. Don't you think our siblings will take sides again, the way we did with Lillian and Rafe? Our families are just starting to get along better." She thought of Cris enjoying breakfast conversation with Peter's brothers the day after the wedding. They might never be best buddies, but it had been a promising start. "Do we really want to risk ruining that?"

He looked like he wanted to argue, the muscles in his jaw bunching and jerking as it clenched. In the end, he let out a resigned sigh, his entire body deflating. "Damn it."

His unspoken agreement that pursuing a relationship between them was foolhardy should have made her happy. Instead, she felt an unpleasant knot thread its way through her belly. Like she'd just made a terrible mistake.

The remaining few bites of her burger suddenly held no appeal, but she took one anyway, then crumpled her napkin and dropped it on top of the rest as she struggled to swallow without choking. Peter seemed similarly disinclined to finish his food. Which, having seen his normal appetite, told her just how upset he was despite his blank expression.

"You finished?"

She nodded, and they both dumped their trash before heading out to the parking lot. Neither of them spoke, the silence as thick and heavy as the previous day's storm clouds, and just as highly charged. She wouldn't be at all surprised to see lightning bolts come shooting out of his eyes at any second.

With every tense step, she tried to convince herself she'd done the right thing.

Every word she'd said was true. The two of them having a bad breakup could upset the fragile balance between their joined families. But what she hadn't said was that she knew, deep down, that a bad breakup would do much, much worse.

To her.

Nathan had hurt her. She was pretty sure Peter, given the chance, could destroy her.

And still, there was a wailing sense of loss inside her head. One that was making her second guess her choices, and their consequences.

They reached her car first. He slowed to a stop, reluctance written in every line of his rigid body. "Well, I guess this—"

"What if they didn't know?" The blurted question came out of nowhere.

He froze, looking caught between confusion...and hope. "What?"

"What if we did give it a shot, see where things went with us, but we just didn't let anyone know about it?"

"You mean sneak around?"

"I wouldn't put it..." She huffed. "Okay, fine. What if we snuck around? That way, we wouldn't have the added pressure of family watching our every move, and if we decided it wasn't working out and ended things, no one would even know, so they wouldn't be able to get upset or take sides. Win-win."

His eyes narrowed slightly, as though he were running her words through his puzzle-solving brain, checking to see if she'd come up with a sound solution. After the longest minute of her life, he gave a slow nod.

"It could work."

Before she could get too excited, he added, "Just to be clear. We're talking about real dating. Like, going places and doing things together, not just holing up in my apartment, watching Netflix and having 'wild afternoon delight' sex."

Heat spread in a languid flush from below her navel to the rest of her body at his deep voice saying those words back to her.

"Yes." She cleared her throat and tried again. "Yes, real dates. As long as we're not going places where we'll run into anyone we know."

"For now."

She hesitated. Nodded. "For now."

The storm clouds finally blew away from his beautiful eyes. He stepped into her, giving her time to protest, before he wrapped his hand around the back of her head and lowered his mouth to hers for a long, thorough kiss to seal the deal. "Mmm. Spicy."

She thought he was teasing until he licked his lips as though they were actually tingling with heat. Only then did she remember the peppers on her burger. "Sorry."

"Don't be. It's like you. Hot and a little uncomfortable, but well worth the burn." He kissed her again before she could protest that assessment, leaving her grinning against his mouth instead.

When he finally released her, she pressed a hand to his hard chest, slightly breathless.

"Just to be clear, dating means we're still having sex, too, right?" Because there was zero chance she could be around this man and not want to lick every inch of his body. Twice.

Something sparked in his gaze, heating it to molten chocolate. "Oh, absolutely."

Thank god.

As she followed him back to his place, anticipation and unease rolled through her in alternating waves. She'd meant what she said. The last thing she wanted was for their families to end up at odds again, especially if she had the ability to prevent it. Rafe and Lillian didn't deserve to have their newlywed bliss blow up in their faces before they'd even knocked the honeymoon sand out of their suitcases.

But selfishly, she hadn't been able to do the right thing. She hadn't been able to let Peter go. Instead, she'd just agreed to actually *dating* the man, which both thrilled and terrified her. It might be a mistake.

No, it was definitely a mistake.

But it was one she had to make, no matter how badly it might end.

At least this way, the only person she was putting at risk was herself.

Chapter 13

"Damn, am I glad we're off tomorrow." Dropping onto the locker room bench, Sam Garcia let out a happy sigh that turned into a groan of relief as he pulled off his uniform boots. "Tourists, man. It's like people go on vacation and suddenly lose their freaking minds or something."

Peter grinned as he laced up his trainers. "Welcome to the summer season."

Which was only slightly less exasperating than the winter season, when Boulder was invaded by snow-sport lovers from around the world. Tourists might be a big part of the city's identity, but they were a huge pain in the ass for the men and women who had to gently remind them that being on vacation didn't mean a free pass to act like an inconsiderate moron.

Of course, next month when their schedule flipped from first shift to second and they were patrolling the three-to-eleven hours, it would be even worse. The only thing more frustrating to deal with than crazy tourists were crazy *drunk* tourists.

But there still wasn't another job he'd ever want more than this one. Except, of course, detective.

A goal he was one step closer to today.

Excitement hit his system like a shot of Jameson. The notice for the promotion board interviews had gone out at noon. In a little over two weeks, he'd be able to complete the final piece to his promotion puzzle. The only thing he had to do between now and then was focus on keeping his nose clean and his badge shiny.

"You meeting us at the Downer tonight?"

"Sorry. Other plans." The anticipation of which zinged through his veins with even more vigor than the interview posting had. Three days without seeing Isabella was four days too long.

"Again? You bailed last week, too."

"What can I say? I got a better offer." He couldn't keep a grin from playing at the corner of his mouth. A *much* better offer. One that involved candlelight, dinner, and one spicy woman he still couldn't believe was his.

"Damn, man! You've been holding out!" Sam threw a balled-up t-shirt at him, which Peter caught before it smacked his face and lobbed back. "You hooked up with one of those badge bunnies after all, didn't you?"

"Nope." He closed his locker and grabbed his gym bag from the bench. "They're all yours."

"The new blonde in Admin? She's been giving you the eye for weeks."

"Nope."

"Then who?"

"No one you know." He was pretty sure Sam and Isabella had never met, anyway.

"Come on, man! You're not even going to give me a hint?"

"Nope."

"You suck, Beaumont. I thought we were friends."

Knowing the other guys in the locker room were following the exchange with unconcealed amusement, Peter gave only a grin as he left. He knew Sam was just busting his balls. If the situation was reversed, he'd have been doing the same to him. Nobody took more pleasure in riding you hard than your friends.

But the truth was, only ten days after he and Isabella had started quietly dating, he was already beginning to chafe under the terms of their agreement. He kept reminding himself there were legitimate reasons for them staying on the down-low for right now.

Good, sensible reasons.

"Hey, Beaumont."

Reasons like the one walking toward him.

Rafael Delgado.

Fight or flight kicked in for a split second before he nailed it down and smiled at his brand-new brother-in-law, who looked happy, tanned, and disgustingly relaxed. It was his first day back after his honeymoon.

And the first time Peter was seeing him since he'd started sleeping with his sister.

He'd known this initial encounter with that secret hanging over them would be awkward. Uncomfortable, even. But he hadn't expected the total freak-out of panic which blasted through him as he shook Rafe's hand, and prayed his palm wasn't sweaty.

"Hey, Sarge. Welcome back. How was Fiji?"

"A-*ma*-zing."

There was a satiated gleam in his eyes that warned Peter he wanted no more details than that. He'd done his very best to *not* think about what his friend and his sister had been doing for the last two weeks.

Just like right now he tried not to think about what he and his friend's sister had been doing during the same time.

"So, how have things been while I was gone? Anything new and exciting happen?"

An innocent enough question, given Rafe's extended absence. But for some reason, the hairs on his neck stirred in warning.

He shook the feeling off. That was just the paranoia and guilt talking.

"Nope. Well, other than Garcia having to coax a tourist off of Ralphie this morning."

"How's that news?" The affectionately named buffalo statue on the downtown Pearl Street pedestrian mall was a popular selfie spot. Sometimes—more often than it should—people thought "riding" the CU mascot would make for a better picture, despite the signs asking them not to.

"Oh, did I forget to mention she was only wearing—and I use the term loosely—hot-pink lingerie at the time?"

A snort escaped before Rafe got his expression back under control. He gave a sober, Sergeant-like nod. "Garcia's kind of call. Leftover drunk?"

"You'd think, but no. Just some crazy woman who enjoys taking semi-nude videos of herself at different public places she visits and posts them on some subscription social media site. She thought we should be grateful she was drumming up interest in our 'boring little city' with her followers, not threatening her with public indecency and trespass if she didn't put some clothes on."

Rafe rolled his eyes. "Freaking tourist season."

The eye-roll made him grin even more than the echoed sentiment about tourists. It looked like Rafe was already adopting some of his wife's bad habits. That was one of his sister's favorite facial expressions.

He glanced at his watch. Damn. He'd have to cut his workout short at this rate to not be late meeting Isabella.

"Sorry Sarge, but I gotta run. Maybe we can catch up another time?"

"What's the hurry? Got a hot date?"

"Damn straight he does." Sam and his shit-stirring grin chose that moment to join their little hallway group. "Not that the SOB is saying with who, though. He's being all secret squirrel and shit about it."

Fuuuck.

Maybe Rafe wouldn't bite. He wasn't just one of the guys anymore. He was a rank above them now. Technically their boss. Ball-busting wasn't something bosses did, was it?

"I bet it's the new blonde in Admin."

It looked like they did.

"Right? That's what I said!" Sam turned to give him a "cough it up" look, which Rafe mirrored with one of his own.

Great. Now they were going to tag-team him on this. Just like old times.

And just what he didn't need.

"I told you, it's not Gretchen, or anyone else you know." He made sure he was looking at Sam when he said it. Because he'd promised himself he wouldn't outright lie to anyone in his or Isabella's families if he could help it.

It was a fine line, but he'd dance on it for as long as he could before he fell off.

"Ooh, so it's *Gretchen*, huh?"

"Dude, get your own love life and leave mine alone."

"Why would I do that when talking about yours clearly bugs the shit out of you?"

Peter dropped his head back and stared at the slightly discolored ceiling tiles for a second. God save him from annoying friends.

"Whatever. I'm late meeting John at the gym."

"Gotta pump up before your date?" Rafe smirked at Peter's scathing *"et tu?"* look. "I'm sure you want to look your best for your *bella dama.*"

The hollow echo of Isabella's name rang in his ears like a death knell.

The fuck? Rafe *knew*?

Then common sense and his language skills kicked in. He hadn't said "Bella." He'd said *"bella dama."* Pretty lady.

He swallowed back the sour taste of panic and managed a credible scowl, since that would be the correct reaction to the good-natured jibe. "Ha-ha, funny guy."

For a second, he didn't think Rafe was buying it. The look he leveled on him was too intense. Too probing. But then, that might have been the guilt burning a hole in his gut making him paranoid again.

A grin finally softened the hard line of Rafe's mouth. He cuffed Peter on the shoulder with a soft fist. "Have a good time, Romeo. Oh, and when you finally come up for air—" he gave his eyebrows a lecherous wag, "—give your sister a call. She wants to have the family over for dinner sometime soon." With a nod of goodbye for Sam, he continued down the hall.

The guilty hole in his gut burned even hotter. Rafe joking about his upcoming sexual exploits, not knowing they would involve his baby sister...yeah, that was a new low he hadn't expected to ever hit.

And probably something Rafe wouldn't forget once he found out, either.

"Fuck."

"I thought you liked family dinners. Or is it that you just don't want to come up for air?" Sam tried to mimic Rafe's waggling brows, with limited success.

He scowled harder, hating this damn secret more with every passing second. "Just...shut up."

Rather than look insulted, the sharp retort only seemed to amuse his friend as they walked a few feet down the hallway to the intersection with another short hall leading out to the parking lot.

As they rounded the corner, he saw the back of a familiar cheap suit walking at a fast clip in the same direction they were.

Lister. Exactly the guy he *didn't* need to deal with right now.

As they hit the doors and stepped into the afternoon sunshine, he tried to remember seeing Lister walk past them in the hall, but couldn't. Which meant he'd just come into the building. But then why was he heading back out again?

He mentally shrugged it away. Lister probably forgot something in his car. Which was a lucky break, since it saved him from what was sure to be another fun-filled encounter with his nemesis. Right now, he had more important things to worry about.

Like telling Isabella how much he hated lying, even by omission, to her brother. And how much worse it was going to get with every interaction. Lying was not his strong suit. Which was why, as a rule, he avoided doing it.

And then there was this dinner party Lillian was planning.

Knowing her, when she said 'family,' she meant *everyone*. Beaumonts and Delgados, all together under one roof, at one table, with a nosy sister at one end and a matchmaking mother at the other.

Somehow, someway, he had to convince Isabella they should go public before that happened. Otherwise, it would be a recipe for certain disaster.

⚬

THE DOOR TO THE small room off the restaurant's kitchen which served as her mother's and brother's office was open. Bella gave it a light tap with her knuckles.

"You wanted to see me?"

Looking up from the list she was making—probably planning the next day's specials based on what she'd been able to get at the farmer's market this morning—her mother smiled and put down her pencil. "Bella, *mija*. Close the door and sit."

The smile soothed the niggling worry she'd done something wrong as she took the chair next to the desk. It was a tight fit. Originally a storage closet, the space had been repurposed when her brother had joined their mother in the kitchen after culinary school.

Personally, she and her sister both felt Cris had only insisted they needed one so he could feel more important. "I'll be in my office" sounded a lot better than "I'll be in the corner," which was where their mother had kept her small desk for as long as Bella could remember.

"So, what's up?" At least she was almost sure she wasn't going to be voluntold to work tonight on her day off again. That could have been relayed in the text, instead of the request to stop in to the restaurant between the lunch and dinner rushes.

Only it wouldn't have been a request. It would have been a given.

Except she had dinner plans with Peter tonight.

And she wasn't sure she'd be willing to break them.

That shocking realization was followed by another. She couldn't think of a single other instance when she had even *considered* saying no to her parents when it came to the restaurant. That she would think it now, because she wanted to spend time with a man? With a *Beaumont*?

Inconceivable.

Even so, relief mixed with frustration when her mother's next words confirmed this summons had nothing to do with her donning her waitress uniform.

"I want to talk to you about your sister."

She groaned. "Do we have to?"

"Bella." Nobody did disappointed tongue clucking like Lucia Delgado. "Do you think I haven't noticed how you two have been going out of your way to avoid each other lately? It's obvious you had some kind of disagreement."

No, a disagreement was arguing over whose turn it was to do the dishes. What they'd had was a complete and total nuclear melt-down.

"We did argue." No sense denying the undeniable.

Her mother waited, an expectant look on her face. When it became obvious no further explanation was forthcoming, she sighed. "Well, it's gone on long enough. You need to apologize."

Surprise—and a pinch of hurt—snapped her spine straight.

"I have to? How do you know she shouldn't be the one to apologize?" Which she was. The betrayer should have to offer the first olive branch. No question.

Although right now, she was still pissed off enough she just might beat her sister over the head with it if she did.

"Well, one of you has to. Let me call her in here, and the two of you can work this out."

"No!" God, no.

It was hard enough living in the same house with Bria at the moment. Locked in a small room together, with only a flimsy door separating them from the kitchen staff prepping for dinner on the other side?

They might as well sell popcorn.

"Mom, this really isn't the place to be having that kind of discussion." The screaming, throwing things kind.

"Well, I would have preferred to have it at home, but you've been running out the door every morning to avoid your sister before I could bring it up."

She was only half right. On Thursday and Friday, Bella had run out so she could spend every possible minute their schedules aligned with Peter. The rest of the days she was doing food truck research, a.k.a. eating and asking questions of the other people eating at them with Kinzley.

Avoiding her sister had merely been a bonus.

"We'll talk when we're ready, Mom. Right now, I'm still too angry to forgive her." Honestly, the last time she'd felt this betrayed was...well, when Rafe had gotten engaged to Lillian Beaumont.

"I don't like it when you girls fight this way."

"We haven't let it affect our work." Things had been frosty but still professional when their shifts bumped up against one another. "Don't worry, *Mami*, we'll work it out."

Eventually.

A sound that wasn't agreement or disagreement was her mother's only response.

Bella glanced at her watch and rose. "If that was it…"

"Actually, no. There was another reason I wanted to talk to you." Her mother opened the top desk drawer and pulled out a familiar spiral-bound packet.

Gaze locked on her business plan, she sank back into the chair with a mixture of confusion and restrained hope. "Okay."

"I've been looking at this, and *mija*, you did a wonderful job. It's so well put together. Very elegant and eye-catching."

A shimmer of pleasure raced through her. "Thank you."

"And it made me realize perhaps we've been overlooking your potential. After all, you did go to school for this sort of thing. Why shouldn't we make use of your expertise?"

Pleasure turned to excitement. This was happening. Her ideas were finally being acknowledged as having worth. This was really happening!

"Which is why I've decided—and your father agreed, which is no small feat since you know how much he hates change—that we should let you redesign all of the restaurant's menus and advertisements."

Excitement screeched to a confused halt.

"You want me to…what?"

"Well, just look at how lovely your graphics are." She flipped the packet open to a page of colorful mock-up ideas she'd played with for the food truck to show how it could tie into, yet still be distinct from, the established Bayamo branding. "You would do a wonderful job."

She took a long, slow breath of air redolent with the scents she'd grown up equating to comfort and happiness. Neither of which she was feeling right now.

"So, you want me to use my *business* expertise from my *business* degree to design *menus*. Do I have that right?"

Please, god, let me not be right.

"After how upset you were when your father rejected your original idea, I thought this would make you happy."

It hadn't just been her father doing the rejecting, but she let that slide for the moment.

"So, this is like a consolation prize."

"A compromise." Her mother smiled.

Smiled.

"No, Mom. A compromise is when two sides each give and take before meeting somewhere near the middle. This"—her hand slashed through the air—"is throwing me a bone to try and make up for totally disregarding my ideas in order to keep doing the same old things the same old way. Dad isn't the only one who doesn't like change in this family."

"Isabella Maria Delgado, you do not speak to me in that way!" It took a lot to get her mother's temper up, but she'd clearly reached the snapping point.

She hadn't felt closer to snapping back in her life. But some last shred of sanity—or self-preservation—sealed her lips over the sharp retort that would have gotten her mouth washed out with soap when she was younger.

Instead, she drew her purse strap over her shoulder and stood, her body so rigid it felt like it might crack if she bumped into anything on the way out.

"I'm sorry for being disrespectful." The apology came through clenched teeth, but she meant it. "But you're disrespecting me, too. You admit I have potential. Expertise. And then all you want me to use it on is designing menus."

An ugly laugh forced its way out. "I've always known I'm not as important as Bria or Cris in the grand scheme of things. But by not giving me an actual place in the business like they have, *anything* here to call my own, you're making it very clear I'm not important to you, or Bayamo, at all."

Her mother stared at her, mouth open, but for once nothing came out. Bella took advantage of her momentary shocked-silent state to slip out of the office, closing the door behind her with a quiet snick.

Her mother's words drummed through her head as she drove home.

Menus! That was the biggest part of the business her parents were willing to entrust to her? What her 'expertise' was worth? They should have just saved their money and not bothered sending her to college at all, then. What was the point of an education if she'd never be allowed to use it?

It wasn't until she turned the car off she realized she was in the garage under Peter's apartment building. With a groan, she leaned her forehead against the steering wheel. She'd meant to go home, where she could lose her shit in private. Instead, her subconscious had brought her here. To him.

Stupid subconscious.

Of course, he wasn't even here, given that his parking spot was empty. A check of the time told her he was probably still at the gym, something her stupid subconscious hadn't considered when it had hijacked her destination. Which meant she was heading home after all. Only now it would take her twice as long to get there.

Which was a lot longer than she'd be able to hold her splintered emotions together.

Except...

The key to his apartment was in her purse.

She'd felt super weird about it when he'd given it to her, along with the alarm code, the last time they'd gone out. But with their schedules being so at odds and the fact they always met at his place, even she had to admit it made sense for her to have it, just in case. Although she'd sworn to herself she'd never use it except in an emergency.

Since her other option was to sit in her car until Peter got home and risk having his neighbors witness her bawling her eyes out—which was *so* not a pretty sight—it looked like today was going to be that day.

Chapter 14

IT FELT LIKE A million years before Peter's key rattled in the door.

Roscoe's thick body, tucked up tight against hers as she sat on the floor in front of the couch stroking his soft head, twitched at the sound. But other than an enthusiastic tail thumping, he stayed right where he'd been since Bella had let herself into the apartment.

Hugging on the pooch hadn't been nearly as good as having Peter's arms around her while she cried. But the dog's warm, steady presence as she alternated between disjointed rants about the oh-so-many problems with her family and drenching his fur with tears had been the next best thing.

But damn, she was glad he was finally here now.

He wore a pleased smile mixed with a tinge of chagrin as he walked through the apartment toward her. "Isabella, I saw your car downstairs. I'm sorry you had to wait. Did I get the time wrong for dinner?"

"No, I got here early. I'm sorry. I used your key." She shifted herself to her feet, using the motion to hide the fact she was wiping her cheeks for any stray tears Roscoe's tongue might have missed.

Of course, Peter noticed anyway.

Then again, it could have been the swollen eyes and pile of used tissues that gave it away.

His smile shifted instantly to concern. "What's wrong? Are you okay? Did something happen?"

Despite the ache that lingered in her chest, his rapid-fire questions in that unnerved tone most men got when faced with a woman's tears made her smile.

"Nothing worth talking about."

He stepped in closer and cupped her chin with his hand, thumb gliding across her damp cheek. "It was enough to make you cry, so I'd say it's definitely worth talking about." His thumb made a stop on her lips. "Tell me. Please."

It was more than a simple request for words. He was asking for her trust, to share her pain and problems with him.

So, she did.

She thought she'd cried herself out already. But when she finished talking, she found there was still enough moisture left in her for one last tear. Sitting close beside her on the couch like his presence could protect her from the pain of her own words, he gently wiped it away.

"I obviously don't know your mother as well as you do, but I don't think she meant it as an insult."

"I know she didn't. Which only makes it worse. She honestly had no idea why I was so upset." She ran a hand over her face, suddenly exhausted. "Maybe it's me. Maybe I'm the one with unreasonable ambitions."

"Do you believe your business plan is solid?"

She didn't even have to think about it. "Absolutely."

"Would it benefit the restaurant?"

"According to all of my market analysis, yes. Almost certainly." Because there were no absolutes in business. Or life.

"Then don't start doubting yourself now. Keep trying to make them listen to you."

"How?" She hated how it came out like a whine. "My parents have just shown the extent of what they think I'm good for, and Bria's more concerned with becoming part of Team Alejandro than backing me up." That still hurt more than she'd thought it could.

"What about Cris?"

She snorted. "You mean my brother 'the chef'? He'll never agree to attach the Bayamo name to anything as *pedestrian* as a food truck. He's too much of a food snob."

"Have you ever considered…" He hesitated.

"What?"

"What if it wasn't attached to Bayamo? What if it was something completely yours?"

It took a few seconds to sink in.

"You mean, run a food truck of my own?" The thought had never even occurred to her. "I don't know. I mean, my entire business plan is built on having the brand association of an existing restaurant. And its resources. I don't know if I could make it work as a stand-alone. Or even if I'd want to. This was always about me finding my own place in the family business, not breaking away from it."

"It's just an idea."

One both tantalizing and terrifying on the same level.

Because if her parents thought being chief fill-in girl and menu designer was the highest rung of the Bayamo ladder she could grab onto, she was going to have to give some serious consideration to whether or not she could live with that.

Or if it was time to take her own advice and start thinking outside the family business box and see what else might be out there for her.

Like she did with anything that threatened to rock her emotional boat, she shoved the problem to the bottom of her brain and focused instead on something a lot less daunting. "Here's another idea. Let's go to dinner. I'm starving."

He took the change of topic without a blink.

"We can't have that." He stood, holding out a hand and pulling her to her feet, where he laid a light kiss to her lips. "Although I still need to walk Roscoe, take a shower, and get dressed."

Too bad, since his damp gym clothes made him look extra yummy despite the faint whiff of sweaty man.

"Okay, you do that, and I'll go home, change, and come back. Or I could just meet you at the restaurant. It would save time."

The determined tilt of his chin told her he didn't like that option even before he said, "But that's time I'd lose out on spending in the car with you."

It was silly, but she got a girly tingle at how much he wanted to spend every minute he could with her. Even if it was doing nothing more than talk during a drive.

"Option one it is, then. Maybe you should call and see if they can push our reservation back an hour."

He played with the fingers he still held in a loose grasp.

"Or I could cancel them altogether, and we could stay right here and have a nice, quiet evening, just the two of us." Roscoe chose that moment to bump his large head against Peter's leg, making them both laugh as he gazed up at them with adoring doggy eyes. "Sorry, pal. Make that the three of us."

God, it felt good to laugh. "Yeah, staying in would be great."

"Okay. It's settled, then." He pressed a quick kiss to her lips, then to her fingers, before letting go so he could get his phone from his gym bag.

She curled her tingling fingers, holding them against her chest with her other hand as she watched Peter talk. He was always doing little things like that. Touches. Kisses. Tiny gestures that said more than words how much being with her affected him. How much she meant to him.

It was enough to almost make her believe they could make this work.

Almost.

Hanging up, he said, "Reservations canceled."

A twinge of guilt crept in to spoil her good mood.

"I'm sorry I ruined our plans." He'd put a lot of thought into choosing a restaurant that was both well-reviewed but also far enough from town they probably wouldn't risk running into anyone they knew. And she'd spent way too much time picking the perfect dress to wear, wanting to look sexy and sophisticated for him.

Her sunflower-print tank top and wrinkled yellow capris did neither.

"You didn't ruin anything. The point of the evening was to spend it together. I don't care if that's having dinner at a fancy restaurant or scarfing down pizza right here watching tv." His serious gaze caught and held hers. "All I want is to be with you."

Something warm spread through her chest at not only his words, but his expression as he said them. He really meant that. He wanted to be with her. Not for sex. Not for how she was or wasn't dressed, or where they did or didn't go.

He wanted her for who she was. As she was.

And, god help her, she felt the same way about him, too.

As *almost believed it could work* tipped toward *did believe*, a flash of panic swept through her, keeping her from sliding all the way over into something she was pretty sure she wasn't capable of handling yet. So, she shoved it deep down in the 'examine it later' pile along with the solo food truck idea and summoned up a grin instead.

"Throw some beer in with that pizza, and you've got a date. Although, I am going to miss getting to see you in a suit and tie."

"You are?"

"Well, yeah. With as hot as you were in that tux of yours?" She shook her hand in the universal 'hot stuff' gesture. "You would have looked *good*."

"Um, thank you?" He cleared his throat and, was that a blush? "Let me just take a quick shower. Give me five minutes."

He was out in four.

Her mouth watered as the light blue tee clung to his less-than-fully dried back, muscles bunching and flexing as he bent down to snap on Roscoe's harness and leash. Yup. No suit required. The man was dangerously hot in anything he wore.

Or in nothing at all.

Down, girl.

On the return loop of their walk, they swung by and picked up the pizza he'd ordered on his phone. Their timing was just right, the pie hot out of the oven and going into the box as they arrived.

"Do we need to stop for beer?" She shifted the fragrant box away from Roscoe's inquisitive nose as they waited at the corner for the light to change.

Peter touched Roscoe's snout and said 'no' in a soft but firm tone before answering. "I've got some IPAs in the fridge. Or if you want wine, we can make a quick detour."

"No, the beer is good." Wine made her sleepy. And she wanted to be wide awake for what she had planned later on.

"Don't let him give you any of that crappy craft stuff that tastes like chocolate and marshmallows," a laughing voice said from behind them.

A laughing *woman's* voice.

Bella's eyes narrowed as they both turned and Peter gave the woman, a petite blonde with short, messy hair and a faded black Metallica t-shirt, a wide smile and a quick buss on the cheek.

"You just have no sense of adventure." His teasing words held a sense of familiarity that made something squiggle uncomfortably inside her belly even as he turned back to her. "Isabella, this is Gina. She lives in my building. Same wing, different floor."

Well, wasn't that just...wonderful.

"How nice. To meet you," Bella added seamlessly. Well, almost. Peter might not have caught her catty verbal slippage, but the twinkle in the other woman's eyes said she'd heard it loud and clear.

"You, too. And for the record, I have a fantastic sense of adventure. I just prefer my beer to not taste like something that belongs between two graham crackers cooked over a campfire." She made a face that would have made Bella laugh if she wasn't still trying to figure out the strange, uncomfortable dynamic going on.

Peter wasn't acting like he'd just introduced a former lover to his current one, which had been her first thought. And her second. And third. Still, there was something about the way the woman was looking at her that put Bella's nerves on edge.

"That was a perfectly good stout," Peter protested. He looked at Bella. "I'll pick some up for you to try sometime. You'll see."

She managed a half-credible smile. "Great."

Come on, light, change already. Put me out of my misery.

"So, where's my best little girl today?" Peter asked as Roscoe stuck his nose in the air and started snuffling around the bottom of the huge purse looped over Gina's shoulder.

Even before she could come up with any horrible possibilities attached to his words, a tiny furry head popped up in the open-topped purse. The Yorkie's button eyes blinked in the sudden light, then looked down at Roscoe, who was staring up with the same adoring expression he'd worn when gazing at Peter earlier.

She laughed. "I think someone's got a crush."

"Oh, that's no crush. Roscoe's in complete and total doggy-love with Bubbles."

Bubbles?

Gina threw her hands up as though she'd said it out loud. "Don't blame me. I wanted to name her Pixie. Omar picked Bubbles. He said a name should be about her personality and not her size."

"Omar is her fiancé." Peter held Bella's gaze for a few meaningful seconds.

Okay, maybe he wasn't as oblivious as she'd thought.

Suddenly feeling much more charitable toward the both of them, she smiled. "I think Bubbles is a cute name."

The miniature pooch, pink tongue peeking out, leaned her head further out to peer down at Roscoe. With his height and Gina's lack of it, the dogs could touch noses without either of them needing to strain much. The oh-so careful way Roscoe interacted with the much smaller dog, who probably weighed about as much as his head, was a total *aww* moment.

The light finally changed in their favor, and they set off with the other people around them. Roscoe kept throwing anxious glances up at the purse, which Bubbles had ducked back into as soon as Gina started moving.

"It looks like she enjoys being in there."

"She does. And she's perfectly safe." She shifted the bag to show the mesh covering on the end Bella hadn't noticed before. It would provide Bubbles with plenty of air and a perfect view. "She's a spoiled little princess. Aren't you, sweetie?" she added in a baby-talk tone. A sharp yap answered.

"And whose fault is that?" Peter laughed at her disgruntled scowl. To Bella he said, "She may say she's taking the dog for a walk, but what she really means is she's taking her for a carry."

"Hey! She starts out walking. But she's got tiny little legs. She gets tired. Don't you, baby? Yes, you do."

"So spoiled," Peter mouthed, making Bella bite her lip to hold back a snort of amusement.

They rode the elevator together, Gina and Bubbles getting off on the third floor, much to Roscoe's moaning disappointment.

"It was *really* nice to meet you, Isabella."

"Um, you too." She pretended not to see the supposed-to-be-discrete-but-wasn't look Gina gave Peter before the doors closed, but it puzzled her. Since working those out were Peter's thing, not hers, she didn't waste any time after they'd settled at the small metal table on his balcony. "So, you and Gina?"

"Just friends and neighbors." The answer came with no hesitation. Being a smart man, he'd probably been waiting for her to ask. "She and Omar moved in a little after I did. We hang out sometimes. *All* of us." He twisted the top off the beers. "She works from home, so she walks Roscoe for me when I'm hung up at work. And Bubbles stays here whenever they go away for the weekend."

She wasn't sure she liked the part where Gina had free access to his apartment, but couldn't argue with the logic of having a plan for Roscoe's care. Slipping a gooey slice of fully loaded pizza from the no-peppers half onto a plate, she slid it over to him. "I bet Roscoe loves that."

"Are you kidding? He lives for Bubbles' sleepovers. He mopes for days when she goes home."

Having seen the avid devotion in his gaze for the little Yorkie, she didn't doubt it.

Eyes on the food as she plated her own fragrant slice, she said as casually as she could, "I'm not sure she liked me. Gina, I mean."

"What? Why would you think that?"

"I don't know. It just seemed like she was trying to figure me out."

"Probably because she wasn't sure who you were, exactly. I didn't introduce you as my girlfriend, but she knows I don't invite women I'm only casually dating to my place."

"You don't?"

He shook his head. "It's my home. I don't open it up to just anyone."

"But...you gave me a key."

"Yeah, I did."

The import of that had her shoving the slice in her mouth to hide the fact he'd left her speechless. It hadn't felt like a big deal when he'd given her the key. He'd downplayed it, saying it was only practical, given that he could sometimes run late if he got stuck doing reports at the end of a shift. But now?

It definitely felt like a big deal.

A *really* big deal.

How big a deal could it be? Gina has a key, too.

It wasn't the same thing, she told her cynical side. There was a practical reason for that.

Practical, like you not having to sit in your car waiting for him?

Damn, she hated when her cynical side made sense.

Confused, and annoyed with herself because of it, she tore another bite off her slice, barely tasting the savory pepperoni and sausage toppings. She needed to stop reading meanings into things where they didn't belong. That was what had gotten her into trouble with Nathan.

She ignored the part of her that insisted it wasn't the same thing at all.

"So, uh, speaking of people not knowing we're dating." Peter gave an odd little grimace. "I ran into your brother at the precinct today."

The bite she was swallowing seemed to triple in size on the way down.

"And?"

"And it was...awkward."

"How awkward?"

"When he started quizzing me about my 'hot date' for the evening? Very."

Her breath caught. "What did you tell him?"

"As little as possible without coming right out and lying."

Air came out in a whoosh. "Good."

"No, not good." He tossed his balled-up napkin on the table. "Isabella, I don't like sneaking around about us. I don't *want* to sneak around about us. I'm proud to be dating you, and I don't care who knows it."

Panic flared. "We agreed—"

"I know we did. And I won't go back on my word. I won't say anything until we both agree it's the right time." His voice gentled as he reached over and put his hand on hers. "But sweetheart, it'll have to be the right time *sometime*."

Her heart pounded with a hummingbird beat in her chest.

"I know. It's just...not yet. Please."

Something which might have been disappointment flickered in his expression. But he smiled and it was gone.

He gave her hand a squeeze. "Okay. I'll wait as long as I have to. I just want you to know I'm ready whenever you are."

Relief gave her an instant of light-headedness. But as they finished their meal, that flash of disappointment on his face ate at her in nasty little nibbles. She knew she was asking a lot. But with all the discord currently ripping through her family, and with the possibility of more to come if she continued to pursue her plans, this was one more worry she didn't need to deal with right now.

Once she worked out everything else, then she could figure out the right time and place to make their dating status public. Once she knew they weren't going to crash and burn, or just plain fizzle out when they realized they really didn't have all that much in common after all.

Once she was certain she wasn't making the same mistakes all over again.

Chapter 15

"Oh my god, these seats are amazing!"

Peter didn't bother hiding his grin at the enthusiastic way Isabella was taking in everything about the Club Level seats he'd scored for them at Coors Field to watch the Rockies play the Braves. Her reaction was even better than he'd hoped.

"I know you said you always wanted to sit right behind the home team dugout for a game, but I couldn't get tickets there on such short notice." Well, he probably could have from a scalper, but he couldn't bring himself to do it. Not even for the bonus points it would have earned him.

"Are you kidding?" She wiggled her butt in the padded seat and made a sound of pleasure deep in her throat. "I think I can deal with the disappointment."

It took a slow count to five for him to beat his unruly libido under control. The woman still had no idea what she could do to him with a simple hip-swivel.

"Good, because it gets better." He hooked a thumb behind them. "There's a private enclosed concourse with food and bathrooms just for this section and the suites above us. Or, if you don't want to miss any of the game, you can order from right here in your seat."

"Okay, stop. You had me at private bathrooms."

He knew she was joking, but having seen the long lines snaking from the women's restrooms at public events, he also knew she kind of wasn't. It seemed the way to a woman's heart—or this woman's, anyway—wasn't through premiere seating and gourmet food, but easy bathroom access.

Go figure.

"Are these your usual seats? Because if so, I can't believe you haven't brought me to a game before this."

If he'd known it would have gotten her to come to Denver, he would have.

"Unfortunately, no. They belong to one of Theo's friends, Nolan. He's a transplanted Brit, and it's like he's trying to make up for all the baseball he missed out on as a kid. He bought season passes, and hardly ever misses a game."

"And he just gave you his tickets for tonight?" She raised a skeptical brow.

"Not exactly. I traded him my seats for a future Avalanche game of his choice." Which in hindsight hadn't been his best bit of negotiation, since the vague terms meant Nolan could wait and see if the Avs went to the playoffs next season and nab one of those games.

That's what he got for making a deal with the devil—uh, lawyer.

"You have season tickets?"

"Yeah. Well, my brothers and I share them."

"Huh. I would have thought you'd have a whole suite or something. Being, you know…"

He cursed to himself. Sometimes he just couldn't tell how she was going to react to things that reminded her of his family's money. The subtle digs had all but disappeared over the past few weeks, but there were times he still felt like he was walking through a minefield, waiting for one wrong step to blow everything up in his face.

Like now.

"Beaumont Investments has a suite at the arena." He needed to emphasize that. "It's a place to bring clients, and sometimes a perk for employees. And they use it for foundation events a couple of times a year, too. But that's all for the business. We—me, Richard, and Theo—prefer to be down where the action is, right at the glass."

Which was why giving up those tickets hurt so much. The only place closer to the action was out on the ice itself. But seeing the smile on Isabella's face as they'd come out onto the second deck made it totally worth the sacrifice.

Of course, she wasn't smiling much right now.

Maybe he should have gone with the scalped tickets, after all.

"You know, I'm not much of a hockey fan, but...maybe you could take me to a game sometime next season? Just to see what it's like?"

The suggestion threw him for a second. Not because she wanted to go to a hockey game, although yeah, that was a bit of a shocker since she'd once referred to it as Gladiators on Ice. No, what had his head spinning was that she was asking about doing something in the future.

Months in the future.

Together.

It was the first hint she'd given him she wasn't thinking of them as day-to-day, or even week-to-week anymore. That she was maybe, just maybe, able to see them as long-term, the same way he did.

Not that he was very good at expressing it.

His attempt when he gave her his apartment key two weeks ago had certainly been a spectacular fail. He'd been trying so hard to play it cool and not freak her out that he might have been a little *too* convincing with his 'it's just the practical thing to do' reasoning.

And then last week, after she'd actually used the key for the first time, he'd tried again, in a not-saying-it-straight-out kind of way. Telling her how rare it was for him to open his private space to a woman. Hoping she would make the next logical assumption. Only...

She didn't.

Or, if she did, she hadn't acknowledged it. Which wasn't totally unexpected. He'd known it would take a lot of patience before she'd be comfortable accepting their relationship was real. Solid. That they were made for the long-haul, like Lillian and Rafe, and Theo and Rachel, and Richard and Amber. They might be opposites in a dozen different ways, but they were alike in about a dozen more.

Together, they just *worked*.

It didn't mean it hadn't hurt, though, when she didn't come right back with a 'you mean that much to me, too' declaration. But he'd told the truth. He'd wait as long as it took for her to say she was ready.

And now, it seemed she was.

In her own not-saying-it-straight-out kind of way.

Happiness, and not a little relief, flowed through him as he threaded his fingers with hers. "I would love to take you to a hockey game next season."

"Good." She smiled sweetly at him. "It's a date."

"Yeah, it is." Risking another emotional retreat, he put everything he was feeling in his gaze as he lifted their joined hands and pressed a kiss to the back of hers.

She swallowed, hard. But she didn't look away. Didn't change the subject. Didn't do any of the little things she usually did when things got too real between them.

She just held his gaze and smiled the sweetest smile he'd ever seen.

It wasn't "I love you," but it was a start.

Which was a good thing, since he was pretty damn sure he was partway—no, make that almost all the way in love with her. Something in all his twenty-eight years he'd never felt before. Not like this.

Oh, he'd loved Kylie Cooper, his high school sweetheart. And he'd loved a few girlfriends over the years since. But he'd never been *in* love with any of them. All he had to do was imagine the rest of his life without Isabella in it to know the difference.

The end of those relationships had been sad. Painful. Losing Isabella would be like an asteroid strike right at the center of his life, sending up geysers of suffocating ash and debris.

Total extinction event.

The waiter's arrival to see if they wanted anything before the first pitch was a welcome reminder they were in public. Any further exploration of this new emotional accord would have to wait until later, when they were alone back at his place.

And explore it they would.

Deeply, and with great vigor.

By the second inning, he'd discovered something surprising about Isabella. She really knew her baseball. Player stats, their hitting averages for the season so far, even the matchup stats between hitters and pitchers from both teams.

He wasn't the only one impressed, either. She got into a spirited debate with the people sitting in front of them about the uneven track record of their high-priced starting pitcher, which ended with one of the guys giving Peter an awed look, saying, "Dude, you've got yourself a keeper."

Yeah, he did.

The nachos and beers had been great, but by the fifth inning it was time for something a little more substantial. He was looking around for the waiter to find out what was available when Isabella touched his arm.

"Why don't we go look for ourselves? Hitting the concessions is half the fun of eating at the ballpark." She bit her lip and added in a softer tone, "And I need to check out those other perks you mentioned."

Ah. The bathrooms.

Thankful for the aisle seats so they didn't have to climb over anyone on their way out, he walked behind her up the wide concrete steps leading to the glass-enclosed concourse behind them. It was tough, but he managed to refrain from ogling her swaying denim-clad ass as she climbed.

Okay, maybe he peeked once or twice. He was only human.

After they both made use of the facilities, they walked around the air-conditioned concourse looking at the food options. Fresh pasta. Tossed salads. Hand-carved sandwiches sliced to order by toque-wearing chefs.

"Anything look good?" He already knew the answer, because it was undoubtedly the same as his.

"Well, it all looks *good*. It just doesn't look like what you eat at a ballgame. To me, anyway." She gave him an apologetic shrug. "To be honest, I kind of had my heart set on an Xtreme Dog."

His mouth watered thinking about the foot-long hotdogs and their menu of unique topping combinations, piled so high you needed a fork to eat it. "I could go for one of those myself."

"Yeah?"

"Yeah. And a big-ass pretzel."

"Oh god, yes." She glanced around. "Are we allowed to bring that to our seats, or are the food police going to nab us when we come back for sneaking in outside contraband?"

He laughed, even though he wasn't a hundred percent sure she was joking despite the twinkle in her eyes. "I'd be more worried about the guys sitting in front of us trying to jump us for it when we sit down." They hadn't seemed the tossed salad kind, either.

They took the elevator that connected the Club and Suite levels to the Main Concourse below. The line at the Xtreme Dog stand was long but moved fast, the workers hustling to serve the hungry fans snaking through the roped queue.

The closer they got, the more the tantalizing aromas made his stomach growl in anticipation. They eventually reached the counter, placed their orders, and walked away with their prizes safely secured in long, cardboard containers.

After a quick side trip to the pretzel stand where she shoved the wax-paper bag into her backpack purse for easier carrying, they were back on the almost-empty elevator heading up to their level.

"You know, I was sure you were going to get the Diablo Dog." He'd started sweating just reading the toppings from the big menu on the wall.

"Well, normally I would. But I thought I should plan ahead for later. I wouldn't want my mouth to cause any discomfort anywhere…" Her gaze flicked down to his crotch and back, her lips curving into a saucy grin, "…tender."

A jolt of desire had 'anywhere' perking up with an inconvenient level of interest.

"Jesus, woman." He shifted his weight and forced himself not to check and see if anyone had overheard. "You make me crazy."

"You say that like it's a bad thing."

"No, it's not." He wrapped his free arm around her shoulders and pulled her into his side, nuzzling her ear. "I like it."

"Then I guess I'll just have to keep doing it." She gave a shiver and a tiny gasp when he nipped her earlobe as the doors slid open.

They waited as the other people exited ahead of them before stepping off the elevator into the enclosed concourse. As they walked through the small crowd of people waiting to get on, he glanced toward one of the nearby bar concessions.

"Should we grab some beers now, or order them after we get to our seats?"

"Why don't we—"

"Bella?"

Isabella went stiff and stopped short. "Nathan."

The tightness of her voice matched the rigidity of her body, putting all of Peter's instincts on immediate red-alert.

His training had him assessing the situation with a critical eye, taking in the man staring at Isabella as though he'd just seen a ghost. Late twenties. Product-tousled chestnut hair. About six-foot, with a lean build that said tennis and golf rather than weights and hoops. Everything he wore screamed money, from his designer casual clothes to the silver and blue Piaget watch on his tanned wrist.

But it was Peter's gut that told him he'd just come face-to-face with the "who" part of the reason Isabella had always disliked and distrusted wealthy people so much.

It was the "why" that would determine if he needed to kill the bastard or not.

NATHAN.

Was here.

Right now.

Standing three feet in front of her.

Bella's heart thrummed triple-time in her chest as she absorbed that fact like a body blow. Never in a million, zillion years had she expected to see him here. Or anywhere. Ever. She made it a point to avoid Denver for exactly that reason, coming only when absolutely necessary, and sticking to places he was least likely to show up when she did.

Like here.

Damn it, why was he *here*? At a ball game? He didn't even like baseball. At least, he'd never mentioned he did. Then again, there were a lot of things he hadn't talked about during their whirl-wind six months together.

Like his fiancée.

"Isabella?"

Peter's soft voice was a welcome jostle from the momentary paralysis that had overtaken her. With a mental shake, she looked up at him, not sure what she was supposed to say or do. This wasn't the same as running into Gina. She *had* slept with Nate, and this was an introduction she did *not* want to make.

But it was clear from the question in his expression there was no avoiding it.

"Peter, this is Nathan. Nathan, Peter."

Please let that be enough. Just walk away.

Her silent pleas went unanswered as Nate's focus remained fully fixed on her. His shocked expression gave way to one of the boyishly sweet smiles she remembered all too well. The kind that had once made her heart skip and her belly tingle.

"Bella, my god, I can't believe this. It's so good to see you!"

She didn't know why he'd think so. She certainly didn't.

Seeming undeterred by either her lack of response or Peter's arm around her—was he blind or something?—he gave her a much-too-intimate-for-the-situation look. "You're as beautiful as ever."

"How's your wife?"

Okay, maybe it was petty of her, but she enjoyed his flinch.

Direct hit.

"Bella, please, can we talk?"

"We don't have anything to talk about, Nathan. Not now. Not anymore." No, the time for talking had been four years ago. Only he'd taken the easy way out.

"I wanted to call you. After...you know. To explain."

"But you didn't." She'd been so sure he would. That he wasn't that much of a spineless bastard.

Turned out he was.

Then again, in the end, so was she.

Hating the reminder of her own cowardice, she squared her shoulders, glad for the comforting weight of Peter's arm across them. "We're missing the game. Goodbye, Nathan."

"But..." He gave her a pleading look. "Bella, *please.*"

She hated herself for it, but for a split second she wavered.

Four years. Four long years of imagining a hundred different ways he would come crawling back to her, begging forgiveness. Telling her he'd made the biggest mistake of his life in letting her go. In not choosing *her*.

It was a hard fantasy to let go of.

But now that she was face-to-face with him, and not the glossed-over hearts-and-flowers version her memory had painted of him, she was struck by the realization she had no interest in hearing what he had to say. What apologies he might make. What excuses. Because honestly, none of it mattered anymore.

She glanced up into the watchful eyes of one of the biggest reasons for that and gave him a small smile. "Let's go."

As they turned and started walking, Nate called after them, his voice thin and a little desperate. "I'm sorry for what my father said to you. He was wrong. I know that. I always knew that."

She paused to look over her shoulder at him. "Did you tell *him* that?"

No. It was easy to read in his shamefaced expression he hadn't. Which really came as no surprise, since Nate had never once stood up to his father about her. Or about anything. He'd just put his head down and done what was expected of him as a Brooks. Even when it meant marrying a woman he didn't love.

Although he'd looked pretty damn happy the day she'd seen them together.

Without another word, she turned her back on him and continued walking.

"What did he mean by that?" Peter asked when they were out of earshot.

"Nothing. Just forget it." But the hateful words Nathan Brooks Senior had spat at her kept ricocheting around inside her head like barb-covered marbles, still able to draw blood after all this time.

"Isabella."

She drew an unsteady breath. She could lie, but it didn't seem worth it.

"Fine. His father said I was nothing but a low-class slut looking for someone rich to fuck so he'd pay my way through life, and it wasn't going to be his son."

Alarm raced through her as Peter started to turn back. "Where are you going?"

"To kill the little prick for letting him talk to you like that."

"No." She tugged on his arm with a strength borne of sheer desperation. "Don't. He's not worth it."

"He's not. But you are."

The fire in his eyes and the heat of his words soothed her lacerated pride.

"Let's just eat our dogs and watch the game and forget about the little prick." She used his term deliberately to try and tease a smile out of him. It didn't work, but at least the muscles in his arm loosened enough so it didn't feel like she was gripping a slab of granite.

Back in their seats, the guys in front of them demanded to know where they'd gotten the dogs the second they opened their containers and the delicious aroma wafted out. She managed to choke down a few bites, but her stomach rebelled and she ended up closing the container back up and tucking it under her seat.

Damn Nathan. After all this time, he was still ruining things for her.

Peter leaned closer. "Do you want to leave?"

She should say no. It would feel too much like running away. But her heart wasn't in the game anymore. Even with the score tied going into the bottom of the seventh, all she could think about was Nate probably sitting up in one of the cushy glass-fronted suites overhead, looking down at her.

And didn't that just say everything about their relationship right there.

"Would you mind?"

He leaned even closer and pressed a chaste kiss to her cheek. "Let's go."

Despite her expectation the questions would start as soon as they settled into the half hour drive back to Boulder, Peter seemed content to let the silence stretch. Unfortunately, her nerves stretched with it, until when he finally spoke she was ready to tell him anything he wanted to know.

"I just need to know one thing."

She swallowed. "What's that?"

"How did you ever date a douche like him?"

She stared at him for a few long seconds, trying to process the unexpected question, then burst into laughter. It held a slightly hysterical edge to it even she could hear, but hey, at least she wasn't crying.

Chapter 16

THE LAUGHTER HELPED RELIEVE some of the tension churning in her belly. But the closer they got to home, the more it built again. She knew she owed him some answers. He'd explained about Gina. How could she not do the same?

Only, it wasn't the same. At all. Gina was a friend and neighbor. Nate was...well, he was a lot of things, but the biggest one was a mistake. A huge, humiliating mistake it seemed she was going to have to pay for at least one more time.

Damn him.

A bit of enthusiastic squirmy love from Roscoe brought another smile to her face. There was something to be said for having someone in your life who couldn't ask questions.

"I need to give him a quick walk."

"Go ahead. I'm gonna wait here, if that's okay." She could use a few minutes alone.

He gave her a slightly wary look. But after a firm, almost commanding kiss, he clipped on the leash, throwing her one last searching look over his shoulder as he left.

As soon as the door closed behind him, her stomach cramped. Had she really thought a little time alone would help her figure out how to explain about Nate without sounding like a fool? Impossible. Because she had been a fool. A great big stupid naïve one.

The urge to grab her car keys and make a run for it rode her hard.

Which was probably what that look had been about when Peter left. Somehow, he'd *known* she was a flight risk. And yet, he still left without saying anything about it. Without demanding any promises she stay put until he got his answers.

Stay or go. He'd left the decision entirely in her hands.

As much as she dreaded the impending conversation, having the choice helped quell the itch to bolt that had her twitching like a nervous Chihuahua as she paced the living room. Needing a little air, she unlocked the glass balcony door and stepped outside. She curled her fingers around the smooth metal railing and took deep breaths of warm summer air.

She could do this.

She *needed* to do this.

She was still trying to convince herself of that when the glass door clicked open a short while later and Peter stepped out onto the balcony behind her. The affronted whine when he closed it again, presumably in Roscoe's face, made her smile into the darkness. When she turned, the smile faded at the serious look he wore.

"I thought you left."

The quiet admission made her realize what the empty apartment must have looked like to him on his return. Three steps closed the gap between them. Placing her hands on his face, she went on tip-toe in her sneakers and kissed him, long and soft and filled with apology.

"Sorry." She breathed the word against his cheek as the kiss turned into an embrace. The feel of his strong arms around her felt so good. So right. "I was just feeling a little closed-in inside."

His arms tightened. "We don't have to talk about it."

"Yeah, we do. *I* do," she amended, stepping back from his embrace with great reluctance. Snagging his hand, she tugged him toward the wicker outdoor couch. They settled against the forest-green cushions and let the quiet of the night spill in around them for a few long moments before she took a deep breath and began.

"I met him the summer after I graduated high school, when a few of my girlfriends and I went to Denver for the day. The weather turned crappy, so we ended up going to a movie. Nathan was sitting in the row behind us with two of his friends, who were being noisy jerks."

"They were probably trying to impress you."

She snorted. "No, they were just jerks." Rich jerks, who thought it was funny to annoy perfect strangers because they were a bunch of younger girls too timid to say anything. "Nate was the only one to apologize. And he got them to shut up and behave."

Mostly, anyway. His friends had continued to make obnoxious observations under their breath all the way through the movie. Usually when there was a lull in the action on-screen and they'd be sure to hear them.

That should have been her first clue to what the only thing men in his social circle thought the women in *her* social circle were good for.

"His friends left when the movie was over, but he stuck around to apologize again for their behavior. He seemed genuinely embarrassed by it. He offered to buy us all a drink, but when he realized we were only eighteen, we ended up going for coffee instead."

"Which means he was at least twenty-one."

She nodded. "A few months shy of twenty-two." A sound of disapproval rumbled through his chest. "Four years isn't a lot."

"It is when you're only eighteen."

"I was almost nineteen." Why she felt she needed to point that out, she didn't know. "And there's five years between us, you know. I don't see you having a problem with that."

Peter looked like he had something to say, but pressed his lips together and remained silent instead.

Smart man.

"Anyway, we kind of hit it off that night, and he asked if he could take me out sometime. And I said yes." It had all seemed so easy. So magical. So damned perfect.

God, was I naïve.

"We dated all summer. He'd just graduated Stanford, and was taking a few months off before starting at his father's law firm, and I didn't start college until mid-August. I was working at the restaurant a lot to put away as much as I could before then, but I still managed to get to Denver to see him at least once or twice a week."

"So, you were working, he was goofing off, and *you* were the one who had to go see *him*?"

Peter's incredulous tone made her temper ripple.

"It's not like he could come here."

"Why the hell not?"

"Because…"

He answered the question himself when she didn't. "Because your family didn't know you were dating him."

"Hello? Have you met my father? Or my brothers? Rafe had been on the force a while by then. He would have made Nate's life miserable. And mine. Knowing him, he probably would have followed us around on our dates just to make sure nothing happened. Or had one of his cop friends do it."

Peter muttered something that sounded like "nothing wrong with that," but before she could ask what he meant, he asked, "What about his family? Did they know?"

Annoyance slithered through her. But at her younger self this time, not him.

"At the time, all I cared about was being together. Nothing and nobody else mattered. So, I never even thought to ask. Or question why we never went out with any of his friends. I was too happy having him all to myself." She gave a disgusted snort. "Stupid."

"No, trusting. And innocent. And he used both to his own advantage."

She wanted to argue. But it was the truth. Though not all of it.

"I don't think he meant for it to be secret in a bad way. I mean, yes, he didn't want anyone to know we were dating. But I think it was because we'd created this perfect little bubble with just the two of us in it, with no interference from our families or friends, no social pressures or expectations, and he was afraid if anyone did find out, the bubble would burst."

"Why do you say that?"

"Because that's exactly what happened." The memory still hurt, but at least it no longer drew blood the way it once had. "It was right before Christmas. His father's firm closed for the last two weeks of the year and the family went to Europe on this big trip, so we'd already exchanged our gifts early."

She'd been so awed by the diamond tennis bracelet he'd given her she hadn't even questioned his going rather than staying home to spend the holidays with her. One of many things she should have noticed as a sign of how tightly bound to his family he actually was despite his declarations of wanting to break free of their stranglehold and live his own life.

With her.

So, so naïve.

"The day after he left, this man showed up at the door. He said he was a lawyer, and he needed to speak to me about Nathan."

Peter stiffened at her side. "He came to your home?"

"Yeah. Thankfully, my parents had just left for the restaurant."

"I'm sure that was no accident." His expression darkened. "He wanted you alone."

She'd never considered that. It made sense, though. Much easier to intimidate an impressionable teenager that way. "You're probably right. But I wasn't thinking about any of that at the time. My first thought was there'd been an accident or something, and

Nate was hurt, and he, I don't know, wanted me to come to him or something."

A self-deprecating laugh slipped through her lips. "But no. He was there to inform me my 'association' with Nathan was over, and I wasn't to try to contact him ever again. At first, I couldn't figure out what he was talking about. It was when he handed me a check for ten thousand dollars I finally caught on. His father must've found out about us, and this was his high-handed attempt to get me out of Nate's life."

"What did you do?"

"I laughed at him. Told him money couldn't buy what Nathan and I had. We were in love and no one could stop us from being together. And that Nate would say the same exact thing when he got back and found out what his father tried to do. Which was when he dropped his next bombshell. That Nate was engaged."

El hijo de puta.

"Son of a bitch."

She shouldn't have enjoyed the viciousness of his guttural words echoing her very thought, but she did. It helped take some of the sting out of the rest of the story.

But not all.

There weren't enough curses in any language to do that.

"That was the purpose of the trip, according to him. Valerie was the daughter of one of the other partners, and she and Nate had supposedly had an 'understanding' since he was eighteen. The plan had always been to make it official when he joined the firm, and he was going to give her the ring while both families were away on holiday together."

Just one big, happy group of rich people circling the wagons to keep anyone who wasn't one of *them* safely on the outside.

"I'm guessing he never mentioned this 'understanding' in the months you were together?"

"Not a hint. Which was why I was so sure the lawyer was lying." That, and all of Nate's words of love and devotion. He'd been extremely convincing. "I told him to take the check back to Nate's father and tell him his plan wouldn't work. It didn't matter what he said, I wouldn't lose faith in Nate. He left it anyway, but right before I tore it up I decided to hang onto it so I could show it to Nate. It was the only proof I had of his father's underhanded attempt to break us up."

Peter grunted his approval.

"I tried to message him, but I didn't get any response. But he'd said he might not be able to answer since he wasn't sure there'd be good cell service or internet where he was."

Which, considering the type of five-star hoity-toity resort his family would have stayed at, should have been another clue something was a little off with his story.

"So, I packed all of my paranoia and worry away and waited for him to come home, which was supposed to be January second. I was on winter break from college, but I was working at the restaurant. The holidays are always crazy, so I was too busy to even think about it, anyway."

Lies.

She'd thought about it constantly.

"Then I got this last-minute hand-delivered invitation to a New Year's Eve party at the country club I knew Nate was a member of. I was so relieved. I thought, see? He'd not only come back early because of what I'd told him in my text message, but he was making a statement by inviting me to be seen with him in public, as his date, in front of all of his friends and family. I was so excited at being proven right, I never even questioned why he hadn't called me, or replied to my texts, or why he wanted me to meet him there rather than coming to pick me up."

"Because the invitation wasn't from him, was it?"

Her stomach twisted at the gentle question.

"See, you could figure that out. But me?" She shook her head. "I was so damn blinded by my trust in him. Or maybe by that point it was simply desperation to be right about him. About us. Either way, I went, hoping for a magical evening. A real 'Cinderella goes to the ball and gets the prince' ending."

Instead, she'd gotten a painful dose of how the world really worked.

Fingertips pressing into the tattoo on her hip, she forced herself to finish, even though she was pretty sure Peter had guessed the rest by then.

"When I showed my invitation at the door, I was led to a small room off from the main ballroom and told Mr. Brooks would join me in a minute. I was so excited. I thought we were going to have this romantic reunion, then make our grand entrance together. Only, it wasn't Nate who showed up."

"It was his father," Peter murmured, then looked chagrined. "Sorry."

"Don't be. You're right. And in hindsight, I should have suspected *something*. But..." She sighed. "He was so smug and condescending. Telling me his son was meant for great things, to follow in his footsteps and have the next generation of Brooks heirs. And while it was perfectly fine for Nate to have 'a cheap piece on the side,' it didn't mean I should start thinking I would ever be anything more to him than that."

Every razor-sharp word from his mouth had sliced another layer from her already fragile composure. It had taken everything she had not to turn around and run, or break down in tears. But she'd had just enough self-respect to keep from doing either.

Barely.

"I told him I didn't care what he said, that Nate loved me and I wanted to see him immediately. I was surprised when he agreed and pointed to the door into the ballroom."

Now, she couldn't stop hearing Star Wars' Admiral Ackbar's cry of "It's a trap!" whenever she thought about that moment.

Then, she'd been a gullible lamb to the slaughter.

"When I opened the door, I was near one end of the room, and I could see Nate and a woman sitting at a table on a small raised dais, and a great big "Congratulations" banner hanging behind them. I was about to go to him when I saw him put his arm around her shoulders and give her a kiss. And then I realized, it wasn't just a New Year's Eve party. It was an engagement celebration."

She swallowed down the remembered bitterness of seeing him kiss *that woman*, smiling and looking so damned happy. The exact same way he used to look when he'd kissed her. It had crumbled the last of her confidence in him—and in herself—to dust.

"His father just stood there with this smug smile while I watched the two of them. Then he said, 'Now do you believe me?' and told me it was time for me to leave."

"The bastard might have wanted to make sure you knew the truth, but he was cruel on purpose. He enjoyed seeing you hurt."

She'd thought the same thing.

"You really are good at puzzling people out, aren't you? Maybe you should rethink that job with the FBI."

His wide chest rose and fell under a deep breath. "What did you do?"

"What could I do? I left." But not before Nathan's father had offered his commentary on her status as nothing but a cheap slut looking for a meal ticket.

"Did you try to get any answers from the bastard afterward?"

"No. His father's parting words were if I caused any trouble, he'd be sure to do the same for my parents' business." She had no problem believing he meant it, either. "So, I just sent back everything Nate ever gave me. No note. No explanation. If he'd wanted to, he could have called me and explained. Or at the very least, apologized. But he didn't. Complete radio silence."

"I was right. The guy's a total douche."

Her lips twitched, almost smiling. Something she'd never have thought possible while telling this particular bit of history.

"There was one thing I didn't send back, though."

"The check?"

She nodded.

"Good. I hope you used it for something special."

"I did, but not the way you think."

After a second of indecision, she stood and unbuttoned her jeans. Folding down the left half, she exposed the black and blue heart tattooed on her hip and angled her body so he could see it better in the light from the nearby lamp.

Peter reached out a tentative hand and stroked a finger over the image, sending a shiver across her skin. "You got a ten-thousand-dollar tattoo?"

"Sort of. I burned the check and had them use the ashes in the ink, so I'd always remember."

His fingers froze before dropping away. She felt the loss immediately.

"How much you loved him, and how much he broke your heart."

"No. I mean, sure, it felt like it at the time. He was the first...well, my first everything. And at that age, that seems way more important than it really is." Her thumb grazed the tattoo. Her touchstone.

"No, I got this to remind me that broken heart or not, he didn't break *me*. Him or his father. And that regardless of pretty words and expensive gifts, no one was going to sneak inside my heart and hurt me like that ever again. Not unless I handed them the key myself."

She knew the instant he saw what she meant. His fingers reached out to brush against the heart and the keyhole almost hidden at the center of the delicate filigree design. The reminder that her heart was locked up good and tight.

Safe.

Another shiver ran through her as he leaned forward from his seated position and pressed a kiss to the inked heart. Pulling back, he looked up at her, his expression solemn and steadfast.

"I will never hurt you like that. I promise."

Staring into his unwavering gaze, she really hoped that was true. Because he'd slipped past most of her protective walls already. It wouldn't take much more for him to own her completely.

Chapter 17

"Did your dog not come with an off switch?"

Bella might have asked it with a laughing tone as she threw the soggy tennis ball for the ten millionth time, but she was kind of half serious. Her arm was becoming the consistency of the flan she'd baked Peter for dessert the previous night.

Lounging beside her on the blanket spread on the grass of the remote part of the park they'd claimed for their own, Peter laughed as Roscoe came galumphing back up and spit the ball out at Bella's feet. Again. "I told you, he'll keep chasing for as long as you keep throwing. All you need to do is stop, and so will he."

"I know, but..." She eyed the dog's eager body language as he danced in place in anticipation, eyes firmly fixed on the ball. "Look at him. He's so happy. How can I say no to that face?"

With a sigh, she picked up the ball and threw it before collapsing next to Peter. Then shrieked in laughter when he snaked an arm around her and pulled her all but on top of him.

"You're such a soft touch." He nuzzled against her ear, laying a kiss to the shell and making her squirm. "I love that about you."

There was that word again.

In the week since her moonlight confession about Nathan and the currently locked status of her heart, he'd started using it more and more often. He loved her cooking. Loved her long hair as it brushed against him when they lay naked in his bed. He even said he loved the way her nose crinkled from the cold when she ate ice cream.

But he'd been very, very careful never to come right out and say he loved *her*.

Breath hitching as he nibbled his way down her neck, she knew that was her fault. She'd spooked him. Or at the very least, made him cautious.

Talking about past boyfriends was never a good idea, but it had felt important he understand her mistrust of rich people and the power they wielded stemmed from a legitimate, painful source. So he'd know why she continued to hold him at arm's—okay, maybe half an arm's—length.

But he hadn't walked away. If anything, he'd made an even more concerted effort to spend as much time as he could with her. To prove her wrong? Or wear her down?

Either way, it was working.

And when he went back to work tomorrow and his shifts changed from seven-to-three to three-to-eleven, she had a feeling he'd be using their more synchronized schedules to ensure they spent even more of their time together.

Not that she was complaining. Spending time with Peter was rapidly becoming her favorite thing to do. But her mother was already getting cranky about how often she was gone without explanation. Even more was going to raise questions she wasn't sure she was ready to answer. Not yet, anyway.

But maybe...maybe soon.

As Peter's lips crested her chin and zeroed in on her mouth, she let out a soft moan and pushed that worry away for another day. Today, she'd just enjoy the hours they had alone together before she had to get ready for work.

The soggy, smelly ball dropped to the blanket right next to their faces, reminding her they weren't *exactly* alone.

"Eww." She reared back, nose wrinkling. "Talk about a mood breaker."

Looking torn between disgruntled and amused, Peter shook his head as he sat up. "Roscoe, we really need to work on your wingman timing." He hefted the ball once, twice, as the dog's keen gaze tracked its every move. "Okay, bud. Last one."

With a deceptively lazy toss, he threw the ball and Roscoe bolted after it with a joyful bark. Even from his seated position, it went twice as far as her best attempt had.

"Show off." She snorted at his wink, then started gathering up their things as he folded the blanket. By the time Roscoe came prancing back with his prize, they were ready to go. Ever hopeful, he dropped the ball at Bella's feet.

"Be strong."

Rolling her eyes at the teasing advice, she picked it up and tucked it inside the nylon pouch with the water bowl and treats. "Sorry, Roscoe. No more." The pleading puppy eyes almost got her, but she held on.

Although she did slip him a liver treat. Which Peter saw, judging by his grin, but wisely chose not to comment on as he hooked the leash to Roscoe's harness.

It took a good ten minutes to walk from the isolated spot they'd chosen so Roscoe could play off-leash before they got far enough around the lake to encounter other people. Close to Peter's apartment, they'd been to the park enough times in the last few weeks that she started seeing some familiar faces.

One face in particular wore a broad smile as they walked toward each other along the paved main walkway running through the north edge of the park.

"Hey, you two!" Wearing one of her signature heavy metal t-shirts—today's was Def Leppard—Gina readjusted the oversized purse on her shoulder after leaning in to give them each a quick hug. "We missed you at the fire pit last night."

Hopefully, the bright sun would be blamed for the pink she could feel heating her cheeks. They'd planned to join Peter's friends on the building's sky deck after finishing dessert. They'd just gotten...distracted.

And yeah, maybe she'd kind of done that a little bit on purpose.

As if sensing her discomfort, Peter simply said, "Maybe next time," with no further explanation.

Not that Gina needed one, judging by the smirk on her lips. "Sure."

Ignoring the humans, Roscoe was in an intense nose-to-nose greeting with Bubbles where she stood next to Gina's feet. Well, more nose-to-head. But as he always did, he held his greater strength and size in full check, careful to let the tiny Yorkie take the lead and move at her own pace as she sniffed, then darted out her little pink tongue in a swipe of approval across his larger snout.

Roscoe gave a low moan of adoration.

"So, I guess your dog really does have legs," Peter joked, leaning down to give the Yorkie a pat.

"Ha-ha." But Gina grinned, because she knew as well as they did she spent more time carrying the dog than walking her. "We're going to the crêpes truck parked at the end of the walk. Want to come with?"

Normally, Bella would have said yes, eager to check out yet another of the successful local food trucks and do an impromptu poll of its loyal customers like Gina. But right now, she had other plans that involved Peter and a private space with a bed.

Peter was clearly on the same wavelength. "Thanks, but—"

"Maybe next time," Gina finished with him. Her smirk grew. "You guys are too cute." She gave a little finger wave. "Later." She led a prancing Bubbles away while Roscoe watched them go with a heartbreaking whine.

Partially hiding her burning face with one hand, she burrowed into Peter's side with a groan. The arm he wrapped around her helped, but the low chuckle she could feel rumbling through his chest didn't. "It's not funny."

"Of course, it's not." The right words, but the wrong inflection since she could practically *hear* the smile in them.

She sighed. It didn't really bother her Gina knew they were acting like two sex-crazed minks. So why was she so embarrassed?

As they continued walking, she chewed on that question. It wasn't like she was a prude. She'd had a few other lovers in the past. Okay, two, not counting The Douche, as Peter now referred to Nathan. But other than Kinzley, because they always talked about everything, no one had ever openly acknowledged the state of her sex life before.

Well, other than Douche Senior, in his own spectacularly offensive way. *"With a tight, young body like that, I'm sure you've given my boy quite a ride, girlie. Hell, I might have even been tempted myself. But don't think a snug pussy is your ticket up the social ladder. Not at the expense of my family name and future bloodline."*

Well, screw him and his inbred bloodline. She was done letting either father or son influence the direction and happiness of *her* future.

Feeling like a weight had been lifted, she gave Peter's hand a squeeze, smiling up at him when he bent a quizzical look at her. Before she could explain, dual cries of "Doggy!" rang out as the Edler twins nearly dragged their mother off her feet to get to Roscoe, who accepted their heavy-handed pats and hugs with his usual quiet stoicism.

Stephanie mouthed a 'sorry' to Peter as her daughters lavished their boisterous form of love, then smiled with a look Bella was coming to recognize a little too well from Peter's neighbors. "We missed you two at the fire pit last night."

Before she could think of a different excuse, since the blush had only just drained from her face, a furious scream split the air that had even the twins freezing in place. Eyes wide, everyone turned to look. Peter took a step to put himself more firmly in front of them all, his entire posture changing in some subtle way she couldn't define.

"Stop! Thief! Someone stop him!"

There was a disturbance in the flow of the people walking or pushing strollers along the paved walk as they either turned to look or moved out of the way of whatever was coming. Almost before she could react, Peter shoved the blanket and leash into her hands.

"Stay here."

She wasn't sure if he was telling her or the dog.

Before she could ask, he took off at a slow jog back in the direction they'd come. She exchanged a wide-eyed look with Stephanie, who gathered her girls up against her and moved them a few steps to the side, out of the way.

Of what, Bella couldn't see for a few more seconds. Until a teenager came zipping through the late morning crowd. Like a linebacker carrying the ball toward the end zone, he zigged and zagged around people in his way, looking over his shoulder as the shouts of "Stop him!" continued to follow, presumably from the owner of the purse he had clutched to his chest.

Unlike everyone else scrambling out of the way, Peter planted himself directly in the purse-snatcher's path. "Police! Stop right there!"

Surprised, the teen's sneakers practically left skid marks as he changed direction, cutting right, off the paved path onto the grass and through the trees. Without missing a beat, Peter was right behind him.

A great big hand gripped Bella's heart as she realized the danger he was putting himself in. He had no radio to call for help, no bullet-proof vest, no weapons to defend himself with. The teen could have a knife, or a gun, or friends waiting out of sight somewhere. Peter might be strong and well trained, but he was only human. He could be hurt. Or worse.

The hand gave a hard squeeze.

She could lose him before she ever really had him.

The sound of feet pounded closer, and a blonde wild-woman ran through the still frozen groupings of people, eyes searching around her frantically. "Where is he?"

"Oh my god, Gina!" Bella hurried to her side, Roscoe at her heels. "Are you okay?"

Hands on knees, she could barely drag in enough breath to pant out the words. "Sat on a bench...to eat...my food. Put my bag...next to me. Bubbles..." She broke off on a ragged sob.

Bubbles.

Who wasn't at Gina's side on her leash.

Who usually rode in Gina's purse.

A purse the thief now had possession of.

"Oh no!" The devastating impact of that realization had her snapping her head in the direction Peter and the thief had gone. They were no longer visible, but she could still hear Peter's shouts to stop.

"I'm calling 911!" Stephanie yelled, waving her phone before putting action to words. For once, her daughters stuck to her legs like they were made of Velcro, big blue eyes wide with confusion and a hint of fear.

The faint quiver in Roscoe's muscular haunches was the only warning Bella got before he bolted. The burn of the nylon leash being yanked from her hand made her cry out in pain, but she was more worried about what might happen to Roscoe running loose to care.

"Roscoe, no! Shit!" She dropped the blanket and ball bag, and took off after him in the same direction Peter had chased the teen. Stumbling over roots and rocks as she threaded through the patch of trees, she somehow managed not to land on her face before breaking through into the open again. Right onto the paved jogging path along the edge of the lake.

Sucking in air as hard as she could—she really needed to start going to the gym or something—she kept running. Roscoe was quickly gaining on Peter and the teen, who was losing his lead as Peter's long legs continued to chip away at the steadily shrinking distance between them.

The teen must have realized his chances of escape were dwindling. He heaved the purse away from him as he changed directions onto a path leading away from the lake. Peter followed, not even giving the purse a second look as it sailed through the air.

And landed in the water.

"No!" She tried to yell it, but it came out more of a strangled wheeze. Peter didn't know Bubbles was in the bag, and she was too far away. Too far to shout and tell him. Too far to get to where the bag was slowly sinking before it was too late for the tiny, defenseless dog trapped inside.

No, no, no, no, no.

Not Bubbles. Not like this.

She put every ounce of strength she had left into making her legs move faster.

Way ahead of her, Roscoe veered from his pursuit of the two humans and made a splashing dive into the lake. Strong legs paddling, he closed in on the bag as it bobbed, semi-submerged now. He snagged the large loops of the shoulder straps between his teeth with the same precision as he'd snatched those ten million tennis balls out of the air earlier and started paddling back to land.

By the time she made it to the edge of the water, Roscoe was dragging his prize on shore. He released the straps as soon as Bella reached for them, letting out a whine of concern as she reached inside and pulled out the soggy bundle of fur.

Soaking wet, the already tiny dog seemed even smaller cradled in her hands as she knelt on the muddy bank. "Please, please, please be okay. Bubbles, sweetie, come on." She gave the Yorkie a gentle jostle, praying for some sign of life.

Could you do mouth-to-mouth on a dog? She wasn't sure, but she was more than willing to give it a shot if she had to.

Running a hand over the dog's delicate ribcage to feel if it was moving, she pushed Roscoe away with her elbow as he snuffled and nudged the still body with his nose. Undeterred, he pushed his way back in and gave the Yorkie a few fast licks, rough enough to rock her little body within the cup of Bella's hands.

With three quick sneezes, tiny button eyes blinked open, dazed and unfocused.

Relief made her entire body quiver. "*Gracias a Dios.*"

"No!" Gina's wail split the air as she stumbled off the jogging path and fell to her knees beside Bella.

"It's okay. She's alive." She held out Bubbles, who was still blinking and looking around groggily, like she'd just woken from a two-day bender. With gentle care, she transferred the dog into Gina's trembling hands.

Looking like she almost didn't believe it, Gina stared down at her dog as tears leaked from her eyes, leaving rivulets of mascara streaking her cheeks. "She's okay? God, I thought..." Her breath hitched, and she tucked Bubbles against her chest, pressing a kiss to her little head. "Thank you. You saved her."

"Roscoe saved her. Didn't you, big guy?" Bella wrapped her arms around him, not caring that he soaked her blouse or smelled like low-tide. "What a good boy. You deserve an extra special treat."

"He deserves a freaking steak. For, like, the rest of his life." Gina reached over and rubbed the top of his head as she sniffled. "Thanks, Roscoe."

He was too busy keeping a worried eye on Bubbles to do more than flick an ear at either woman's praise. But he did look up past them both a minute later at the sound of approaching footsteps.

Bella looked over her shoulder and nearly sagged with relief at the sight of Peter leading the purse-snatching teen back along the path with a firm grip on his arm. He looked fine, but confused by the two of them kneeling on the ground.

Until his gaze jumped first to the wet purse beside them, then to the shivering Yorkie wrapped in the bottom part of Gina's tee as she cooed and sniffled. Bella could almost hear the pieces snap into place for him like one of his giant jigsaw puzzles.

She also saw the second self-recrimination hit.

Oh no, you don't.

"Bubbles is fine. Roscoe got her out. You didn't know," she added when the guilt refused to leave his face.

"You little bastard! You nearly killed my baby!"

Bella thought she might have to hold Gina back from strangling the sullen teen. Thankfully, she didn't seem willing to give up her hold on Bubbles long enough to follow through with the murder sparking in her narrowed eyes.

Roscoe, on the other hand, needed a firm grip on his collar to keep him from going for the kid's throat. It was the first time she'd ever heard him growl like that. He seemed more than willing to exact vengeance for his doggy-love's near drowning.

The teen must have thought so, too. His eyes widened and he stepped back into Peter, who didn't give an inch.

"Hey, I didn't know there was a dog in there, lady. I wouldn't hurt no damn puppy."

Nobody seemed mollified by his words, least of all Roscoe.

After uniformed officers showed up to take the teen into custody and take their statements, Peter fussed over her sore hand, which had started to throb a little now that the adrenaline rush was over.

He gave Gina a big hug, Bubbles a finger rub on her soggy head, and the both of them another apology for not nabbing the teen sooner. Gina just shook her head and swatted his arm, calling him an idiot.

Roscoe got so much praise he even tore his adoring attention from the Yorkie long enough to give Peter a tail-wag and a quick face lick.

As she watched him fuss over everyone he seemed to consider under his care, Bella felt a shift somewhere deep inside. He could say he became a cop because he enjoyed solving puzzles, but he was more like Rafe than he knew. A natural born protector. Someone who would always put others first, no matter what.

Peter Beaumont might come from money, but that didn't define him. At his core, he was good, and sweet, and trustworthy. The kind of man she could feel safe loving.

And with that realization, the lock on her heart finally cracked open.

Chapter 18

"LOCAL DYNAMIC DUO FOILS Dognapping."

Laughter and good-natured hoots of derision rang through the locker room as Sam read the headline from his phone. Peter finished buttoning his uniform shirt without comment. He'd been expecting someone to dig up whatever ridiculous puff piece the reporter who'd shown up at the park the day before had printed. At least it was buried in the online edition, not the print version.

He'd checked.

"Off-duty policeman Peter Beaumont and his trusty dog, Roscoe—" More hoots of hilarity echoed around the room. "—were enjoying one of their regular walks in Pagosa Park when desperate cries for help shattered the peaceful morning calm. Without a moment's hesitation, the brave pair leapt into action, giving chase to the thief who had snatched an unsuspecting woman's purse." Sam gave Peter a smirk, knowing he was hating every minute of his recitation and taking pleasure in it all the more for the same reason.

Friends sucked sometimes.

Peter gave him the finger, then did his best to ignore him.

"When the thief threw the purse into the lake to try and affect a clean getaway, Officer Beaumont instructed his faithful canine companion to retrieve it while he completed his apprehension of the fleet-footed felon. That quick thinking saved the life of the victim's dog, which had been sleeping inside the purse at the time it was viciously stolen. After resuscitating the half-drowned Yorkshire Terrier named Bubbles, the officer returned it to its grateful owner, Gina Hicks, who declared both man and dog 'true blue heroes.'"

A gagging sound came from the other side of the row of lockers. Probably Quinn. Their friendly rivalry over the coveted detective slot had gotten a bit strained over the past month. No doubt thanks in part to the number of times he'd seen Lister whispering in his ear.

But he took the wordless ribbing without offense. He'd gagged a little, too, when he read the treacly words, which he knew for a fact had never passed Gina's lips. Not to mention all the other inaccuracies and half-truths the article was riddled with.

"For the record, it wasn't all me. There were a couple of Good Samaritans who stepped up, called 911, and helped save the dog. I had nothing to do with that part."

He hadn't even known the bag the perp threw was Gina's, or that Bubbles was in it. An oversight which still made his gut do a flip when he thought about what might have happened.

"Then why weren't they mentioned?"

Because Isabella had begged him to keep her name out of the paper if he could. She'd said her family, especially her parents, would freak at any hint of her involvement with the purse-snatching. That everyone's overprotective genes would kick into high gear and drive her crazy.

Personally, he had a feeling it might have more to do with her not wanting them to see her name associated with his and start asking questions she didn't want to answer. But he'd kept that opinion to himself and let her bounce after they gave their statements, before the reporter got hold of him.

He shrugged and closed his locker, ignoring Sam's amused gaze. "The reporter already had her headline before she even talked to me. She just made the rest of the facts fit it." Showering him with undeserved praise which would be fodder for his friends and coworkers to razz him with for the next week.

A price he'd willingly pay for keeping Isabella's anonymity the way she'd asked. But man, he was getting really tired of the sneaking around and secrets.

Giving Sam a look laced with promised retribution—which only made his friend grin and blow kisses in response—he left the locker room and headed for the break room to snag an energy drink from one of the vending machines.

He'd slept like crap the night before, the same way he always did the first night before his shift changed. His head knew he didn't have to get up at oh-fuck early, but his body hadn't gotten the memo yet. It was going to be a long day.

"Well, if it isn't the king of the canine rescue." Rafe did a mocking slow clap as he walked into the break room. "Bravo, Beaumont."

Groaning, he gave his brother-in-law a sour look.

"For fuck's sake! Does everyone here read that stupid online rag?"

"Nah. Garcia forwarded the link."

"To you?"

Rafe's grin grew. "To everyone."

Sam, you're a dead man.

"Great." Chugging the almost too-sweet drink, he lobbed the empty can into the recycle bin with a little extra force.

"Come on, you should be used to being in the papers by now."

"Yeah, and it did me so many favors the last time it happened." Fury still sparked as hotly as it had a month ago about the cause and effect of that damn wedding picture being printed for the world to see.

Or rather, one particular jackass with a grudge to grind.

Rafe instantly sobered.

"I hate that that ass tried to shake you down with some bullshit assault story. Like you'd ever have put hands on him over a woman. Or for any reason. And I really hate he claimed it happened during my damned wedding reception."

"Yeah, it's fucked up. But it was taken care of."

Once the lawyers had gotten involved and made it damn clear there'd be no "nuisance" payoff to make him go away, which was probably what he'd been hoping for. If he wanted a single cent, he'd have to bring his case to court and prove it.

As usually happened with slime, he'd oozed back through the cracks and disappeared after that.

"I'm just sorry it put any kind of smudge on the memory of yours and Lil's day."

"Not your fault there are greedy assholes out there. But I won't say I'm sorry you were there to help Bella out." Rafe's lips thinned. "Especially when she shouldn't have been in that bar in the first place."

"She had every right to be there." Catching Rafe's raised eyebrows at his sharp tone, he backtracked. "I mean, she's legal, after all. She wasn't doing anything wrong. No woman deserves to be harassed just for walking into a bar by themselves."

"Still."

Still what? He was starting to see why Isabella felt forever doomed to be regarded as a child by her overprotective family. But pointing out Lillian had been the same age Isabella was now when Rafe started dating her would only open up a line of discussion he had no desire to pursue.

So, he turned the conversation back to the article.

"Anyway, it's not the crap I'm taking from all you assholes over that ridiculous story that really ticks me off. It's that now I have to avoid going to that park for a while. Which sucks, because it's one of the few places in the city I can let Roscoe off-leash to run besides the dog park."

Rafe's wince said he understood. Without meaning to, the reporter had publicly outed someplace Peter went to regularly.

"Sometimes privilege has a suck-ass price." Rafe's words held a sour tone.

Probably because he'd paid that price himself when his romantic Fiji honeymoon had been invaded by a security team camped out—discreetly, of course—in the adjoining bungalow. After one of the more rabid social media influencers who was a self-proclaimed fan of Lillian's artwork had somehow found out their destination and made it public on a Live seen by millions, they hadn't had a choice.

Safety over privacy. Always.

"You knew what you were getting into when you joined the family."

"Yeah, I did." Rafe grinned. "And it's worth every pain-in-the-ass minute."

Peter was glad he thought so. He just hoped that didn't change as time wore on and the constant precautions and protocols started to chafe.

The way they would for Isabella.

The uncomfortable thought popped into his brain as they headed for the door to go to lineup. She hated how her family scrutinized and tried to control her every move in the name of safety. Would she find the often intrusive security measures he had to follow just more of the same?

Exiting the room, he came to an abrupt halt at the sight of Lister lounging against the wall right next to the open door, empty coffee cup in hand. The usual faint curl of his upper lip like he'd smelled something bad expanded to include Rafe, who stopped as well.

"Got nothing better to do than hold up the wall, Detective?" Rafe's tone was his neutral Sergeant's voice, but the stiffness in his posture said he hadn't missed the derisive look.

"Just waiting for you two to finish your private little coffee klatch so I could get a refill. Wouldn't want to intrude on important *family* business."

Peter couldn't be sure if the comment meant he'd been eavesdropping, or if it was just one of his usual digs at the Beaumont name. At least Rafe's rank would help insulate him from the worst of the jackass's vitriol if he decided being married to a Beaumont warranted the same level of harassment as being one by birth.

Not wanting to expend the emotional bandwidth to engage, Peter walked away without replying. But of course, it could never be that simple with Lister. He always had to get in one last swipe.

"I'll see you bright and early Monday morning, Beaumont."

It took a lot, but he didn't give in to the urge to flip the asshole off. It wouldn't have done anything to help, and likely would have only made things worse by letting Lister know he'd struck a nerve.

But damn, it would have felt good.

"Don't let him get inside your head. He's a dick, but he's still only one person on the interview board. Just concentrate on staying calm, cool, and focused. Your record speaks for itself."

"I know." He really did. But the itch at the back of his brain was telling him Monday wouldn't be easy, no matter how Zen he was. Or how good of a pep-talk anyone gave him. Not even his brothers, who were no doubt planning to impart the wisdom of their interviewing prowess at lunch to help him prepare.

Inspiration struck.

"Hey, I'm having lunch with my brothers tomorrow before work. Why don't you and Cris join us?" He might not be able to do anything about the potential havoc Lister could wreak on his own career dreams. But maybe he could help advance Isabella's while he waited to see what fresh hell the man had up his sleeve.

———— ◆O◆ ————

"Officer Beaumont, please have a seat."

Resisting the urge to tug his uniform any straighter than it already was, Peter walked to the chair that faced the five members of the interview panel, concentrating on not looking like he was marching to his own execution. The last time he'd felt this uncomfortable and exposed was onstage at his mother's charity bachelor auction.

At least this time, no one was going to ask him to take his shirt off.

Stowing away that cringe-worthy memory, he settled on the hard wooden chair and focused instead on the calming breathing pattern his brother Theo had shown him at lunch yesterday. Supposedly, it helped center and ground him whenever he got to a particularly hairy spot on a rockface he was climbing.

Peter just hoped it kept him from sweating through his extra-strength deodorant, because his pits were already feeling a little swampy.

Cal Walters, the Deputy Chief of Police, got the ball rolling.

"Officer Beaumont, you've been a member of the department for seven years now, and in that time you've had an exemplary, if unremarkable, record as a patrol officer. So, tell us, why do you want to be a detective? What makes you the best candidate for the job?"

It was tough not to wince at the 'unremarkable' label. Maybe he'd worked *too* hard trying to fit in and not draw attention to himself.

"Well, sir, I've always had an aptitude for problem solving and getting to the heart of a mystery. I believe my deductive powers and determination, in addition to both my schooling and work experience, would lend themselves to the position. And while I enjoy regular police work, being able to solve crimes where the who, how, when, and why aren't immediately evident would be even more fulfilling."

There was more that wanted to spill out, but he sealed his mouth and stuck with the short version he'd practiced the night before.

His boss, Captain Leia Yamana, went next. "What would you consider the least favorite part of your job?"

It felt like an ambush question. And it was. Putting him on the spot was as much about seeing how he handled the situation as it was about how he answered. Maybe even more so. Still, that didn't mean he had to like answering this one.

Especially when that answer was sitting at the other end of the table.

Forcing himself to not even let his eyes flicker in Lister's direction, he said, "I guess that would be having to adjust to the shift changes every month. It takes a while to get everything back in synch and makes it tough to have a regular schedule for things."

Was it his imagination, or was there a glimmer of amusement and maybe even approval in her gaze before she looked down to jot something on the papers in front of her? Perhaps his problems with Lister hadn't gone as unnoticed as he thought.

Detective Sergeant Eileen Porter, one of the people he'd be working for if—no, *when*—he got the job, tapped her pen lightly against her palm. "Officer Beaumont, what would happen if you pulled over a speeder and it turned out to be a member of your family? Would you give them a ticket or let them off with a warning?"

The head of the detective unit, Warren Vance, had a deep baritone voice that, though soft, commanded attention. "Do you find the question amusing, Officer?"

He wiped the beginnings of a grin from his expression.

"No, sir. It's just that I actually *have* written my brother a ticket." Back when Richard was single and first gotten the Ferrari 488 Spider he lovingly referred to as 'Baby.' He'd been seduced from his normal stick-up-the-buttness by the turbo-charged V-8 that could go zero-to-sixty in three seconds flat.

Richard had been so blissed out by the experience of all that power at his fingertips, he'd accepted the ticket with a smile which would have been more appropriate to a post-coital moment than a joyride on a deserted road outside of town.

Lister went next.

"What would you say is your greatest weakness?"

Thanks to Richard's experience doing interviews, he'd been expecting that question to come up. But it figured Lister would be the one to ask it.

"Probably that I don't consider a job done until I'm completely satisfied, even if it means spending too much time looking into the minute details." He wasn't the total perfectionist his brother was, but they definitely had the same genes.

Lister looked like he wanted to roll his eyes. He settled for making a note on the file in front of him.

More inquiries followed from each person, alternating between hypothetical situations and how he'd handle them, and probing questions about both his professional and personal life. Every time it was Lister's turn, his stomach clenched, anticipating the worst. But to his surprise and relief, Lister stayed within acceptable bounds. He even put forward some of the best hypothetical scenarios.

Which was his only excuse for not immediately realizing that had changed when Lister asked, "How would you handle a stressful situation that included a friend? Say, a confrontation in a bar where someone was putting unwanted moves on a woman you know. Would you use your authority as a police officer in order to make him back off?"

That felt a little too close to home, but he answered without hesitation.

"First, whether or not I knew the person would be irrelevant. If I saw *anyone* being harassed, I'd try to defuse and deescalate the situation, making it clear the attention was unwanted, or if that didn't work, removing the woman from the immediate area to ensure her safety. My being a police officer would have no bearing at that point as long as no laws were being broken, and mentioning it might escalate the tension rather than ease it."

"What if they persisted, or maybe followed you out of the bar later and confronted you? You're a big guy. You could do a lot of damage to someone without even trying. Would you use intimidation or physical force to get your point across and make him back off if he continued to get in your face?"

Son of a bitch.

The scales fell from his eyes as he caught the glimpse of malicious glee in Lister's expression and realized he'd been sandbagged. This was no hypothetical scenario. Somehow, Lister knew about what had happened the night of the wedding.

Rage, and a bit of panic, bubbled up from the acid pit in his gut.

Before he could get out a reply, Lister added with a cutting tone, "Or would you depend on your family's money and influence to have it 'taken care of' and make it all go away?"

Words, always so easy to trip off his tongue when needed, suddenly abandoned him, leaving him feeling like a landed fish, hook sunk deep into the corner of his useless, gaping mouth.

Captain Yamana glanced between the two of them, a glint of concerned confusion in her expression. "Is there something going on here we should know about?"

Peter glared at Lister, who simply smirked and stayed silent, leaving it to him to answer. And while he'd love to say there wasn't and move on with the rest of the questions, his bubbling gut was telling him he couldn't. If Lister mentioned anything about it after he didn't, it would look like he was lying, or had something to hide. Or both.

The perfect damned-either-way situation.

And he'd let Lister maneuver him right smack into it.

I'm going to fucking kill him.

"I believe Detective Lister is not-so-subtly referring to something that happened last month at my sister's wedding to Sergeant Delgado. I helped extricate one of Rafe's—Sergeant Delgado's—sisters from an uncomfortable situation with two men who didn't understand the word no. Later, one of them tried to claim I'd assaulted him in an attempt to extort money from my family."

Commander Vance's brow pulled low over his dark eyes. "I didn't see anything about this in your personnel file."

"Neither did I." The deputy chief glanced down at the file in front of him with a frown.

Damn it.

"Because no charges were ever filed, sir."

"Because your family money made it 'go away'?"

He couldn't help it. Peter's gaze flicked to Lister as his words came out of Vance's mouth. He had no idea if the man shared Lister's 'Beaumont is a spoiled rich kid' animosity, but it felt as though he might be leaning that way.

Which, since he would be his boss if he got the job—and it was definitely feeling like *if* again—could cause him a world of problems in the future if he didn't straighten that lean out right now.

"No, sir. The person in question dropped the issue as soon as the lawyers contacted him and told him to go ahead and bring me to court, because it was all a lie. And neither I nor my family pay to make lies go away. We fight them with the truth."

"So, you have proof this person is lying should he decide to file charges at some later time? A witness to your movements on the evening in question?" Deputy Chief Walters asked.

Molars threatening to crack from the grinding he was giving them, he took one of Theo's calming box-breaths. It didn't help. He understood why the question had to be asked. Any hint of something that could put his integrity in question was a huge black mark against his credibility for any future cases he might handle.

He understood it. That didn't mean he had to like it.

"I wouldn't need one, sir, since I never touched him."

Walters didn't look happy with his answer. "But you'd have one you could produce if you needed to?"

"I..." Uncertainty stalled his words. He'd made a promise to Isabella. But neither of them could have anticipated their secret relationship could become the lynchpin his promotion might hinge upon.

Even so, his word was his bond.

He cleared his throat. "I do have someone who could alibi my movements that evening, sir. But I can't elaborate any further at this time." If he ever needed to, he and Isabella would surely be past the point of keeping secrets.

He hoped, anyway.

The silence that followed was troubling. All the panelists shared the same dissatisfied expression at his evasive answer. Except Lister. His look was more contemplative, which was even more worrisome.

Porter's pen tapped against her palm again. "Do you find this becomes an issue often, Officer Beaumont? Your family's wealth and notoriety?"

"No, ma'am. I'm not as in the public eye as the rest of my family is, a deliberate choice for exactly that reason. And while I can't totally divorce myself from my name, when I put on the uniform, I'm a police officer, period."

"I can attest to the fact the Beaumont name hasn't been an issue on the job." Captain Yamana cast her gaze at the four people beside her as she spoke, lingering on Lister as she added the 'on the job' caveat. Satisfied by his scowl and squirm, she sat back and gave Peter a tiny nod as if to say *I got your back on this one.* "In all my years as Officer Beaumont's supervisor, there's never been an instance where his family connections have interfered with his ability to do his job."

Porter nodded, as though satisfied. Vance jotted something on his file.

With a look at his watch, Walters said, "Officer Beaumont, do you have anything you'd like to add before we conclude this interview?"

The carefully prepared recitation of his qualifications and potential contributions to the detective division suddenly seemed trite and a little tone-deaf under the current circumstances. Instead, he forced himself to hold back the frustration threatening to choke him and find the right words to mitigate Lister's dirty tactics.

"Yes, sir. The seven years I've been a police officer with this department have been the most fulfilling of my life. When I chose law enforcement as my career path, my parents weren't sure I was making the right decision. But I've never doubted that choice for a single minute. I'm a good cop, and I have the skills and the drive to become an even better detective. I know I'd be an asset to the department should I get the job."

He paused, uncertain if he should say what was pressing on his chest, wanting to get out. It could either help him, or hurt him.

Fuck it.

"I know there are two other excellent candidates vying for this position. They're both good cops, with more time on the job than I have. And if you decide one of them is more qualified, then so be it. All I ask is that when making your decision, you base it on my job performance and what I can bring to the table for the department and the city, and not on how many times my family name gets printed in the newspaper. Yes, I am a Beaumont. But the name doesn't define who I am, or what kind of detective I can be. Those records"—he gestured to the files in front of each of them—"and my integrity do. Thank you for your time and consideration."

Walters nodded. "Thank you, Officer Beaumont. The board will have a decision after all of the interviews have been conducted. You're dismissed."

He stood, and with a nod to the panel, escaped the room with an even stride and straight back. But no matter what he'd said, the damage was already done.

And there was nothing he could do to fix it.

Chapter 19

"What the fuck was that?"

Tracking Lister down in the empty break room in between interviews probably hadn't been his smartest idea. But the fury slowly building like a volcano getting ready to blow didn't care about being smart. All it wanted was a target.

And that was the asshole with the shit-eating grin on his face, pouring himself a cup of coffee like he didn't have a worry in the world.

"Problem, Beaumont?"

The taunting tone ratcheted his temper up another hundred degrees.

"Yeah, a big one. What the hell were you doing, bringing up that bullshit about what happened at the wedding? Hell, how did you even know about it?"

"It's called investigating, Beaumont. It's what a detective does." He blew on his coffee. "Maybe that's something you should be familiar with if you want to be one."

But he'd have to know there was something to investigate first. How would he...

The memory rose of Lister lurking outside the breakroom door two days ago. When he'd been talking to Rafe about his name being in the newspaper for the mugging, and the bullshit assault accusation laid against him from the wedding had come up.

"Fucking eavesdropper." He shook his head in disgust, partly at himself. He'd wondered at the time if he'd been listening to their conversation. He just never considered the potential consequences if he was.

Idiot.

Lister shrugged, leaning one hip against the counter to sip his coffee. "Not my problem if you talk about shit someplace where anyone can hear it. You should probably be more careful about that."

"Why bring it up today if you knew the whole thing was a bullshit bid for money?" Because he would have had to hear that being discussed, too.

"You mean, why throw a little dirt on your *exemplary* record?" Lister sneered the word like it tasted bad. "Poor golden rich boy. Welcome to the real world with the rest of us poor slobs who don't have our daddy's money and lawyers to smooth things over when the shit hits the fan."

"The attorneys only got involved because the guy was targeting me *because* of my family's money. I've never used my name or the connections that come with it to help advance my career in any way."

"Yeah, like the fact the chief of department plays golf with your brother hasn't helped you at all."

"It hasn't. He recused himself from the interview board and sent Deputy Chief Walters instead for exactly that reason. And I'm getting really sick of you pushing whatever grudge you have against me every chance you get to anyone who'll listen. I wear the same uniform as you. Do the same job. Bring home the same paycheck you do. Less, actually, *Detective*. I don't get treated any different because of who my family is or who they know."

The sneer on Lister's face turned nasty. "Oh, yeah, you're just like me. Please. I saw that penthouse your brother lives in featured in one of those lifestyle magazines a few years ago. The place is a fucking palace."

Peter gritted his teeth. "That's my brother. I live in a two-bedroom condo."

"Should I feel sorry for you about that? Try living in a shoebox studio with a pull-out couch and bad plumbing. Because after my ex-wife gets her cut of my paycheck every month, that and a crappy ten-year-old Malibu are all I can afford. So don't give me this 'I'm just like you' shit. How you live is still miles above what I've got. And it doesn't change the fact you live like you do because you want to, not because you don't have any choice."

Well, fuck. Much as he'd love to argue, the bastard had a point.

"You're right. My life is pretty damn good." He could see he'd surprised Lister with his easy agreement. "But it's not my fault if yours isn't. And I'm getting damned tired of being blamed for whatever sucks for you. You want to resent me? Fine, have at it. Resent away. But don't use your crap attitude to try and manipulate the truth and tank my career."

"Oh, you want to talk about manipulating? What the hell was that stunt with the mugger and the dog? Trying to pad your record with a last-minute atta-boy?"

"You don't seriously think I somehow staged a mugging to make myself look good!"

Lister shrugged. "Is it just coincidence the 'victim' is a friend of yours?"

"Yeah, it is. Hell, I didn't even know it was her purse that was stolen until after I'd collared the kid."

"So you say."

His back teeth got another workout as he struggled against his temper. At this rate, he'd be needing a trip to the dentist before the day was out.

"Look, I don't care what you believe. I know what happened, and so does everyone else who was there."

A gleam he didn't trust entered Lister's eyes. "Right, your witnesses. That would be another one of your neighbor-slash-friends, and..." He looked up as if dredging through his memory. "Oh, yeah. One of Delgado's sisters."

"How the fuck—" Damn it. He must have pulled the arrest report and seen the names on the witness statements.

Son of a bitch.

Lister cocked his head as though having an epiphany.

"Wait, wasn't that the same sister you 'saved' from the guy who said you hit him at the hotel bar? Quite a coincidence, wouldn't you say? Her being there for both those things. With you?" A sly smile curled his lips. "I wonder what other things she was around for. Like, maybe the alibi for that night you don't want to 'elaborate' on?"

His heart started chugging like a runaway freight train.

How the hell had he put that together?

"You don't know what the fuck you're talking about."

"Don't I?" Pushing away from the counter, Lister glanced at his watch. "Well, gotta be getting back. Jackson's interview is up next." As he walked by, he murmured barely loud enough to be heard, "You just never learn, do you?"

Peter turned to ask what he meant, and froze when he saw Rafe standing inside the open doorway, a confused expression on his face as he stepped aside to let Lister leave.

"Not my problem if you talk about shit someplace where anyone can hear it. You should probably be more careful about that."

Hell. Maybe he *didn't* deserve to be a detective.

"What was all that about?"

"Nothing. Just Lister being an ass, as usual." Maybe, if he was really lucky, Rafe hadn't heard enough of what was being said to matter.

"What did he mean about Bella being a witness to the park mugging?"

Damn it.

So much for luck.

"She was."

"What do you..." His expression hardening, Rafe looked behind him into the hall, then closed the door. Proving he was much smarter than Peter was. "What do you mean, she was there?"

"She was there. She helped pull the dog out of the water. That's it."

"That's it? What the hell, Beaumont? My baby sister was involved in a violent crime, and you never thought to mention it? You sat across a picnic table from me for two hours yesterday and it never once entered your mind this was something I should know about?" Rather than rising, his voice got softer as he spoke, in stark contrast to the vein bulging at his temple.

This was bad.

Rafe's temper didn't pop often. It was part of what made him such a great cop. But it seemed even a whiff of danger involving his sister, and reasonable Rafe went right out the window, replaced by seriously pissed Rafe. Who looked like he was ready to go full-on berserker at any second.

"She wasn't involved in it. All she saw was the guy running, and me going after him and arresting him. She was never in any danger."

"You don't know that," Rafe spat. "Anything could have happened."

"But it didn't."

"So, if it was no big deal, why lie and keep it from me?"

"I didn't lie. I just didn't bring it up." Okay, that was splitting a non-existent hair.

Rafe thought so, too, judging by his disgusted expression.

He sighed. "She asked me not to tell you, okay?"

Rafe had the nerve to look surprised. "What? Why?"

"Maybe because she was afraid you might do something like, I don't know, overreact and turn into a crazy, overprotective lunatic for no reason?" He waited until Rafe's expression eased from livid to chagrined before he let out the breath he was holding.

"I still should have known about it before now," he grumbled.

"Maybe. But can you blame her?"

"Her? No."

Well, shit. They were back to it being his fault.

Before Rafe could launch into round two of the big brother blame-game, the break room door swung open and two officers walked in, ending their privacy. Rafe muttered a gruff 'talk to you later' that sounded ominous and left, letting Peter off the hook.

For the moment, anyway

That didn't mean Lister's well-timed verbal 'slip' wouldn't still bite him in the ass later. Because at some point, Rafe's temper would have time to cool, and he was going to come up with other questions he hadn't thought to ask. Like why had Isabella been in the park with him in the first place. Or if Lister had guessed right about her being his alibi for that night at the hotel.

And all the implications that went along with it if she was.

⸎

WHEN BELLA PULLED INTO the parking lot behind Bayamo Wednesday afternoon, she had a brand-new stack of business proposals on the seat beside her and a swarm of butterflies in her belly. What did they call it when you kept doing the same thing over and over, and expected a different result?

Oh, right. Insanity.

Well, crazy or not, she wasn't giving up on her idea without a fight. Not even after the demoralizing counter-offer her parents had come up with about the menus.

252

Maybe especially not after that.

She checked her phone and smiled. Peter had sent a text that read simply *You can do this* followed by an adorable hug gif.

He'd wanted to give her one in person, but the man was much too distracting for her peace of mind. She needed to be focused on her presentation, not daydreaming about the way he smelled when she tucked her face into the curve of his neck. Or of the light prickle of his morning beard against her skin when he waited until just before going to work to shave.

Kind of like she was daydreaming right now.

See? Dangerously distracting.

Blowing out a breath, she grabbed up the packets and gave herself one last pep talk as she walked to the Employees Only door and let herself in. She was going to nail it this time. Her family was going to give her ideas serious consideration, or else...

What?

What could she possibly do if they didn't start taking her seriously? Go buy her own food truck to prove them all wrong? The idea was ridiculous.

Intriguing, but ridiculous.

She'd only come up with the food truck plan to secure her place in the family business. Branching out on her own had never been a consideration. Not until Peter had planted the seed in her brain a few weeks ago. But it wasn't something she'd ever seriously consider doing.

Was it?

Unsettled by her own traitorous thoughts, she was less focused than she wanted to be when she walked into her father's office. And of course, everyone was already there waiting like they never were. Which only threw her even further off her game.

Not an auspicious start.

You can do this.

Squaring her shoulders, she smiled and stood at the head of the table. "I know you weren't convinced the last time a food truck was something that would enhance and expand the Bayamo brand. So, I've done some extra data research and market analysis to confirm there's both a need and a desire for the kind of quality product we'd be offering."

She handed out the packets as she spoke.

"While it's only a small sampling, I conducted in-person interviews with current food truck patrons to see what it is they consider most important, by ranking, when choosing a place to eat, and what it would take to entice them into trying a new vendor. That's now Appendix D." She opened her packet to the correct section.

No one else did.

An uncomfortable sense of *déjà vu* prickled along her skin, like someone walking over her grave. Or, rather, the grave of her idea.

Swallowing to get some moisture flowing in her mouth, she soldiered on.

"I also conducted some online polling about people's current eating habits. Where and when they were most likely to eat outside of the house, sit down versus takeout, and traditional takeout versus food truck takeout. That's Appendix E." She flipped the page. "I think you'll see that, on a whole, there's a greater-than-average interest in food truck dining within the more urban environs of the downtown area, with an additional spike when connected to special events and/or specific locations."

"Oh, wow," Bria muttered, eyes on the phone in her lap, thumbs flying as usual. "You printed up a few new graphs. That changes everything."

To Bella's surprise, Cris reached over and plucked the phone from Bria's hands. Ignoring her outraged expression, he placed it face-down on the table, out of reach. "Bella's put a lot of work into this. I think we owe it to her to listen to what she has to say this time."

She wasn't sure which shocked her more. Cris's reproachful words, or that he seemed to include himself in their censure.

Who are you, and what have you done with my unreasonable brother?

Her father shifted in his seat. "I don't—"

"Javier." There was a whip to her mother's tone that was rarely heard but always heeded. She gave her husband a long, speaking look before smiling at Bella. "Go ahead, *mija*. You have our full attention."

She drew a shaky breath.

"Okay. Well, Bria's right. There isn't much new information I can give you. That's because what was already there is rock solid. Even you said it was a good business plan, *Papi*."

He looked uncomfortable at the reminder, but nodded. "It is. Very good."

That might have given her a warm and fuzzy feeling if it hadn't been so obviously painful for him to admit. "Then I'm not quite understanding why everyone is so reluctant to at least *consider* the idea. Is it because it's coming from me?"

Her mother gasped. "Isabella! How could you even think such a thing?"

She gave her mother a solid stare. "Menus."

It was all she had to say.

Things hadn't exactly been all sunshine and puppies with either of her parents since that horrible argument three weeks ago. They'd all been walking on eggshells around each other, both at home and at work. Although no one seemed inclined to actually address the issue.

Including her.

But at least some of what she'd said that day must have had time to sink in, since her mother's shocked expression morphed into regret.

Bria looked confused. But there was a hint of compassion in Cris's eyes that made her wonder if her mother hadn't told him about what happened. Was that why he was suddenly on Team Bella? Out of sympathy?

Humiliating, but she'd take the support any way she could get it.

"I looked over your projections," Cris said, fingering the corner of the plastic cover on the packet in front of him.

He had?

She was almost afraid to ask. "And?"

"Starting up a new business, because that's essentially what this would be despite the tie-in to the restaurant, is a huge risk. Not just financially, but because if it fails, that tie-in means it has the potential to bring down Bayamo's reputation and brand right along with it."

That was the part that scared her the most. "You're right, it could. *If* it failed. But what if it doesn't?"

Her father stirred again. "That's a big gamble to take with the family's sole source of income, *mijita*."

"I know, *Papí*. But you always said half the success you've had was because you knew how to adjust to what people wanted. So, isn't it just as big a risk *not* to change and grow with the times?"

It was clear he didn't like his own words being used against him. Pursing his lips, he gave a quick look to her mother before tipping his head in what might have been agreement.

Bria's mouth pressed in an annoyed line. "Just because you have all of those certificates in food service and whatever doesn't make you an expert, you know. You don't know the business side of the restaurant the way *Papí* and I do. It would be—"

"Stupid of us not to consider it." Cris looked at both their parents, but his gaze lingered the longest on their father. "I think there's potential here to tap into something we've been overlooking."

"As do I." The way her mother said it made her wonder if it was the food truck they were talking about, or something else.

Some*one* else.

Her chest got a little tight.

Her father stared down at the packet in front of him, one blunt finger tapping the table in a slow, steady beat.

"*Papi*?" She bit her lip, waiting.

The tapping stopped.

"I'll want to look at this more closely, but...yes." He looked at her, pride and a hint of apology in his eyes. "We'll consider it."

The rush of relief and excitement that swept through her was almost enough to make her wobble on her feet. "Thank you." She included Cris and her mother in her gratitude. When she glanced at her sister, though, she wasn't surprised to see resentment reflected back at her. "Bria?"

"Well, looks like you got what *you* wanted." Bria snatched up her phone, and with another molten glare, stalked out.

Yeah, definitely no olive branches from that direction anytime soon.

The meeting broke up after that, with her father retreating to his desk and her mother following Bria with a determined look on her face. To Bella's pleasure, Cris carried the business plan with him into the hall.

"You know, I'm not one to look a gift horse in the mouth, but...I have to ask. The last time I brought up the topic, you were very vocal in your opposition to any kind of food that came from a 'roach coach.' What made you change your mind?"

Cris rubbed the back of his neck, looking a little abashed. "Well, that was before I actually ate some. I know, I know. It was hypocritical of me to object when I'd never even tasted what they offer."

"Yeah, it was. I'm just surprised you were willing to give it a try."

Shocked was more like it. Getting his chef's jacket seemed to have given him sudden amnesia about growing up loving chili dogs from the pushcart at the park near their home.

"To be honest, if I'd known that's all there was to eat where Rafe and I met Theo, Richard, and Peter for lunch the other day, I probably wouldn't have gone. But I'm glad I did."

"Theo and Richard? *Beaumont?*" Okay, she deserved the *what kind of stupid question is that?* look he gave her. "I mean, I'm just surprised, is all. I didn't realize you'd gotten so...friendly with them."

"Come on, Bell. They're not bad guys. And they're all family now."

"Not really," she muttered before realizing it. But she meant it. Family was so *not* how she thought about Peter.

"Change and grow with the times, Bell. Isn't that what you said? Just give them a chance. You'll see. Now, I need to get back to the kitchen." He leaned in and gave her a side hug. "You did good with this food truck thing, sis. I'm proud of you."

She grinned. "Thanks. I'm proud of me, too."

And still in a bit of disbelief. There were no guarantees the idea would ever get off the ground, but her family had taken it seriously. They'd taken *her* seriously. She couldn't have asked for a better outcome.

Sliding into the car, she wanted nothing more than to drive to Peter's apartment to share the news and celebrate, but he was probably getting ready to head to work. So she called instead.

He answered on the first ring. "Well?"

"They're going to consider it. I mean, seriously consider it." Her stomach did a little butterfly dance, still not used to the idea.

"That's great! I knew your parents would come around."

"Actually, it was Cris who changed sides first." She paused, the question hovering in the back of her brain becoming too insistent to ignore. "Did you take him to Rayback and try to convince him to support my idea?"

"All I did was invite him and Rafe to lunch. I never brought up you or your business proposal. I just let him eat some of the excellent food there, see how popular and busy the trucks were, listen to the people rave about them, and draw his own conclusions."

In some corner of her brain, she wanted to be annoyed with his interference. But she wasn't that much of a fool. He hadn't tried to "fix" things for her like a macho jerk. All he'd done was provide an opportunity to show her brother he might be letting unfounded prejudices blind him to something potentially incredible and...

Hello, lightbulb moment.

A little stunned by her sudden epiphany, it took a few seconds to realize he was asking if she was still there.

"Yeah. Yes, sorry. I just...the phone cut out for a second." More like her brain had. "Thank you for doing that. He never would've seen what he was missing on his own." She gave a self-deprecating huff. "We Delgados can be a bit pig-headed about things sometimes."

Understatement of the year.

She'd been dragging her feet for weeks, saying it was worry over how their families would react if they found out she and Peter were together. When all along it had been her own issues, the ones she'd thought she already put to rest, that were holding her back. Keeping her from accepting the truth. That what they had was real.

Maybe even potentially incredible.

After all their time together, after everything he'd done for her. How sweet and loving and understanding he'd been. How *patient*. After all that, she'd still been clinging to the same warped yardstick she'd been measuring men by since Nathan had shattered her trust in them. And in her own judgement.

Her hand crept to the inked touchstone on her hip. How long was she going to keep letting Nathan Brooks and his spineless snobbery continue to ruin her life?

Finally, she knew the answer.

Not one damn minute longer.

Chapter 20

"THIS HAS GOT TO be the best job *ever!*"

Peter barely held back a laugh at the excited pleasure in Isabella's declaration as they watched the herd of puppies romping around in their covered enclosure in manic puppy fashion. Not even having to pick up their many, not to mention aromatic, poops before they could roll in them could detract from the adorable side of the job.

"Yeah, Mom really came through."

In more ways than one.

Not only had she assigned them both to the puppy meet-and-greet booth, which had turned out to be *the* most sought-after booth to volunteer for at the entire fundraiser event. But she'd also put them on the same shift.

It could have meant nothing. But knowing his mother and her creepy sixth-sense match-making abilities when it came to her children's love lives...

Yeah, it meant something.

And he was totally okay with that.

More than okay, if he was being honest. It felt like he and Isabella had turned some kind of corner in the last few days with their relationship. After wearing themselves out with a long, lazy morning of sex on their joint Thursday off, followed by an afternoon of wearing Roscoe out at the dog park, she'd actually been the one to suggest going out to dinner. Together. Downtown for once, not to some out-of-the-way spot like they usually went to avoid bumping into anyone they knew.

Which, as it turned out, hadn't happened anyway. He still wasn't sure if he was disappointed or relieved. But the fact she'd been willing to risk it gave him hope she was *finally* ready to take their relationship public.

God knew he could use something good to focus on while he waited out the promotion board's final decision. Although, after Lister's little stunt, he had a pretty good idea what that was going to be.

Or, rather, what it wouldn't be.

He did his best to ignore the way his gut cramped at the too-familiar certainty he'd blown his chance at detective. It had been a very long week at work of keeping a calm face amid people trained to ferret out the truth. He was due a little down-time.

Spending it with Isabella was just what he'd needed to climb out of his black mood.

"Mommy, look! Puppies!"

The squeal of another child spotting the yapping balls of fluff brought a smile to both of their faces despite the eardrum-piercing pitch. As the little girl hung on the top of the railing to get a better look at the romping maniacs, Isabella launched into an explanation of how all the puppies would one day grow up to be service dogs. But before that could happen, they would each need a volunteer foster-family to help socialize them, teach them all of their basic commands, and take them to obedience classes.

As had happened more often than not, the parents looked interested until they realized they'd have to return the dog once it was time to begin the more intensive and personalized preparation for becoming someone's service animal.

"I don't know if I could give a dog up after raising it for a year," the father said with a sad shake of his head. His wife looked pained by the thought. "I think we'd all get too attached."

Peter nodded. "Totally understandable. It's not for everyone." He wasn't sure he'd be strong enough to do it, either, even for such a good cause. "But if you have any friends who might be interested, please let them know about the program."

He handed the couple a card with the service dog foundation's information, as well as one for the local shelter his brother Theo and his fiancée had become involved with after adopting their own dogs from it.

"Just in case..." He tipped a glance at the girl speaking baby-talk to the little golden retriever staring up at her with bright eyes and a lolling pink tongue.

The father smiled. "Thanks."

After letting their daughter stuff a five-dollar bill into the donation box, the couple lured her away from the puppy corral with the promise of cotton candy. Peter shuddered.

"Not a fan?" Isabella asked at his reaction.

"Not anymore. A few hours of working with that stuff can get spun sugar in a lot of places you just don't want sugar to be. My whole body was sticky." One of the most disgusting sensations he'd ever encountered.

"Really?" She leaned closer and lowered her voice to a purr. "Well, I bet you would have been delicious, then. In fact, I think I would have wanted to eat you..." She brought her lips close to his jaw. "Right. Up." The nip of her teeth had him jerking back in surprise.

"You..." He sucked in a shuddery breath, battling the rush of lust that nearly left him lightheaded. "You're a dangerous woman, you know that?"

Judging by the smile that spread across her slightly flushed face, she liked that idea.

God, he loved this woman.

His heart sped up, but not in fight-or-flight terror. It raced because the realization *didn't* scare him. He'd known weeks ago when they'd gone to the ballgame he was getting in deep. That he was more than partway there.

But somewhere along the line, he managed to slip right over the edge and fall firmly and comfortably all the way in love with her without even realizing it.

And damned if that didn't make him one happy bastard.

Slipping an arm around her waist to tug her closer, he murmured against her lips, "How about you show me some of that sass when we get back to my place later?" He took the groan that pulsed from her mouth into his as he stole a kiss as agreement.

When their shift ended, they headed through the park the foundation had taken over for the day toward where the food tents were set up. Before they got there, he was surprised to see two familiar faces making their way through the crowd.

"Vic!" As they clasped hands and did a quick one-armed chest bump/hug, he took extra care not to step on the toes of the yellow Lab standing patiently at his friend's side. "I thought you already left."

"I was going to, but your mother started talking to me and, well..." With a hand missing the tips of his last two fingers, he rubbed the back of his neck under close-cropped brown hair which had begun to gray prematurely. "Don't take this the wrong way, but that woman's a force of nature."

"Tell me about it." If anyone knew the power of Patricia Beaumont's force of will, it was her family. "Well, I'm glad you're still here. I want to introduce you to someone. This is Isabella Delgado, my..."

Crap.

He'd walked right into that, hadn't he?

"His girlfriend." She said it with a firm certainty.

"My girlfriend," he echoed, his surprise surpassed only by his giddy pleasure. *Finally*, she was making it public. He smiled down at her like a loon. Could the day get any better?

Vic raised a brow at the strange by-play, the gesture pulling at the shrapnel scars marking the left side of his face from forehead to chin. As if realizing how the expression highlighted the damage, he wiped it blank again. The middle of Peter's chest ached for him, knowing the facial scars were just the most visible of his friend's wounds.

Hoping to distract him from his obvious discomfort, he continued the introductions. "Isabella, this is my friend Vic Marlowe."

"It's nice to meet you, Vic." Isabella extended her hand with a smile.

After a small hesitation, Vic took it, keeping the contact brief and impersonal. Peter counted it a sign of how far he'd come. There had been a time his self-consciousness about his appearance made him avoid any physical contact with, or even talking to, someone he didn't know well. Especially women.

"You, too." Vic gestured to the dog, and his gruff tone lightened. "This is Miss Molly."

At her name, the Lab's tail beat a quick rhythm through the air, but she didn't move from her spot at Vic's side. With the yellow vest almost disappearing against her similarly colored fur, it wasn't immediately obvious she was a service dog—something Peter had a feeling was no accident. But her training and demeanor left no doubt as to her role.

Or to how vital a part of Vic's ongoing recovery she truly was.

Isabella smiled at the dog, not making a move to pet her without an invitation. "Hello, pretty girl." Getting another tail wag, she transferred the high-wattage smile to Vic. "We were on our way to get something to eat. Would you like to join us?"

Peter saw the instant Isabella's concentrated attention became too much for his friend. It was like a switch flipped. All animation drained from his expression, leaving his eyes dark and panicky, his breaths turning quick and choppy.

"No. Thanks," he added, voice once more gruff and as stiff as his posture. Molly whined and leaned heavily into his leg until he reached down and buried his fingers in the ruff at her neck. "I need to go."

"Oh. Sure. Maybe another time." Isabella looked confused, and even a little hurt though she kept smiling. "It was nice to meet you."

Vic jerked his head in what might have been agreement, although he couldn't seem to get the words out. Eyes down, he walked away, Molly glued to his side.

Shit.

Not good.

With a look of apology to Isabella, Peter started after him. "I need to check on something. I'll catch up with you at the food tents, okay?"

"Um, sure." She didn't look sure, but he didn't have time to explain he was worried about Vic's sudden change of headspace. The way Molly had reacted, so was she.

"Vic, wait up." He stretched his stride and caught up in a few steps. "You okay?"

"You're dating *her*, Beaumont? Are you fucking kidding me?"

Peter shushed him and snapped a quick look behind them, but Isabella had already turned away. Thank god she hadn't overheard. "What the fuck, Vic? Why not her?"

"Maybe because she's Rafe Delgado's baby sister? You know, your friend? Your boss? Your *brother-in-law*? Jesus, man, what the hell were you thinking?"

"That I like her." He paused. "No. That I love her."

Vic came to a sudden stop to stare at him. "Shit. You're serious."

"Completely."

"Huh." His damaged hand rubbed over Molly's head as she leaned into him again. "And Rafe's okay with it?"

"He doesn't know. Yet," he added at Vic's narrowed gaze. "But he will. Everyone will. Soon." At least, he damn sure hoped so. He was ready to shout it from the rooftops the second Isabella gave him the go-ahead.

"Don't dick around, Beaumont. Life's too short for that shit." His fingers tightened on the dog's fur for a second before straightening away from her. "Go back to your girl. You should never keep a lady waiting. Especially not to talk to a beat-up old reject like me."

"Beat up or not, you're still my friend. And you never answered my question. Are you okay?"

"Define okay." Vic gave a brief show of teeth in what might have been a smile if one was being generous. "I'm as good as I get these days."

"You sure? You started looking a little...tense back there."

Freaked out was more like it.

Vic lifted a shoulder. "Too many people. Too many curious stares that slide away when I catch them looking at the scars. I hit my limit. Not Isabella's fault I went into meltdown because she gives good eye contact and has a killer smile."

Something inside him bristled that his friend had noticed. It must have shown, because Vic gave another of those sort-of smiles.

"Man, you do have it bad." He clapped Peter on the shoulder. "Go find her. And apologize for me, would ya? Tell her I'm not usually that much of an ass."

"Can't do it, bro. I make it a point never to lie to her." He grinned when Vic snorted and made an obscene gesture before walking away. He watched for a minute, but Molly's relaxed demeanor was a pretty good indicator any potential crisis had passed.

Cutting through the crowd, he wished he'd thought to tell Isabella a specific spot to meet. The excellent turnout for the fundraiser would be a boon to the service dog groups it would help support, but it was going to make it a pain to track her down among the wide swath of food vendors and tables set up for eating.

A quick trip through the area netted him zip. Rather than chance walking in circles around each other for the next ten minutes, he stepped over into the shade of some trees, pulled out his phone, and called her. As it rang, he caught the faint strains of iPhone chimes from not too far away. Which he might have thought was a coincidence if it hadn't stopped at the same time his call dumped over to voicemail.

Frowning, he dialed again. Once more, the distinctive chimes rang out nearby. This time, he paid closer attention to where they were coming from before they stopped, following the sound through the small stand of trees.

Where he found Isabella and Rafe on the other side, in what looked like a pretty intense discussion.

Shit.

There were several reasons Rafe might be giving his sister grief. None of them good, and most of them having to do with him. He prepared to step out of the cover of the trees to back Isabella up, regardless of which it might be.

Only to be brought to a shocked stop when he heard what she was saying.

Watching Peter's friend Vic leave like he couldn't get away from her fast enough left Bella confused and her feelings a bit bruised. Having Peter abandon her to go with him had only made it worse.

But it was overhearing how appalled Vic had sounded about her and Peter's relationship—*You're dating* her, *Beaumont? Are you fucking kidding me?*—that had hurt the most. Much more than she would have thought they would, given she'd known the man all of two minutes.

Or maybe it was because they were exactly the sort of words she'd always expected to hear that caused the dull ache to settle into her chest, making it hard to breathe properly as she walked blindly through the crowd. Wasn't that why she hadn't wanted to run the chance of bumping into any of Peter's friends when they went out? To avoid this kind of embarrassment and pain?

And here it was, right out of the mouth of the first person they'd admitted their relationship status to. *The very first one*. Well, what had she expected? He was Peter freaking Beaumont, after all, and she was just the spare Delgado. She must have been dreaming to think they could pretend that didn't matter.

Okay, she knew she was overreacting. A little. Knew it was only one person's opinion, and it didn't matter. Shouldn't matter, anyway.

But it did, damn it.

And it hurt. A lot.

The scent of barbeque made her stomach give a sudden cramp of revolt. Looking around, she realized she'd gotten to the area of the park with the food tents despite her total inattention to where her feet were taking her. Starving only a few minutes ago, there was no way she could eat anything now. In fact, breakfast seemed to be having thoughts about coming up for a return visit.

Not knowing where the restrooms were, she hurried past the crowded picnic tables to a small group of shade trees. If she was going to boot, it would be in privacy.

A girl could only take so much humiliation in one day.

The trees provided a buffer of isolation from the crowds, as well as some much-needed respite from the sun. Her nausea eased almost immediately. The only things that would have made it even better were some ice-cold water, and Peter.

"Bella?"

For the briefest second, she thought her wish had conjured him to her side. Then reality clicked into place as she recognized the voice even before turning around.

Damn it.

"Rafe. Hi. What's up?"

A frown marring his handsome face, her brother gave her one of his patented *I'm here to get answers* looks. "Actually, I was going to ask you the same thing."

"What do you mean?" Although she had a feeling she knew. Peter had told her Rafe found out about her being at the park when Gina was mugged. She'd known it was only a matter of time before he'd want to talk to her about it.

"I swung by the house the other day to see you, but you weren't there. In fact, *Mami* said you're hardly ever home anymore. That you're always out, but won't say where or what you're doing."

Or who you're with.

Oh yeah, she could read that in his expression without even trying. It was the same big-brother expression he'd been giving her since she was six years old. After their father's mugging, she and Bria hadn't been able to take a step outside the house without either Rafe or Cris getting all up in their business. Which had been understandable when she was six.

Now? Not so much.

"I do have a life, you know. I don't have to give *Mami* an accounting of every minute of my day." *Or you.* She put that unspoken addition into the glare she gave him.

Not that it seemed to do any good.

"No," he drew the word out, "but you definitely should have mentioned the minutes that had to do with you being in the middle of a mugging in the park last week."

"Oh, god," she groaned, pressing a hand to her rebelling stomach, "do we really have to do this now?"

When his unrelenting look said yes, she sighed. Better to just get it over with than have him follow her around the rest of the day. Or worse, pop up at the house again where their parents might get involved, turning it into a game of dogpile-on-the-daughter.

"Fine. Yes, I was there when Gina had her purse snatched. But I wasn't 'in the middle' of it. I never even saw it happen. All I saw was the guy running away with her purse afterward. So, you can get your panties out of their wad. I was in zero danger."

That much, at least, was true.

"Until you decided to chase after him." Something a little wild flared in her brother's eyes. "I read the statement you gave. Do you know how reckless and irresponsible that was? What could have happened to you?"

"I didn't chase after *him*. I'm not stupid, despite what you seem to think. I was chasing Roscoe, after he got away from me." To run after Peter and the thief. And okay, now that she'd put it together like that, maybe she hadn't been thinking of what might happen if the kid had somehow backtracked in their direction.

Damn, she hated when her brother was right.

Not that she was going to tell him that, of course. There'd be no living with him afterward.

"The dog. Right. And how was it exactly you came to be holding his leash?"

"Peter gave it to me when he went after the purse snatcher."

"And you just *happened* to be there?" He raised one dark eyebrow. "In a park on the opposite side of town from where you live? At the same time and exact spot Peter Beaumont was, so he could hand off his dog to you?"

Uh-oh.

"It's a really nice park." Okay, even she knew that was weak.

"Bella."

The whip in his voice, so like their mother's, pushed her "oh no, you don't" button like it was dispensing free candy. Snapping her head back to glare at him, she jabbed a finger into his chest. Hard.

"Don't you 'Bella' me. You're my brother and I love you, but I am so done with being treated like a dimwitted little girl. Yes, I was at the park. Yes, I was there with Peter. Yes, maybe chasing after the dog wasn't the smartest thing to do. But at the time, all I was thinking about was that he was my responsibility and I didn't want him to get lost or hurt. And if I hadn't done it, Bubbles might have drowned."

"So, you risked your life for a couple of dogs?"

She tipped her head toward the sky.

Dios, give me strength.

"I did what seemed like the right thing at the time. Please tell me you don't give every Good Samaritan who steps in to help this much grief, because that would be totally sucky of you to do."

The tightening around his mouth said louder than words he didn't like being called out on being a hypocrite. "You're my sister. It's my job to worry about you, damn it."

Some of her anger deflated.

"Like I said, I'm not a little kid anymore. I can take care of myself."

"I know. It's just...you're my *sister.*" He sounded so adorably frustrated and a little sad. She couldn't hang on to her temper, however righteous it might be.

Hadn't she felt that same mix of confusion and melancholy after he got married, when she'd realized everything about their relationship was changing? It seemed he was only just figuring the same thing out for himself now about her growing up.

With a sigh, she wrapped her arms around him in a hug.

"I know. And you're my brother. Which is why I'm not tearing a strip off of you for being such an overprotective dumbass."

He huffed a laugh against her hair, which had started to frizz in the heat despite the French braid she'd secured it in that morning. "Hey, Bell?"

"Yeah?"

"What happened the night of my wedding?"

The softly asked question had her stiffening before she pulled from the embrace to stare at him, heart picking up its pace like a startled rabbit. "W-what?"

"You heard me. What happened the night of my wedding?" The look in his eyes said he already knew. But what did he know? About her escaping up to the lobby bar in the middle of his reception? Her sharing a couple of drinks there with Peter?

Oh, god! He couldn't possibly know about her going back to Peter's hotel room.

Could he?

Ignoring the threatening gurgle her stomach made, she struggled to remain calm. There was absolutely no way her brother could know about that. Any of it. Not unless someone told him. And since she and Peter were the only two someones who knew...

"If you're going to get on me about drinking too much of that incredible wine they served with dinner at the reception, I'll remind you I'm legal. And I didn't get drunk."

Maybe just a tiny bit buzzed.

Just enough to let her normal inhibitions loosen their belt a little and say yes to a night of hedonistic pleasure she might have otherwise missed out on.

"What's going on between you and Peter?"

Dear god, he really *was* a mind reader.

"What do you mean? Why would anything be going on?" Did she sound as panicked to him as she did to her own ears?

"You were together at the reception."

"You paired us up in the wedding party, remember?"

"Let me rephrase. You were together in the hotel bar *during* the reception. You were together at the park when the mugging happened. You've been sneaking out of the house—"

"I don't *sneak!*"

"—for hours, sometimes entire days, at a time and won't tell anyone where you've been. Can you see where I'd be a little concerned about what's going on?"

Despite her temper spiking right back up to its previous teapot-steaming boil, one thing her brother said echoed in her head louder than the blood pounding in her ears.

You were together in the hotel bar during the reception.

That was way too specific to be a guess. Which meant someone had told him about it. And since that someone wasn't her, it left only one other someone it could be.

The bitter taste of betrayal rose in her throat.

So much for promises.

"There's no need for you to be concerned, because there's nothing going on. I mean, come on! He's Peter freaking Beaumont. What would I be doing with someone like him?" Which hurt a lot less than asking what would someone like *him* be doing with *her.*

"Okay, sure. We've been spending a little of our free time together lately. So what? We both have weird schedules and days off during the week. It doesn't *mean* anything!"

Rafe lifted that stupid eyebrow of his again, pissing her off even more. Because without saying a word, he was right. She was full of crap.

"It doesn't!" she insisted.

"Then why are you yelling?"

She was, wasn't she?

Taking a breath, she lowered her voice and spoke in as calm a tone as she could dredge up from the chaos rioting inside her. "Because you're not listening. Yeah, Peter is a nice guy. He's smart, and honest, and has a protective streak almost as wide as yours." A trait that should have been an immediate turnoff, but instead had become rather endearing.

"But?"

"But he's still a Beaumont. I'm not trying to diss your wife," she said, putting up a hand as his eyes narrowed. "I'm just saying that from my experience, a relationship crossing that kind of massive difference in backgrounds rarely works out well for the person without the trust fund behind their name. Money trumps everything. Even love."

For the first time, her knee-jerk mantra for the past four years didn't feel right. It didn't even feel honest. It felt...like she was making excuses to cover up her own feelings of inadequacy.

Wounds she'd thought finally healing had had their scabs ripped right back off by one careless comment from Vic. Just one. From a guy she didn't even know. And here she was, right back to being the defensive, wounded wuss she'd been after Nathan and his father had done a clog dance on her self-esteem. God, did she really think so little of herself?

It seemed she did.

Her stomach did a massive flip at the realization.

Pressing a trembling hand to it, she took a deep breath in through her nose, willing the returning nausea away. Unfortunately, the heavy scent of various foods hanging thick in the air had the opposite effect.

She swallowed hard before speaking. "I'm not saying it doesn't work out sometimes. I'm just saying that sometimes, it just can't."

"And are you saying you and Peter are one of those that can't?"

"I think I'd like to hear the answer to that as well."

Horrified, she spun around at Peter's softly spoken words as he stepped from the trees behind them. Which proved a mistake, since her stomach chose that moment to complete the rebellion she'd been fighting, and tossed its contents up onto the ground at his feet.

Humiliation level: complete.

Chapter 21

"I really am sorry."

There was a moment of stony silence from the other side of the SUV before Peter replied. "You don't have to keep apologizing."

Yes, she did. But it seemed none of her multiple attempts on the drive home from the park had made a difference. Which was entirely her fault. She had so many things to apologize for, she didn't know where to start. Once she got the first words out, she floundered, not knowing what to say next.

Pathetic, Bella. Really pathetic.

Her hand tightened around the bottle of water the EMT in the medical tent had given her to sip on. Both Peter and Rafe had insisted she get checked out after her inglorious hurl, even though she knew exactly why it had happened. Heat and jumbled nerves had created the bubbling bouillabaisse in the pit of her stomach.

Peter's sudden appearance at the worst possible time had just been the kicker that made the pot boil over, so to speak.

She'd expected to have to deal with the two of them hovering over her through the entire needless process. But to her shock, after a long, silent stare-down, Rafe had deferred to Peter to take her to the medic by himself. Although he had made a point to say he'd check on her later. A comment that seemed more for Peter than her.

Not that he reacted to it. He'd kept the same stone-faced expression he was wearing now—his cop-face—giving away nothing about what he was thinking or feeling.

She hated it.

Which was why she kept trying to apologize.

She'd screwed up. Big. Huge. And she needed to fix it, fast, before it got past the point of being fixable. If it hadn't already.

Pulling into the empty driveway of her parents' house, she tensed when he put the SUV in park but didn't turn it off. Determined not to let him dump her and run without getting one solid apology out first, she asked, "Will you come inside so we can talk? Please?"

The firm jaw she so admired made an intimidating profile as he sat staring through the windshield. After a few endless seconds, he hit the ignition button and reached for the door handle. Not once did he look at her. Not even a glance.

Not good.

Once through the front door, she tried to think about where they should go to talk. The farthest from the door was probably best, so she kept walking until they got to the kitchen, where she dropped her purse and the bottle of tepid water on the table.

"Do you want something to drink? Or eat? We never had lunch. You must be starving. I can—"

"Is that what you really think of me?"

Ookay. It looked like they were jumping right in.

"What do you mean?"

"'Peter freaking Beaumont. What would I be doing with someone like him.'" He did a fair mimicry of her derisive tone.

Good enough to make her close her eyes on a silent groan.

Damn it.

She'd been wondering how much of their conversation he'd overheard. Figures he'd shown up in time to witness the worst part of her stupidity.

"No, I don't."

"Then why say it?"

"Because...because I used to think it." A lot. "But that was back in the beginning. Before I—" She barely stopped herself from doubling down on her mistakes. Now was not the time to blurt out she'd fallen in love with him. "Before I figured out you weren't like Nate. At all."

"But you still said it today."

"I know, and I'm sorry. I am," she insisted when his mouth twisted in disbelief. "It was a knee-jerk reaction. Rafe started asking a bunch of questions about us, and I got mad you told him about us being together that night when you said you wouldn't, and it made me worry what else you might have told him, and your friend Vic thought I wasn't good enough for you, and—"

"Whoa, whoa, whoa." He waved his hands like a home plate umpire calling for time. "I told Rafe about what night?"

"*That* night. In the bar." She willed him to deny it.

But of course, he couldn't.

"Right. Well, actually, Richard was the one who told him about it."

Her head snapped up so fast she heard her neck crack. "Richard? How did he know? And why would he tell...never mind." This was so much worse than she'd thought. "How many people did you tell, exactly?"

"A few. But not about *us*." He sounded very firm about that. "Only that we both went into the hotel bar around the same time. *Separately.* And how you were cornered by those two jackasses, and that I walked you away from them before it became an even bigger problem than it was. Which it did anyway," he muttered, looking annoyed.

Annoyed? *He* had the nerve to be annoyed?

"Because it got you tangled up with someone like me?"

"Because it got me targeted for a trumped-up lawsuit when the jackass in question saw my picture in the paper the next day, realized who I was, who my family was, and decided to cash in. He accused me of tracking him down later on and making my point about staying away from you with my fists."

"What? That's crazy! Besides, you couldn't have done any such thing. You were..."

Upstairs having mind-melting sex with me.

A hot blush scalded her face.

"Yeah." He looked momentarily sidetracked, possibly by the same thoughts, before he shook himself out of it.

"Anyway, Richard knew because the lawyers had to get involved. And Rafe needed to know since he might get some blowback from the hotel, even though the whole thing disappeared when the jerk learned he wasn't getting any easy go-away money. But that's the *only* part anyone knows about."

There was a flicker of uncertainty in his eyes that worried her. But first things first.

"Why didn't you tell me about any of this? And don't you dare say because it didn't concern me, because it very clearly does."

"You're right. It does. And maybe I should have mentioned it. But honestly? I was afraid to bring it up, because it would have been just one more thing to remind you about my family's money. One more reason for you to push me away, just for being a Beaumont."

"I wouldn't have done that."

Would she?

"Of course you would. You've had one foot out of this relationship since before it even was one. And the sad thing is, I was willing to put up with it, because it meant I at least had a shot at convincing you I was worth taking a chance on."

He gave a half-laugh filled with derision and pain. "But I never did, did I? No matter what I do or say, how much time I give you,

you're never going to see past my name to *me*. I'm always going to be 'Peter freaking Beaumont' to you."

"I told you, I don't see you like that anymore. But that doesn't mean other people won't look at the two of us and see this huge gulf between who you are and who I am. I mean, come on. Even your friend Vic said something to you about it, when he left the picnic rather than eat lunch with us. The guy barely even wanted to shake my hand."

And why did that still bother her so damn much?

Peter stared at her for a long second, the ghosts of emotions chasing across his face. Finally, he shook his head.

"You see what isn't there because you always expect the worst from people. Or maybe it's just the people associated with me." Before she could argue, he went on. "Vic doesn't like to shake hands with anyone he doesn't know well because of the damage to his fingers. It makes him self-conscious."

"Oh." She'd seen the facial scars, but hadn't noticed anything wrong with his hands.

"And he left because he was on the verge of having a panic attack. Didn't you see the way his service dog was acting?"

She hadn't been paying attention to the dog. All she'd known was that same gut-crawling sensation of being judged and found as less-than that Nathan's father had treated her with the night of the New Year's party. But now that Peter said it, she did recall Molly's insistent whining right before Vic bolted.

God, she was an idiot.

"I didn't realize. But still, he asked why'd you get involved with someone like me?"

"Not like you. *You*. He thought I was crazy to get involved with the sister of my friend, who also happens to be my boss *and* my brother-in-law."

"Oh." She seemed to be saying that a lot. But really, what else could she say? Except... "I misunderstood. I'm sorry." Another thing she was saying a lot of.

"Yeah, me too." He turned and started walking out of the kitchen.

Panic lanced through her chest. "Wait! Where are you going?"

He stopped but didn't turn around.

"Back to the picnic. I have things I'm responsible for there I need to do."

"Oh. Right." She swallowed, hating talking to his back. "Well, will you call me later? After you're done?"

"I don't think so."

"Why not?" She didn't even care how pathetic that sounded. All that mattered was that it felt he was slipping through her fingers right when she'd decided she wanted to hold on with both hands.

When he turned, the flatness in his eyes made her want to cry.

"I've spent my entire life being judged by who my family is instead of for myself. And honestly, I'm sick of it. I deserve better, especially from someone—" His jaw worked like he was chewing his words. "Especially from you."

"Peter—"

"You can say my being a Beaumont was the problem all you want. But the truth is, the only one who ever made it one was you. I've tried to show you *me*, who I really am. I let you in deeper than any woman's gotten, ever. Hell, I gave you the key to my apartment, the place that's my sanctuary, and you didn't even know what that meant. But if all that's not enough for you, then I don't know what else I can do to get through to you. I guess maybe your heart really is locked up too tight for anyone to get inside of. Even me."

He turned and started walking again, and this time he didn't stop when she called his name.

As the front door thumped closed, she sank onto the chair, the heart he'd accused of being locked up tight feeling like it had just stopped beating. Because he was right. She'd spent far too long finding reasons to keep him at a distance, worried about him damaging that fragile organ if he ever got too close to it.

When in the end, it turned out she'd done that all by herself.

***

Tipping the golden bottle of Corona back for a long swallow, Peter contemplated all the ways his life had gone to hell in the past twenty-four hours.

When he'd woken up yesterday morning, he'd been on top of the world. The biggest problem on his horizon had been wondering how to steal a few kisses from Isabella during the picnic in full view of both their families and not get caught. And today...

Today, life sucked big hairy donkey balls.

From his spot next to Peter's chair on the balcony, Roscoe let out a soft exhalation that was part whine, part sigh. He hadn't left his side since he'd come home the night before, slamming things and stalking around the apartment like a surly bear who'd been bee-stung trying to steal honeycomb from an angry hive.

Not a totally inaccurate analogy, all things considered. Hearing Isabella denying their relationship to Rafe so emphatically, just minutes after the word 'girlfriend' had passed her lips, had certainly felt like he'd been attacked. He just hadn't thought the barb of her words would strike so deep.

Or hurt so much.

"Live and learn." He saluted his own dumbassery with the beer and swallowed the last of it down before reaching over to soothe Roscoe's worried-looking brow with a slightly off-balanced pat.

"It's okay, pal. We were fine before we had her. We'll be fine again without her. Who needs her, anyway?"

When the stubborn little voice inside his head answered "We do," he decided another beer was in order. Clearly, he hadn't had enough to drink yet if he could still feel anything other than blessed numbness.

Taking the empty into the kitchen, he grabbed the last bottle from the six-pack he'd picked up earlier on the way back from the dog park. He'd just popped the top when there was a heavy knock at the door. Since anyone who knew him would assume he was at work, he almost ignored it.

But some small, ridiculous part of him that thought maybe, possibly, it might be Isabella had his feet turning in that direction before he could convince himself it wouldn't, couldn't be her.

He was right.

"I can see you're making the most of your sick day." Rafe's dry tone didn't mask his disapproval as he shouldered his way past Peter into the apartment.

"Best medicine ever. I'd offer you one, but this is my last. Unless maybe you want to go out and get us some more?"

"Pass."

With a shrug, he turned to head back outside, nearly tripping over Roscoe, who'd trailed after him like a shadow.

"Are you drunk?"

He righted himself and gave the dog a pat of apology.

"Not yet. But I'm working on it." The balcony seemed too far. He dropped onto the living room couch instead. "So, Sergeant Delgado, are you here looking to bust me for abusing my sick time?"

"No, jackass. I'm here because I wanted to check and see how you were doing." He sank into the chair across from Peter with a sigh. "I'm sorry, man. I really thought you'd get it."

Funny how the call from his captain a few hours ago letting him know that Tawnya Jackson had gotten the nod from the promotion board was only the second worst thing on his 'how my life has gone to shit this weekend' list.

"Yeah, me too, but shit happens." He tipped the bottle and let the sweet, cold beer wash away the sour taste of disappointment.

Rafe eyed him with one of those looks he used when he was trying to suss out what was going on inside a suspect's head. "Just so you know, some people think the reason you called out sick today was because you knew you didn't get it."

"Some people named Lister, you mean." He let out a bitter laugh. The hits just kept on coming. "That bastard won't be happy until he destroys every shred of my credibility on the job." All because Peter was a have, and he was a have-not.

Fucker.

"The captain shut it down as soon as she heard about it. Reminded everyone that no one knew until this afternoon the decision they'd made, but…"

But once an idea got in someone's head, it was next to impossible to get it out again.

The way Isabella couldn't get past her preconceived ideas about him.

And damn it, there he went, thinking about her again. He looked at the half-empty beer in his hand. Nope. A six-pack wouldn't be nearly enough.

Annoyed—at Isabella, at Lister, at the beer that wasn't doing its job—he snapped, "Yeah, well, people can think whatever the hell they want about me. Doesn't make it true."

Any of it.

He didn't even care right now about the damn promotion. He'd called out this morning because he was too screwed up by what happened with Isabella yesterday to have his head in his work. His usual ability to compartmentalize one part of his life to focus on the other totally abandoning him when he needed it most.

It would have been foolish, if not downright dangerous, to don the uniform in that condition.

Instead, he'd gone for a quad-punishing run in the building's gym to burn off some of his mad. When that hadn't worked, he opted for door number two. Drinking until he just didn't care anymore.

Since that was failing, too, he wasn't sure what to try next. But damn it, there had to be *something* that could help dull the pain screaming like a wounded beast inside his chest.

Peter freaking Beaumont.

And he'd thought Golden Boy was bad.

Fuck me.

He guzzled the icy beer and wondered if the liquor store down the block delivered.

"So, if this"—Rafe gestured to Peter, unshaven and slumped on the couch, almost empty beer in hand at four in the afternoon—"isn't about the promotion, then I'm gonna guess it has something to do with my sister, and whatever the hell happened yesterday."

Seriously.

Fuck. Me.

"Whatever happened is between me and Isabella."

"She's my sister."

"Still doesn't make it your business." Although he felt like a hypocrite saying it, since he knew if their roles were reversed, he'd be the one sitting there demanding answers about Rafe's involvement with Lillian.

Oh, wait. He *had* done that.

"She admitted she's been spending time with you."

"She also said it didn't mean anything. In fact, she was pretty insistent about that."

"Bella being that insistent usually means she's either nervous or hiding something." Rafe's gaze tried to burrow into Peter's brain again. "Or trying to convince herself she's right."

"Yeah, well, it sounded like she was doing a damn fine job of it to me." She'd certainly convinced him.

Rafe was silent for a long moment.

"See, here's the thing about my sister," he said finally, leaning in like he was about to impart some important nugget of knowledge. "When she gets an idea in her head, she tends to put her teeth into it and not let go, no matter how old or worn it might get."

Yeah, that was Isabella to a tee.

"Now, I don't know exactly what happened, but I do know she got hurt by someone a while back. And from the way she acted and the things she said when Lil and I were first together, I've always figured it was some rich asshole who broke her heart."

A rush of resentment rolled through him at the memory of that spineless bastard giving Isabella puppy-dog eyes at the ballgame. Like he hadn't sent her entire life into an emotional tailspin with his actions.

"It's not my story to tell, but...yeah, pretty much."

Rafe let out a pent-up breath. "Damn it. How did I not know it when it happened?"

"She made sure no one did." When he got an expectant look, he shook his head. He'd only said what he did because Rafe had already guessed that much. No matter the state of his relationship with Isabella, he wouldn't betray her trust.

Looking annoyed but resigned, Rafe continued.

"My point is, Bella's had a long time to stew in whatever happened back then with this guy." The promise of retribution flashed in his eyes. "And it's clear from the way she's acted around you and your family since Lil and I started dating, she's been hanging on to that bitterness all this time. I honestly wasn't sure she'd make it through the wedding week without exploding from all the snark she was stuffing down inside for my sake."

Peter had had the same thought a time or two during their forced proximity. And yet, it had been a different kind of explosion between them that had set the past six weeks of insanity in motion.

He would have been better off if she *had* just pushed him into the creek.

"So, you can see where I'd be a little confused to find out the two of you are suddenly spending all this time together. Willingly." Rafe's lips twisted. "At least tell me I'm not a big enough idiot that I missed you actually getting along all that time before the wedding."

He understood his friend's self-directed frustration. He'd been feeling the same way about his own faulty powers of observation and deduction since hearing *Peter freaking Beaumont* pass through Isabella's lips.

"No. Only since the reception. Something just...changed that night."

"And would that *something* have anything to do with the alibi witness for that night you haven't been willing to elaborate on whenever anyone asks?"

Well, hell. He'd walked right into that one, hadn't he?

Stupid mouth.

Stupid beer.

Stupid him, for forgetting how good a cop Raphael Delgado was.

"You know I'm not gonna answer that, right?" Which he knew was an answer in itself. So did Rafe. But at this point, outright denial would just be absurd.

Anger darkened Rafe's eyes. "Was she drunk?"

"No! Of course not." He never would have gone upstairs with her if she was.

"Were you?"

"No."

The muscle along Rafe's jawline tensed and flexed. Somehow, he seemed to wrestle his temper under control, the heat cooling from his gaze until only a shadow of banked fury peeked out. "She's. My. Sister."

"And I love her."

Stupid fucking beer.

Cocking his head like a raptor studying its prey, Rafe gave another of those brain-burrowing gazes. "What?"

He couldn't take it back. But he damn sure wasn't saying it again.

"Doesn't matter now, anyway. I can't change who I am, and she can't accept me *because* of who I am, so..." He sucked down the last drops of his beer and put the bottle on the end table with a thump. "Yeah. Doesn't matter."

"Right. Got it."

This time, it was Peter's gaze that narrowed. He didn't trust the quick dismissal of that line of questioning. But Rafe's face gave nothing away, so he decided not to pick at it. The last thing he needed was to encourage more questions.

"Look, I appreciate you coming over, but don't you have a wife to get home to or something?"

"Yeah, I do, actually." He glanced at his watch. "She's making dinner, and I still have to stop and pick up a few things at the store."

Peter snorted. "My condolences." Cooking had never been one of his sister's talents. He could tell Rafe was working hard not to grin by the way his lips pressed together as they both got to their feet.

"So, you gonna be okay here by yourself?" Rafe gave a meaningful look at the empty beer bottle.

"Yes, Mom. I'm fine."

He was so not fine.

"And you're *sure* you're not drunk?"

"Yeah, I'm sure." Unfortunately. "Why?"

"Because if you were, I'd feel bad about this."

The punch he never saw coming caught his jaw and sent him sprawling back onto the couch in a messy heap. He could just make out Roscoe growling low in his throat over the throbbing heartbeat of pain in his face as he glared up at Rafe.

"What the fuck, man?"

"That's for sleeping with my baby sister." He shook out his hand, grimacing. "Now we're even."

It took his muddled brain a second to figure out what he was talking about. Way back when Rafe had once been Lillian's unofficial bodyguard, Peter had slugged him when he found out he was sleeping with her.

Hand gingerly probing his tender jaw, he gave a slow nod. "Fair enough."

Rafe reached out a hand which, after a second's hesitation, he took to help him to his feet. "So, we're good?"

"Yeah, we're good."

"Think you could tell your dog that?"

He sounded blasé about it. But when Peter glanced at Roscoe, he was surprised to see the normally happy-go-lucky mutt laser-focused on Rafe, ears pinned back, ruff up. Another low growl rumbled deep in his throat.

"Roscoe, leave it. Down. It's okay, pal. Friend."

He went to one knee and ran a hand over the dog's head, smoothing the raised brindled fur on his neck and giving him hugs and pats until his tense muscles eased to their normal relaxed state. "Good boy."

Roscoe's tail thumped the floor as he gazed up adoringly at his human.

Rafe shook his head. "Huh. No wonder he took off after you in the park."

"Actually, I've always thought he went after Bubbles. Long story," he said when Rafe raised a questioning brow. After another pat, he got up and walked with Rafe to the door. He opened it, but Rafe paused on the way through.

"If you really do care about my sister, you won't let things end over whatever stupid thing she said or did."

Peter couldn't keep the surprise off his face.

"I know my sister. I love her, but sometimes she can be too stubborn for her own good." Rafe gave a self-deprecating grin. "Family trait. So...try to learn from my mistakes, huh? Don't let anything—or anyone—get in the way of trying to make things work. Not even yourself."

Closing the door behind his friend, Peter thought about his parting advice. He had a point. Anything worth having was worth fighting for.

He just wasn't sure he could handle one more blow if he failed.

Chapter 22

"You know you can't hide out here forever, right?"

Bella slouched lower in the plastic chair on Kinzley's doll-sized balcony and pretended she was enthralled by the view. Although since the only thing to see was the street sweeping machine slowly making its way down the block, she was pretty sure her friend wasn't buying it.

"I'm not hiding. I'm regrouping."

The snort she got in answer echoed the one from the irritating voice inside her head. She sighed. It was tough to sell a lie to someone when you couldn't even convince yourself.

Especially when that someone knew you as well as Kinzley did.

In the matching chair beside her, her friend slid one bare foot propped on the railing over to nudge hers, careful not to smudge the fresh polish they both wore. "Want me to do your fingernails, too?"

Despite her misery, she grinned. In Kinzley's mind, nothing couldn't be made better with a good mani/pedi. She wiggled her toes, watching the iridescent blue polish shimmer and change colors in the Monday morning sunlight.

"Thanks, but I think this is enough sparkle for me."

"There's no such thing as enough sparkle." Kinzley tipped her head so the blue-tipped black hair shifted to reveal her multi-pierced left ear.

Bella leaned closer. "You got another piercing?"

"Yup." She fingered the crystal dangling from the tiny gold hoop in the uppermost curve of the delicate shell. "Like I said. Never enough sparkle." She got a thoughtful look. "You know, maybe you should—"

"Nope. One each is my limit. You know I'm a wuss about pain." Which she'd heard only increased the higher the holes went on the ear.

"Says the woman with the tattoo on her hip. Now *that* had to be painful. This?" She pointed to the hoop. "One zing from the gun and"—she snapped her fingers—"you're done."

The thought of anything zinging through tender cartilage made her shudder.

"No, thanks. And besides, I was highly motivated when I got that tat. It was well worth the pain." Although if she'd known beforehand just how much it would hurt, she might have found some other way to memorialize her vow about protecting her heart.

God knew this way hadn't worked out so well.

She slumped back into her seat at the reminder of the mess she'd made with Peter. Everything he'd said after dropping her at home had been true. She'd been too quick to judge. Too quick to assign the worst explanation possible to people's words and actions toward her because they were his friends.

And worse, not quick enough to find the right words to tell him he was wrong before he walked out. She didn't see him as Peter freaking Beaumont anymore, no matter what he'd heard her say to her brother. She saw him as the man she'd let sneak past all her defenses and remind her how to feel again. Trust again.

Love again.

And then she'd gone and screwed it all up.

I am such an idiot.

She knew it. She just didn't know how to fix it.

"Stop." Kinzley's foot nudged hers again. "You were just starting to smile, and now you're all sad and frowny again."

"I deserve to be sad and frowny. I hurt him. A lot." The look on his face before he'd left still haunted her. Like she'd stuck a meat cleaver in his chest. "He's right, you know. He deserves better than me."

"Pretty sure that's not what he said."

"Close enough."

Kinzley heaved a gusty sigh and looked skyward. "You can be such a drama queen."

"Am not!"

"Then stop pouting and go apologize."

"I'm not…" Okay, maybe she was. "I don't think it'll be that simple. He was pretty upset."

"Rightfully so. It doesn't mean he won't forgive you. Especially if you grovel. A lot. And maybe cry a little. You could try—" A knock at the apartment door changed her focus mid-suggestion.

Careful of her still-tacky toes, Kinzley got to her feet and duck-walked inside. "When I get back with the pizza, we're going to sit here and brainstorm until we come up with at least one good plan to get your man back."

She wasn't sure any plan could work that little miracle. But the stubborn part that had kept her from giving up on her food truck idea reared its head and dug in steel-spiked heels. If there was a way, any way at all, to fix things with Peter, she'd try it.

Even if it meant groveling.

"I forgot how tiny these balconies were."

The sound of her brother's voice from the open doorway nearly tipped her off her chair as she turned to stare at him in surprise. "Rafe! What are you doing here?"

"Looking for you." Stepping outside, he slid into Kinzley's vacated seat, angling it away from the metal railing so he didn't bump his knees.

"Why?" If he needed to tell her something had happened to anyone in the family, he wouldn't look as calm as he did. Which only left one other reason he'd go to the trouble of tracking her down. "If you're going to pick up where you left off the other day giving me grief…"

"I'm not."

She eyed him with deep suspicion. "Okay. Then why *are* you here?"

"I went to see Peter yesterday."

"Rafe!" Her feet slid from the rail and slammed to the ground.

He raised his hands. "Just hear me out for a minute."

Like she had a choice. He'd effectively blocked any chance of easy escape when he shifted his chair. Okay, yes, she could demand he get out of the way, and he would. He wasn't a total jerk.

But the stubborn part of her that was demanding she figure out how to fix her mistakes thought she might need to hear what he had to say. Leaning back in her seat, she put her bare feet back up on the rail, crossed her arms, and gave him her best squinty-eyed glare.

"One minute."

His lips twitched, which meant the stare hadn't had the desired effect. Then again, Rafe had probably been stared down by much scarier people than her.

"How much do you remember about when *Papi* was robbed?"

"What? What does that have to do with Peter?"

"It's my minute. Indulge me."

After letting out a *hmph*, she shrugged. "Not much, really. I think most of what I know is from listening to other people talk about it over the years. I was only about what, six? Six and a half? So, all I understood at the time was some bad man had hurt him, and everyone was scared, so I was scared, too."

That part she remembered clearly. Not wanting to leave the house. Being startled by something as innocuous as a dropped spoon. Always being on edge, and never really understanding why until she was much older.

Rafe nodded. "Yeah, we were all scared. And not just for *Papi*."

"I know. You and Cris followed me and Bria around like guard dogs for months." And though she'd never admitted it, it had been the only thing that got her out the front door those first few weeks.

"Do you know why?"

"Because you're an overprotective control freak?"

"Because I saw what *Papi* looked like in the hospital."

"So did I. He had a bandage here"—she touched her forehead—"and his eye and lip were all bruised and puffy."

"No. I went in with *Mami*, before they let you, Bria, and Cris see him. Before they cleaned off the blood and stitched him up. I was fifteen, and I remember looking down at him and thinking, he's my father, he's supposed to be invincible. But seeing him like that, I suddenly realized he could have died." He closed his eyes for a second, as though to block out the memory before continuing.

"That was the day I understood bad things could happen to anyone. Even good people who didn't deserve it. Innocents like you and Bria. The thought of something like that happening to either of you..." Something dark and scary passed across his normally placid expression.

"But it didn't. And it hasn't. You've spent our whole lives making sure of it. You and *Papi* both." Which had been both a blessing and a big, fat, overbearing curse.

"And yet, I clearly didn't do a good enough job, since you went and got your heart broken by some *cabrón* when I wasn't looking."

"Peter is *not* a bastard! And if anything, I think I might be the one who broke *his* heart." She bit her lip at Rafe's raised eyebrow, her spiked temper plummeting as fast as it had risen as her brain caught up with her mouth. "Oh. You weren't talking about him, were you?"

He shook his head. "But it's pretty telling your first thought was to defend him."

"Yeah, well, maybe I shouldn't have, if he went and told you about Nathan."

"He didn't tell me anything. I'd guessed a while ago you had a nasty breakup with someone who came from money. It was the only explanation for how much you disliked Lillian, and all the Beaumonts."

Guilt sat in a sour lump in her throat.

"I was wrong about her. And I really am sorry for my part in almost breaking you up."

"You know, that's about the hundredth time you've apologized for that, but it's the first time it felt like you actually meant it. Thank you."

Some of the guilt dissolved, and she managed a small smile. Which only lasted until he opened his mouth again.

"Does that admission include being wrong about Peter, too? I mean, you did just admit you broke the guy's heart."

She groaned.

"Rafe, I love you, but you need to learn when it's time to butt out."

"I can't. Somehow, I feel like whatever happened between the two of you is partly my fault."

Since it kind of was, she didn't bother denying it to make him feel better.

But no, that wasn't fair, either. His wedding may have thrown them together. His interrogation at the picnic may have set the spark to the fuse. But it was her own cowardice and insecurities that had blown everything up between them.

This was on her.

"I guess that means you know he and I were, um…"

"Seeing each other? Yeah, I kind of figured that out."

Her stomach squirmed as she wondered what else he'd 'kind of' figured out. She might be an adult and free to live her own life, but there were still some things that needed to remain behind the veil of feigned ignorance within a family.

Especially with your big brother.

"I appreciate you wanting to help, but honestly, I kind of feel uncomfortable talking to you about this. I mean, you're my brother, but you're also his friend. Isn't that, like, a conflict of interests or something?"

"Only if you don't want the same thing."

"That's just it. I don't know if we do or not. I want to try and fix things, but I don't know if he does, or if he's already given up on us. On me. It isn't like he's called or anything," she added on a mutter.

"And have you called him?"

She gave him a petulant scowl. "No."

"Why not?"

"Because...I haven't figured out what to say yet." And maybe because she was more than a little worried when her name showed on the screen, he might not answer the phone. "Wait, didn't you say you went to see him yesterday? How was he? Did he say anything? About, you know, us?"

She hated sounding so needy. But damn it, she had to know.

Speculation glimmered in Rafe's eyes. "He said...a few things. I won't say what, that's between you and him. But I can tell you he was pretty wrecked, and it wasn't just because he didn't get the promotion."

Her bare feet slipped from the rail with a squeal as she sat forward in shock. "What? He didn't get it? How is that even possible?" Peter had to be devastated. Becoming a detective had been his dream. "I need to call him. No, I need to go over and see him. Why wouldn't he have called and told me? I could have—"

Once more, her brain caught up to her mouth.

She slumped back in her seat. "No, I guess I'm the last person he'd want commiserating with him." Especially after everything he'd done to help further her attaining her own dreams, while his were a smoldering pile of rubble.

"Bell, don't feel bad. It's not your fault he didn't get the promotion. He knows that."

"Wait, what? Why would it be *my* fault?"

Mild panic flooded his expression. "Umm..."

She narrowed her eyes. "Rafe?"

"I, umm...damn it." He let out a harsh breath. "I thought you knew."

"Knew. What?"

His gaze flicked over the railing as though weighing the risk of a third story jump before he muttered something under his breath about good deeds and punishment.

Finally, he sighed. "At least tell me you know about the guy who hit on you at the bar trying to squeeze some money out of his family by threatening a bullsh—crap assault allegation."

"I only found out about that on Saturday." Smack in the middle of their relationship going nuclear. *"I was afraid to bring it up, because it would have been just one more thing to remind you about my family's money. One more reason for you to push me away, just for being a Beaumont."*

And she very well might have, too. In the beginning.

She was such a sucky person.

"Well, did you know Peter couldn't provide an alibi for that night after he left the bar? Not even to the lawyers handling the case."

"You couldn't have done any such thing. You were..."

Upstairs having mind-melting sex with me.

"He couldn't?" It came out on a squeak.

"Or should I say, he wouldn't."

"I'm, um, sure he had a good reason."

"Yeah, I'm sure, too." And he did *not* look happy about it.

If a blush could be measured in Scoville heat units, hers would be up around the Ghost Pepper's one million mark.

Just kill me now.

She cleared her throat. "What does that have to do with him not getting the promotion?"

"Maybe nothing. But it came up during his interview last week, thanks to that son of a...Lister." At her blank look he added, "The guy who's made Peter's life miserable for years at work. Somehow, he found out about the assault accusation and made sure to mention it to the board."

"But he didn't do anything! It was all a scam."

"Doesn't matter. By not being forthcoming about his alibi, Peter gave the impression he had something to hide. And any hint of impropriety can put a permanent mark on a cop's reputation, deserved or not."

"Oh, my god." Her stomach contracted in a painful knot. "This is all my fault."

"No, it's Lister's fault for turning his personal grudge into a weapon."

"Why does he hate Peter so much?" And why hadn't he told her about any of this?

"Because he's a Beaumont."

The words felt like a slap.

From the look on her brother's face, he'd meant them to.

"I've spent my entire life being judged by who my family is instead of for myself. And honestly, I'm sick of it. I deserve better, especially from someone— Especially from you."

She looked away, sick with shame. He did deserve better.

"If you were trying to make me feel even worse than I already did, mission accomplished."

The long-suffering sigh he let out was one she was well acquainted with.

"I'm not trying to make you feel bad, Bell. I'm just trying to make you see that even with his promotion on the line, Peter chose to protect you. That's gotta prove something to you. I know it did to me."

"That he was stupid?" She rolled her eyes at his exasperated look. "I know, okay? I know he's more than just his family's net worth. That he's a good, honorable, trustworthy guy who cares about me. Here, anyway." She tapped her head. Then her chest. "But in here, everything keeps circling back to wonder when all the wonderful stuff will go away and I get hurt again when he realizes he's traded down."

Rafe bristled. "Why would you...ah. The guy."

"Yeah, the guy." The lying, spineless, I-can't-believe-I'm-still-letting-him-ruin-my-life guy. "It isn't logical. Even I know that. But...I can't seem to stop myself from going down that rabbit hole of self-doubt." She gave a defeated shrug.

Rafe reached over and took her hands in his.

"Baby sister, I wish I could tell you if you and Peter get back together, things will work out as well as they have for me and Lillian. But I can't. And it has nothing to do with him being a Beaumont, or you being a Delgado. It's because you're both human. No one can dictate how things will go between you except you." He squeezed her hands. "But I do know if you let the opportunity to find out what you might have pass without at least trying, you will always regret it."

Tears thickened her throat. Blinking rapidly to keep them from falling, she gave a small nod. "I think you're right."

To her surprise, rather than get twitchy about the tears, Rafe stood, pulling her to her feet and into a hug. She let his warmth wrap around her, absorbing the comfort and protection he offered, just like when she'd been that terrified six-year-old and he'd been her personal teenaged superhero.

When he finally let her go, she felt calmer than she had in days. "Thank you."

He pressed a kiss to her forehead. "Anytime, *hermanita*." He paused. "So, that guy."

"What guy?"

"You know. Nathan..." He drew the first name out, encouraging her to fill in the blank of his last.

Like she was stupid.

"Oh, no. That's long over and done. No one is doing anything to him."

That got a small grunt of displeasure. "Well, if you ever change your mind..."

"If I do, Peter already called dibs on taking care of it."

Rafe grinned. "I knew I liked that guy."

She answered his grin with a wistful one of her own. "Yeah, me too."

"Then do something about it."

With that last bit of advice, he left her on the balcony, mind and emotions in a whirl with everything he'd told her. She sank back into her chair. Peter had missed out on his promotion. Possibly because of her. Because of her irrational demand to keep their relationship a secret. All because he was a Beaumont.

And she was a spineless coward.

Just like Nathan.

"Oh my god." Her hand rose to her mouth as a horrible realization dawned. "I've been treating him the same way Nathan did me. Like he was my dirty little secret I didn't want anyone to find out about, but didn't want to give up."

And he'd let her. Because those were the terms she'd set, and he'd been willing to put up with them, just to be with her. Just like he'd been willing to endure the accusations against him despite the consequences, to protect her reputation and her wishes.

And what had she done besides hurt him?

"You can say my being a Beaumont was the problem all you want. But the truth is, the only one who ever made it one was you. I've tried to show you me, who I really am. I let you in deeper than any woman's gotten, ever. Hell, I gave you the key to my apartment, the place that's my sanctuary, and you didn't even know what that meant. But if all that's not enough for you, then I don't know what else I can do to get through to you. I guess maybe your heart really is locked up too tight for anyone to get inside of. Even me."

But that wasn't true. He'd not only gotten in, he'd taken it over. Owned every bruised, battered inch. She just hadn't had the guts to tell him so. To give him that much power over her, the way she'd done with Nate.

But he wasn't Nate.

He'd *never* be Nate.

Why had it taken her so damn long to accept that? And at what cost?

"So, that was an interesting..." The plates of cheesy pizza in Kinzley's hands drooped as she walked out and took in Bella's expression. "Bell, you okay?"

"No, not even a little."

"Okay." She dropped the plates onto the tiny plastic table and perched on the edge of her chair. "Which part?"

Knowing her friend had shamelessly eavesdropped didn't bother her. It meant she didn't have to waste time bringing her up to speed.

"All of it. I screwed up so bad, Kinz. And I need to fix it. Now. Before it's too late."

"Yeah, we knew all that. Did you finally figure out what to say?"

"No. I don't think just saying I'm sorry is going to be enough to prove it to him. I need to show him I really mean it. Something he can't miss."

"And how do you plan to do that? Hire a skywriter to plaster "Sorry I was an idiot" all over Boulder and hope he sees it?"

Bella blinked at her friend. The smallest of smiles touched her mouth.

"No, but you just gave me an idea that might do the trick."

Chapter 23

Reducing his life to a series of definable numbers had been what helped Peter make it through the last few miserable days.

Eight hours to get through each shift. Three shifts to endure before forty-eight hours of blessed solitude. Seven hours every night to try—and mostly fail—to slip into the welcome embrace of unconsciousness. Without any alcoholic assistance.

His body was still making him pay for the last time.

Stepping into the elevator in the parking garage, he jabbed the button for the third floor. Three was also how many times one of his friends had needed to talk him off the ledge about doing serious bodily harm to Lister since Monday. The fucker just didn't know when to leave well enough alone. He was in his face, smirking and offering insincere condolences about the promotion going to Jackson every chance he got.

So far, he'd heard no hint of any rumors about the false assault allegation floating around the station. But it was only a matter of time. There was no way in hell Lister would leave a juicy poison arrow like that in his quiver of spite for long. He was probably hanging onto it until it could do the most possible damage. Again.

Bastard.

For the most part, work had been the usual mix of sincere condolences and good-natured ribbing about not getting the promotion. But there had been more not-so good-natured jabs mixed in than he'd expected, too.

Rafe had been right about his calling out sick the same day as the announcement playing right into Lister's machinations. There was a lot of lost ground to make up there concerning his commitment to wearing the badge.

But for the first time since he'd been saddled with the Golden Boy label, he was just too damned tired of the bullshit to care.

Let every person on the force think he was a sulky little bitch because he didn't get what he wanted. Like he'd told Isabella, he was sick of constantly having to defend himself to everyone all the time.

An all-too-familiar ache had him rubbing his chest, like he'd eaten one of those spicy burgers she loved so much. One hundred and six. That was the ever-expanding number of hours since he'd last seen Isabella. Talked to her. Touched her.

And damn it, it was killing him how much that was killing him.

He shouldn't care. Should have been able to consider the whole thing a hard lesson learned and moved the fuck on.

But he couldn't.

Whenever he'd almost convinced himself it was the best thing to do, the only thing to do, Rafe's parting words kept coming back to repeat over and over in his head.

"Don't let anything—or anyone—get in the way of trying to make things work. Not even yourself."

Which would have been a hell of a lot more helpful if he'd bothered to offer any clue as to exactly *how* he was supposed to 'make things work.' For someone who considered himself an exceptional puzzle solver, so far he was scoring a big, fat zero on figuring this one out.

"Just one friggin' hint would be nice," he muttered to the universe as he jabbed his key into the lock. "Is that really too much to ask?" Swinging his apartment door open, his body automatically braced even as his brain registered Roscoe wasn't waiting on the other side with his typical welcome-home tackle.

"Caught you sleeping, huh, pal?" he called as he shut the door and dropped his keys on the kitchen counter. It didn't happen often. Usually, the dog's ears were as good as radar dishes, hearing him coming from halfway down the hall. But sometimes after a really hard run, he was tired out enough he slept like the dead.

And Peter had definitely been giving him plenty of exercise the last few days.

Not that it had worked helping *him* sleep, unfortunately.

The wild thump of Roscoe's tail filled the dim apartment, lit only by the under-cabinet lighting in the kitchen left on when he was working nights. Reaching for the wall switch, he flicked them off and the overhead fixture on with one motion.

"Come on, boy. Who needs to go for a—"

Adrenaline spiked through his veins at the sight of the woman sitting on his couch, Roscoe's big head on her leg as she stroked it.

"Walk? I already took him a little while ago. I hope that was okay."

The sound of Isabella's soft voice after days of only hearing it in his dreams sent a rush of something besides adrenaline through him. Surprise and lust combined to make his tone rougher than normal. "What are you doing in here?"

Her hand paused in its stroking before resuming.

"You gave me the key to your apartment, remember?"

"That's not what I mean, and you know it."

"I know. I'm just...nervous. I had this all figured out in my head beforehand, and now, I'm..." She trailed off as her hand rose and fell in an uncertain gesture.

Picking up on her anxiety, Roscoe whined and rolled his eyes at Peter, accusation in their dark depths. Not about to be guilted by his own dog, he snapped his fingers and pointed to the spare bedroom. "Roscoe, bed."

Reluctance written in every inch of his muscular body, he slunk from the living room, sending one last look over his shoulder at them as if to say "get your shit together, humans."

If only.

Isabella scooted to the edge of the couch, drawing his attention to where her flowy skirt pooled around her bare thighs. The simple cropped white cotton top she wore just skimmed her navel, giving the barest of tantalizing glimpses of skin between the two opposing pieces of fabric as she moved. And though her face looked bare of makeup, her lips were red and full, as though she'd been biting them.

Damn. *He* wanted to be the one nibbling on those lips.

He'd closed half the distance between them before he realized he was moving. With a force of will he wasn't sure would last, he stopped himself well out of touching range from where she sat and planted his feet with the mental command of *stay!*

"Why are you here?" This time, the question was less gruff and more urgent. He'd asked for a clue on how to fix things. Maybe this was the universe throwing him a bone.

"We need to talk."

The four most ominous words in the English language.

"You could have called any time in the last four days."

She swallowed and nodded. "I know. But...I needed to do this in person. It only seemed right."

Hell. Maybe the fucking universe had decided to throw him a curveball instead of a bone.

Right at his head.

He added crossed arms to his stance, making himself as solid a target as possible to absorb whatever blow was coming. "I'm listening."

Opening the hand clenched beside her on the cushion, Isabella held up the key she'd used to let herself in.

"The other day, you said I didn't know what it meant when you gave me this. But I did. I do. You were offering me something so huge that I...I just wasn't ready for it. To have this"—she gestured between them—"be that big. That important. Which is why I never said anything about it. Because I was scared."

"And now?"

"And now...to be honest, I guess I'm still a little scared. But I'm more afraid of not at least trying to see where this can go."

His heart started pounding louder as he heard his own thoughts coming from her mouth. But he refused to let himself hope.

Yet.

"And why should I believe you? How do I know this"—he mirrored her gesture between them—"won't suddenly become too much for you and scare you off again? I'm always going to be a Beaumont, Isabella. I can't change who I am. No, I *won't* change who I am. Not even for you."

He tried not to feel bad for making her wince, but it was the truth. He was done apologizing simply for being born a Beaumont. And if she couldn't accept him as he was, there really wasn't anything left for them to discuss.

"It's a fair question, considering my track record with you and your family." She took a deep breath. "You gave me this key as more than a way into your apartment. It was supposed to be a tangible way to tell me you were giving me a way into your life. Into your heart." She placed it on the coffee table with a soft click. "I don't have a place of my own yet to give you a key to in return. But I think I figured out the next best thing."

With visibly trembling hands, she stood and pulled the elastic waistband of her skirt down low on the left side, all the way to the top of her dark blue panties. Her tattoo sat just above the lacy edge. He squinted at a spot of redness that hadn't been there before. Not sure he was seeing what he thought he was seeing, he took several steps closer.

"Wait. Is that..."

"You said my heart was locked up tight—too tight for even you to get into. Well, it's not. Not anymore. Despite all the roadblocks I threw in your way, all the stupid, stubborn ideas I kept clinging to, you still managed to find a way in, and...well, I guess the easiest thing is to just..."

She squared her shoulders and looked him directly in the eyes. "I love you, Peter Beaumont."

He would have felt less stunned if she'd taken the Yogi Berra-autographed bat down off the wall and brained him with it.

"You do?" She did?

She nodded a little too fast, betraying her nerves. "I really, really do."

His gaze dropped to the addition made to the black and blue filigreed heart on her skin. The thing purposefully left off when it was first created. The old-fashioned key, now attached to the locked heart's flourish of ribbons, had to be one of the most beautiful things he'd ever seen.

And not because of the artist's talent.

There was suddenly too much distance between them. He shoved the coffee table aside and closed the gap for a closer look at the hard evidence of what she was telling him. There, he saw what he hadn't at first.

Worked into the key's design were two letters. PB.

Holy shit.

He had no choice but to believe her now. It didn't get any more real than permanently marking your own body to prove your commitment to something.

The first time she'd done it to prove something to herself.

This time was to prove something to him.

His fingers traced a delicate line along her exposed skin, careful to avoid the area still red and irritated by the fresh artwork. "This isn't the next best thing." Wonder and awe bubbled inside him like uncorked champagne. "It's *the* best thing. Ever."

His hand left her belly and came up to cup her chin, giving her the same direct look she'd given him to say the words. "And I love you, too, Isabella Delgado."

Tension flowed out of her body and a smile nearly split her face in half. "You do?"

"Yeah. I really, really do." His mouth pressed to hers to seal the vow.

It was supposed to be a soft, reverent kiss. But as it often was between them, passion overtook good intentions, and it became an almost frantic tangling of tongues and lips and teeth as they both tried to make up for lost time.

"I'm so sorry," she panted between kisses. "I never meant to hurt you. I was just so scared and confused, and—"

"It's okay. And I'm sorry, too." He couldn't believe he was actually forming words while his entire blood supply was surging south. "I should have stayed and talked things out, not just walked away like I did and left everything unresolved. That was a dick move. No. That was a Nathan move."

"No. Don't bring him up. Ever again. He has nothing to do with us anymore."

He didn't have to question if that was true or not.

The key etched into her skin proved it was.

They stumbled to his bedroom, neither of them wanting to let go of the other, which made undressing more comedy act than act of seduction. Finally, laughing and panting, they landed on the bed, skin-to-skin at last.

God, he'd missed this. Missed her.

Missed *them*.

Pulling his mouth from hers with a reluctant need for air, he skimmed his hand down her body to caress her breasts, then further down to her belly where it came to rest beside the tiny key. "I can't believe you did this."

"I didn't want there to be any doubt in your mind I was serious."

"There isn't." Not anymore. "Does it still hurt?"

"It did yesterday when I got it. Now it's only a little sore." She smiled one of the sweetest smiles he'd ever seen. "But it was worth it."

Damn, did he love her.

The smile he gave her back was more wicked than sweet. "I guess I'm going to have to be very careful, then." He pressed a kiss to her belly beside the tattoo. "And get creative."

"What do you—ooooh."

Her moan as his mouth moved lower was better than applause.

He brought her up to the heights of orgasm twice before coaxing her to her knees and sliding into her welcoming body from behind to avoid brushing against the tattoo. It was like clicking the last piece of one of his mega-jigsaw puzzles into place. This was completion. This was where he belonged.

And he wasn't walking away from it—from her—again.

When she came a third time, the sweet feel of her squeezing him tight in pulsing waves sent him over his own edge with a long groan. Reluctant to let it end, he milked every last drop of pleasure from the moment for them both, until finally he collapsed beside her on the bed in a wrung-out heap.

After they'd both gotten the sensation back in their bodies, Isabella rolled to her side, a satiated smile on her lips as her hand idly stroked his chest and belly. He kept his arm tucked tight around her shoulders, holding her close, absorbing the feel of her like it was a balm to his jagged heart.

If they wouldn't starve to death, he'd be content to stay just like this for the rest of their lives. Just the two of them, with nothing outside these four walls to worry about.

"I heard about the promotion," she said in a low voice as her fingers played around his navel. "I'm sorry."

Oh, well. It looked like the real world was going to intrude, after all.

Raising his free hand, he ran it up and down her arm in a light line, simply because he loved touching her. "Honestly, a small part of me is relieved I won't have to work with Lister every day." He hadn't realized how much the prospect had bothered him until it was gone.

Her fingers stilled for a second. "But being a detective was your dream job."

"It still is. But I can wait till the next opening comes up." An easier setback to accept than the potential of losing her. Amazing how some much-needed perspective could clear up what was really important in life.

"Or...you could rethink the FBI."

This time it was his hand that stilled.

"You know why I didn't pursue that. It would mean having to leave Boulder."

"I know."

"And what about...us?"

"We could try the long-distance thing for a while, see how it goes. And then..." She bit her lower lip. "I could always move to wherever you are."

Okay, whoa. What?

He turned onto his side to face her more fully.

"You'd move? What about your family? The restaurant? Your whole food truck plan? You can't just walk away from all of that."

"Of course I can. I mean, I wouldn't be walking away from my family, obviously. We'd still come back to visit all the time, since your family's here, too. But the rest of it? I only wanted the food truck idea to succeed to prove I'd earned my place in the family business, the same as Cris and Bria. *That* was my dream. And I did it."

He grinned at how smug she sounded about it. "Yeah, you did."

She grinned back, then got serious again.

"If they decide to go ahead with expanding in that direction, I don't have to be the one to do it to know I had a hand in it." A thoughtful gleam entered her eyes. "Of course, I could always open a Bayamo food truck wherever we end up. There are millions of people out there who haven't been fortunate enough to experience my mother's recipes yet."

"They don't know what they're missing." He'd buy her a fleet of food trucks, if that would make her happy.

On second thought, she would hate that. She'd be happier doing it on her own.

"My point is, I achieved my dream. Now it's your turn. And if that's joining the FBI in order to solve crime puzzles, then I'm behind you one thousand percent."

How the fuck did he deserve this woman?

"Dreams change."

Her brow wrinkled. "What do you mean?"

Cupping her cheek with his hand, he drank in everything about her, from her deep brown eyes filled with love to her kiss-reddened lips puckered in a confused frown. "It means I may *want* to be a detective, or FBI, or whatever I end up being where I can use my skills. But I know now I don't *need* it to be happy, or complete. For that, all I need is you."

Her eyes grew moist before she blinked the incipient tears back.

"You have me." She bit her swollen lower lip and gave him a hopeful look from beneath her long lashes. "And maybe you'd like to have me again?"

He did.

Twice.

Epilogue

"ANY OTHER BIDDERS? ANYONE? Going once, going twice...annnd sold to lucky paddle number three two seven!"

Peter joined in the applause for the successful bidder on the bachelor currently onstage beside the evening's auctioneer, Maya Martinez. Convincing the popular local DJ to help with the Everbrite annual bachelor auction had been a stroke of genius. Her engaging personality and sly wit were helping make the proceedings a lot more fun for everyone involved than in years past. Especially the bachelors on the chopping block.

Of which he was happy to not be one of this year.

Just another of the many, many reasons he was thrilled to have Isabella in his life.

"Thank god it's not us up there anymore," Richard said, echoing his thoughts.

"It's not that bad."

They both looked at Theo in disbelief.

"Give me a break," Peter said. "You hated it as much as we did."

"You're just saying that because Rachel is practically in charge of the whole thing now," Richard added.

Theo sipped his Scotch, eyes surveying the packed room with a proprietary sense of satisfaction. "Yes, she is. And she's doing a damn fine job."

Their mother had been slowly transferring more and more of the Everbrite Foundation leadership responsibilities to Theo's fiancé, allowing both of their parents to finally ease into a state of semi-retirement.

Well, their mother had eased, anyway.

Their father she was dragging there one stubborn inch at a time.

Although there were signs she was making progress. The around-the-world cruise he'd surprised her with for their upcoming fortieth wedding anniversary was a good indicator he knew it was time to shift his primary focus from the family business to the family.

And especially his ever-patient wife.

"I still can't believe Rach got 'Maya in the Morning' to be the guest auctioneer." Theo gave a wicked grin. "That woman sure gives good voice."

Peter slugged his arm. "Hey! You're practically a married man."

"Ow. And we have a deal. She gets a free pass drooling over Chris Hemsworth, and I get one for Maya. I mean, come on, listen to that. It's like liquid sex." As the DJ's patter segued into an introduction of the next bachelor, Theo's expression went from rapturous to maniacal glee. "Jesse's up," he hooted. "Sucker!"

Head shaking in amusement, Peter sipped his beer and glanced around the ballroom. Most of the men in attendance had abandoned their tables after dinner and retreated to the bar area once the auction began. A few, like himself and his brothers, had staked out spots close enough to the main event onstage to watch, but far enough to be out of the line of fire.

The bidding was almost always enthusiastic, and sometimes even a little cut-throat.

No sane man wanted to get in the way of that.

While Theo heckled his friend as he strutted the catwalk, Richard asked Peter, "Have you spoken any more with Remi?"

"No."

"Are you still considering it?"

"Maybe. I'm not sure." Their cousin had been trying to convince him to make the move to the FBI ever since Peter made the mistake of calling him with some questions about the job.

In theory, it would be an opportunity making detective one day couldn't compare to. But when he weighed that against the low odds of being assigned to a Colorado field office if hired, the attraction level went way, way down.

And it wasn't all because of Isabella.

He believed her when she said she'd be willing to relocate anywhere with him. Something that still boggled his brain, since she was even more family-centric than him. That offer, even more than the tattooed key, told him just how dedicated she was to making their relationship work.

No, *he* was the one who wasn't sure he could leave his family and everyone he knew behind. And with all three of his siblings soon to be old married people, the chances of some nieces and nephews arriving in the not-so-distant future was almost a given.

He wanted to be here for that.

The thought of Isabella cuddling a newborn with silky hair and big brown eyes sent a streak of longing through him that nearly knocked him off his feet. That. He wanted that. And he wanted it here, with everyone they loved around them. One big, happy, extended family.

The rightness of that picture settled something in his chest.

It seemed he'd made his decision, after all.

The mild disquiet which had plagued him the last few months gone, he turned his attention to the bidding war going on over Theo's friend Jesse. Dressed in a pair of loose linen slacks, palm tree-emblazoned shirt with the top few buttons undone to show his deeply tanned chest, and boat shoes with no socks, he looked more like he should be strolling the California beaches where he grew up rather than a Colorado catwalk. But judging by the crazy stupid money being bid, the women were eating it up.

Score another one for Rachel and her change to the unwritten 'everyone in a tux' rule.

When the winning bid was finally taken, he couldn't help but take a poke at his brother.

"Correct me if I'm wrong, but I'm pretty sure that's more than *you* went for last time, isn't it?"

"Screw you," Theo replied with a rueful grin. "Besides, I still brought in more than you did."

Unable to stay out of the needling, Richard said, "And I brought in more than either of you."

"That's because you Beaumont boys are just too delicious and cheap at twice the price. It was definitely a loss when the three of you went off the market."

Peter rolled his eyes at Des's chirpy observation as he and Michael joined them. "Thanks. I think."

"I thought you were backstage, heading off any potential wardrobe malfunctions for the participants," Richard said.

"I was. But everything is going swimmingly, so I'm taking a small break to come out and see how things look from this side of the stage."

"And raid the dessert tables while the poor catering staff's still trying to set them up," Michael added with an unrepentant grin.

Des raised an eyebrow at his husband. "So, that wasn't a cream puff I saw disappearing into *your* mouth a minute ago, hmm?"

When Michael lifted his hands in mock surrender, Des sniffed, then blew him a kiss before turning back to the others. "Besides, Amber can handle any minor emergencies that may crop up in my absence. The dear girl is magic with a needle."

Richard preened so hard at the compliment about his fiancé, Peter thought he might strain something. "She is good, isn't she?"

"Of course she is. I'd wouldn't expect anything less from a protégé of mine."

"And where's Bella this evening?" Michael asked. "I haven't seen her yet."

Even after three months, the pleasure of being openly linked as a couple still made him bubble up with happiness.

"Last I saw, she was huddled in a corner with Lillian talking about the art for the restaurant's new food truck. They probably won't come up for air until dessert is announced." Because he knew his sister wouldn't be able to resist the siren song of sugar any more than he could.

Lil had seemed a lot less surprised than anyone else when he and Isabella had told their families they were dating. She'd given him a smirk and an eloquent look, like she'd known all along. And who knew? Maybe she had. That twin thing they had could be a little creepy sometimes.

As soon as she'd heard about Bayamo's new venture, she reached out to Isabella and offered her artistic skills to help draw up artwork for the truck. He'd had a moment of worry Isabella might take it the wrong way and get her back up about it. But, recognizing the olive branch for what it was, she'd graciously accepted, and the two had been putting their heads together every chance they had to spitball ideas.

He'd almost be jealous of the time they were spending together if it hadn't been for the results. Some of the mock-ups he'd seen so far were pretty amazing.

Unfortunately, Isabella's rocky relationship with her own sister wasn't mending quite as fast. Bria's selfishness had cut her deep, and it was going to take a while for the rift to fully heal. But he had no doubt it would, eventually. Because, family.

And karma.

Which had smiled when Kinzley's sister moved to California with her boyfriend and his band, leaving her with an open bedroom and half the rent to cover.

Isabella had just finished moving in.

While Bria was still living in their parents' house, waiting for Alejandro to work up the nerve to ask her father's permission for not only her hand, but for her to move in with him before the wedding.

Isabella had tried to be a better person than to revel in the irony of that turn of events. He had no such compunction. Because sometimes, to borrow Des's phrasing, life was just too delicious. And having Bria be the last chick stuck in the family nest instead of Isabella was the perfect kind of karmic payback.

Much like the one that had come Lister's way when his sly machinations during the whole promotion process came to light.

Evidently, there were more than a few ears having poison dripped into them during his smear campaign against Peter. Several recipients had been on the interview board. And more than one had brought the matter up the chain of command on his behalf.

It was nice to know he finally wasn't the only one who saw the man for the toxic asshat he truly was.

Not that anything official could be done about any of it. Lister was nasty and a jerk, but he wasn't stupid. He'd never crossed any lines that could get him into any real trouble with the department.

With his fellow officers was another matter entirely.

For a guy like Lister who thrived on his popularity, being shunned by most of the department was a punishment worse than any official reprimand could have ever been. And while he might eventually work his way back into some people's good graces, he'd never again have their full trust.

Karma for the win.

Unlike Isabella, he hadn't even tried to be a better person about it. He not only reveled in Lister's fall from grace, he'd raised a toast to it and thanked the universe for the assist.

The fact Isabella had taken upon herself to visit his captain and fill her in on the exact nature of Peter's alibi for the night of the bogus assault claim hadn't hurt, either. That information had also filtered up the chain of command with Isabella's blessing, ensuring there would be no shadow calling his reputation or integrity into question in the future.

God, he loved that woman.

And he made sure he told—and showed—her every chance he got.

"Have you heard back from the CDHS about your application yet?" Theo asked, breaking into Peter's plans about how he was going to show her that night after the auction ended.

Des shook his head and made a small moue. "Not yet. The wheels of government grind slowly, I'm afraid. But hopefully soon." His hand caught his husband's for a quick squeeze, betraying the nerves his glib words hid.

"Well, you know you have our support, in any way you need it. You two will make amazing foster parents."

Peter and Richard both nodded in full agreement with Theo's statement. His fiancée had been through the system. If anyone knew how important finding the right kind of foster parents was, it was Rachel. And she adored Des and Michael as much as the rest of them did. She'd actually been the one to suggest they consider it in the first place.

"Any kids will be lucky to have you as their parents," Peter said.

Looking uncharacteristically choked up, all Des could manage was a husky, "Thank you." He shared a loving look with Michael, then cleared his throat and gave one of his trademark over-the-top smiles.

"Well, we should be getting back to our intrepid bachelors backstage. Before anyone makes a run for it now that the waters have been chummed, and they've seen how hungry the crowd is for fresh meat. We'll catch up with you later, dear boys. Enjoy the show." Fingers waggling, he tucked his other hand in Michael's arm and departed.

Hungry was an understatement. The bidding on the current bachelor, this one wearing a cowboy hat and boots with his tux, was reaching a fever pitch. In fact, the two determined women involved in the fast-paced back-and-forth looked like they might just come to blows before it was over.

Peter winced, hoping John wouldn't hate him too much for talking him into participating once his turn onstage came. He might be one of the bravest men he knew, willing to run into burning buildings while everyone else ran out. But this could be the thing that put his courage to the ultimate test.

Society women could be pretty terrifying.

"So, any idea when you're going to pop the question?"

The beer he'd just sipped went down the wrong way. From the gleam in Richard's eyes as he choked, that had been his intent. "We've only been dating four months."

"So? I knew Amber was the one in three months."

"I knew in two," Theo said with a smirk.

Peter shook his head. Everything had to be a competition.

"Yeah, but neither of you 'popped the question' until months later, and that was what he asked. Of course, I already know Isabella's the one. I'm not an idiot. Shut it," he told Theo before he could open his mouth to comment. "I'll ask her when the time is right."

Which would definitely *not* be anywhere close to Christmas or New Year, since those few weeks were intrinsically entwined with painful memories of Nate the Douche. He wanted their life together to be free of any taint of mistakes past.

Richard gave him an approving look. "Good man." He raised his glass. "To finding the people who bring us joy."

Theo added his glass. "Who keep us grounded."

"And make us complete." Peter tipped his glass so all three touched. "They're all we'll ever need."

A Note From the Author

I hope you've enjoyed Peter and Bella's story. I had so much fun writing about the Beaumont brothers and their sassy, strong-willed women. But sadly, this brings us to the end of the Boulder branch of the family.

Of course, there are always those Louisiana cousins we met who make my fingers itch to write about, so who knows what the future may bring? I also have a few ideas about those friends taking part in the bachelor auction at the end of the book. I know I'm curious about what they might get up to with their winning bidders. Aren't you? So, I have a feeling we may be seeing more Boulder and more Beaumonts in the future.

But the next series that will be coming out in 2025 is one that's extremely special to me. It deals with injured military men and women and their service dogs, broken by life and by love. And, of course, about the people who find a way into their damaged, wary hearts. Look for book 1 in the Wounded Warrior Legacy series, Just the Way You Are, early next year.

If you want to know more about what I'm writing, scan the QR code on the next page to visit my website (nikarhone.com) and sign up for my newsletter, where you can also claim your FREE book, available exclusively to my subscribers. Or stay up-to-date on all future releases by following my author page on any of the major book sites.

And finally, if you enjoyed this book, please take a moment to leave a review at your favorite retailer. They're what feeds an author's creative soul. Thank you!

Claim Your FREE book here

Also By Nika Rhone

<u>Boulder Bodyguards series</u>
What the Lady Wants
Finding Forever
Can't Help Loving You

<u>Boulder Beaumonts series</u>
Worth Any Price
Never Let Me Go
All I Need Is You

<u>Wounded Warrior Legacy series</u>
Just the Way You Are (coming 2025)

About the Author

Nika Rhone spent her childhood wearing out library cards as she read her way through the extraordinary worlds far beyond her small hometown on Long Island, NY. By her teens, her imagination was taking her places all on its own, forcing her to learn how to type (badly) so she could get all the stories down on paper. After a long love affair with science fiction and fantasy, she finally discovered romance, fell head-over-heels, and now spends her days crafting happily-ever-afters for the characters who still tell their stories faster (and better) than she can type them.

You can keep up with all the latest book news, events, and giveaways by visiting her website www.nikarhone.com and joining her newsletter.